DUNE

THE LADY
OF CALADAN

THE DUNE SERIES

BY FRANK HERBERT

Dune
Dune Messiah
Children of Dune
God Emperor of Dune
Heretics of Dune
Chapterhouse: Dune

BY FRANK HERBERT, BRIAN HERBERT,
AND KEVIN J. ANDERSON

The Road to Dune (includes the original short novel *Spice Planet*)

BY BRIAN HERBERT AND KEVIN J. ANDERSON

Dune: House Atreides
Dune: House Harkonnen
Dune: House Corrino
Dune: The Butlerian Jihad
Dune: The Machine Crusade
Dune: The Battle of Corrin
Hunters of Dune
Sandworms of Dune
Paul of Dune
The Winds of Dune
Sisterhood of Dune
Mentats of Dune
Navigators of Dune
Tales of Dune
Dune: The Duke of Caladan
Dune: The Lady of Caladan

BY BRIAN HERBERT

Dreamer of Dune
(biography of Frank Herbert)

DUNE
THE LADY
OF CALADAN

Brian Herbert

and

Kevin J. Anderson

TOR

A TOM DOHERTY ASSOCIATES BOOK

NEW YORK

DUNE: THE LADY OF CALADAN

Copyright © 2021 by Herbert Properties LLC

A Tor Book
Published by Tom Doherty Associates
120 Broadway
New York, NY 10271

www.tor-forge.com

Tor® is a registered trademark of Macmillan Publishing Group, LLC.

The Library of Congress Cataloging-in-Publication Data is available upon request.

ISBN 978-1-250-76505-5 (hardcover)
ISBN 978-1-250-76506-2 (ebook)

Our books may be purchased in bulk for promotional, educational, or business use.
Please contact your local bookseller or the Macmillan Corporate and
Premium Sales Department at 1-800-221-7945, extension 5442,
or by email at MacmillanSpecialMarkets@macmillan.com.

First Edition: September 2021

Printed in the United States of America

0 9 8 7 6 5 4 3 2 1

DUNE

THE LADY
OF CALADAN

In her mind and heart, Jessica found herself at the bottom of an abyss. Each moment took her farther from Caladan, Duke Leto, and Paul.

After receiving the Bene Gesserit ultimatum, and the threat against her family, Jessica had crossed star systems in a Spacing Guild Heighliner, ordered back to Wallach IX like a recalcitrant child. She felt no warm homecoming as she rode a shuttle down from the huge orbiting ship to the Sisterhood's dreary, cold homeworld.

Would she ever see Caladan again? Or Leto or Paul? She shifted her position on the hard seat of the shuttle. Maybe the answer to that question depended on what Mother Superior Harishka wanted from her.

Exceptionally strong side winds buffeted the vessel, which made the pilot change his descent and swoop around, rising higher until the turbulence abated. Other passengers muttered a drone of unease, but Jessica remained silent. She had her own turbulence to deal with.

As she looked out the diamond-shaped windowport, the roiling clouds mirrored her troubled mind. She resented the iron control that the Sisterhood exerted over her. She had been separate from them many years, imagining herself independent on Caladan, but they had cracked the whip. The Bene Gesserit summons had left no room for discussion. Reverend Mother Mohiam had threatened to destroy the Duke and the future of House Atreides if she didn't obey, and the Sisterhood certainly had the means to do so.

They wanted Jessica for their own purposes, had withdrawn her—permanently?—from Caladan. Never in her life had she felt so dismal, separated from everyone and everything she loved. But she did not intend to meekly comply.

The shuttle rocked again in the unsettled air and began to descend again after circumventing the storm, and Jessica saw they were approaching the Mother School complex below. Through a veil of tangled clouds, she made out the ancient buildings and new annexes, the angles of red-tiled roofs, the low underbrush that covered the grounds. The foliage had turned a bright scarlet and orange with autumn colors. The structures were connected, like the countless women in the Sisterhood, all part of an intricate and powerful political machine.

Jessica had been raised here from infancy, parentless, and the Sisterhood had raised her, indoctrinated her, and enfolded her life from birth until her inevitable death. The Bene Gesserit *owned* her.

Using some of the very methods taught to her at the Mother School, Jessica concentrated on a breathing exercise that brought clarity and calm. She felt her muscles relax. She had to be at her best and sharpest to face whatever came next.

As she centered herself, the turbulence around the shuttle smoothed, and the remaining clouds parted over the landing zone on the perimeter of the complex. Still wearing garments from Caladan, Jessica felt out of place, but soon they would make her change into the school's traditional dark garb, to remind her that she was still one of them, always one of them.

Wallach IX, with its weak sun and chill climate, had long been a place where young women of the order either rose to the challenges, or failed. Jessica felt an odd nostalgia for the ancient training center, torn by her loyalties to the Sisterhood and her family. She had spent so many years here, soft clay for them to shape as they chose, finally assigning her as the bound concubine of a young Duke with great potential.

And now she was back. She felt a deep sense of foreboding.

MOTHER SUPERIOR HARISHKA greeted her in person on the tarmac. The Mother Superior had piercing eyes and a severe, uncompromising demeanor. Despite her age, the old woman's skin was remarkably tight and smooth, possibly from the geriatric effects of the melange she consumed regularly. She had filled the same role for decades, after a lifetime of service to the order. "Come with me. You are needed immediately." She didn't explain about the urgent matter that had turned Jessica's life upside down.

Despite her advanced years, Harishka set a brisk pace, moving like a military commander leading a charge against enemy lines. They entered a large new administration building that had been built with a generous donation from old Viscount Alfred Tull, whose name was on a plaque by the entrance. "I want you to see this first, before you attempt to settle in. We may not have much time," Harishka said. "You need to know the reason you are here, and why it is so important."

Yes, she thought. *I need to know that.*

As Jessica followed her up wide stairs and down long corridors, she absorbed peripheral details, but did not ask questions, though a desperate curiosity clamored inside. In an isolated section of the third floor, Harishka led her to a viewing window that looked into a large medical chamber with a closed door. Two other Sisters remained there, outside the plaz like guardians, but Jessica stepped up to the window, determined to see.

Harishka explained, "The room is sealed and barricaded, but do not underestimate the danger. This is clear armored plaz, and she can see us now if she is alert enough, but for our protection we can always set it to one-way plaz if necessary."

With all the precautions taken, Jessica expected to see some kind of caged monster inside. Instead, she saw an ancient woman stretched on a bed, tossing restlessly in her sleep. She wore only a medical gown, with tubes and monitors connected to her. Her face was drawn back in a grimace, and she cried out, but the thick plaz blocked all sound. Despite the wrinkles on her age-spotted neck, arms, and hands, her face was not nearly as shriveled as her body.

Jessica didn't understand. "She . . . is the danger? What does this have to do with me?"

The Mother Superior gave an oblique answer. "This is Lethea, a former Kwisatz Mother. Now she serves in a different capacity for as long as she remains alive . . . and for as long as she withholds what we need."

Kwisatz Mother. Jessica remembered Shaddam Corrino's first wife, Anirul, who had been present during Paul's birth, who had been greatly interested in the boy child. Anirul had been a Bene Gesserit of "hidden rank," while quietly holding an important, secret title. She had died very shortly after Paul was born.

"And what does a Kwisatz Mother do?" Jessica asked. *And why did she have the power to summon me?*

"Like a Guild Navigator foreseeing safe pathways throughout the stars, so a Kwisatz Mother can see each thread in the immense tapestry of our breeding plans. Lethea was relieved of duty due to mental instability. She is still useful—even if she is dangerous."

Jessica couldn't tear her gaze from the crone writhing on the medical bed, locked away alone. Lethea seemed barely able to move. "Dangerous?"

Harishka stared ahead, as if her gaze could bore through the barrier. "She has already murdered several of us. Hence the need for all the security."

The Mother Superior nodded to one of the two women stationed there to watch Lethea. She was in her thirties with black hair and an olive complexion. "Sister Jiara has watched Lethea closely, but I'm afraid she has few answers."

Jiara looked through the plaz. "Her mind is crumbling, but it is still incredibly powerful." She paused just a beat. "Enough to kill several Sisters through her sheer force of will."

As if sensing their presence, Lethea's eyes opened to narrow slits, and she stared directly at Jessica from the other side of the armored room. Jessica shuddered. "Why do you need her?" she asked the Mother Superior. "What is so important?"

"Lethea has a special prescience the Sisterhood needs, a predictive ability about the future of our order. It has proven to be accurate, and valuable to us, enabling us to make calculated decisions. That is why we keep her alive, despite the danger. But her mental gift comes and goes, and Lethea is losing control of it."

"She is out of her mind," Jiara added, sounding bitter. "But she insisted that we bring you here."

Jessica had so many questions that she could no longer contain them. "What does this have to do with me? I've never met this Kwisatz Mother."

Harishka turned toward Jessica and said, "You are here because Lethea said, 'Bring her here. Our future depends on it.' And she insisted that you be separated from your son. According to her, you could bring about the end of the Sisterhood."

Jessica felt as if she had fallen off a ledge. "Separate me from Paul?" This made absolutely no sense at all. "Why? For what purpose?"

Harishka's expression fell. "We need you to discover the answer. She predicted horror, bloodshed, disaster. That's why we called you here so urgently."

Behind the plaz wall, Lethea's gaze held on Jessica, then shifted to glare at Mother Superior Harishka, Jiara, and at the other Sister. Finally, the old woman closed her eyes and sagged like a rag onto the medical bed.

"She's a crafty one," Jiara whispered. "Look at her. She wants to kill more of us, if given the chance."

"Is she really asleep at last?" the other Sister asked.

Harishka touched a button on the wall, and with a quiet hiss the door to the medical room opened. She called for three Medical Sisters, who rushed down the hall. "Attend to her now, quickly, while you can." The trio hurried in, rolling a machine and hooked it to the old woman, adding tubes and lines, but trying not to disturb her. Two of the Sisters took readings, while the third remained alert, as if ready for an attack.

"Intravenous feeder," Harishka explained to Jessica. "Lethea refuses to eat on her own. We keep her alive, no matter how much she objects. And we expect you to pry answers from her."

The two women worked quickly, but as they were unhooking the feeding tube, the patient stirred. Alarmed, the Medical Sisters abandoned the feeding machine and bolted for the door.

Lethea snapped fully awake and called out in a strange way, "Stop!"

Jessica recognized the irresistible power of Voice. Was this how she killed?

Two Sisters had made it through the door, but the third, the one who had been guarding them, jerked to a sudden stop. Terrified, she struggled, but could not move, as if snagged by a lasso. Her companions turned and grabbed her, dragging her out into the corridor, then slammed the door behind them.

Thrashing on her medical bed, Lethea glowered at the window.

"We have to send in teams of three," Harishka said. "She only seems able to control the mind of one Sister at a time, and this way, the other two can stop a victim from killing herself."

"It's a game to her," said Jiara, "seeing if she can catch one of us alone."

Lethea shot a hostile, terrifying gaze through the window at Jessica, but Jessica refused to turn away, meeting the stare with her own. "Is that why Lethea demanded to see me? Because she wants to kill me?"

"It is possible," the Mother Superior said. "Very possible."

House Atreides has always measured its worth in terms of our honor, not the extent of our holdings. In what matters to us, we are far richer than any other House in the Landsraad.

—LETO ATREIDES, upon assuming the title of Duke of Caladan

All primary Guild routes eventually made their way to Kaitain, the glittering Imperial capital.

Traveling aboard a Heighliner from distant Caladan, Duke Leto Atreides rode in his family's lavishly appointed frigate. His staff of retainers, far larger than he needed, wore green and black, each tunic or jacket sporting the prominent Atreides hawk. This show of ostentation was not at all what the Landsraad had come to expect from the Duke of Caladan.

After the recent Otorio terrorist attack, the rules of the Imperium had changed. And after the trouble involving Jessica . . . He felt a wave of emotion. After Jessica, Leto himself had changed. He was a different man with a new purpose and priorities. He had embraced long-ignored ambitions for his House and his son, and he clung to that new determination. It was all he had left.

The Atreides protocol minister, a thin and unconfident man named Eli Conyer, filled out forms during the transit, and when the Guild ship dispatched the mob of frigates, shuttles, and passenger craft into Kaitain orbit, Conyer broadcast an announcement of the Duke's arrival. He insisted on the proper welcoming formalities, transmitting notices to the Landsraad secretary and the Imperial Palace as well as to news and informational outlets.

On the passenger deck of the Atreides frigate, Conyer could not hide his smile. "Everything as befits your station, my Lord. The capital will know that the Duke of Caladan has come!" He said it as if some messiah had arrived.

Not long ago, when he had attended the inauguration of the garish Corrino museum on Otorio, Leto had rolled his eyes at the popinjay nobles who flaunted themselves in hopes of being noticed by Shaddam Corrino IV. Now he was in danger of acting just like them.

Leto was not comfortable with so much attention, but this was, after all, what he had instructed the minister to do. This was his first foray into building more prominence for House Atreides. "Doesn't every Landsraad noble do the same thing?"

Conyer huffed. "It is common practice, Sire, but you have not previously done so. Therefore, this visit is noteworthy."

All his life, Leto had been content to be a good leader of his own people, choosing the course of honor and raising his son in a similar fashion. Because of that, though, much wealth and power—and therefore security for House Atreides—had slipped through his fingers. He had missed many opportunities. What if he had diminished his legacy for Paul? Leto wondered if other nobles secretly considered him inept in the realm of political games.

The terrorist attack by Jaxson Aru had left numerous vacancies in the Landsraad, and nobles vied for them like pigs at a feeding trough. Leto refused to be like that, but he realized he didn't have to be weak either. He had come to Kaitain to claim some of what House Atreides deserved. It was long overdue.

Conyer studied a screen and smiled. "I arranged for a reception guard and an escort to meet us at the Imperial Spaceport, Sire." He looked away, seemingly embarrassed. "It was a contract service, but well within our budget."

"You did well," Leto said as the ornate ship settled down in its designated zone. "Have adequate guest quarters been arranged for me and my retinue?"

Conyer looked offended. "Of course, my Lord! In the Promenade Wing of the palace, a fine suite with adjacent rooms for your retainers and security staff. You will be seen and noticed whenever you go about your daily business."

The capital city was a showcase of governmental buildings, monuments, museums, towers, statuary, fountains, prisms, obelisks, archways, and sundials under clear blue, climate-controlled skies. The cacophony and visual overload made Leto pause as he emerged from his own flashy frigate. He missed the sound of the outgoing tide on Caladan, the waves curling around the docks in the harbor town. He remembered walking with Jessica among the tide pools, pointing out sea anemones, scuttling crabs, and spiny starfish. He recalled a storm far out at sea, flashes of lightning in the clouds. . . .

Now, he steeled himself as he looked across the vast city and remembered his purpose here. As soon as he became a more powerful lord with expanded holdings, he could enjoy the ocean-side splendor of his ancestral planet again.

But it wouldn't be with Jessica, not anymore. That relationship was broken irreparably, and the Bene Gesserit had formally recalled her to Wallach IX. He wondered if he would ever see her or speak with her again.

A squad of rigid troops marched toward the Atreides frigate looking like palace guards, but these were just the contract escorts that Conyer had arranged, so that Leto could make a big impression. A pair of bannermen held up a scarlet-and-gold flag with the Corrino lion alongside a green-and-black flag with the Atreides hawk. One guard bellowed out in a resonant voice, "Kaitain welcomes the Duke of Caladan!"

Twelve uniformed escorts bowed in unison, displaying well-practiced respect. On nearby landing zones, Leto noted additional passenger shuttles and private noble frigates, all landed from the same Heighliner. Similar contract reception committees greeted those visiting noblemen.

As his retainers followed him out of the frigate, Leto swept back his dark hair and raised his chin. With his aquiline nose and strong jaw, he cut a striking profile. He spoke a hard command to the hired escort guards, "Take me to the Imperial Palace, where Emperor Shaddam will see me." He had no idea if that was true, and the haughty tone felt unnatural to him, but the uniformed attendants snapped to attention and whisked him off. Leto's personal staff would transport his belongings to his new quarters.

He thought of his fourteen-year-old son, Paul—his heir, even though Paul was the child of a concubine rather than the issue of a legitimate marriage. Leto had refused to play those marriage games. His one attempt at such a political play had ended in bloodshed and tragedy at the wedding ceremony, and Leto had vowed never to put his family through that again. His *family.*

So much had changed.

Instead, Leto had turned his attention to reviewing possible marriage candidates for young Paul, but he had discovered to his surprise that some other nobles did not consider House Atreides important enough for a marriage alliance. A flash of anger heated Leto's face at the memory of when Duke Fausto Verdun had sneered at the very idea that his daughter might marry Paul Atreides.

If he succeeded in his goal on Kaitain, though, that attitude would change.

As he entered the spectacular Imperial Palace, Leto was only one of hundreds of equally important visitors. The escort guards ushered him into the cavernous main foyer, but there they left him, their commission discharged. He suddenly felt like one petal of one flower in a broad mountain meadow. He drew little attention in the bustle of the Emperor's court.

A surprisingly close voice startled him. "Ahhh, hmmm, my dear Duke Leto, I hoped I would intercept you here!" He turned to see a lean, dark-haired man with narrow features, large eyes, and a weak chin. The man's black-and-purple garments had all the accessories expected of an important man at court. "Allow me to welcome you. I will assist you, as I can."

Recognizing him, Leto gave a brief bow. "Count Fenring, I appreciate the gesture." He paused, realized this was an unexpected opportunity. "You may be able to help with my business here on Kaitain."

Hasimir Fenring was one of Emperor Shaddam's closest friends and advisers. His formal title was Spice Minister on Arrakis, but he also spent much time scheming at court. He could certainly be a powerful ally for Leto, but he was not a man to be controlled, except by Shaddam. Why had he made a point of Leto?

The Count made a quick bow again. "Neither the Padishah Emperor nor I will ever forget how you saved us from that madman on Otorio. We escaped only because of your warning, and I am certain Shaddam will grant any favor you request."

"Thank you. I came to Kaitain to try a different approach to earn a little more respect for House Atreides." Leto drew a breath, pushed back his annoyance.

"More respect?" Fenring raised his eyebrows in question.

Even amid the colorful noise of the huge reception foyer, Leto spotted a dark-robed Bene Gesserit and froze—Reverend Mother Mohiam, the Emperor's Truthsayer, gliding in close enough to eavesdrop. The wound of what the Sisters had done to Jessica, and to him, remained deep and raw. Leto pointedly shifted his position so that she looked only at his back.

"I apologize for my abrupt tone, Count Fenring. My family recently received a personal insult from another noble house, and I am quite upset." He squared his shoulders, straightened his green-and-black cape.

Fenring didn't seem to notice the old Reverend Mother. "An insult to your family? Ahhh, so it is kanly, then?"

The idea startled Leto. Duke Verdun may have disparaged him and his son, but Leto did not intend to escalate the bloody feud. "No, that is not my purpose here. Apparently, House Verdun considers my son unworthy as a suitor, and Duke Fausto does not deem House Atreides important enough in the Landsraad. I am here to see about expanding my wealth and influence so I can rectify that impression."

"Ahhh, hmm . . ." Fenring's lips curved in a smile. "Noblemen usually work around the edges and behind the scenes to gain influence, but you are so direct! I like that. Perhaps I can help you, Duke Leto. I have certain influence of my own and, of course, I have the Emperor's ear." He chuckled. "But I would not worry about Duke Verdun!"

Out of the corner of his eye, Leto noticed the Truthsayer gliding closer. He asked, "Why is that?"

Fenring raised his eyebrows. "Ahhh, because House Verdun has been annihilated. Duke Fausto was a rebel and a traitor, working with the Noble Commonwealth rebellion. Emperor Shaddam punished him, and his entire family is dead."

Leto caught his breath. He had not expected this.

LATER THAT AFTERNOON, inside Shaddam's private contemplation quarters—where the Emperor did very little contemplating—Fenring revealed what Leto Atreides had told him about his purpose in coming to Kaitain.

With her raven hair, large eyes, and full lips, Empress Aricatha had Shaddam wrapped around her little finger. She remained by the doorway, intending to listen, but Fenring gave her an impatient look. He still hadn't decided whether she was an ally or an enemy.

Shaddam lounged in a casual uniform that had far too much brocade to be comfortable. He made a dismissive gesture. "Let us have our discussions, my love. I will tell you anything you need to know afterward."

Because he was watching so closely, Fenring saw the flash in Aricatha's eyes before she gave a quick nod and slipped out the door.

When she was gone, Shaddam said, "So, my cousin Leto is finally interested in the power he could have had long ago. Shall we throw him a reward now for what he did on Otorio?" He ran a finger along his lower lip. "It would look good to the rest of the Landsraad."

"Seeking power seems out of character for him," Fenring said. "Is he setting himself up for some other purpose? Could he quietly be involved with the Noble Commonwealth himself? Leto Atreides is exactly the sort of noble the rebels would want to recruit."

Shaddam scoffed. "Leto Atreides? A rebel and a traitor?"

Reverend Mother Mohiam also sat primly in a chair, waiting. Now she spoke up. "I was observing, and I can attest to his genuine shock upon hearing the fate of Duke Verdun. I studied his expressions, the tension in his muscles, his tone of voice. His antipathy was not feigned. If Fausto Verdun was a member of the rebellion, Leto Atreides did not see him as an ally."

"I did not have a high opinion of Verdun either," Shaddam said. "He was a hard man to like." Then he laughed. "But the good and noble Duke Leto? I've often wished the man would display a bit more ambition and show a darker side to his personality. Then I would truly understand him."

"That would make him more human," Mohiam agreed. "Now that his concubine is gone, he will have time to consider other priorities."

Fenring scratched the bridge of his nose. "Perhaps he is good at concealing his true nature, hmmm?"

Mohiam considered for a moment, then shook her head. "No, he is direct and authentic."

The danger posed by an enemy is directly proportional to the fear he instills.

—Sardaukar battle training manual

Imperial gunships marked with Corrino scarlet and gold swarmed down on the planet Elegy. This was not a diplomatic entourage, but a terrible show of force. The Emperor's Sardaukar troops would ensure the planetary governor's cooperation and flush out the violent rebel leader Jaxson Aru.

Colonel Bashar Jopati Kolona was not even convinced that the terrorist was on Elegy, but Shaddam pursued every rumor swiftly and without mercy. Ten troop carriers holding hundreds of warriors under Kolona's command landed like an avalanche on the Elegy spaceport. They filed no flight plans and requested no permission from the planetary control towers. The Sardaukar simply forced commercial traffic to get out of the way. Kolona did not so much issue orders as watch his wishes unfold with a deadly inevitability.

On the way down from the battle frigates in orbit, the colonel bashar had calmly transmitted his demand for Viscount Giandro Tull to meet the ships at his spaceport. Tull would find a way to be there, and to cooperate fully, or else face the consequences.

As soon as the ten gunships landed and opened their hatches, troops rushed across the landing zone, moving in a natural lockstep drawn from years of precision training. The gunships kept their weapon ports ready, and gunners monitored the targeting controls, ready to obliterate the entire spaceport should their commander give the order.

As he emerged from his flagship carrier, Kolona's eyes adjusted to hazy sunlight. He drew in a deep breath of the oddly perfumed air from the ubiquitous lichen forests for which the planet was famous, then stepped forward, getting down to business.

As expected, Viscount Tull came to greet him. The nobleman had even managed to erect a staging area and a ribbon-bedecked reception platform at the edge of the landing field. He acted as if the Sardaukar crackdown was some kind of parade.

As a Sardaukar who had endured ruthless survival training on Salusa Secundus, Kolona was hyperaware of his surroundings, alert for any threat. His focus was like a lasgun targeting cross, centered on the Viscount.

Giandro Tull stood on the raised platform dressed in shimmering fabrics derived from the distinctive Elegy lichens that grew in prominent rock formations. The nobleman's auburn hair was shoulder length, his features lean and handsome. His smile was artful, but artificial. He stood stock-still while Kolona approached in a dress uniform that was the epitome of military finery, the creases so crisp and sharp they could have been used as weapons.

Kolona and his honor guard of thirty soldiers wore personal shields and carried an array of long blades and short daggers, curved execution hooks, and throwing knives. Giandro Tull had brought only advisers dressed in lichen-scale finery; they stood uneasy, clearly hoping not to escalate the situation. Good, exactly as Jopati Kolona preferred.

The Viscount's calm smile did not falter, and Kolona was impressed with his controlled demeanor. "To what do we owe this unexpected honor, Colonel Bashar?"

He answered with equal formality. "The Padishah Emperor sent us to investigate troubling reports that the criminal Jaxson Aru has been seen on Elegy. I am here to discover whether or not the rebel movement has contaminated your planet."

Tull did not look shaken at all. "Wherever did you hear such nonsense?"

"I'm not at liberty to reveal the sources of our intelligence, my Lord." Kolona did not actually know where the report had come from, but Shaddam had begun to see conspirators everywhere. Suspicion was reason enough to scrutinize, and the officer followed orders.

"I'd be happy to discuss this further." Tull gave a brisk bow. "Let me invite you back to my manor house. I will provide a fine dinner, and you can share any evidence you may have against me. I am a loyal subject of the Imperium."

The invitation took Kolona aback. "I am not here on a social visit, sir. That much should be apparent."

The handsome Viscount's voice hardened. "I am neither blind nor foolish, Colonel Bashar. I know that your Sardaukar already obliterated House Verdun on Dross, and the same thing could happen to my holdings." His false smile widened. "Unless you feel there is a need to make this unpleasant, I prefer to have a cooperative conversation. You and your Sardaukar will have any reassurances you may need to dispense with this nonsense, so you can be on your way as soon as possible."

Kolona gestured to his honor guard. "My troops will disperse throughout the city and travel to smaller villages where Jaxson Aru or his rebels may be hiding. The Sardaukar will commence observations and conduct any necessary interrogations."

Viscount Tull swallowed visibly. "Please reassure me that your soldiers will follow strict protocol and cause no unnecessary damage."

Kolona gave the only possible answer. "They are Sardaukar."

His soldiers swept out like flechettes from a scattershot weapon and descended upon the Elegy capital, chasing down whispers and gossip. Viscount Tull was very careful in his actions, and Kolona appreciated that. The colonel bashar hated to inflict needless violence, death, and destruction as had happened to House Verdun.

He also remembered how, years ago, a similar swift and unexpected operation led by Duke Paulus Atreides had obliterated the Kolona family and their holdings. . . .

INSIDE THE MANOR house, the lavish banquet did not impress Jopati Kolona. A life spent subsisting on nutrient-dense rations had erased his appreciation for gourmet tastes, but the officer played his role as if he were enduring a military function. Knowing it would not be in Tull's interest to poison him, Kolona took an adequate number of bites so as not to be considered rude, and he was not interested in light conversation.

The two men sat alone in a private banquet room decorated with ornamental mist-fountains and sawtooth bouquets of lichen. Without speaking, servants delivered plate after plate of food, setting the courses down and then departing.

"I could take you to my stables to show you my fine horses, the rarest of breeds from bloodlines traced all the way back to Old Earth." Tull smiled. "A military man such as yourself should appreciate the exceptional quality of these mounts."

"Sardaukar do not often ride beasts," Kolona said. "And this is not a social visit." His Sardaukar would find out any truth to the rumors.

Still waiting for explanations, Tull finally said, "So, will you reveal why I've come under the Emperor's suspicions?"

"Many reasons. Primarily because you were conveniently absent from the Otorio gala during Jaxson Aru's terrorist attack. Many Landsraad nobles attended to show their support for the Emperor, yet you were noticeably absent— and therefore survived. Did you perhaps know ahead of time about the imminent attack?"

Now Tull lost his composure. "My father had just died, sir! All of Elegy was in shock, and I had to secure political control. You think I somehow concocted his death as an excuse?" His voice broke with anger.

Kolona did not let his expression change. "It is a possible scenario. Knowing about the attack, you could have seized the opportunity to overthrow your father and take control of House Tull."

Tull looked convincingly sick. "I find that suggestion offensive not only from a Sardaukar officer, but simply from a human being."

Kolona picked at his food before continuing. "Also, the Emperor's Truthsayer voiced certain suspicions regarding your new tenure at House Tull. She claims to see hints in your mannerisms, things that only she could detect. The Emperor listens to her."

Now the Viscount scoffed. "Reverend Mother Mohiam's comments are tainted. She is a Bene Gesserit, and the Sisterhood has an open dispute with me. The motives of the Bene Gesserit are childishly transparent, and I would place little stock in them."

He sniffed, then continued, "The witches had my father in their thrall all of his life, and he gave them large sums, which they used for construction at their Mother School. A waste of our family fortune, if you ask me! When my father died, I cut off their funding and expelled his concubine. The witch tried to seduce me before my father's bed was even cold." Tull appeared nauseated, and his voice seemed harsher. "If you do not already know these things about me, Colonel Bashar, I am not impressed with your abilities as an investigator."

Kolona gave a nod of respect. Of course he had known those details.

Viscount Tull waited, then pressed with an edge in his voice, "Anything else?"

"The Emperor is concerned about your close business ties with House Verdun. According to CHOAM public records, your commercial activities are intertwined."

"Naturally they are. Despite the beauty of our capital world and the profits we make from cultivating our rare lichens, we focus on extraplanetary industries. We extract base metals in our asteroid belt and send the ores to Dross for processing." Tull's expression darkened. "Your strike on House Verdun was a severe commercial blow to my people, and I have filed a formal complaint with the Landsraad Council."

"How do we know your supposed commercial activities are not a way to fund the Noble Commonwealth movement?" Kolona asked.

Tull retorted, "How do we know that Fausto Verdun was a traitor at all? I have yet to see any proof shared with the Landsraad after the summary execution of the Duke and his entire family." His anger was barely contained.

Kolona maintained a neutral expression. He was highly skeptical of Verdun's guilt, but a Sardaukar could not express any reservations about what the Emperor commanded him to do. "The evidence was sufficient in my view."

Tull looked openly angry. "All those people slaughtered, no trial, no evidence presented, no chance for appeal, and I am just supposed to take your word for it?"

"Take Emperor Shaddam's word for it," Kolona said, and that effectively ended the conversation.

They ate and drank in silence. In a subdued, bitter voice Tull said, "Investigate here all you wish, Colonel Bashar, but you'll find no evidence of rebellion." He pushed aside his plate, signaling that the meal was over. "Unless you fabricate it."

Kolona again gave the implacable answer. "We are Sardaukar." It was not an outright denial, but he meant it as such.

The officer took his leave of the extravagant manor house and returned to the personnel carrier at the spaceport, where he set up a field command post.

His troops remained for four more days, thorough in their inquiries, but they found no damning evidence. Jopati Kolona was secretly relieved.

To be a good leader it is necessary to informally—and constantly—assess the psychological well-being of all those around you.

—Admonition from MUAD'DIB

I *am in charge, but not in charge,* Paul thought—the young Master, with the burdens of a Duke.

At age fourteen, this was the first time he had filled the role alone. In his father's absence, he weighed the great responsibility on his shoulders, and accepted it. Although he understood he must temporarily act as Duke, Paul couldn't fathom what had happened with his parents. Why had Leto and Jessica abruptly gone their separate ways?

On a misty morning, the young man stood on one of the seaside battlements of Castle Caladan, an ancient defensive wall that was of little practical use in modern times. A chill wind blew in from the sea.

He had called his four closest advisers and teachers to join him. With Duke Leto away, Paul needed to establish parameters under which he would fill his role, even assert his authority, should it be necessary, although he hoped that no crisis would strike Caladan. These four would help him be the best leader.

He had always looked to Thufir Hawat, Gurney Halleck, Duncan Idaho, and Dr. Yueh as his mentors. Even though he was the ducal heir, they would scold him and correct him if they saw him about to make a fatal mistake. At any other time, the young man would have also relied on his mother's sage counsel, but the Lady Jessica was gone, too. . . .

Paul didn't understand what happened.

Before Duke Leto had left for Kaitain, he was odd and terse, worried in a way that made the young man concerned. So much was in turmoil, and he didn't have all the answers he wanted. His father had been away from his holdings before, most recently for the Emperor's gala on Otorio—and the proxies and chain of command were well established. Yes, Paul was technically the acting Duke, but his mother had always been a pillar of wisdom, even if Paul was seen as too young. No one had ever been concerned about leadership on Caladan before.

But she wasn't here.

From the battlement wall, he gazed out on the sea, remembering all the generations of Atreides that had ruled here. Behind him, the others waited, saying nothing, but certainly curious about what he wanted to do. Paul spoke, while gazing out to the gray clouds and choppy water. "While my parents are gone, I'm the acting Duke of Caladan. This is the first time I've done this alone."

"Not alone, young Master," Duncan Idaho interjected. "We're here for you."

Paul turned to look at them. "Would each of you follow any command I might give to you?"

"Aye, young Master." The troubadour warrior, Gurney Halleck, had brought his baliset over his shoulder, always ready to play the strings or quote an appropriate verse from the Orange Catholic Bible. "Unless you intend to ask us to jump off a cliff into the sea!"

Paul remained serious, pushing the boundaries. "Even that, Gurney. What if it came to such a situation? Hear me, I'm not joking. If I am acting as Duke, would you follow any command, as if it came directly from my father?"

Duncan stepped closer to the young man. The Swordmaster was deadly and intimidating, and one of Paul's closest friends. "Of course. We would die for House Atreides." He gave a curt bow.

"But would you die for *me*?"

Despite the seriousness of the question, Duncan gave him a wry smile. "Without question. You are House Atreides. But if we do our duty correctly, that should not be necessary." He was a head taller than Paul, with hair in tight dark curls and eyes that flashed with curiosity.

Looking over at Thufir Hawat, Paul noted that the aged warrior Mentat was pensive as he rolled the question in his mind, calculating possibilities and assessing Paul's tactics. "Are you conducting training exercises and thought experiments yourself now, young Master? Turning the tables on your instructors?"

Paul faced the Mentat. "Do you agree with what they said?"

The grizzled old man seemed to be in the midst of one of his mental exercises. "Like everyone here, I am at your service, just as I served your father and the Old Duke before him. We are sworn to House Atreides. It is my duty to advise, and then it is my obligation to obey."

The only one who had remained silent until now was the sallow-faced Suk doctor, who seemed more perplexed than troubled. Dr. Yueh was thin, smaller in stature than the other three, and no warrior. His long hair was bound with a silver ring into a ponytail behind him. A diamond tattoo on his forehead indicated that he had completed the most rigorous Imperial conditioning. As the Atreides doctor, Yueh had tended Paul's scrapes and bruises, had even saved the young man's life recently, when Paul nearly died from moonfish poisoning. Yueh was stiff and formal in contrast to the warm loyalty of the others.

The doctor stood in front of a crenel, a lower section of the wall from which ancient soldiers could fire their weapons. Paul placed his hands on Yueh's shoulders, put pressure on them. He maintained his grip even when he felt the doctor tense up. "And you, Dr. Yueh? You would follow my commands, whatever I say as acting Duke?"

"If they are good commands, yes, my Lord."

Paul was surprised by the vague answer. "And if they are bad commands?"

"Then I would consider it my duty to advise you."

Paul appreciated the complexity of the answer. "What if I disagreed with you?"

"Then I would assume I must be wrong, and I would follow your orders, Sire."

Paul remained where he was, nodding. The others watched him, wondering what he was up to. He continued to grip the Suk doctor's shoulders, both of them standing at the edge of the high wall above the crashing waves. "If I commanded you to leap off this battlement into the sea, would you do it?"

Yueh blinked, startled, but he did not move. "As with all the people of Caladan, my life is in your hands . . . uh, my Lord. You could simply shove me over the edge. You are in your father's position now." He and the others looked quite uneasy.

Paul released him, marched back and forth in front of the men. "What if I ordered all of you to jump from this high place right now? Would you?" He looked at them all. "Of course not! Because such a command would be capricious and immoral, and as such, you should not obey it. I am in my father's position, but he would never order such a thing. You should only obey lawful and moral commands, even from me."

Thufir's brow furrowed, and Duncan smiled with relief. Gurney laughed out loud.

Finally, Yueh said, "As a doctor I have studied not only physical illnesses, but mental infirmities. Few people are more dangerous than an unstable commander." His lips tightened into a hard line. "But you are not mentally unstable, Paul Atreides. This was a test for us."

"And for me," Paul said.

Gurney added, "We have known you your entire life, lad, and you would never issue such a command. That would be a . . . a *Harkonnen* thing to do."

"So, as my closest advisers and the top officials in House Atreides, it is your duty to make sure I am not mentally infirm—correct?"

With light steps, he sprang to the top of the parapet, a high point on the low wall. On the other side, he looked straight down to jagged rocks and the sea. One moment of insanity, and Paul could die.

Gurney moved forward like a prowling animal, swift yet cautious.

Thufir barked out, "Young Master, I insist you get down."

"You always warn me against risks, Thufir," Paul said. Then he added in a singsong voice, "Don't sit with your back to a doorway. Trust your instincts. Always leave yourself a way out. Never let your guard down. Am I right?"

The warrior Mentat nodded. "At this moment, I would also counsel you not to be on top of that wall."

Paul glanced at Gurney, who looked genuinely worried. Dr. Yueh regarded him with a slight scowl. But he saw a twinkle in Duncan Idaho's eyes.

"Duncan has been training me to push myself, to face danger, to be ready for any real circumstance. All of life is training—isn't that what you say, Thufir?"

The Mentat remained stony. "And a life cut short would certainly end your training."

Paul laughed. "Duncan and I climbed the cliffs below the castle, holding on by our fingers, scaling the impossible precipice. He encouraged me."

The Swordmaster grimaced. "I saved you from complete foolishness."

"And now I know I can do it. Thus, I do not doubt myself."

With complete confidence, Paul leaped across one of the crenels to the other side, then skipped along the wall with swift grace, dancing over the crenels. Then he misjudged, slipped on a section of mist-slick stone, caught his balance, and barely kept himself from going in the wrong, and fatal, direction.

Gurney and Duncan, bounding along as spotters, reached for Paul, but the young man had already saved himself.

Thufir Hawat called, "I would also counsel you not to leap across crenels! I do not find this amusing."

"You have given me advice all my life, and I appreciate what you have done for me, but today I declare myself a man, able to make my own decisions, good or bad." With his back to the sea, he held his arms wide, palms open. "Only a man can rule a planet. It is not something to be left to a boy."

"Your actions here do not give us great comfort, lad," Gurney chided.

Grinning, Paul sprang down to the ground. "I wanted to teach you something about me. Duncan and Gurney always insisted that I train to the limit, that I take risks in order to improve myself—*calculated* risks. I have never walked on the wall like this before, have never leaped across the gaps. But I thought I could do it, and I did."

"For the most part," Duncan said.

Paul walked up to them, running his hands through his wind-blown black hair. "Thanks to your training and counsel, I had the ability to save myself from a slight misstep. I am responsible for my actions and decisions, facing the consequences of what I do . . . but I am also responsible for listening to my advisers. I will continue to depend on each of you. Though I have blustered a bit today in my declaration of manhood, I still need all of you. I could not rule without you."

They bowed.

"House Atreides has enemies, and if they decide to attack us, there will be no warning. Logically, with my father away, Caladan is at greater risk. Thufir, place the military on full alert, and keep your eyes open—just in case."

The old Mentat chuckled. "You are wise beyond your years, Master Paul. But yes, I have already done that."

WHEN PAUL ENTERED his father's study in the old castle, the finely appointed chamber seemed empty without him. In fact, the whole castle seemed hollow without its Duke and without the Lady of Caladan.

Paul did not sit in his father's chair, oddly reluctant to be alone in the study. He touched the top of his father's bulky elaccawood desk, noted the marks from years of use. It had belonged to Paul's grandfather, and to other Dukes before that. So many important decisions had been made here in this room.

He caught himself, wondered why his feelings about everything were so intense. His father would be away on Kaitain no more than a month or two, and he hoped his mother would return as well, despite their quarrel. He wanted life to return to normal.

Hearing a sound, he turned toward the open doorway to see it filled by the form of Thufir Hawat. The old Mentat's hair looked mussed, and his expression seemed just as rumpled. A bright red stain on his lips showed that he had just consumed another vial of sapho juice.

Thufir locked his hands behind his back and delivered a report. "My Lord, we just received alarming news." He paused a moment as if to let Paul prepare himself. Had something happened to his parents? "House Verdun has been destroyed on Dross. The Duke was declared a traitor, and Sardaukar legions completely obliterated the lord and his holdings. All family members were killed."

Paul blinked. Duke Fausto Verdun? His daughter, Junu Verdun, had been considered an acceptable future wife for Paul. Leto had even dispatched an offer of betrothal, which had been insultingly rebuffed. But . . . traitors? All dead? Even the pretty, talented, and intelligent young girl? "How, Thufir? Why?" He straightened, cleared his throat. "Explain."

The old Mentat seemed unsteady, as if his assessments hadn't provided an acceptable answer. "The Emperor believes Duke Verdun was involved with the Noble Commonwealth movement. He preemptively dispatched an overwhelming military force to strike their home without warning. The capital city was leveled, the entire noble family killed in the attack."

Paul tried to process the completely unexpected news. "Junu Verdun . . . she had to be innocent."

"All dead, my Lord. It is a terrible loss."

Paul hardened inside. "Were they really rebels? When you were studying betrothal prospects, did you not extensively research the Verdun holdings? Did you miss something?"

Thufir looked deeply troubled. "I found no evidence against the House, sir. None whatsoever. Perhaps the Emperor will explain in due course."

Paul had never met the young woman, only seeing her images in the dossier compiled by his mother and the warrior Mentat. This incident must be a political bloodletting of some sort, outright murder ordered by Emperor Shaddam. Such things had happened before in Imperial politics.

And Duke Leto had traveled to Kaitain to be in the thick of it.

Paul slumped into his father's chair after all. "Thufir, please give me time alone to consider this dire news."

The loyal Mentat bowed. "I will review our forces, attend to security measures, make certain Caladan has no vulnerabilities. There is no reason for the Emperor to attack us, especially not after your father saved his life on Otorio, but, well . . . these are dangerous times."

"Yes, they are."

After the Mentat left, Paul swam in his own thoughts. Now he would never meet Junu Verdun . . . whose father had rudely spurned the offer of marriage, declaring Paul unsuitable. Even so, the young woman had done him no wrong. She had been an innocent bystander, a child of the wrong noble family. She had not deserved such a terrible fate.

Thinking of Junu, his prospective wife, brought to mind a girl who had been visiting him in his dreams. *Tell me about the waters of your homeworld.* . . .

That was the young woman he needed to find.

He leaned over the wooden desk, found several sheets of blank paper and a stylus. Deep in thought, he tried to sketch the girl, but he couldn't get the drawing right. He crumpled the paper and tossed it aside, then made another attempt.

Duncan Idaho slipped into the study, approaching the big desk before Paul noticed him. "Never let your guard down, young Master," he said. His sword was unsheathed, and he brandished it. "It's time for your lesson downstairs. I came to see what's keeping you."

Paul was not concerned, too determined to get the drawing right, to capture the face that haunted his dreams. He had once caught a glimpse of the girl in Cala City near the castle, or at least he'd thought so, but had not been able to find her again.

Duncan sheathed the sword and leaned over the desk, curious to see what the young man was doing. "That's a pretty girl there. You have artistic skill, as Gurney has musical skill." He gently pushed Paul's hands to the side so he could see the entire sketch. "Is that a desert in the background?"

"Each time she comes to me in my dreams, I see her in a sandy place, with rocks and dunes. And don't scoff at me, Duncan Idaho. Dreams are important."

"I wouldn't think of scoffing at you, even though they may just be the vivid dreams of a young man. But dunes on Caladan, hmmm. Ah, I know of such a spot, south along the coast. With your father we flew over it once in a military 'thopter. If this dream girl is surrounded by dunes, I can't imagine a better place to look."

Paul was surprised, but didn't let his hopes rise too high. "You think she might be there?"

"It would be worth finding out, my Lord. We can go there together. No harm in looking . . . if it helps solve the mystery that haunts you."

Even trust is a commodity to be bought and sold.
—Secret Noble Commonwealth
communiqué

Though a fugitive, Jaxson Aru traveled freely. With long-standing connections and CHOAM resources, he had many channels available to him. His mother was the Ur-Director of CHOAM and his brother the figurehead President.

Even if his family had disowned him, he was able to buy the secrecy he needed. The Tleilaxu would certainly maintain his secrets.

Disguised as a simple businessman hoping to purchase biologically engineered grain, Jaxson traveled to the Thalim system and disembarked onto an orbiting station where all outside visitors were required to quarantine. Without this procedure, no "unclean powindah" were allowed to set foot in the sacred city of Bandalong.

Other business representatives from the Guild transport filled out forms and let themselves be taken into isolation on the station. Jaxson pretended to be just one of them, but they would give him special treatment. He had a privileged relationship with these people.

In less than an hour, his sealed cell whisked open to reveal two robed Masters, short in stature with a corpse-like pallor to their skin. Both men had gaunt features, narrow chins and noses. Over countless generations, the genetic wizards had selected for such attributes, giving their race a kind of homogeneity. Jaxson found it strange the Tleilaxu wouldn't choose a more traditionally attractive appearance, but perhaps their fanatically religious race took their odd appearance as a badge of honor.

The answer was not important to Jaxson. He was used to being reviled, too. The entire Imperium wanted him dead after Otorio, but that shocking massacre of Shaddam Corrino's sycophants had shone a brighter, more compelling light on the rebel cause than his mother's parlor-room plans had managed to accomplish in decades. And the Tleilaxu were a great asset, even if the broader Noble Commonwealth movement didn't realize they sympathized with the movement.

The two hooded men looked coldly at him from the doorway, and Jaxson offered a perfunctory bow because he did not wish to antagonize them. "You're here to escort me down to Bandalong," he announced, not making it a question. "Master Arafa blessed my visit."

The men frowned in unison. The one on the left said, "*Approved*, not blessed." The other said, "Follow us before anyone sees."

The quarantine station smelled cold, oily, and unwelcoming. Separate window-less corridors held waiting rooms like prison cells. He wondered why these people feared outsiders so much. Explaining nothing, they placed him alone in a shuttle, which departed for the planet. The shuttle's interior had no windowports, so he could not see the city during the bumpy ride down to the surface.

Jaxson refused to let himself feel intimidated. He needed the Tleilaxu, and the Tleilaxu needed him.

When the shuttle landed and the hatch opened, Jaxson saw a city skyline of domes and sharp towers, geometric architectural experiments that offended the eyes and sensibilities. Bandalong's sky was a hazy gray gloom.

Another Tleilaxu Master met him at the shuttle, his appearance so similar to the other two that it was hard to tell the differences. Jaxson gave a perfunctory bow. "Are you Master Arafa?"

The hooded man turned close-set eyes toward him with a glare of suspicion. "You have to pass more layers of security before you are allowed to see him."

Jaxson endured an intrusive personal bodily search and passed through a scanning portal that mapped his skin and features and penetrated deep to the bone. The Master announced, "Your disguise is insufficient to fool us."

Jaxson snapped, "I am not trying to fool you—merely the rest of the Impe-rium. That's one of the primary reasons I came here and why I need to see Master Arafa."

The Tleilaxu didn't understand. "Your associate Chaen Marek dispatched a message that you wished to review genetic modifications to the barra ferns."

"I am a complex man," Jaxson said. "I have more than one interest, and the Tleilaxu can fulfill more than one need. I am the most-wanted man in the galaxy, and I've placed my security in your hands. I'm the one who should be suspicious!"

The unnamed Master extended an accusatory finger. "But the Imperium de-spises our entire race. If any hint leaked out that we secretly support your cause to unravel the Corrino reign, then all Tleilaxu would be eradicated."

Jaxson smiled. "So if either of us slips, it is mutual annihilation—the best way to guarantee trust and cooperation." He made an imperious gesture. "Now take me to Master Arafa."

They reached the armored greenhouse laboratory, and his guide gave him a breathing film to place over his mouth and nose.

He passed through the transparent air lock, and finally met Master Arafa. Jaxson noticed a prominent hook to the man's thin nose and a lumpy scar above one eyebrow. Arafa also wore a breathing membrane.

"You took great risks to come, Jaxson Aru. But you are safe here."

"We both forge a dangerous path," Jaxson said.

Arafa placed his hands together. "It is as God wishes. We are the agents of God's will."

Jaxson had no interest in a theological discussion, so he agreed. "We are the agents of God's will." *Just as you are the agents of mine.*

The Tleilaxu Master gestured him inside. The armored greenhouse laboratory was like a mad scientist's garden filled with a writhing botanical infestation of plants, all of which were decidedly *wrong*. Some specimens looked monstrous and repulsive; others were beautiful yet subtly insidious.

Arafa mused, "I understand your drug operations on Caladan experienced a great setback, your lucrative barra fields destroyed by Leto Atreides."

"It was a setback, true," Jaxson said. "But I have other plans for Duke Leto. I'll grant him that victory."

Arafa remained skeptical. "Ailar is what financed all of your plans . . . and ours."

"I have other sources of money, for now." Jaxson narrowed his eyes. "And I can continue to pay, if that is of concern to you."

Arafa made a quiet, dismissive sound, which was not a denial. It reassured Jaxson that the Tleilaxu Master had indeed been concerned.

"Chaen Marek will rebuild his growing operations from scratch, with your assistance," Jaxson said. "Barra ferns are natural plants on Caladan. We cultivated them and expanded their use as a source of the drug ailar, adapting it from local religious purposes. But Marek got greedy and sloppy. His enhanced ailar was dangerous and out of his control, and it poisoned enough people to draw unwanted attention and thus exposed our operations."

"Marek will fix it, just as we will fix it," said Arafa. "We have new, better barra ferns. Only rarely do they contain the lethally high concentration of the drug."

They passed a group of brilliant red flowers like giant lips that trembled and smacked. A misty perfume wafted out, and Arafa bent close, trusting his breathing film to protect him. "Beautiful flowers with a deadly nerve toxin." He raised his eyebrows, making the small scar dance. "Genetically configured to affect only women."

"Why?" Jaxson asked.

"God's purposes are often mysterious. We provide the products, and others employ them to their own purposes."

Other sections of the greenhouse contained bulbous fungal growths, twisting reeds that made a hypnotic humming sound, thornbushes that glistened with venom-filled needles, vines that struck out toward any motion.

Finally, they reached a growing area covered with curling prehensile ferns, some of them splotched and mottled, some vibrant green. Several ferns stretched taller than a man, studded with vicious spines.

"Here we experiment with barra fern variations under closely monitored conditions. We can grow a few specimens in our facility, although the ferns thrive only on Caladan."

Jaxson nodded. "Marek has already staked out a new growing area on the isolated southern continent. I told him to be unobtrusive." He stepped closer to the monstrous plants. "These giant ferns are untenable in large commercial operations."

Arafa smiled. "Most of these specimens are much too toxic and unstable for your use. They would never be a viable alternative for the ailar trade."

"Then why waste the time and effort? We have critical needs and a tight timescale."

The Tleilaxu Master spread his hands. "In our work, we learn the most by pushing to extremes."

Jaxson digested this as he stared at the exotic foliage. "Good," he said, finding a way to turn the conversation to his true purpose. "Then I have another extreme for you to investigate. I need a new disguise. Emperor Shaddam's henchmen hunt me relentlessly. For now, I have places to hide and a secret base of operations, but I need more freedom of movement."

Arafa gave a slow nod. "Yes, we easily detected your disguise when you came here. It's fortunate that we are not your enemy."

"I understand you have a technique—facial cloning, I believe you call it."

Arafa reacted with surprise. "This is the other matter you wish to discuss?"

"Facial cloning. Grow me a new face that is more than a disguise, one that goes as deep as my cells."

"Ah, there are many surgeries available that offer similar results," Arafa suggested. "Your features could be reconfigured in numerous ways."

"Facial cloning," Jaxson insisted. "No scars, no surgery. Just new skin and features that extend down to the genetic level. I believe it was an offshoot of your ghola program, growing new bodies from the cells of a dead person."

"Yes, we have grown new faces," Arafa admitted, but did not explain further.

"I brought the cells with me." From his pocket, Jaxson removed vials containing loose hairs, two clipped nails, and a flake of skin that he had found after a painstaking search, the tiniest speck at a time. "My father died of a stroke on our Otorio estate. He is lost, but I will never forget him. He was my mentor. He shaped me. If I must wear a disguise, I want to be reminded of him every time I look in a mirror."

Arafa accepted the vials, squinted at the contents. "The result will be a combination of your features and his, something unique and on no existing records." Behind him, the thorny barra fern twitched and unfurled, but the Tleilaxu was too intent on the cellular specimens to notice. "There will be a substantial cost."

Jaxson drew a deep breath through his membrane. "There always is."

One can be intimidated by the spice melange—its unique benefits, its monetary value, the pervasive demand for it throughout the Imperium.

One can be frustrated by the spice, the fact that it is found in only one planet in the known universe, that its extraction must be done under hellish conditions, that the greatest powers vie for the Emperor's favor to work the spice sands on Arrakis.

But one cannot deny the spice. That would be like denying air and light itself.

—CHOAM Company précis

Standing in the heat and dust, Baron Vladimir Harkonnen ignored safety measures by removing his mouth and nose coverings. Reveling in the astonishing aridity, he closed his eyes and inhaled a long, steady breath, drinking in the dryness. He ignored the noisy chaos of the Orgiz refinery operations in the isolated canyon.

He just absorbed the distinctive cinnamon aroma, sharp, potent, and heady. It burned his nostrils and his lungs with a delicious richness. *Spice!* . . . everywhere. And it was his—especially here, because even Shaddam IV did not know about the Orgiz refinery, nor did the Emperor impose his damnable spice surtax on it.

After only a few seconds, though, the crackling dry air began to irritate his nose and throat. He took one more breath and rolled his tongue around the inside of his mouth. Spice out in the open was raw and primal, but he preferred it to be served in purified form, in controllable quantities and in a more civilized setting.

He replaced the mouth covering and filter plug. The skin of his rounded face was rough with grit, starting to tighten and dry already. Once he got back to his Carthag residence, he would enjoy a steam bath and command one of his attendants to apply lotions. Soon, he would be off to Kaitain to see the Emperor, but right now he had to finish his inspection of the illicit refinery.

Orgiz had been built by his father eighty years ago, when House Harkonnen first received the siridar-governorship of Arrakis. The refinery was in a rugged, mostly unmapped line of mountains, a box canyon with high walls that widened into a sheltered arena, where an entire operations center could remain hidden from all but those who knew where to look. Under the management of Dmitri Harkonnen, Orgiz had produced a great deal of melange.

Then a rogue sandworm had found its way into the blind canyon—or had it been maliciously led there by Fremen?—and wrecked the place. The refinery had remained abandoned for decades, erased from all charts.

The Baron looked around at the new spice silos, packaging lines, and compression cannisters, the newly repaved landing field that could accommodate even a large carryall. With extensive effort over the past few months, the Baron had restored the complex for his new scheme with CHOAM. Already the metal silos looked tarnished and pitted from the Arrakis environment, but the equipment functioned, and it produced spice. Nothing else mattered.

To the rest of the Imperium, Orgiz was long forgotten, and its new output was recorded on no Imperial ledger, not noted by the hawk-sharp gaze of Count Hasimir Fenring, the Spice Minister. None of the facilities or ships flaunted Harkonnen colors or insignia, and no worker had any connection to the Baron. Orgiz produced a secret supply line of spice to fulfill his agreement with CHOAM's Ur-Director Malina Aru. In the buzz and bustle of activity around him, he heard only a sweet musical drone of profits.

His nephew Rabban stepped up, wearing no formal rank insignia. The burly man was covered in dust, and a dark smear of soot or oil marked his left cheek. His deep-set eyes were as hard as the canyon walls around him. He removed his mouth covering, coughed enough to loosen phlegm, and spat on the ground, a gesture that would have startled the Arrakis natives.

"Two more shipments ready to go, Uncle." With a jerk of his heavy chin, Rabban indicated the landing field where a pair of nondescript cargo craft sat with warm-up lights glowing and suspensor fields humming. Heavy groundcars delivered pallets of packaged spice into the open holds. "A load of melange, unmarked, untraceable to Orgiz, and certainly unconnected to House Harkonnen."

The Baron made a noncommittal sound through his nose. "Melange? You mean 'sterilized geological samples bound for researchers on Hagal.'" It was a ruse they had used to mark other shipments, drawing no attention.

Rabban let his greed show. "Now that suspicion has been removed from our operations, shouldn't we take advantage of it? We could double our production here, increase our secret sales to CHOAM." He paused to chuckle. "We can always build new treasury buildings if we make too much profit."

"Don't slap the face of a miracle, Rabban," the Baron said. "Fenring mistakenly thinks he caught and executed the smuggler ringleader. Let us not provoke more trouble."

He was still relieved that the Harkonnens had somehow dodged certain exposure. Emperor Shaddam, along with Count Fenring and his annoyingly eccentric failed Mentat, Grix Dardik, having inferred the existence of a secret operation not under Imperial oversight, had concluded that a great deal of spice money was being embezzled, right under the Emperor's nose.

The Baron thought he'd covered his tracks carefully, and Malina Aru certainly hadn't left loose ends dangling for Imperial Mentat accountants to find, but Fenring had poked around . . . and somehow blamed the wrong person for the illicit operations. Rulla, the wife of known smuggler Esmar Tuek, had been fingered as the responsible party, "proven" guilty, and executed. The piracy ring had been disbanded, and now, at least officially, the Imperium was no longer looking for any spice black market. Too convenient all around.

Inexplicably, the Baron and CHOAM had dodged a mortal blow, and he did not intend to waste the reprieve. "We continue with greater caution, Rabban. We've had a scare. The Ur-Director is on edge."

"She still wants our spice," Rabban pointed out. "As much as we can send her."

The Baron saw that the groundcars had finished loading the two cargo haulers. "Everyone wants our spice. And if we intend to remain in control, we need patience."

Though Rabban's expression darkened, he nodded. He followed his uncle's orders, whether he liked them or not.

"I leave you in charge, nephew. Continue the spice operations, with increased caution." The Baron paused and smiled. "And continue to earn great profits. We have our industries on Giedi Prime, the whale fur and fisheries on your Lankiveil, but there's nothing like melange." He gave one last look at all of the busy operations.

Rabban wasn't an imaginative or insightful manager, but he was competent, so long as he was pointed in the right direction and not pushed beyond his abilities.

"I'm off to Kaitain to see the Emperor," the Baron said. "I will reassure him that all is well, so he will find no need for his Spice Observer to watch us too closely."

Rabban turned to shout at the workers over the industrial noise. The Baron watched his nephew for a few moments longer, to reassure himself, then left for an unmarked 'thopter that would take him back to Carthag.

After leaving Lethea's secure medical chamber, Jessica was taken to the
fourth floor of the residential building, a special floor for visitors. *Visitors* . . . Jessica wondered how long they would hold her here. Would she ever
leave? What did Lethea want to do to her?

Her quarters consisted of a small room with a single bed, a nightstand, a
soft, tattered chair, a wall-mounted glowglobe, and a little bookcase containing
filmbooks and shigawire reels. The spartan room reminded Jessica of her younger
days of hard training at the Mother School under Mohiam.

Seeing her new home, she thought of her long journey, her tension. How
many days had it been since leaving Caladan, since leaving Leto? In her wardrobe, she found a black Sister's robe to wear. Other than the few items she had
brought with her, including a sentimental set of coral-gem earrings and necklace,
she had nothing that would make her look like a Duke's lady. Here, she was just
another Sister.

If the Bene Gesserit had permanently withdrawn her as the Duke's bound
concubine, and if Leto had truly broken with her, then she could no longer use
her former title. *Lady Jessica.* Even so, her mind and heart would not let go. It was
not something the Sisterhood could strip from her.

I am still the Lady of Caladan.

THE NEXT MORNING, the Mother Superior summoned her again to Lethea's room. Four women clustered in the corridor in front of the large observation window. Harishka whispered to a mysterious woman who wore a dark hood
and an obscuring mesh over her face. Beside them, the brunette Sister Jiara spoke
in low tones to a Reverend Mother who had light brown hair, a pasty face, and
a harsh expression.

As Jessica joined them, the mysterious veiled woman quickly departed down a side corridor, while Jiara, Harishka, and another Reverend Mother named Ruthine stared through the armored window as if studying a dangerous specimen in a zoo.

The Mother Superior turned to Jessica. "We need you to uncover some answers." Her face tightened as she ran her gaze up and down Jessica's features. "She demanded you come here. She insists on seeing you—she refuses to tell us. Find out what she wants."

Ruthine scowled. She had gray-brown hair in ringlets, and her face was an unmemorable mix of bland features, but she seemed anything but bland. "Maybe she just wants to kill you. We could have done that without nearly so much trouble."

Inside the chamber on her medical bed, Lethea writhed. Her wild, unfocused eyes darted around as if she were a caged animal.

Pointedly ignoring what Ruthine had said, Jessica replied, "I don't know anything about her. What can I possibly do?"

"You're going in there with her," Harishka said, her tone cold. "Ask her. We will all be waiting to hear her answer."

"Yes," Jiara said, looking at Jessica. "We'll observe from here."

Jessica forced herself to take a calming breath and pressed her lips together. "If she has already coerced several Sisters into killing themselves, this is like throwing a mouse into a snake's cage."

"True, but I think you're a mouse who can possibly outsmart the snake. We have deemed this mystery important enough that we are willing to risk your life."

Jessica stiffened. *But how important do you consider my life in the first place?*

"Horror, bloodshed, disaster," Ruthine said. "Something about you or your son."

She remembered the many tests she had endured here at the Mother School. "So, this is another gom jabbar." She took a heavy step toward the sealed door. "I survived the first test that Mohiam gave me. I will survive this one."

Ruthine turned to her with a gaze like sharp fragments of diamond. "Are you afraid?" Something about this woman set her on edge as much as Lethea did.

Jessica steeled herself, knowing that she was required to do as the Bene Gesserit commanded. Perhaps if she could complete her task here, they would let her return to Caladan to salvage what she could. She turned to Harishka. "I am not afraid, Mother Superior."

Ruthine scoffed. "You should be."

"Remember the oath you took," Jiara warned. "A Sister must take *every* measure possible to safeguard and advance the Bene Gesserit."

"I remember my oath, and I know what it means," Jessica said, then lowered her voice. "It means I am expendable."

"We all are, in the broader sense," Harishka noted. "There are no exceptions. But Lethea thinks you or your actions could end the Sisterhood. Find out why, or we may have to resort to other actions."

"We can't take the risk," Jiara muttered.

Jessica remained outwardly calm, but inside her mind, she pushed back. So, an ancient woman who struggled with violent inner demons had summoned Jessica from across the Imperium. In her prescience, or dementia, she had seen something vital, some key decision or action that would alter the course of history. *Why separate me from Paul?*

Lethea wouldn't simply kill Jessica the moment she entered the room. Would she?

All senses alert, Jessica went to the closed door of the confinement chamber. "Fear is the mind-killer . . ."

The Mother Superior gave her a smile of respect. "Recite the entire Litany if you wish."

"That will not be necessary." Jessica looked at a wall control panel for the door. "I'll do my duty, and I hope the Sisterhood remembers that."

Ruthine seemed to be resentful toward her. "You have not always done your duty for us, though. Perhaps this will make up for it."

Jessica remained outwardly calm, not giving them the satisfaction of showing her bitterness. She activated the door and entered the room. An unpleasant odor assailed her nostrils, and she heard the rushing hum of air circulators. When the door closed and locked behind her, she felt as if she had entered a combat arena.

Even though the medical equipment continued its quiet electronic whispering, and the fans thrummed in the background, a hushed void seemed to open up when she entered the room. Jessica froze just inside the door.

Lethea paused in her struggles, raised her head, and glared at Jessica. Her eyes were passionless, dead, as if she were visualizing what to do with the intruder.

Jessica waited, facing the old woman strapped to the bed. Lethea thrashed, and she became surprisingly lucid. "You don't like the smell! I can tell by the look on your face. Are you here to change my bedclothes?"

"I am Lady Jessica of Caladan," she responded with cool formality. "You summoned me."

Abruptly, Lethea lurched up with enough strength that the restraints groaned and creaked. "You!" She tried to reach out, desperate to attack with her bare hands, but could not.

Jessica remained where she was, well out of reach. "Why did you call me? What do you want?" *Why did you tear me from my home and family?*

As if a switch had been flipped, the crone settled back and appeared calm. A smile crept across her face. "Let's do something together, shall we?"

The Mother Superior demanded answers from her, and Jessica needed to provide them before she could ask to be released. She took a cautious step closer to the medical bed. "Explain yourself. What have I done to draw your attention?"

"What have you done? Or what will you do? Are you the danger, or is it your boy?" She squirmed on the medical bed. "Help me change my sheets. We'll do it together. Release my restraints."

Jessica was not fooled. "That is not why you called me all the way from Caladan."

"Send someone in here to take care of it, then." Looking peeved, Lethea lay back and stared at the ceiling.

"I'll do that after you give me answers. Mother Superior Harishka is listening."

The old woman made an annoyed sound. "They are all listening. Always listening. They know what I said. There are countless paths to the future, but thanks to you and your son, so many of them end in cliffs for the Sisterhood."

Taking a gamble, Jessica moved close to the bed and adjusted the pillow under Lethea's head. "Is that more comfortable?"

A wry smile crossed her cracked lips. "Look around you, Lady Jessica of Caladan. Does this room look like it was designed for my comfort?"

"No, it doesn't. I'm sorry."

"You are sorry?" She made a rude sound. "You could destroy us all!"

"Yes, I am sorry."

"Have Harishka come in here and tell me she's sorry! She and I used to be friends, you know." Lethea twisted her head to glare through the plaz barrier at the Mother Superior who waited out in the hall, made a childlike face at her.

Jessica continued to assess the danger posed by this volatile personality. "Why am I here?"

"Because I know!" Lethea said. "Because of you, your son . . . the danger to us all!" She lowered her voice. "Be safe, be done with it. Kill your son."

Jessica covered her shock. She didn't even have to think about her response. "No. I will not."

"Then we are all doomed." Lethea fell back and closed her eyes. She seemed to slip into another portion of her mind. "Or maybe I just dreamed it all. Dreams can be very vivid, you know." Moments passed, and Jessica watched her face, her motionless fingers and toes. Then Lethea's eyes opened to slits, and she looked long and hard at Jessica.

"I will not kill my son," Jessica repeated in a firm tone. The old crone could feel the strength of her determination.

Lethea babbled in a rapid whisper, as if speaking to someone inside her head, so low that Jessica could not make out the words. Perhaps a flood of Other Memories had surfaced inside her, the disembodied voices of past Reverend Mothers driving her insane. It had happened to others.

Lethea jerked awake and thrashed against her restraints. She looked up with a blank stare and shrieked, "Jessica of Caladan! Bring me Jessica of Caladan!"

Jessica forced herself to remain calm and focused on bringing her senses to heightened awareness. "I am here. Explain yourself!"

Harishka and the other observers would be hanging on every word.

The crone's face shifted, little by little, and her mouth turned down before she spat words up at Jessica. "You! It is already too late!" Her expression changed again, and she cackled. "They get what they deserve."

"Who does? Tell me what you saw?"

Lethea looked at Jessica with a knowing smile. "We shall spend more time together, you and I. Harishka fancies herself a leader who needs facts to make decisions. She is a logical person, too logical at times. We shall see how she fares . . . if she will do what needs doing."

"You are placing my son in danger." Jessica felt more urgency. "Why did you need to take me away from my son and Duke?"

"We are all in danger!" Lethea yelled. "Go!"

Without showing emotion, Jessica went to the door and waited until Jiara unlocked and unsealed it.

Harishka waited outside the room, curious, worried, confused. She stood with hands on hips. "Lethea is unpredictable. She thinks it keeps me off balance."

"The answer seemed clear enough," Ruthine said.

The Mother Superior rounded on her. "Nothing is clear! Lethea is brilliant, but she is also vindictive. I do not trust any of her motives . . . or anything she said."

"And yet I am here," Jessica muttered, "taken away from everything I hold dear."

"Not everything," Jiara said. "You still have the Sisterhood."

From inside the chamber, Lethea screeched, her voice muffled through the monitoring speakers. "You're confined just like I am, but in a different way, because I have something you want. I'm in control here!"

Harishka sent a signal, and an automated needle flicked out from the medical bed and stabbed Lethea's upper arm. The crone arched her back and hissed, but the tranquilizer sent her into a stupor.

Harishka said, "She did not give us all the answers we need. Therefore, you will try again, and again, until we are satisfied."

Jessica struggled with the ravings, feared what some other Sisters might do in response. "My son is no threat, not to the Bene Gesserit, not to anyone. He's only fourteen."

The Mother Superior stalked away without answering.

A man is composed of his memories, his history, his actions, and his reputation.

     —DUKE PAULUS ATREIDES, in a letter to his son

After settling in at the Imperial Court, Duke Leto focused on his project as if it were a military operation. First, he connected with Archduke Armand Ecaz, a friend who was also at the Imperial capital on Landsraad business. The one-armed nobleman had been an Atreides ally for years, and he was one of the few who had escaped Otorio, thanks to Leto's warning.

The two men stood outside the imposing Landsraad Hall, where the façade's fluted stone columns towered as thick as Ecazi bloodwood trees. Along the main boulevard, poles flew the colorful flags of noble houses. Scattered among them, some flags flew at half-mast, belonging to families that had suffered losses on Otorio.

Leto had to use a directory to locate the green-and-black banner of House Atreides, far down the street. Seeing the obscure location, Armand suggested that Leto file a formal petition requesting that the Atreides banner be moved to a more prominent place closer to the Hall.

During the governmental session, many seats were empty because the day's agenda had no particularly important business. At Armand's suggestion, Leto chose three innocuous bills to support. He sat in the section reserved for House Atreides, and when the agenda items came up, Leto signaled his intention to speak. He rose, booming out so that all could hear, "Duke Leto Atreides of Caladan supports this measure."

"So noted," replied the Hall parliamentarian, and Leto's name went on the records of the proceedings.

He didn't feel he had done much, but now that they were leaving the session, the Archduke gave a sad smile. "You accomplished the most important part, which was to be seen and noticed. Some Landsraad families have a representative vote yes or no on every single bill brought to the floor, whether or not it has anything to do with them. The result is that their representatives are frequently chosen for important subcommittees because they were visible."

Leto imagined how such tedious work would distract from his true calling on Caladan. "Being on numerous subcommittees is a good thing?"

"A *prominent* thing, and it lets their representatives influence certain policies. Not all matters are irrelevant, Leto. Many nobles here, particularly Rajiv Londine, have been lobbying to overturn the Emperor's spice surtax—unsuccessfully so far."

Leto said, "I've heard the complaints, but the surtax does not affect me. House Atreides has nothing to do with spice." He did recall, however, his recent experiences with the dangerous new drug ailar that had established itself on Caladan and then spread among the Landsraad, taking many lives.

Armand gave him a serious look. "Vent and complain in front of me if it makes you feel better, but I know you are not so naïve about politics."

"Oh, I understand all too well. That is why I left home and came to Kaitain," he said. "Count Fenring has even offered to help me gain more prominence here."

The Archduke replied carefully, "An interesting prospect. Hasimir Fenring can indeed help you gain influence at court, but use caution with that one. He may help you get what you want, but not in a way that an Atreides would find acceptable. I know how much honor means to you—you would not want to make a deal with the devil."

Leto's chest tightened. He had thought the same thing, and nodded. "Understood, old friend."

Weary of crowds, he returned to the palace, intending to write a letter to Paul and prepare a report of his own activities for Hawat. As he crossed through the busy common areas, though, he was intercepted by a man in an elaborate courtly uniform.

"Empress Aricatha would be pleased to have you join her for spice coffee and conversation," said the messenger. He gave Leto the exact time to arrive, which was less than half an hour hence. Leto barely had time to get to the proper wing, so he rushed off, glad that he'd worn formal clothes for the Landsraad session.

A polite, silent retainer guided him into the Empress's private drawing room. Aricatha waited for him at a small, intimate table with only one other chair, and her expression was warm and welcoming. She wore a spun-gold dress bedazzled with green gems. "I am pleased to see you again, Duke Leto Atreides, and under much better circumstances than the frantic evacuation of Otorio. One of my duties as Empress is to know my husband's most important subjects."

He bowed and took his seat. A fine china cup of steaming dark liquid sat at his place, apparently poured only seconds ago, and he immediately caught the sharp but alluring scent of strong coffee mixed with aromatic melange. "It is my honor, Majesty."

"I also wanted to express my gratitude. In the chaos after Jaxson Aru's attack, we may not have been generous enough with our thanks."

Leto shifted in the chair. "Emperor Shaddam made his thanks abundantly clear, Your Majesty. You have no reason to worry." When she took a drink of her spice coffee, he politely sipped his own. Energy tingled inside his mouth and throat, and a rush of warmth went through his chest.

Her eyes sparkled when she saw his expression. "Do you like our recipe?"

An embarrassed flush rose to his cheeks, and he felt like a bumpkin. "I have had spice coffee only a few times, but this is delicious."

"Many in the Imperium would not be able to live without spice in some form," she said with a hint of disappointment. "At least the Imperial treasurers are quite happy, as well as House Harkonnen."

At the mention of his family's archenemy, Leto hid his reaction behind another sip of coffee, but this time the energetic rush wasn't so pronounced.

Aricatha continued speaking in a casual way, but she'd apparently planned out every word of the conversation. "Despite the terrible events of that night, I recall that earlier you spoke with such obvious fondness for Caladan. I looked at images, but I wanted to hear more." She folded her hands in front of her on the table. "Tell me about the oceans of your world, Duke Leto. Why is Caladan such a special place?"

Aricatha's question made him homesick for the familiar activities of the castle, listening to the problems of his people. Perhaps they were mere parochial concerns, but they mattered greatly to the people of Caladan. Paul was there handling it all now. . . .

Leto described the dance of tides, the annual fishing harvests and festivals, the chains of isolated islands. He talked about the beautiful northern wilderness where he had recently taken his son, though he did not mention the drug fields they had found there. He told her about the burgeoning moonfish industry and promised that he would send her a special shipment so she could taste the delicious fillets, just as she had given him spice coffee. As the words poured out of him, he felt uplifted.

The Empress laughed, seeming to enjoy his company. "And tell me of your lady love, Jessica. I've done my research about you! Very few powerful nobles have had such a stable, long-lasting relationship. Though she is only a bound concubine, the Lady Jessica seems a perfect match for you."

Leto could not hide the dark flush on his face. "Jessica is no longer my concubine. She was recalled to the Mother School on Wallach IX, I think permanently. She made it clear that her ultimate loyalty is to the Bene Gesserit, not to me." His bitterness was obvious, and Aricatha sat back, looking troubled.

An attendant entered during the moment of awkward silence and announced that the Empress had another visitor on her schedule. Leto rose, bowed, thanked her for her time, and retreated to his suite in the Imperial Palace.

HE FELT DISORIENTED for hours after the Empress mentioned Jessica. It was a reminder to him that the Landsraad knew little about the internal affairs of House Atreides, and even if they did, how many other nobles would care about his emotions? A concubine was just that, someone who provided a service, and Jessica had performed her service very well for many years. Leto had convinced himself that their relationship was different, but now that only made him a fool. If her original Bene Gesserit assignment had been to worm her way into his heart, then Jessica had done an admirable job indeed.

He didn't want to believe that. But how could he not?

As he sat alone in his quarters, deep in thought, he recalled some lessons from his father, his role model. Duke Paulus had taught Leto to rule and had also taught him nobility, to embrace a solid core of honor. Yet Leto had seen his father condone things that Leto refused to accept under his own rule.

He remembered once sitting before the old Duke in his private study, which Leto now used as his own. He'd only been fourteen at the time . . . Paul's age now. In the previous year, House Atreides had worked with Emperor Elrood to overthrow House Kolona, a noble family that was supposedly plotting against the Imperial throne. Elrood had allied with Paulus to declare a vendetta, and Atreides forces attacked the Kolona planet, Borhees. Leto had never understood the strategy or reasoning for that move, expending such a huge Atreides force of ships, weapons, and fighters. The attack had obliterated House Kolona except for a handful of scattered survivors who lived as guerilla fighters in the hills.

"That action doubled the size of our holdings," Paulus had explained to his son, but he sounded disappointed in himself rather than triumphant. "Now all the income generated by House Kolona is ours." He seemed to be justifying something to himself.

The old Duke had leaned forward on the centuries-old desk. "Understand, son, that crushing House Kolona was never my ambition. And while we gained an important holding because of it, the price I had to bear . . ." He looked up, and Leto saw his father weighed down with responsibility and guilt, not the flamboyant man who entertained the people of Caladan with his public spectacles. "But Elrood forced . . ." Paulus shook his head and didn't explain further.

Not long afterward, Paulus had been killed in the bullring, and Leto became the Duke of Caladan. Some years later, he uncovered troublesome documents that his father had locked away. Although he never determined how old Elrood blackmailed Paulus into doing his bidding, Shaddam IV had taken over the Golden Lion Throne, and everything changed.

Leto had surprised the court by surrendering the fief of Borhees to distant survivors of House Kolona, claiming that he didn't want the tainted wealth. Shaddam could not comprehend why he would do such an inherently foolish thing, but Leto clung to his principles.

That was who Duke Leto had been, but now he'd come to Kaitain seeking something else.

An image of Jessica came to his mind, and he wished for her counsel right now, but he caught himself and hardened his heart. Obviously, many things had changed. . . .

AT NIGHT, THE Imperial Palace was lit brighter than any constellation. No matter the hour, the garish symphony of activity played on. People came from all worlds and all time cycles. Music emanated from bubbles and small stages around the vast palace. Out in the streets, spectacular fountains burst with light and water.

Leto dressed in flashy evening garments and left his quarters to be seen in the capital city. Accompanied by his coterie of retainers and functionaries, because a nobleman without an entourage was clearly unimportant, Leto let himself be swept through the grand galleries and wings. The hardest part was for his own retainers not to gawk too much at the spectacle.

With no specific destination in mind, Leto suddenly heard his name bellowed out. "Duke Leto Atreides! Stand where you are!" He turned, looked for anyone he recognized, and saw a storm of a man sweeping toward him. The man was half a head taller than Leto, and built like a bear. His florid face was accented by a thick mustache.

"Leto Atreides, Duke of Caladan, I challenge you!" People turned to look, and the milling crowd swirled closer to this new entertainment.

With a sinking feeling in his gut, Leto recognized Lord Atikk, whom he had met only once during the gala reception at the Corrino museum. Afterward, Leto had learned that his addict son had died from an overdose of ailar, and Atikk blamed Leto.

"In front of these witnesses, I invoke kanly," Atikk roared. "I hold you and your Caladan drug responsible for the death of my son."

Everyone stared as Leto struggled to remain calm. "I'm deeply sorry for your grief, Lord Atikk, but House Atreides had no knowledge of the drug operations on our planet. Once we learned about them, we eradicated the fields of barra ferns." He sighed. "I cannot bring back your son, but I can guarantee that no one else need die from ailar."

"Lies!" Atikk sneered. "You put on a grand show of burning some isolated growing areas so you could flaunt Atreides honor, but it was just a ruse. You fool no one! The drug distributors are already making overtures to ailar users around the Imperium. Nothing has changed. The only way to stop this is to stop you." He stepped even closer. "Again, I invoke kanly. I challenge you to a duel at a time and place that I will determine—face-to-face! The forms have been obeyed, and you, Duke Leto, will face justice for what you have done."

Atikk and his entourage stormed away.

Knowledge is a commodity. Knowledge is a weapon. Knowledge is a threat. And we can never get enough of it.
—CHOAM circular from Ur-Director MALINA ARU
to Inner Circle of High-Echelon Directors

Even in broad daylight, the Imperial observatory on Kaitain offered a spectacular view. The Emperor's "infinite city" rolled off to the horizon in every direction, and the air was crystal clear and meticulously scrubbed of pollution. Colorful buildings showcased the architectural styles of thousands of worlds, and each competed for attention.

The skyline made Malina Aru's eyes ache.

Though she held the most power in CHOAM, the Ur-Director was not often required to make public appearances. She preferred to remain behind the scenes. Few people understood that power did not require flash and dazzle.

But ever since her volatile son Jaxson had attacked Otorio and inflamed the entire Imperium, Malina had been cautious. Forced to grovel before the Landsraad, she had disowned her son and begged forgiveness because it was the only way to salvage the vital mission of the Noble Commonwealth. The quiet rebellion had worked for centuries to break the Corrino grip on absolute power. It was a long game plotted by the best politicians and historians—until Jaxson had swung in like a wrecking ball, scattering the carefully positioned game pieces. Though he was her own flesh and blood, sometimes Malina wanted to strangle him.

"I keep working at the task, Urdir," Empress Aricatha told Malina in a low voice. They conferred outside the observatory in the shadow of the eggshell dome, pretending to take in the view. "I have a great deal of influence, especially with my dear Shaddam, but I cannot be too overt. You understand that."

"I understand, and you are playing your role perfectly—for now." Malina kept her dark brown hair sensibly short and wore a trim business outfit in contrast to the ostentatious fabrics worn by the Empress. The Urdir lowered her voice further, even though Chamberlain Ridondo was out of earshot inside the observatory, adjusting the scopes. "But why didn't you warn us about what was going to happen to House Verdun? We could have salvaged something, maybe rescued a couple of family members. At the very least, we could have planted false records or erased damning information."

Aricatha's full lips were a liquid garnet color, and her irises were like stained wood mixed with the dark between the stars. Though she was the Empress, she flinched at Malina's words as if a schoolteacher had scolded her. "My husband does not always tell me what he intends to do. He meant to shock the entire Landsraad by obliterating House Verdun."

Malina frowned even more. "At least that barbaric act diverted some attention away from my son." She shook her head. Because of Jaxson, Malina could not speak out against the injustice of what had happened to Duke Verdun and his family. Let other Houses proclaim the Duke's innocence or, more likely, disown House Verdun, call the family heinous rebels, and write them out of Imperial history.

Empress Aricatha, Shaddam's newest wife, had been placed in her position through the quiet machinations of CHOAM. Under a different name and identity, the young woman had served as a concubine to doddering old Count Uchan on Pliesse. When it became apparent that Shaddam was losing interest in Firenza, his latest wife in a strictly political marriage, CHOAM's expert trainers transformed Aricatha into a perfect companion for the Padishah Emperor, while Malina's own daughter married Count Uchan and wrapped him around her finger.

Lady Anirul, the Emperor's first wife and the mother of his four daughters, had lasted the longest of the wives, but she had been killed fourteen years earlier. Aricatha thought she could do better. Designed to be the perfect woman for Shaddam, she played his strings expertly. Thus CHOAM realized its best-case scenario: Aricatha had the ear of the most powerful man in the known universe and was obligated to pass along all vital information to CHOAM.

Duke Fausto Verdun, one of Malina's true Noble Commonwealth conspirators, had been targeted and executed. Now the Ur-Director feared that other secret rebels might be discovered, too.

Neither Shaddam nor his ruthless Sardaukar forces realized that the Noble Commonwealth had two factions, nor would he likely care. Somehow, Verdun had been sloppy, and he had paid the ultimate price. But had he left any loose ends that might endanger other members of the movement? Malina and her fellow conspirators were understandably on edge, and Aricatha was their only source of information.

"What evidence did Shaddam have against him?" she pressed the Empress. "The Landsraad is in an uproar. A Great House was accused and obliterated, but the Emperor presented no proof. More importantly, how did Verdun let himself get caught? We must know."

Aricatha lashed out in a whisper, "How do you know he had any evidence at all? It's not unlike my husband to create a spectacle just to make a point."

Both women suddenly looked up as they heard the chamberlain moving inside the observatory, and the dome began to pivot on its suspensor tracks. The wide opening turned toward a different part of the daylit sky.

The Empress lowered her voice and asked, "Why are you so interested, Urdir? House Verdun's holdings will be taken by some other noble family, and CHOAM will assign a new Directorship."

Aricatha did not know—did not *need* to know—any significant details about the rebellion, or that the Urdir and CHOAM were in any way involved. Malina said, "Verdun was one of my most important inner-circle Directors, and now I have to carefully rebalance the percentages." She calmed herself, spoke encouragingly to the Empress. "Use this as an opportunity. Express your displeasure that Shaddam didn't consult with you, tell him that you want more important assignments and that you want to become his most . . . intimate adviser."

"I do my duty," Aricatha said with a smile, then drew out the anticipatory silence. "I did learn unexpected information on a different subject, however." When Malina motioned for her to continue, she added, "Do you have any interest in Duke Leto Atreides from Caladan? Apparently, he had a falling-out with his bound concubine, the mother of his son and presumed heir. In a power play, the Bene Gesserit summoned her to Wallach IX against his wishes, and it's not clear whether she left voluntarily or under duress. The Duke is deeply wounded and alone, and he holds great resentment toward the Sisterhood."

"That leaves him open to manipulation." Malina absorbed the information. "House Atreides does not figure in our plans at the moment, but I will keep my eyes open for an opportunity. After Otorio and the redrawing of the Landsraad holdings, the Emperor's own shares in CHOAM are close to an unshakable majority . . . and we cannot have that." She rubbed her temples. "Right now I miss my beloved spinehounds, but court officials apparently find them intimidating."

"Where are they?" Aricatha asked.

"I left them in the Silver Needle with Frankos until I can depart from Kaitain." Her older son, the figurehead CHOAM President, would care for Har and Kar. Across the sweeping panorama, her eyes locked on the graceful spire of CHOAM headquarters, which rose like a dagger nearly as tall as the Imperial Palace.

The lanky, lantern-jawed chamberlain emerged from the observatory. "It is ready at last, my Ladies. The scopes are adjusted and aligned, and the view is quite spectacular. Come, you must see for yourselves."

"Even in daylight?" Malina already knew the answer, but this gave Ridondo the chance to explain to them, which helped him feel important.

"Our lenses can penetrate the atmosphere, and you will see several Guild Heighliners in various orbits. The activity is astonishing."

"That will be lovely," Aricatha said with an innocent brightness as she played her charming role. The two women followed the chamberlain into the building.

Inside, three astronomer-functionaries moved the large-aperture penetrative scopes and adjusted the display. Aricatha led the Urdir to an eyepiece fitted with a soft-cushioned rim.

Chamberlain Ridondo stepped back and folded his hands together, letting them take turns at the view.

Through the eyepiece, Malina watched the tiny blips of spacecraft, shuttles, cargo ships, and dump boxes emerging like sparkles from a cavernous Heighliner. Malina assessed the space traffic, the commercial activities of hundreds of Houses, thousands of individual ships, and uncounted billions of solaris in trade—all wrapped in the web of the CHOAM Company. She drank in the view for a long time.

She was surprised to hear a familiar voice as someone else entered. "Ridondo said I would find you two here. Always scheming, I assume."

Malina found Emperor Shaddam's words annoying, but Aricatha quickly answered in a warm tone, "Conducting business, my love, and solidifying my friendship with Ur-Director Aru. I wouldn't call that scheming."

"Call it what you will," Shaddam said.

"We were discussing the terrible fate of House Verdun," Malina added.

"A fate of their own making." Shaddam turned sour. "And the same fate will befall any other House that sympathizes with the violent rebels. Everyone must know how vigilant I am."

"They all know now, Sire," Malina said.

Aricatha fawned over the Emperor. "If I have a close bond with the Ur-Director of CHOAM, my dear, then I can help you as well. We're good friends."

Shaddam, who was not easily moved by flattery, imagined he knew what Aricatha was doing to him, but her training was so subtle that he had no idea.

Malina stepped away from the scope and gestured to the eyepiece. "Would you like to see, Sire? It will remind you of all the ships, trade, and people that come to Kaitain because of you."

He smiled. "I think about that every day." He bent over the eyepiece, concentrating closely. Aricatha excused them, leading Malina away from the observatory.

The Ur-Director tried to imagine what Shaddam would do if he ever discovered Baron Harkonnen's illicit spice operations and how he was plotting with CHOAM to cheat the Emperor out of his spice surtax. She decided she needed a fallback plan for her own survival.

*Combat at close quarters is not unlike fighting in a much larger arena. In
each case, it is wise to know your battlefield, and adapt to it.*
—Bene Gesserit instruction manual

Before departing for their trip down the coast, Paul and Duncan walked
around the ornithopter to visually check its fuel supply, wing connec-
tors, ailerons, structural fasteners, windscreen, and the lightweight metal skin
stretched over the frame. Duncan insisted on the routine as a necessary mark of
a good pilot, and Paul followed suit.

A low fog lay over the sea, but only a few wisps touched the high turrets of
the ancient castle. The pair were heading off to the Caladan sand dunes in hopes
of finding the mysterious girl who kept appearing in Paul's dreams. Although the
young man doubted he would find her there, he wanted to see the plantings and
the ecological experimentation, and he looked forward to visiting a new part of
his world. *The business of being a Duke. . . .*

Duncan looked up to the clearing sky. "A fine day for flying, young Master. A
little breeze to stir the senses, but you can handle it." He climbed into the copilot
seat. "Take the controls."

Paul settled in and activated the engines, feeling the craft become part of him
as he tested the articulated wings, tucked them against the fuselage as the swift
craft rose, then picked up speed. He extended the 'thopter wings to their full
extent, and they moved in a graceful rhythm. Looking through the expansive
plaz windscreen, Paul could almost envision himself as a spreybird, soaring high.

"You never know what we'll find out there," Duncan said. "Where else will
we see sand dunes on Caladan? You told me the dunes were a clear part of your
dream with that particular girl. Maybe you'll learn something about your premonitions." He gave a knowing smile.

Paul mused as they rose above the castle and followed the line of the coast.
"Maybe." Duncan seemed more convinced than he was.

The dunes were an hour's flight south from Cala City, where a quirk of unusual terrain collected wind-borne sand. A village named Alorence had been
established on the northern tip of sand, on what had once been verdant forest

and farmland until encroaching dunes swallowed up the fertile terrain. Over the past century, the villagers had built high masonry walls to keep the sand from inundating their buildings and streets, but their efforts were in vain. The village was saved when an agriculturalist discovered that planted poverty grasses could stabilize the slip faces of the dunes and keep the waves of sand from encroaching farther on arable land.

Paul guided the 'thopter toward the village structures ahead and the sweeping swath of sand just beyond. Some of the dunes were covered with a burst of incongruous grass, as if the sinuous hummocks had grown a crop of woolly gray-green hair dotted with yellow flowers.

"Sand-heather," Duncan said.

Paul looked over from the controls. "Why, Duncan, you're more of a scholar than I realized."

The Swordmaster scoffed. "I looked over your shoulder yesterday while you were reading a filmbook. You were so focused that you didn't even notice me there."

"Thufir would be scandalized to hear that you managed to sneak up behind me." Paul chuckled. "Or maybe I knew you were there all the time."

Circling over the village then traveling out to the first line of dunes, they looked down on a planetology research camp on a hardened pan, which was naturally protected by rock hoodoos like the gnarly heads of fairy creatures guarding the area. People in khaki outfits and wide-brimmed hats were trudging up the face of the nearest dune. Paul flew low, and several members of the party waved to him, undoubtedly noticing the hawk crest on the fuselage.

Paul looked at Duncan. "Did you inform anyone in the village that we were visiting? Are they expecting us?"

Duncan glanced out the windowplaz on the copilot's side. "I thought this was just a quick trip, me and you. If I sent word to Alorence, then it would become an event, and the town leaders would meet you, the planetology teams would want to take you out to the plantings. Were you willing to spend a few days here? Thufir can arrange it if you need to take your time and look for that girl."

Paul shook his head as he kept flying, feeling uncomfortable. "No, I just want to have a quick look." He peered out at the sandy landscape, the grass plantings, the cloudy sky. He had awakened from the dream so many times, and this felt . . . wrong. He sighed in disappointment. "These are dunes, all right, but the terrain isn't the same, and the . . . sunlight is different from my dreams."

"The sunlight is different? How can sunlight be different?" Duncan scoffed. "The sun is the sun. But the best way for you to look for this particular girl of yours is to meet with the locals." He reached teasingly toward the comm. "Should I let them know who we are?"

"Today, let's just be an unscheduled overflight. I'd prefer to visit on my own terms." He altered course toward a broad, unplanted dune away from the camp, beating the wings slower and slower as he came in for a smooth landing far from any other people. Sand whipped around them, swirling like tan mist.

"Nicely done," Duncan said.

"Now let me have a look at these dunes on Caladan." He sharpened his memory of his dreams, the quality of light and shadow, the starkness, the sense of inevitability. There was much more to his dream than just that lean, beautiful girl. Feeling a strange sense of wonder, Paul stepped out onto the sand. At first he expected shimmering heat, even though clouds studded the sky, hiding the sun. He drew a long breath, and the air was full of moisture with a sharp tang of salt. In his mind he had a quick image of wispy thermals rising over a salt pan, with dunes and rock formations all around. Bending down, he scooped up a handful of sand, let it sift through his fingers. It was not warm at all.

This wasn't right.

Duncan joined him, but Paul concentrated hard on his surroundings, placing his thoughts into his dream self and feeling an odd intensity. He looked at the nearby rock escarpments that formed a half circle around his chosen landing area, then turned to face the undulating, encroaching dunes, like a sandy incarnation of a Caladan sea. These dunes were not nearly high enough to be the ones in his dreams, and the rocks were the wrong shape, the wrong color. And it was cold here, not hot, as it should be.

This is not the right place, he thought. *She is not here.*

Disappointment struck him harder than he expected. He tossed the sand, rubbed the remaining grit off his hands. "Let's go."

Duncan was taken aback. "Already, young Master?"

Paul needed to leave. It was a powerful feeling—not a premonition of danger, but something else. "This isn't the right place—or time." He shook his head slowly. "I'm sorry, Duncan. I know you tried, but this isn't where I'm supposed to be."

Duncan's brow furrowed below the tight black curls of his hair, but he didn't try to understand. "As you say, my Lord." He swung back up into the aircraft. "But I still think we should go to Alorence, visit the people, see if any girl catches your eye."

"I'm not looking for a girl to catch my eye," he said, climbing back into the cockpit. He fired up the engines, set the articulated wings in motion. "Right now, I have to think like a Duke."

After lifting off, Paul cruised over the expanse of dunes, the experimental sections covered with grasses. He looked down at the work crews moving over the sand, and his vision blurred with images of countless people—an army?—crossing a vast and different desert. When the 'thopter began to wobble, he shook his head to clear his vision.

"Are you distracted, Paul?" Concern was clear in Duncan's voice.

Paul concentrated on the controls. "This region is too benign, too safe."

"Too safe?" Duncan laughed.

But the young man was firm. He gazed into the distance at the flight path that lay ahead of him, and he expanded it to the path of his future life. "The place I'm looking for is bigger than this—much, much bigger."

*Business is an illusion and wears many disguises. Profits and influences,
however, are immutable.*

—BARON VLADIMIR HARKONNEN, internal
spice operations report

"Present your report, Baron—and your excuses, if you have them." The Emperor looked down at him with a grim, stony expression, and then, surprisingly, he smiled. "But I already know the results, and I am pleased."

In the cavernous Imperial throne room, Baron Harkonnen felt countless eyes on him. Whenever Shaddam held court, the chamber filled with courtiers, ministers, advisers, and endless functionaries who served no purpose that he could identify. Many of today's spectators had come hoping to see the great Vladimir Harkonnen dressed down.

The Baron wore his best finery, black adorned with his orange-and-purple family colors, and a griffin crest emblazoned the cape over his shoulders. His fat fingers sported many rings, although he had removed several so as not to appear too ostentatious before the throne. His suspensor belt diminished his weight so that he could walk gracefully to the dais, although his girth made it impossible for him to give a proper bow. Instead, he spread his hands and leaned forward. "As always, Sire, I do my best to honor you and the Imperium."

His mind raced as he gauged the Emperor's reaction. Fortunately, Shaddam was talkative. "Those spice thieves were a constant thorn in my side and cost the treasury a significant sum, using up half of the spice surtax." He stroked his clean-shaven chin. "Hasimir tells me that you two found the culprits and punished them accordingly. I congratulate you on these laudable efforts." He lounged on his massive Hagal quartz throne, shimmering with blue-green translucence. "I saw the images of their ringleader being fed to a giant sandworm. Quite remarkable!"

Count Fenring was not the Baron's friend by any means, but in certain matters their interests aligned, such as ensuring that the spice operations ran smoothly. Fenring had his own schemes with sanctioned smuggler bands, and the Baron would play along for now and discuss with the Count later. The Emperor was satisfied the problem had been taken care of, and that was all that mattered.

The Baron said, "House Harkonnen worked closely with your Spice Minister to root out and destroy this band of pirates, Sire. All melange production operates under your purview."

But Shaddam's mood changed again, and his voice turned harsh. "The problem would not have occurred in the first place if you had been monitoring more closely! You let this happen right in front of you, Baron. I expected more diligence from House Harkonnen."

He swallowed and could feel the audience's attention turn back toward him.

The Emperor raised a hand like an orchestra conductor and continued, "But Hasimir's peculiar Mentat uncovered all those illicit sales, when my own Mentat accountants couldn't detect them. So very subtle and so very careful." Shaddam's nose narrowed as he sniffed with contempt. "What was her name? Rulla Tuek? I'm amazed that a dirty desert woman could have been the mastermind of such an elaborate scheme."

The Baron's pulse raced. Did Shaddam know more than he was letting on? He would never have remembered the name of Rulla Tuek unless he meant to make a point. "The Fremen rabble are devilishly clever, Sire," he admitted. "They've committed many destructive acts, sabotaged our equipment. I thought they were little more than animals, but obviously some of them are great schemers." He used the name intentionally as well. "Like Rulla Tuek and her entire operation."

Shaddam tapped his fingers on the thick arm of his throne. "Obviously." He sounded skeptical, annoyed. "Still, my spice surtax has been collected, which is quite a significant amount of wealth to be put to good use. In fact, I intend to host a large physical display of this money, a show for the masses, just to make a point. To awe them."

The Emperor's lips quirked in a smile again as he enjoyed his plans. "Real solari coins, a huge cargo load of them, to demonstrate the largesse of the Golden Lion Throne. My people will talk about it for generations." He seemed wistful, preoccupied, then his focus snapped back to the Baron. "This entire matter of the black-market spice channel points out shortfalls in your leadership, Baron. One band of spice thieves has been dealt with, and Count Fenring assures me there is no longer cause for concern, but I will be watching much more closely from now on. In fact, my Mentat accountants have found certain irregularities in your operations, reports, and expenses."

The Baron realized he was sweating. The number of curious observers in the throne room seemed to have doubled, all staring at him. He cleared his throat, lowered his voice. "Shall we perhaps discuss this in private, Sire?"

"Maybe public exposure is more appropriate."

The Baron's emotions whipsawed. Had the Emperor been trying to trick him with his good mood? Trapped now, the Baron had to find a way out. He attempted to bow again. "How can I improve my operations so I might better please you?"

"Your equipment losses are unacceptable," Shaddam said. "The number of spice harvesters, carryalls, and scout flyers decommissioned in the last year is significantly above the previous average."

"It was a terrible year for storms, Sire. Coriolis winds, abrasive sand, and magnetic discharge wreak havoc on electronic systems."

The Emperor's gaze pierced like a sharp blade. "You've written off fifteen percent more large equipment than in previous years, and at great expense."

"That equipment was outdated, Sire. We kept the carryalls and harvesters running well beyond their projected lifetimes, but they still eventually fail. We had to decommission all that large machinery to build a superior work fleet."

"I have seen the numbers," Shaddam said, "and the cost."

"An expense primarily borne by House Harkonnen, Sire. I can't have my spice crews using substandard or damaged equipment. The safety of my people is paramount." He tried to sound sincere.

In truth, the Baron had marked much of that old equipment as scuttled and dismantled for scrap, but each of them still had a year or more of functional lifetime, and he used the machinery in his undocumented spice work for CHOAM. Very dangerous, but highly profitable.

He gave a conciliatory smile. "We will monitor the new equipment more closely, Sire, conduct more frequent maintenance to keep it in service longer. Arrakis is one of the harshest worlds in the Imperium, but we do what we must for spice."

The Emperor pursed his lips. "Yes, we do what we must for spice." He lounged back on his crystal throne. "That is all I wish to discuss, Baron. Know that I am watching you. I expect greater efficiency and diligence from this point forward. You are dismissed."

The Baron approximated another bow and turned away, feeling light-headed. He was eager to leave the Imperial Palace. Next, he would speak with Malina Aru in CHOAM headquarters here on Kaitain, and then go to his beloved homeworld, Giedi Prime.

He refused to acknowledge the suspicious glances of the courtiers and advisers as he made his way out of the crowded throne room, but he abruptly halted when he saw the Bene Gesserit Reverend Mother lurking near a towering column—the Emperor's Truthsayer. He hadn't noticed her at first, but Mohiam was listening, analyzing his every word for any hint of deceit. She moved toward him, and he felt a flash of alarm as he tried to recall exactly how he had answered Shaddam's questions, which specific words he had used. Had he uttered an actual falsehood? Mohiam would catch him at it. Damned Truthsayer witch!

"You seemed uneasy, Baron Harkonnen. I listened to your words."

"Everyone here was listening," the Baron retorted.

"But they do not hear in the way a Truthsayer hears. When discussing how Count Fenring dealt with the spice thieves, I sensed evasion in your answers. Perhaps we should investigate further. Ask more questions."

He tried not to show his panic. "Count Fenring led those investigations. Ask him your questions. He identified the culprit and took care of the matter. If you sensed anything, it is because I am dubious about his methods and his conclusions. But if the Emperor is satisfied that the matter is ended, then so am I."

Mohiam's dark, intense eyes bored into him, and he did not want to speak further, lest he make a mistake. "If you hear anything questionable in my words and tone now, witch, it is because of my great dislike for you."

He did not hide his revulsion. Reverend Mother Gaius Helen Mohiam was a despicable person and a manipulator who had blackmailed him many years ago, forcing him to impregnate her, per the Sisterhood's orders. That disgusting act had given him an incurable disease that turned him into this fat mockery of the lean and muscular man he had been.

He stalked off, heart pounding, hoping she would not report her suspicions to Shaddam.

Just before he passed under the arched throne room entrance, he halted abruptly again. A handsome, dark-haired man in Atreides green and black stood with Archduke Armand Ecaz, watching him with icy wariness.

Duke Leto Atreides.

The Baron reeled, momentarily unbalanced on his suspensors. Leto directed his gray eyes at the Baron as if they were weapons. The resentment on his face was palpable.

Fortunately, they were separated by many others in the crowd. Having no desire to approach the Atreides, the Baron left, feeling his skin burn. He needed to get out of this snake pit.

When a Kwisatz Haderach fails to develop, it is a traumatic event, not only for the candidate but for the Kwisatz Mother in charge, who has so much invested in the program. Our records are littered with the names of the fallen, in both categories.

—Secret Bene Gesserit breeding archives

Jessica remembered this dining hall from her years in the Mother School, growing up, becoming an acolyte, completing her training as a Sister, before being sent as concubine to the Duke of Caladan.

So many years ago, another lifetime. *Leto . . .*

As she entered, she saw that the large, old hall had been expanded with a new annex building connected by a short passageway, for additional seating. Many women moved about in the bustle of the mealtime, but they seemed to be avoiding her. Was it widely known why she was here? Jessica remembered all too well the harsh gossip and innuendo. Did they now believe she posed a danger to the Sisterhood, even if no one knew the reason why?

As she considered where to sit, another Sister came up beside her, striking up a conversation. "It depends on if you feel traditional or modern." The tall woman had soft bronze hair like her own, an oval face, and feline blue eyes. Her fluid movements showed smooth muscular control; she looked a year or two older than Jessica. "I am Sister Xora." Jessica noticed that other women at the dining tables were looking in their direction. Xora lowered her voice. "They are curious about you."

"I am Jessica . . . Sister Jessica, here from Caladan."

Xora smiled. "Everyone knows who you are. It is the talk of the school. The arrival of the Mystery Woman. That's what they call you. They're curious to know why you're here, and what that murderous old Lethea wants with you. Apparently, you are the embodiment of bloodshed, horror, and destruction."

Jessica was surprised. "And why didn't Lethea kill me, like the others? She had the chance."

"She didn't kill you *yet*." Xora pointed to a nearby table in the old hall and added in a bright voice, "Would you mind if we ate together?"

Jessica looked around at the other Sisters, decided it might be best if she didn't eat alone. She didn't have any friends here. "I'd welcome that—if you aren't worried about the Mystery Woman."

"I'll risk it." Xora chose a table, marked it as taken, then led Jessica to the serving area. "This is the only fare I've eaten for seventeen years. I remember some banquets at the Imperial Palace, a long time ago . . ." The other woman sounded distracted and wistful as she directed them to the long serving buffet. "I recommend the Wallach porridge, hearty greens, and spices, prepared with or without highland pork. I prefer the meat version." She smiled mischievously. "To keep my teeth sharp."

Jessica smiled, but exercised instinctive caution with this woman. Maybe Xora was just trying to be friendly, or did she have another reason for seeking out her company? "A good soup would be nice, considering the cold weather here." She thought longingly of the summer rainstorms on Caladan. . . .

The two served themselves porridge and wedges of hearth bread, then carried their trays to a dessert table. Jessica watched another Sister spray mist onto a potted sapling in the middle of the last serving table. As the liquid doused the leaves, the small tree glowed and stirred, and presently, a bright yellow fruit emerged. The Sister plucked the fruit, put it on her tray, and walked to her table.

Jessica was fascinated. "A most unusual lemon tree."

"They have softer, sweeter flesh than lemons. The tree only produces fruit when it is given water," Xora said. "A quid pro quo, water in exchange for something to eat."

Xora repeated the procedure, and soon, they both had fresh fruit of their own and had returned to their table. Before eating her porridge, Jessica couldn't resist tasting the fruit. A harmonious blend of flavors burst in her mouth, one after the other, building to a bold combined taste. "Delicious!"

Xora responded with a sardonic expression. "Remember the Mother Superior's basic admonition: Don't eat your dessert before your meal."

The memory made Jessica smile, and she realized that she had actually started to relax.

Xora leaned over the table, sharing gossip. "A lot is happening at the school now. You and Lethea are subjects of much conversation, but there is also a financial crisis of sorts going on. House Tull, our largest benefactor for years, has cut off our funds. The old Viscount used to pay huge donations to the Bene Gesserit—you saw a lot of the new construction here, the modern buildings— but he recently died, and his successor pulled all funding, saying his noble house had given enough. That came as a shock to the Mother Superior. We've offered to send a new concubine for the new Viscount, but he has refused." Xora paused. "I'd like to be the one sent there, if they'll give me the chance. I hear Giandro Tull is very handsome, and I am the perfect age to be an appropriate companion."

"Can you ask for the assignment?"

Xora responded with a rueful smile, and Jessica saw that she was quite pretty, with high cheekbones and full lips that gave her an interesting, intelligent range of expressions. "No, all any Sister can do is her best and hope she is selected for something interesting."

"Yes." Jessica tasted the succulent highland pork in the porridge and enjoyed the rich flavors. Long ago, she'd had no say about being offered to Duke Leto, and he had been highly dubious about accepting her.

Xora took another bite, pondered, then said, "Tell me more about yourself, Mystery Woman. I'm eager to get to know you better."

Jessica was automatically guarded. "Isn't my situation common knowledge? Old Lethea demanded that I be torn from my home, from my son. Because she had a bad dream."

Xora let out a commiserating snort. "Lethea! That vile old woman has caused chaos around here for some time." Her smile was kindly, but intense, as if they shared a secret. "Forgive me for pushing myself on you. I sought you out on purpose, because I know some of your mystery. We . . . have something in common." She lowered her voice and looked around. "Like you, I was a concubine once . . . and I, too, had a son that the Bene Gesserit did not authorize."

Astonished, Jessica put down her spoon. Her service as Leto's bound concubine was known to the Sisters, but not her breach of instructions. Did they know she had been told to bear only daughters? She thought only Mohiam and other high Reverend Mothers knew about that. She felt cold and remained silent.

Xora nodded solemnly as she continued her own confession. "At least you got to stay with your Duke. For my terrible transgression, I was hauled back to the Mother School seventeen years ago. I have not left since, and that's a waste of my abilities. I have high-level skills, but the proctors reassigned me to teaching Acolytes."

Jessica could not stop herself from asking, "What happened to your son? Is he . . . far from here?"

The woman's face filled with emotion. She closed her eyes for a moment, then reopened them. "No, he is very close, but I'm not allowed to be a mother to him. He doesn't even know me."

Jessica couldn't imagine what that must feel like. "I'm truly sorry. Tell me what happened."

"I was assigned as concubine to Baron Onar Molay, back when he was young, romantic, and fresh-faced. I was his second Bene Gesserit concubine. He'd gotten tired of the previous one, Sister Jiara—you'll see her here at the Mother School. The Mother Superior decided to replace her with me."

Jessica certainly remembered Jiara from outside the armored medical room. Since ancient times, the Bene Gesserit leadership had moved concubines around like chess pieces. Jessica's assignment to House Atreides and Xora's to House Molay were not unusual occurrences.

"In service to my nobleman, I spent a few months at the Imperial Court on Kaitain." She paused, chewed at her lower lip. "While I was there, Lord Molay was entwined in politics. I was lonely and made my own connections. I had an affair with a young Sardaukar officer and fell in love with him, as you did with your Duke. That broke all sorts of rules—not only of the Sisterhood, but of the court and the Sardaukar."

Jessica was surprised, but Xora continued, intent on telling her story. "When I got pregnant, my Sardaukar was disgraced and sent off to some planet in the hinterlands, and I was recalled here as punishment. Baron Molay was furious to be so publicly cuckolded, and Harishka sent one of her most seductive breeding mistresses to mollify him. I had my baby son here on Wallach IX."

Jessica's heart ached for what Xora had endured, and the pain increased with the resonance to her own situation. "Like me, you fell in love when it was forbidden, and had a child you were not supposed to have."

Xora looked at Jessica. "We may be the only Sisters here at the school who have that in common."

Jessica touched the other woman's hand, then withdrew before anyone could see. Emotions were a thing to be watched carefully and held in check. All emotions.

I have come to see that the trappings and masks throughout the Imperial Court are false, yet mutually accepted, a shared illusion. This is far removed from real life.

—DUKE LETO ATREIDES, letters to his son

Lord Atikk's formal kanly declaration arrived on an etched ridulian sheet, as cold as ice. Leto read the details with a sinking heart and knew there would be no negotiation, no reparations, no apologies. He had to face the man in a traditional duel, where blood needed to be spilled for blood.

While waiting to learn the terms, he spent his time studying Landsraad rules and the laws of the Imperium. He pored over *The Assassin's Handbook,* trying to find some way out, but in the case of a declared blood feud, Leto's possible responses were limited.

He was willing to make overtures to heal the breach, but Atikk would accept nothing less than a deadly fight. Already, heated rumors rippled through the court, and excitement echoed in the halls of the Imperial Palace. Leto knew that further bowing, pleading, or conciliation would make him look weak.

Lord Atikk was known to have considerable combat skills and had used them more than once. Leto practiced his fighting techniques in the palace exercise arenas. He hired combat opponents who worked him into a sweat, but none proved to be nearly as challenging as Thufir Hawat, Gurney Halleck, or Duncan Idaho. He was not eager for the fight, but he was prepared, a highly skilled fighter in his own right.

Leto had learned not to travel through the arched galleries or the prism-lit palace wings without his entourage of Caladan guards and retainers. While he maintained a proud, aloof demeanor, he noted the averted glances, the mouths covered to hide whispers.

When he'd first arrived on Kaitain, the court had buzzed with news about the eradication of House Verdun, but now the chatter was about Atikk's challenge and the impending duel. Many whispered suspicions and conspiracies about Leto, while others spoke plainly, as if they wanted him to overhear.

"Very convenient . . . one of the few survivors from Otorio."

"He escaped while so many others died."

"I hear he stowed aboard the Emperor's escape ship and left other nobles to die in the explosion."

Leto whirled, infuriated by the suggestion, but the crowd shifted, and courtiers folded around whomever had spoken.

Surprisingly, Count Fenring defended him, lashing out at the gossipers. "Thanks to the sharp eyes and quick thinking of Leto Atreides, our Emperor survived the heinous attack! Ahhhh, without Duke Leto, it would have been too late for so many of us." The Count swept his glare across the cowed sycophants. His words sliced like thrown razors. "He is beyond suspicion!"

"Then why did Lord Atikk declare kanly on House Atreides?" someone called out.

"Because Atikk is an ungrateful fool, hmmmm," Fenring said. "He himself is only alive because of Leto's warning. Atikk owes his life to the Duke, and it is outrageous for him to challenge a man known for his honor."

Leto wasn't sure how to embrace the support of a man like Fenring. He kept his voice neutral. "Thank you for your kind words, Count, but I don't think Lord Atikk will change his mind."

"Of course not, hmmmm," Fenring said. "He will need to be dealt with."

Leto fingered the cold declaration in his pocket, thought of the imminent duel. "I know when this will be over."

Fenring stroked a finger along his weak chin. "Hmmmm." He waved a hand at the staring courtiers. "Go and leave Duke Leto alone. You must have other nonsense to attend to."

The people scattered, and Fenring strolled off. The members of Leto's Caladan entourage could not hide their smiles.

His satisfaction was brief, though. Reverend Mother Mohiam stood near a marble statue of an ancient hero, regarding him with her bright eyes. He had avoided her so far, but after overhearing what Fenring had just said, she stepped forward. "Your quick thinking on Otorio saved me as well, Leto Atreides." Her voice was dry and raspy. "Technically, I am among those who owe you my life, although the Sisterhood does not acknowledge such debts."

"I didn't do it for you." His emotions turned to stone. If this witch had been killed at the Corrino museum, she could not have pulled Bene Gesserit strings to manipulate Jessica. The Sisters were all treacherous, and he now imagined his bond with Jessica might have been as illusory as the holographic light shows around the Imperial Palace.

He could feel himself being dissected by Mohiam's probing gaze. She understood his emotions and the course of his thoughts. "Rest assured, Jessica is safely back at the Mother School. She will be well taken care of and is no longer your concern. You need not worry."

"Jessica made her choice. She showed her true loyalty, and I learned an important lesson."

Mohiam smiled and intentionally misunderstood him. "I am glad you were pleased with her services for so many years. Jessica was a student of mine when she was young. I trained her well."

"Too well."

"The Sisterhood could always provide another concubine for House Atreides. I'd be happy to assist in the selection." She gave a bow that somehow seemed mocking. "I can find a woman more suitable to your needs."

Anger flared in Leto, and he turned away. "That will not be necessary. Castle Caladan needs no more witches."

SOON ENOUGH, THE tides of palace rumors swirled and shifted with the arrival of another controversial Landsraad noble, a source of freshly inflamed gossip. After an absence of many years, Baron Onar Molay appeared on Kaitain with grand ceremony, as if nothing had happened in the intervening time. He flaunted his presence, which sparked countless conversations about his prior disgrace and shame, how his Bene Gesserit concubine Xora had cuckolded him by having a blatant affair right at the Emperor's court with a Sardaukar officer.

The people of far-off Caladan paid little attention to politics and scandals at the Imperial Court, but even Leto had heard the outrageous story that shook the ranks of the Sardaukar and the Emperor's own personal guard. The resounding controversy had rocked House Molay and the nobleman's standing in the Landsraad, and he had only been mollified when the Sisterhood provided new concubines for him. He had kept a low profile for nearly two decades.

Now as he boldly returned to Kaitain after a long absence, Baron Molay seemed either defiant or oblivious. Leto watched him interact with uneasy nobles as if they were old comrades. He pretended that the betrayal was all the fault of his concubine and the soldier, and none of the embarrassment even registered with him.

The situation made Duke Leto think of Jessica and the far subtler ways she had hurt him. He also remembered what Mohiam had said. Should he salve his hurt by picking a succession of other concubines, just to forget her? Leto knew that wouldn't work, and it would certainly cause great pain to Paul.

He focused his mind on his current priorities: his son and the imminent duel.

AFTER COMPLETING HIS investigation on Elegy, Colonel Bashar Kolona was glad to be back at the Imperial Court. As a Sardaukar, he was duty-bound to quash the rebellion, just as he had obliterated all vestiges of House Verdun, but he had found nothing suspicious in the household of Viscount Tull. When he delivered his report to Shaddam, he could tell that the Emperor was disappointed, but Kolona would not fabricate evidence.

Wearing his formal uniform, he stood at attention inside the throne room and was surprised when Baron Molay returned to the palace after so many years. Molay held his chin high and walked with a beautiful Bene Gesserit concubine on his arm. Kolona had not thought about his disgraced comrade in a very long time, but Jopati Kolona could never forget how he had been ruined.

They had trained together under the harshest conditions on Salusa Secundus, and then both had secured assignments here in the Kaitain court, along with other Sardaukar. While life in the palace was filled with distractions and temptations, Kolona could not understand how the other soldier had let his training and his honor slip, how he could have been lured by Baron Molay's concubine.

The affair harmed a wealthy Landsraad noble, ruined the Sardaukar's career, disgraced the concubine, and created instability at the Imperial Court.

The young soldier had been sent away in shame while Baron Molay retreated to lick his wounds and rebuild his reputation, staying away from Kaitain. Apparently, he thought that seventeen years was enough.

But Jopati Kolona had not forgotten, nor had the rest of the Imperial Court. The colonel bashar stood at attention in the throne room, his gaze fixed ahead.

ON THE MORNING of his duel with Lord Atikk, Leto awoke with dread and a sense of inevitability. He had not slept well, but otherwise, he felt prepared. He dressed in loose garments displaying the hawk crest. He had brought a ceremonial sword from Caladan, but today it would serve as more than ornamentation.

Leto emerged from his guest suite, wondering if he would ever return. He had already left final instructions for Thufir, Gurney, and Duncan in case he did not survive the combat, and he had recorded a message for Paul. When old Duke Paulus was killed in the bullring, Leto had not been ready to become Duke, but he had stepped up to the responsibility nevertheless. Paul would do the same, if necessary. His son would be a good and honorable Duke.

Leto felt caught in a web of Imperial power games. Maybe he had been a fool to play them.

His entourage was somber. Dressed in formal green and black, they escorted Leto through the echoing halls toward the assigned rendezvous, outside of Atikk's spacious rooms.

As they approached the site of the combat, though, he saw that the court was astir, filled with shock, horror, and even more excitement. Leto was taken aback to see a Suk doctor and several attendants carrying a pallet, on which lay a big man's body. His skin was mottled, his face drawn back in a rictus of pain, his open eyes bulging, shot through with red hemorrhages.

Whispers swirled like a building thunderstorm. "Lord Atikk is dead!"
"On the day of his duel."
"Poisoned! In his own chambers."
"I never expected that from Leto Atreides!"

Leto froze. "What is this? Someone explain what happened."

Fenring emerged from the dead nobleman's quarters and strolled along be-hind the stretcher. "Ahhhh, hmmm, unfortunately, the poison snooper in Lord Atikk's dining chamber was faulty, and somehow, an odorless and tasteless chau-mas was introduced into his favorite dessert." The Count grinned, as if he wasn't at all shocked.

Leto felt cold inside. "You're saying that someone poisoned him just before he was scheduled to duel with me this morning?"

One of the courtiers snickered. "Someone!"

Fenring slid in beside him. "It does follow the rules of kanly, my dear Duke. *The Assassin's Handbook* clearly allows the use of targeted poison when one has declared a blood feud, all in an attempt to limit collateral damage. Hmmm."

With growing alarm, Leto squared his shoulders and raised his voice. "I did not poison Atikk! I came here prepared to fight him. I face my own problems." He raised his sword, indicated his shield belt. His anger rose. "I did not ask for this duel, and I did not kill him."

The crowd just stared at him.

Fenring added, "Again, allow me to point out this is a perfectly acceptable end to a kanly challenge. The matter has been resolved without the need for a bloody and disruptive sword fight." He raised a hand in a salute. "Kudos to Duke Leto Atreides!"

Leto's cheeks burned. The members of his entourage appeared stunned. While secret poisoning might be an acceptable tactic, and his own Master of Assassins, Thufir Hawat, might consider it necessary under some circumstances, Leto would never have killed his noble peer in such an underhanded way. The kanly challenge placed his own honor on the line. To him, it smacked of cow-ardice.

Far from looking uncomfortable, Fenring actually seemed pleased. "Well, ahhhh, no matter who did it, the conflict is neatly settled, and now we can get on with other Imperial business." Leaving the corpse to be handled by the Suk doctor and attendants rushing away, the Count lowered his voice. "He was not worth your time, Leto. I see great potential in you."

I have many business associates, because CHOAM is a vast company with connections everywhere. I have fewer allies, because maintaining them requires long-term planning and a certain level of mutual trust. Fewer still are those I call friends. They are truly precious, but also extremely dangerous, because they know too much. I do not often take that risk.
—CHOAM Ur-Director MALINA ARU

The Silver Needle thrust into Kaitain's sky like a sword, unmarred by windows or superstructure, although the one-way metal let company bureaucrats survey the city view from inside. Externally, the CHOAM Company headquarters appeared bright and impenetrable, just like CHOAM itself.

The spire was supposed to convey the subliminal message of an assassin's dagger, so that the Emperor would never forget who truly controlled power. Shaddam Corrino had seen the Silver Needle all his life, but Malina Aru wasn't convinced he noticed, or heeded, subtle messages.

Before she returned to her quiet sanctuary on Tupile, the Ur-Director had business to conduct with her son Frankos in the headquarters building. During her time on Kaitain, she had testified before two Landsraad committees, sworn—honestly, with the Emperor's Truthsayer present—that she'd had no direct contact with Jaxson since his attack on Otorio and suggested (though she didn't believe it for a minute) that Jaxson might have gone renegade, heading outside the boundaries of the Imperium, never to be seen again. She had shown herself to be a model of cooperation in the hunt to bring Jaxson to justice, and she was the aggrieved mother, a heartbroken parent whose son had gone wrong.

Inside the Needle, Malina discussed these matters with Frankos. The Otorio incident had provoked outraged retaliations from the Emperor, but Jaxson's sheer audacity had also generated support for the movement, which showed the deep-seated dislike for House Corrino. Many noble families with long-standing grudges now quietly embraced the rebellion. Although many Landsraad Houses might sympathize with the Noble Commonwealth, Malina realized that the glacial pace of change had made the overall movement seem weak and ineffective. Powerful potential allies had not offered their support because they doubted the Noble Commonwealth would ever succeed. Jaxson's bloody attack, though, had added urgency to the calls for change.

Malina still disapproved of his tactics, but the obvious results gave her food for thought. She needed to be open to possibilities.

In the President's spacious office at the tip of the Needle, the one-way metal granted her a spectacular, unobstructed vantage of the capital city. Right now, inside the main boardroom, Frankos presented his briefing for the Urdir, condensing and summarizing hundreds of trade deals into significant points. Her older son knew how to curate the most important information, so as not to waste her time.

While she listened, Malina's attention strayed to her beloved spinehounds at her feet. Though their home was rugged Tupile, they weren't native creatures to that volcanically unstable planet. Har and Kar had been specially bred for her on Tleilax. Because of their many secret dealings with CHOAM, the Tleilaxu owed her favors.

The two spinehounds were lean, muscular, and wolflike, their fur composed of sharp silvery needles, but when Malina stroked in the proper direction, they felt as soft and rare as precious metal. Har and Kar were content to rest on the penthouse floor beside her.

Frankos sifted through printed papers and finished delivering his summary. She would peruse the compressed files on her trip back to Tupile in an unmarked CHOAM transport.

She remembered Frankos and his sister, Jalma, when they were just children, and the plans she and Brondon, her husband, had made as parents. Ambitious CHOAM administrators, they had such high hopes for their three children. With Frankos now the President and Jalma ruling House Uchan on Pliesse, at least two of them had not disappointed her.

Jaxson had been problematic from the beginning. Nevertheless, she was his mother and did not give up hope that she could salvage him, bring him back into the fold. . . .

Har and Kar both perked up at the same time, and a resonant growl built in their throats. Frankos looked up from his crystal pad. "Oh, I forgot to tell you about a visitor being ushered in right now. Baron Vladimir Harkonnen. He made arrangements to see you in person."

Malina was alarmed. "There can be no record of official meetings between the two of us."

"He was on Kaitain meeting with the Emperor and asked to discuss matters relating to his CHOAM Directorship, both on Arrakis and Giedi Prime." Frankos gave a conciliatory shrug. "It is a legitimate reason."

Malina's thoughts raced. "Wipe all records that show he entered the Silver Needle, just to be sure. No one should know that he was here."

But Frankos looked dubious. "Mother, the movements of Baron Harkonnen are hardly unobtrusive."

Thinking of the enormous man and his gaudy clothes and suspensor belt, Malina knew her son was correct. "Then change the log to reflect that he met with some minor officials on the lower levels and that I was unavailable for him. We can't let other ambitious nobles think they can just drop in for a social visit with the Ur-Director of CHOAM."

Frankos busily scribed notes on a clean sheet of ridulian crystal.

The Baron arrived at the penthouse office, moving with an unexpected grace that managed not to be comical. His great body was like a cargo ship covered with folds of fat, buoyed up by suspensors, but his feet were delicate as they touched the carpet and moved him forward. He had overheard Malina's last comment. "You should always find time for me, Ur-Director, considering our important business together."

The spinehounds crouched, ready to attack, but Malina remained seated. "I find time for you, Baron, but I don't want everyone else to know. Since House Harkonnen does have legitimate business activities with CHOAM, you can justify coming to our headquarters, but we can't let anyone notice that we pay unusual attention to each other."

The Baron shot a sidelong glance at Frankos, as if questioning whether the CHOAM President should be there. Malina scoffed. "Of course my son knows about our confidential arrangement. We may speak freely."

Har and Kar remained tense, their silver spines bristling, and the threatening growls seemed to delight the Baron. His spider-black eyes sparkled. "Fascinating creatures."

He turned back to the Urdir. "Emperor Shaddam just put me through a very incisive interrogation about the spice thieves, and I handily answered all of his questions. Nothing we need worry about. He is perfectly happy to accept that Count Fenring rooted out the criminals who were shipping spice on the black market. A smuggler woman and several of her compatriots were framed and executed." His gaze bored into Malina's. "All scapegoats, chosen by Fenring for some reason. I believe he is making a show to protect himself, and we scoop up the benefits."

This was indeed a surprise. "You say that the Emperor is satisfied?"

"Shaddam clearly is, but I cannot understand Fenring's game. Does he actually believe he caught the perpetrators? That man is not easily duped. Previously, I tried to deflect attention by cracking down on smuggler activities, but Fenring insists that Esmar Tuek's band must be left alone, that they are sanctioned by him." He clicked his tongue against his teeth. "No matter, the Emperor has stopped breathing down our necks, at least for now. We can improve our operations and make certain there are no mistakes."

The spinehounds circled Malina's chair, continuing to lock their predatory eyes on the Baron. "Lovely creatures," he said again.

Malina did not relax, despite his reassurances. "And if Fenring or the Emperor should choose another scapegoat—you, perhaps?—have you made contingency plans? I must consider the future of CHOAM. If you are withdrawn from Arrakis, who will we deal with? Who is your heir apparent? You are not married. You have no children."

The Baron pouted. "Why do you assume I have no children?"

"I don't care about your sexual prowess. I care about House Harkonnen's line of succession."

"I have two nephews who are both sufficiently Harkonnen. Either will rise to the occasion, at the appropriate time. I am off to Giedi Prime next, and I have already summoned Rabban to join me." He smiled. "I will broach the matter there." He approached the spinehounds, showing amusement rather than fear. "In fact, pets such as these would make a marvelous incentive. How might I procure a pair of them as a gift?"

Malina considered. "Har and Kar were specially bred for *me*." The Baron continued to wait, not accepting that as an answer. After a long pause, she continued, "I can send a request to the Bene Tleilax. Perhaps they would be willing to produce two more for me." She reached down to pet the animals, and they relaxed. They were closely bonded with her every move, attuned to her every emotion. "Your nephew Rabban works the spice operations on Arrakis? Are the hounds for him? Will you designate him your na-Baron?"

The large man frowned. "Rabban is adequate at times, but no. I have higher hopes for my younger nephew, though he will have to prove himself. You met him on Giedi Prime."

Malina remembered the pouting, aloof teenager. "Feyd-Rautha."

"Exactly. Lovely boy! He would adore having his own pets."

Though Feyd had not made a particularly good first impression during their meeting in the Giedi Prime munitions factory, Malina felt it was a small enough concession. "I will make the request."

Life is never static, and each day brings fresh challenges. When facing a novel problem, simple courage may not suffice. On such occasions you must search within yourself for depths of courage you did not know you had.

—LADY JESSICA, private journals

Having heard Lethea's ravings, Jessica was just as desperate as the Mother Superior to learn the root cause of the crone's obsession, so she decided to find her own answers. The half-mad old woman could have tried to kill her the first time, but she hadn't. Instead, she demanded that Jessica murder her own son.

Jessica would face her again, this time without observers.

In the thickest dark of the night, she hurried down the medical-wing corridor on the third floor of the admin building, heading toward Lethea's secure chamber. She couldn't sleep, and she refused to lie awake in bed dreading or second-guessing. She would confront the situation head-on, on her own terms, and the sooner the better. Jessica saw advantages to keeping people off balance. The Sisterhood had certainly done that to her.

Maybe without Harishka eavesdropping, Lethea would reveal more.

With the exception of breeding project archives, external security at the Mother School was not tight. Jessica was sure one or more Sisters would be monitoring Lethea, but she would take advantage of the opportunity to dig deeper into the crone's wounded psyche.

For her own reasons, Jessica needed to know what Lethea wanted from her, why she had issued such dire warnings, and how Jessica could remove the threat. Even with her determination, Jessica nevertheless felt like a fly in the web of a hungry spider.

But I am no mere helpless fly, she reminded herself. She could control this situation, instead of letting it control her. Duke Leto had often told her that he admired her independence, which he had tolerated . . . until discovering that she had interfered with the list of betrothal candidates for Paul. That had been the first big breaking point, resulting in his anger and unwillingness to forgive.

Leto did not know what she had done *for* him, though. She had rebelled against the Sisterhood to give him the son he wanted. Little did he realize the full scale of her defiance, and now she was paying the price.

Paul. She tried to visualize her son's face, but the image would not hold;

his face flickered and faded, as if telling her not to distract herself. When she encountered Lethea, she would need all her strength and faculties. She pushed aside her longing for those she wanted to be with, and marched on.

The corridors were dark, and the school was hushed and brooding, like a crouching animal. Jessica rounded a corner and saw the guarded room, with two white-robed Acolytes standing by the barricaded door. The young women turned toward her in surprise. They appeared to be diligent, but tense with responsibility. They glanced at each other, didn't seem to know how to respond.

"I wish to see Lethea," Jessica announced. "*Now.*" She did not use Voice, because she didn't yet have a measure on these two, but her confidence worked almost as well as a command.

"The Mother Superior isn't here," said one of the Acolytes, Rinni. The girl had an odd, oblong face, and her mouth quirked unevenly down to her right. It gave her an intimidating air. Her companion was smaller but more muscular; Jessica knew her as Asha. Both watched Jessica carefully, and Jessica studied them, assessed them.

"No matter. I will see her now. You know who I am, and you know the Mother Superior instructed me to talk with Lethea. I think I can get more out of her in private."

Asha said, "But it's the middle of the night."

"Therefore, it is the perfect time. I doubt Lethea is ever aware of what hour it is." Jessica approached the door, showing no hesitation.

The Acolytes, though, were clearly doubtful. "We should call in more observers," said Rinni.

"That will only interfere with my work." Knowing she didn't have much time, Jessica barked out in a compelling Voice, "Open the door now, and do not get in my way."

The muscular Acolyte's eyes dulled, though something within her tried to resist and made her face twitch, before subsiding. She unsealed the door, and her companion stood awkwardly by.

Jessica slipped past them into the room and closed the door behind her. She suspected they would call Sister Jiara or some other supervisor, so she had to work fast. She needed answers for herself as much as to satisfy the Mother Superior.

The old crone was awake and aware. With her restraints loosened, probably because she had been so deeply drugged, Lethea struggled to sit up in the medical bed, and looked at Jessica with an expression that was both predatory and hunted. Her bony ankles were secured with straps, and a harness bound her shoulders against the headboard.

"I heard you out there, Jessica of Caladan. You are adept in the use of Voice, too. You should command your son to leap out a high window—I can show you how!" The dry, raspy sound might have been a laugh. "Better yet, you and I should have a Game of Voice—I order you to kill yourself, and you try to make me do the same."

"That would be a waste of our skills," Jessica said.

"And Harishka would hate it." Lethea gave her a strange smile, motioned for the younger woman to come closer.

Quelling her uneasiness, Jessica did so. "I will not kill my son. Do not ask again." She would not show any trepidation, because the old woman would sense it, like an animal. Jessica did not intend to be her victim. She held on to the fact that Lethea needed something from her. "Why would you say such a terrible thing? He's just a boy."

"Just a boy!" Lethea cackled. "But perhaps the Sisterhood deserves whatever happens to them. They have created and planned for their own monster. Let them survive the consequences of their own hubris."

"What monster?" Jessica felt defensive. "Paul is no monster."

"Ah, but he could be. Are you sure he's not the Kwisatz Haderach? Is that what you wanted?"

"The Kwisatz Haderach?" Jessica's voice was hoarse. "Why would you say that?"

"You've thought of it yourself! Do not deny it—if he is what the Sisterhood wants, then that's what they deserve!"

Jessica was unsettled. Lethea's behavior was different, vindictive. This dangerous woman was likely in the throes of dementia, unreliable and volatile. A former Kwisatz Mother, now fallen into madness . . . could the Sisterhood do nothing to help her? Jessica felt the smallest glimmer of pity. "Why do you say that? What did the Bene Gesserit do to you?"

Lethea's eyes went unfocused. "What they do to all of us, what they will do to you." She reached out and grasped Jessica's hand. "My whole life, my heart, my energy, my skills . . . all to be discarded like this. Harishka knows, and yet she still won't see."

Flinching but forcing herself to remain still, Jessica took the old woman's hand and squeezed her grip. She lowered her voice, kept it firm. "I will not let any harm come to my son, no matter what you say."

"Then the path is set." Lethea shuddered, and a line of drool ran out the side of her mouth. "They won't get anything more from me."

Jessica saw madness in her eyes, and she suddenly wondered if the Bene Gesserit themselves had caused this deep breakdown by trying to crack open Lethea's mind and extract the abilities they needed. The clawlike hand squeezed hers more tightly. The papery skin was at first cold, then gradually warmed.

The old woman seemed relaxed, almost normal now, but Jessica wouldn't let down her guard. This might be another private game she was playing. She watched the rheumy eyes carefully, looking for the slightest change.

"I was once beautiful, you know," the old woman mused, "as you are now. I was quite in demand."

"You are still beautiful."

"And you are too kind." She paused, then rasped, "Kindness is a weakness." Jessica stared hard at her. "Kindness is a choice, and I have had to make hard choices. Your kindness caused a great deal of hurt."

The old woman narrowed her eyes to slits and stared away. "And that chain of hurt is only beginning. You will cause much more harm with repercussions that will last for generations!" She released a long sigh that came out as a rattle. "You are the first pebble in the avalanche that will destroy the Sisterhood as we know it. Is it too late to stop the landslide? Maybe so . . . if you won't take the necessary action."

Jessica felt a chill. The reason the Bene Gesserit considered this woman so valuable was because of her specific, targeted prescience about the order's future. "How am I responsible? Why do you want to separate me from my son? What am I going to do that is so terrible?"

"It's already done! Never should have happened, never should have been allowed . . ." She heaved a great breath. "The boy child was nearly killed just after birth, but Kwisatz Mother Anirul saved him! A mistake! A mistake! She was too soft. You are too soft."

Jessica yanked her hand free. "What do you mean?"

"It all flows from your defiance! Arrogant girl. Your foolish act of love will bring ruin to billions."

Jessica's anger overwhelmed her fear. "And your broken mind gives you delusions." She thought of Paul, so earnest as he trained, devoted to his father and to Atreides honor, determined to become a good Duke. "The Sisters should not listen to your ravings." She dropped her voice further. "They should never have listened to you." She could have been home on Caladan now, with Paul, with Leto. . . .

The crone's voice took on an eerie quality, as if she were speaking across a gulf of time and space. She lunged against her restraints to seize Jessica's wrist with surprising strength. Lethea whispered excitedly, "Your son, the son who never should have been conceived . . ." She paused, and then her voice seemed to overlap with others inside her mind. "He has a . . . terrible purpose."

As the ancient woman squeezed hard enough to make her arm hurt, Jessica felt a chill, and a rush of female voices entered her mind, distant at first, but growing louder and more importunate. With the voices came a multitude of faces, overwhelming her vision from within.

With considerable effort, Jessica pulled herself free, and the voices and images stopped. "You're hallucinating. Your mind is shattered, and your body is filled with drugs. Even you don't know what you're seeing!"

"Not entirely your fault," Lethea said in a calm, wavering voice. "The Sisterhood stirred up a whirlwind, and I have been part of it. They planted the seeds of their own downfall, and they will reap a harvest of blood."

Jessica experienced a primal, superstitious fear of this woman, all the multitudes churning within her like an army of raving ghosts.

"I spent a long life in service to the Sisterhood." Lethea slumped back in exhaustion. "I sacrificed much, gave my heart and soul and every breath to the order. When the breeding program reached an impasse, I recalculated the bloodlines and matches, and I found the right path. By bearing a son, you changed that path . . ." Her face twisted in a grimace of pain. "And for all my efforts, Harishka rewards me with betrayal, entrapment, and torture! The Bene Gesserit won't let me die! I curse them with their own inevitable future."

The fatigued old woman appeared to be *crumbling*. She wheezed badly, as if in her last few moments of life.

"You frighten the Sisterhood," Jessica said. "You have threatened them, just as you threaten me and Paul. They have reason to fear. You've done great harm."

In a sudden move, Lethea lashed out as swift as a striking snake and grabbed Jessica by the neck. "I have *killed* people! I could destroy you, too, here and now."

In a calculated response, Jessica struck a nerve center on the old woman's arm, and the grip suddenly went limp. "I would not be so easy to kill as the others."

Lethea slumped back. "Maybe you are exactly what the Sisterhood deserves, for what they did to me." Then her voice ran through a frightening succession of different female identities, one after the other as the multiple personalities of Other Memory threatened to take her over. "What they did to me!"

"*What they did to me!*"

"Did to me!"

One voice said, "There is a good Lethea and a bad Lethea, and both are extremes."

As Lady Jessica touched the old woman's skin, images and voices tried to infect Jessica's mind, imparting glimpses of past lives. She did not pull away, not yet.

Finally, Lethea's own voice reasserted control. "The children I've borne, the daughters I wanted to have! The life the Sisterhood stole from me, the lives they stole from others! They forced me to follow strict rules, never revealing secrets, constantly changing lives—for the worse. With my prescience, terrible glimpses flicker in my mind, the evil collective path of the Bene Gesserit and my part in it. And yours!"

Jessica pulled herself back out of the old woman's reach.

"If one prey slips loose," Lethea said, "there are always others." Her head flopped back against the board, and her watery eyes rolled up at the viewing windows, all of which had been shifted into mirrors. Jessica had no doubt that observers had gathered out there to watch this encounter. No one had come in to help her.

Lethea's gaze glided across the wide mirrored windows and penetrated, even though she could see nothing behind the reflection. "Two Acolytes are out there." Her voice sounded dangerous. "Ah, Mother Superior is coming, along with Ruthine and Jiara—but they are not here yet." Her lips quirked in a smile. "You there—I know you! I sense you, and I know who you are."

Jessica remembered the two young women standing guard. "What are you doing?"

Lethea ignored her. "Acolyte Rinni—hear me, heed me. You are afraid, are you not? I know you are. Recite the Litany Against Fear. It will save you." The old woman's expression darkened, became frightening and malicious. "Remember it. Hold it." Her tone shifted, altered to a specific command interlaced with the manipulative power of Voice. "From now on, you will have no other thoughts but the Litany Against Fear. No other words, no other memories or realities. The Litany is you, the Litany is all there is."

Jessica heard something heavy move on the other side of the plaz, a body falling, and a young woman speaking, louder and louder—reciting the Litany Against Fear.

Jessica glared at Lethea. "What have you done?"

"The Mother Superior thought I could not get to them through the barriers. She was wrong." She laughed again. "*I am the mind-killer!*"

Rushing out of the isolation chamber, Jessica saw Acolyte Rinni sprawled on the floor, her expression hypnotized. Her words flowed endlessly, the same words over and over, locked in an infinite autistic loop, repeating, "Fear is the mind-killer," and the rest of the Litany, over and over and over again, unable to break it.

Jessica dropped beside her on the floor, shaking the young woman by the shoulders. The other Acolyte said, "I sent for help! Medical Sisters and the Mother Superior are coming!" The two tried to break the hold of Lethea's command, but the young woman continued her endless muttering.

Three medical attendants swiftly arrived with a litter. Rinni lay on the floor in a trance, babbling a horrible twisting of the words that had helped so many Sisters over the millennia.

> "*I must not fear.*
> *Fear is the mind-killer.*
> *Fear is the little-death that brings total obliteration.*
> *I will face my fear. I will permit it to pass over me and through me.*
> *And when it has gone past I will turn the inner eye to see its path.*

Where the fear has gone there will be nothing.
Only I will remain."

The words burned into Jessica's brain, but she did not find them comforting. At the moment, they made her skin crawl as medical attendants rushed the poor victim away, still chanting endlessly.

In order to achieve great things, one must first aspire, and that is where most people fall short. They have no spark to ignite the brilliant flame that leads to achievement.

—COUNT HASIMIR FENRING, private conversations
with Emperor Shaddam IV

Though his primary duty was to serve as Spice Minister on Arrakis, Count Hasimir Fenring's mind was not limited by a singular focus. He engaged in countless machinations, pulling puppet strings and nudging opinions on Kaitain and throughout the Landsraad. He kept watch for ways to increase his influence and set game pieces in motion, all to serve Emperor Shaddam, of course. And himself.

Because of his newly revealed ambitions, Duke Leto Atreides caught his attention, as a potential pawn or perhaps even a protégé.

The lanky, well-dressed Fenring strolled through a feathertree hedge maze in one of the palace's many isolated courtyards. His lovely wife, Margot, was beside him, the epitome of poise, beauty, and grace. He adored her. She had blond hair, shining eyes, and a face that would have challenged the talent of the greatest sculptor, yet Margot's mind was her most remarkable attribute, at least to him.

With his narrow face, weak chin, and darting movements, Fenring was not a man who could have won over such a magnificent woman by charm or physical attraction alone. Margot had been trained among the Bene Gesserit and assigned to him when he and Shaddam were both young, ambitious, and reckless. Similarly, the witches had presented Lady Anirul to Shaddam as his first wife, but that marriage hadn't ended well.

Fenring and Margot were perfectly matched, however. He knew full well that she had instructions to watch him and report back to the Sisterhood, to work her wiles as the Sisterhood wished, but he was more than a match for her skills. They were like two puzzle pieces fitting together, close partners, each with their own agendas and deep loyalties, which were often aligned.

Fenring took her hand now, felt her soft skin, her smooth fingers clasping his. Her warm smile was filled with so much love that he believed she was sincere. With the Bene Gesserit, who could know?

As they walked under the shade of the pastel feathertrees, the stirring fronds made whispery sounds. Transmitters embedded among those fronds sent out scrambling pulses to foil eavesdropping devices, and Fenring could be confident in their privacy. "I have an idea, my dear," he said.

"Oh? When have you ever lacked for ideas?"

"I have my eyes set on a possible pupil, someone who has great potential—if I serve as a proper mentor."

"You always see the best in people, husband."

"I am an astute judge of resources."

"And who is this new candidate?"

They passed a mist fountain that made the air sparkle in the Kaitain sunlight. "It may be a surprise, but hear me out. Leto Atreides has changed his priorities, and I think I can help him, mold him."

Margot's expression shifted as she considered.

Fenring continued, "The Duke of Caladan is both defined by his honor and trapped by it. In order to succeed in Landsraad politics, one must see gray as well as black and white. His vision has, ahhhh, improved after what he experienced at Otorio. There have been domestic changes on Caladan as well."

Margot nodded. "It is worth investigating. I remember how brave Leto was during the Trial of Forfeiture years ago, even threatened with losing all his holdings and his life."

Fenring squeezed her hand. "And he did thwart the Tleilaxu at the time, and expose a Harkonnen plot against House Atreides. I have to admire that, and I expect we will see more messiness between the Harkonnens and the Atreides."

Margot stroked the side of his face tenderly, which made him flush. "Then I will watch your workings with interest, as always, darling."

"Let me see what Duke Leto is all about, hmmm." Fenring looked up at the tallest feathertree, where peach-colored spikes were ready to burst with spores. "He has a promising political career, if he has the mettle for it."

EVEN THOUGH LORD Atikk was dead—secretly poisoned in his own quarters—no investigation seemed imminent. Leto struggled with how to react to the assumptions of the other courtiers. Rather than blaming him, people accepted his clever solution to the blustery man's declaration of kanly. The fact that other nobles believed the Duke of Caladan capable of secretly poisoning an opponent to avoid facing him—even admired him for such a neat and definitive solution—made him wonder how they viewed him, and viewed themselves. He found it deeply unsettling.

I already agreed to a face-to-face duel! I do not sneak in and poison my opponents!

He was even more surprised to receive a private dinner invitation from Count Hasimir Fenring. Leto was curious and wary, but saw it as an opportunity. In general, he did not like to conduct business with anyone he didn't trust, but in the web of the Imperial Court, so many rules were different. Reminding himself why he had come to Kaitain, Leto felt duty-bound to understand those rules better. Fenring could help.

He met the Count on a high balcony on one of the palace towers. The elaborate open patio granted a view of the vibrant nighttime vistas. Leto's senses never adjusted to the assault of colors, sounds, and sensations, and he longed for the calm of the ocean and the peace of his ancestral holdings.

The thin, severe-faced man waited for him at a well-set table under the open skies. Count Fenring wore a high collar, ballooned sleeves, and ornate medallions. Leto had heard the man was a swift and smooth assassin, although he looked as if he could barely move in such uncomfortable finery. He could only imagine what weapons the garments might conceal. "Ahhhh, Duke Leto! Thank you for joining me. We have interesting matters to discuss."

As Leto moved to the offered chair, he could hear a hum of transparent shields that formed a bubble over the patio, deflecting possible assassination attempts as well as pernicious nighttime insects. The Duke took his seat. "Thank you, Count Fenring. I'm interested to hear what you have to say."

"Ahhh, hmmm, right to business! I like an efficient man. It makes my work easier." Fenring removed the covers from the dishes, not bothering to call an army of servants. "The food may seem familiar to you. This repast will help me understand you better. Moonfish fillets in taki mushroom sauce, along with pundi rice, a medium-grain variety, even a bottle of Caladan wine." He lifted the bottle with his large-knuckled hands. "A blanq. I hope I chose well."

"If you chose from Caladan, you chose well," Leto said. "Pundi rice is a staple, and the moonfish . . ." He let Fenring serve him a juicy seared fillet that glistened in sauce. "Our market has grown since my father introduced the delicacy to the Imperium."

"Perhaps it is an investment I should consider." After serving himself, Fenring took a bite and smacked his lips. "Remarkable! I must have more of this. In fact, I'll insist that the palace place a standing order and have regular shipments sent to the Arrakeen Residency as well."

"Fish on Arrakis? A pleasant irony." Leto gave a wry smile. "Thank you, Count Fenring. Caladan's moonfish exports have great potential for expansion. We are very proud of it."

They continued an awkward, casual conversation before Fenring leaned close, his dark and sharp eyes boring into Leto's. "I know why you are here on Kaitain. You've spoken at several important Landsraad meetings and made your opinion known on various proposals."

"Taking my civic responsibilities to heart, Count Fenring," Leto said. "I have done nothing unusual."

"Not unusual for any ambitious noble, no, but rather unusual for the Duke of Caladan, hmmmm?"

Leto ate some seasoned rice, and decided that his own chefs at Castle Caladan had superior recipes. "I am considering the expansion of Atreides holdings to benefit my son and our future. There is nothing wrong with that." He realized he sounded defensive.

Fenring chuckled and tasted the pundi rice, washing it down with the fine white wine. "Nothing wrong at all, my dear Duke. In fact, you caught my attention from the moment you arrived at court. I may be able to help you in your ambitions."

"You already hinted as much, and the offer still surprises me. Why would you help me?"

Fenring touched his chest in feigned offense. "You do not think me a compassionate man who wishes to become a mentor?"

After a long pause, Leto replied, "I don't think that's all there is to it."

The Count responded with a delighted grin. "Of course not! But there are always reasons. The tides of power and influence constantly shift, and I consider it an investment in the future to support people I understand, whose gratitude I may earn. The Emperor is deciding how to assign Landsraad holdings, and I have his ear. I can easily make recommendations, if you are willing to join in the game. You have been rather, ahhhh, aloof in the past."

"Not aloof, merely preoccupied with my own people," Leto said, then squared his shoulders. "But I've come to realize that the Imperium is larger than Caladan, and I may have overlooked many opportunities."

"Good! I am glad we can dispense with that. Now, let us state the obvious." Fenring set down his fork and tapped a finger on the tabletop. "One thing holding you back in the Landsraad is your failure to make a marriage alliance."

Leto's brow furrowed. An image flashed across his mind—Ilesa Ecaz in her wedding dress, lying bloody with her throat slashed. "I tried that already, and it did not turn out well."

Fenring dismissed the idea with a wave. "Yes, hmmm, that was quite a debacle, but many new opportunities have opened up since then. The Otorio disaster left several grieving but wealthy widows, with many nobles circling them like wolves. You should seize the opportunity."

Leto stiffened. "My son and heir is fourteen, and I've already begun investigating candidates for his betrothal." He felt a warmth in his cheeks remembering how Duke Verdun had insulted Paul and House Atreides. "That has been my focus. I do not seek marriage for myself."

"Ahhhh, yes, the timing is right for your son, but one cannot limit the approach to only one avenue," Fenring said. "Before this dinner, I took the liberty of studying a few possibilities for you. Let me suggest a marriage that would be greatly advantageous to House Atreides. A perfect match. I'm certain my friend Shaddam would give his blessing, if you helped me take care of a few loose ends."

Leto hesitated. Suddenly losing his appetite, he took a sip of wine to give himself a moment to think. "And who is this perfect woman you have chosen for me?"

Fenring lifted one long finger. "I didn't say *perfect woman*. I said perfect *match*."

Leto could only think of Jessica's oval face, her bronze hair, her green eyes, how it had felt to hold her, how she had often given him her wise counsel.

How she had betrayed him.

How she had left Caladan to rejoin the Sisterhood.

"I'm listening," Leto said.

"Vikka Londine comes from a well-respected noble family, which is led by her father, the annoying Rajiv Londine. Their main holding is the planet Cuarte. An Atreides and Londine alliance would offer many advantages." He swirled his wine, staring into the goblet, and looked across the Kaitain skyline.

Leto tried to recall what he knew of House Londine, came up with very little. "And she is not married?"

"Not currently. She and her husband, Clarton, were estranged, and he chose to attend the gala reception at the Imperial Museum without her. He, ahhhh, did not survive the attack." Fenring smiled as if this were not bad news at all. "If you were to marry into their House, you might provide the right kind of influence, rein in the old nobleman. Shaddam would be very happy."

"I see you've made extensive calculations."

"Ahhhh, always. Vikka Londine is currently right here on Kaitain, and I will arrange introductions. Why don't you review the House Londine holdings, meet her, see if you find her tolerable?"

Leto's stomach tightened. He had promised Jessica he would not attempt to marry again. He'd also told her that he loved her, that she was his bound concubine, that he wanted no other. Because of that promise, he had focused on finding a marital match for Paul instead, but now. . . .

Maybe he would take that burden on his own shoulders after all. Why should he impose a political marriage on his son, if he wasn't willing to accept it himself?

"I'll consider it," he told Fenring.

The Count beamed. "Excellent. Tomorrow I am off for Arrakis on important business, but I will not be gone long. When I return to Kaitain, I'll expect your reply."

After spending several days on Giedi Prime, Baron Vladimir Harkonnen wanted to take care of one last thing before he returned to his lucrative holdings on Arrakis. Malina Aru's prodding about his successor had kept him thinking for some time. *Who is your heir apparent?* He had put off the decision for too long, stringing his nephews along. Though the Baron was by no means ready to retire, or die, he was realistic, and the ambitions and wealth of House Harkonnen went beyond his life span. All the melange in the Orgiz refinery would not make him immortal.

The CHOAM Ur-Director had been right to ask. *Who will we deal with?*

The Baron continued to wrestle with possibilities. He had to make his decision, or at least come closer to one. He had been instructing his nephews for years, grooming them for important duties, but would either Rabban or Feyd serve as a worthy Baron?

Supported by his suspensor belt, the immense man made his way around a large, echoing room he had set up for this specific meeting. His Mentat, Piter de Vries, was there with him, always close, always attentive, but the Baron would issue his own challenge, turn his nephews loose. *Let them impress me!*

Feyd-Rautha and Rabban arrived together, brothers but rivals, curious but wary. Feyd looked around, sniffing the air as if uncomfortable with the long silence and the room's emptiness. "Where are the executives who used to have offices in this wing? Why is everyone gone?"

"Very observant," the Baron said. "Those particular executives are no longer with us."

"Our uncle burned them up," Rabban said matter-of-factly.

Frowning at the interruption, the Baron directed his attention to his younger nephew. "Yes, I invited your brother to watch, because he enjoys beastly things, all the blood and screaming. But you are more sensitive, dear Feyd, and I don't want you to have nightmares."

The younger man gave a petulant frown. "I would have liked to see it, too."

"Perhaps next time. There is always a next time, isn't there?" It was not a question.

"I told our uncle to burn them up," Rabban said. "It was my idea."

Piter de Vries gave him a sharp look, and the Baron knew who had really come up with the idea. Rabban and the twisted Mentat often squabbled, but they somehow managed to work together.

The Baron explained further. "I informed your brother that we needed to clear these offices for today's little discussion, and he came up with how to do it." He looked closer at his handsome young nephew. "If I were to ask *you* how to kill people, Feyd, I suspect you would have offered a different method."

"Incinerating our enemies isn't a terrible idea," Feyd conceded and gave a grudging nod in the direction of his older brother. "A bit dramatic, though."

De Vries flicked his gaze back and forth between the two nephews as if performing a deep scan. "All of the executives in this section were underperforming, individually and as a unit," he announced. "The idea was to provide incentive to other executives in similar situations. In this particular case, a dramatic show was the best way to get the message across to our thousands of workers."

The Baron said, "I had them put to death, along with their assistants. Their desks and everything else they touched were burned in a great bonfire behind one of the warehouses, and they all roasted to death. Quite a spectacle."

"It was wonderful," Rabban said.

"Yes, wonderful," Piter said, although his agreement sounded grudging.

"Besides, I needed this room cleared to show you both something." The Baron motioned to his Mentat, who activated an imager to project looming faces onto the walls around them. The images moved slowly around the room, like fleeing prey, and the nephews easily recognized their Atreides enemies.

At a signal, Piter halted the images. The Baron used a fat, ring-bedecked hand to point at one face and spoke in a professorial manner. "Now, who is this?"

Rabban started to sputter something, but his brother spoke first. "Duke Leto Atreides, our mortal enemy. He is the son of Duke Paulus, who died in the bullring."

"We'll kill Duke Leto, too." Rabban's face was flushed.

"Yes, in due course, we will get rid of him." The Baron blew air through his plump lips. "But first, there are things to do, measures to be taken, clever plans to be made."

"We should just level the Atreides holdings on Caladan," Rabban suggested. "Leave nothing but rubble and smoke."

The Baron glowered at him. "That's not a clever suggestion! I know you are more than just brute force, or I never would have given you responsibilities on Lankiveil and Arrakis." He turned to his nephews, lowered his voice. "Now, I intend for you two to take part in those plans, to contribute to the pain the

Atreides must suffer. It is a game I think you both will enjoy." Without explaining further, he indicated the second image that showed a boy even younger than Feyd. "And this?"

"The Duke's bastard son," Feyd said, sounding proud. "I'd like to kill him myself."

"Yes, young Paul Atreides, the supposed future of House Atreides. We will not only eliminate the present Duke, but also his son."

Piter smiled and nodded, but did not speak.

Rabban was getting worked up. "You want us to destroy Paul?"

The Baron watched his burly nephew's emotions boil too quickly to the surface. Rabban was stockily built, muscled like an armored vehicle, and needed to learn to use his mind as much as his brawn. The Baron patted him on his beefy shoulders, calming him but also warning him. "Your anger and violence are good, but only when properly channeled. Do not go around Harko City with the urge to kill someone today. If anyone needs killing, I will decide and give you the authorization. Right now, control your emotions and listen to me. Details are important, as is self-control."

"Details." Rabban settled down, but only a little. "Leto and Paul Atreides. They are noble, but we hate them."

"And as my two potential heirs, you and Feyd will each have a chance to prove yourselves. Now pay close attention. There are other game pieces you need to know." Piter de Vries cycled from image to image, pausing at each. The Baron pointed. "And this one? Who is she?"

"The Duke's whore," Rabban said.

"His bound concubine," Feyd said. "Mother to his son."

He looked long and hard at the woman's image, had always been intrigued by her appearance. There was something mysterious and interesting about her, even attractive, but he could never put his finger on exactly what it was.

"Should we kill her, too?" Rabban asked, sounding a little more cautious now. "Maybe kill her first?"

"We have reason to assassinate all of them, but an even greater reason to *hurt* them." The Baron flushed, his voice and his annoyance rising in tandem. "I caught a glimpse of Duke Leto on Kaitain. It's been a long time since we were in the same chamber, but he was there when Emperor Shaddam chastised me in front of the court. The damnable Atreides heard it all, and if he had been within reach, I would have stabbed him to death right there."

Now it was the Baron's turn to control his temper, if only to provide an example for his nephews.

Next, Piter showed the Atreides Mentat, Thufir Hawat, and then the Suk doctor, Wellington Yueh. Smiling, the Baron explained that he had already initiated a special plan involving the doctor, but he refused to reveal his secrets.

Rabban identified the next images. "Duncan Idaho, the Atreides Swordmaster, and that one is Gurney Halleck, the troubadour warrior. I gave him that scar." He laughed. "I could beat either of them easily in single combat. I've faced them before."

The Baron knew that the previous encounters hadn't turned out particularly well. Rabban had distorted his own memories.

Feyd sniffed, not letting himself be upstaged by his brother. "I could beat either of them, too. I've had enough victories in the combat arena, eighty kills to my credit."

"Indeed you have, dear Feyd, though I would expect you to find a more devious way to harm House Atreides. Your brother's heavy-handed approach does not always work."

Rabban grumbled at the criticism, but Feyd responded with a crafty smile. "I might use a trick or two. My intelligence, along with my physical skills, will win out."

The Baron mused, looking from one nephew to the other. "If the two of you ever faced off in combat, I wonder who would be the victor. Brains or brawn?"

"I have a brain," Rabban said, his tone defensive.

"A small one," Feyd retorted.

Rabban controlled himself and said in a surprisingly even tone, "Our uncle would not like it if I killed you. You are his fair-haired boy, while I am—how do you put it, Uncle—a tank-brain?"

The Baron was pleased to see Rabban exercising better control of his emotions. "Yes, that's it! My beautiful, lithe Feyd, and the muscle-minded tank-brain, Beast Rabban. You each fill a necessary niche." He remembered what Malina Aru had demanded. *Who will we deal with? Who is your heir apparent?* He needed to know for his black-market spice scheme, as well as for himself.

"You love us both, Uncle," Rabban said, sounding resigned, "but you love him the best."

Hearing this, Feyd gave a little smug smile.

The big man belly-laughed. "Love? What sort of a word is that? *Love!* Ha! You are both useful to me, as is Piter de Vries, and I will keep each of you around for as long as you serve me well. You must always prove to be more valuable than your detriments. It's a balance sheet, and assets must be higher than liabilities." He looked at Feyd's smooth skin, his youthful face. "There are things you do well, and things your brother does well."

Looming in front of the Atreides images, the Baron finally issued his formal challenge. "The time will come, and soon, when I must appoint a na-Baron, my designated heir. I will not leave something so important to chance.

"First, I want you to be in charge of yourselves. Each of you must recognize not only your strengths, but also your weaknesses. Always try to improve. We have great work to do for House Harkonnen, and I need to know that you are worthy. You have a natural rivalry, as siblings." He paused a moment to recall how much he had loathed his own brother Abulurd. "But I want you working as a team, rather than quarreling."

Of course they would quarrel, especially once he set this challenge.

"But only one can become the next Baron. I place value in both of you, in your own way, and in the final analysis, I must make a judgment. Whom will I choose to lead House Harkonnen?"

Feyd and Rabban studied him intensely, like cats about to spring. Piter de Vries squirmed with his own ideas, which he forced himself not to express. The Mentat distracted himself by consuming more sapho juice and slipping a spice lozenge into his mouth.

Turning his back on the gallery of Atreides images, the Baron approached his nephews. "Perhaps you have always assumed I would choose you, my dear Feyd, but never assume anything. I must make a logical decision. I want you both to hone your skills, prove which one deserves to lead our Great House. In my business dealings with CHOAM, it is particularly important to show them that we have a functioning and logical line of succession."

"The Urdir has no right to interfere in our internal matters," Feyd said, "no matter your business relationship with her."

"She gets her spice from us. That should be enough," Rabban added, agreeing with his brother.

"Even so, I see her point, and I intend to accelerate the process. You have obeyed my commands, followed my leadership. Now, demonstrate your own unique skills, imagination, and abilities. Tell me, what is the primary goal of House Harkonnen?"

"Power and wealth," Feyd said without hesitation.

"And death to our enemies," Rabban added.

"Both are correct answers. And to achieve power and wealth, we must inflict great harm on House Atreides. Right now, Duke Leto is on Kaitain currying favor with the Emperor, and I do not like that one bit."

Piter de Vries watched, his face calm, like a blank slate waiting for input.

"So I pose an important challenge to you," the Baron continued after taking a deep breath. "Impress me, my young Harkonnens. Compete with each other and win my decision. Consider how best to seriously damage House Atreides and hurt Duke Leto. How would each of you do it?"

"Take the Harkonnen military and attack them," Rabban blurted out. "Pay the Spacing Guild fee for a troop transport and drop down on Caladan while the Duke is away on Kaitain. They are vulnerable."

"That would bring immediate censure from the Landsraad," Piter explained with barely contained scorn. "The fines we'd face might be half a year's income from spice production."

"A military assault would be too overt," Feyd explained. "Our uncle wants something more subtle that cannot be traced back to us. Imperial politics are devious, and we need to find a subtle way to cause harm." The young man's eyes flashed as he assessed ideas. "We are to show imagination and initiative."

The Baron was delighted with his answer. "Precisely! Each of you, develop a plan and implement it. The best plan wins. Above all, maintain plausible deniability—though Duke Leto must know who has hurt him. Both of you, put your wits to work."

Feyd and Rabban looked at each other like gladiators in an arena.

I'll squeeze them a little, the Baron thought, *and see if they break.*

It is possible to fail in a school lesson and then, using the same discredited data and methodology, to succeed in life.

—*The Wisdom of Muad'Dib*

I think Duncan is upset with me, Thufir," Paul said as the old Mentat watched him engage in fighting stances against an imaginary opponent. Paul danced in and out of a patch of morning sunshine that flowed through the training room's large eastern window. Thufir had his back to the window, so Paul saw him only as a stern silhouette.

"How so?" the Mentat asked. Then he snapped, "Concentrate on your training."

"You told me I need to learn to fight while distracted," Paul replied offhandedly, then went into a deep crouch before he tucked his short sword against his body, rolled on the floor, and bounced to his feet, slashing at the air. "After we came back from the sand dunes, Duncan insisted on our normal training session. He exerted himself too much when we sparred, and I was hardly breaking a sweat. I teased him that if he kept slowing down, I might accidentally kill him in one of our sessions."

The young man sliced a quick counterstroke, then came down for an imaginary mortal blow in the sunbeam. "And then I nicked him on purpose. Just a little, but I've never done that before. I'm getting better each day."

"You hurt his pride. Duncan is a celebrated graduate of the elite Ginaz School." The old Mentat's voice was redolent with the wisdom of intense mental conditioning and the experiences of a lifetime.

"I know. I laughed and reminded him that he taught me everything he'd learned on Ginaz, and I have other teachers!" As Paul moved around the training floor, Thufir did as well, and his face remained shadowy. "With all this knowledge I'm accumulating, I think he's afraid I might turn into some kind of superman!"

"Certainly not a humble one." Thufir's shadowed face tightened. "Perhaps you should learn more caution and tact around one of your most brilliant instructors."

"I was just teasing him! Duncan is my friend." Paul wished he hadn't made the comments, but he and the Swordmaster had an easygoing relationship. "I'm sure he'll get over it. I hope so . . ."

"He will because he must. Duncan is the Swordmaster of House Atreides, and with your father on Kaitain, you are serving in the role of Duke, for now. That duty must come before friendship, or wounded pride. Have you thought that if Duncan does his job properly, as your protector, then you would rarely need to demonstrate your own skills against an enemy?"

Paul contemplated, then nodded. "I will learn better how not to hurt people's feelings. I need Duncan's respect above all else." With a burst of energy, he bounded around the edge of the training room, sprang partway up a wall, kicked off, and rolled before landing smoothly back on the floor. Even he was surprised that he had pulled it off.

"Are you trying to demonstrate that you are superhuman?" Thufir asked. Paul heard no trace of humor in the Mentat's voice.

"Duncan said that arrogance and overconfidence could get me killed. Staying humble would better prepare me to avoid mistakes."

Now Thufir smiled. "I didn't know Duncan preoccupied himself with such deep thoughts, but I agree with him."

"So do I, and I apologized to him."

Now the Mentat looked satisfied. "In the end, your apology was the most important thing you did. It revealed that in your innermost heart, you do not believe your nobility makes you superior to him. Both of you are human beings, but with different stations in life."

"I'm not better than you either, Thufir. The difference between us is simply happenstance, the random nature of birth."

Regaining his focus, Paul performed three acrobatic flips in succession, landing on his feet, except for a brief stumble, from which he quickly recovered.

Thufir gave a slow nod. "I see evidence of your mother's training in how you move, your nimbleness and lightness of foot. It enables you to glide away from danger and then strike back with deadly force. She has taught you well."

Paul felt a deep sadness at the mention of his mother. "I hope she's able to come home and keep training me."

The Mentat made a noncommittal sound. As head of security for House Atreides, Thufir knew more than he was letting on about what had happened between Leto and Jessica. Paul himself had only limited information on what his parents had been quarreling about, but the old Mentat would not breach a confidence.

"All of life is training." Thufir had changed the subject, but not entirely, Paul realized. "I have a new challenge for you. Calisthenics. Consider this conundrum."

Paul braced himself for another one of his teacher's deep mental simulations. "I'm ready."

"For the purposes of this exercise, imagine that your father and mother are of the same social station. Neither has any advantage due to nobility or gender or familial background. They are, simply, your parents."

Paul continued his physical regimen while listening. He felt hyperalert, wondering what the Mentat was doing.

"They are equal in all respects, and you realize that together they form an insurmountable barrier to your life's path. You could reach greatness—not only for yourself, but for humankind—only if you can get beyond the obstacle they pose. There is no way around your mother and father, because they are such a powerful combined force. The only way to attain your glorious destiny and help the human race is to exile one of them forever, send your father or mother to a distant planet and never see that parent again."

Paul froze, just stood there with his practice blade in hand, but his mind was rapidly moving. "I don't understand how those circumstances could occur."

"You don't need to. Just accept the possibility." Thufir's intense, droning voice had a hypnotic quality. Paul watched the movement of his sapho-stained lips. "Which of the two would you exile, young Master? An impossible choice, but it must be done. Which would you send away forever? Duke Leto? Lady Jessica?"

"Neither," Paul said. "As before, I refuse. I do not accept the parameters of the question."

The Mentat scoffed. "An unacceptable answer. A coward's answer."

"A leader's answer," Paul insisted. "You have imposed an absurd, artificial scenario, based on flawed premises." He realized that his mother was gone from Caladan. Had his father considered her a threat to Paul's future? Because of the Sisterhood? Had the Bene Gesserit exiled her because they feared she was a problem? No, not possible.

"Life is often absurd and artificial, and we must deal with it," Thufir said.

As Paul prowled around the sunny training floor, his mind focused on something else that he had only half noticed before. Thufir Hawat, who had long counseled him never to sit with his back to a doorway, had kept the morning sun at his back, preventing Paul from seeing him well. It was a tactical decision an ancient army might have made to give them an advantage in combat.

Does Thufir see me as a potential threat? Paul could not believe this, and yet—

His surface thoughts had triggered a deeper sequence. "In my time here acting as Duke, I shall impartially consider the obstacles I face, the people around me—my mother and father, you, Dr. Yueh, Gurney Halleck, Duncan Idaho. Six people, and four of them have a common trait." He turned to face the Mentat. "Do you know what that is?"

"The student questions the instructor?" Thufir made a respectful acknowledgment as he pondered. "I see what you are doing. You would have me immerse myself in thought now, when you are supposed to be answering a profound question."

"You assemble facts for Mentat calculations, which result in probabilities. Put yourself in my shoes for this exercise, and add your deep mental training." Paul paused and looked at him. "Well?"

"Four of the six have something in common. Very well. I give you a conundrum, and you give me a riddle in return. Five of the six are male and one is female, so that is not it. One is of noble birth and the others are not, so that is not it either." The old Mentat smiled a little, but it was not the confident smile Paul was accustomed to. "You are teasing me, young Master, to throw me off track. Instead of facing the painful decision in the scenario, you choose to play mind games with me."

"Only a fool would play mind games with a Mentat," Paul said. "Unless his conditioning were true and unbreakable."

Thufir's eyes sparkled for a moment, then his expression grew dark. "Now I know the sorting you have made. You speak of the Great Schools, don't you?"

Paul smiled. "Yes, of the six people closest to me, only two—my father and Gurney Halleck—were not trained in one of the major schools."

Thufir was done indulging him. "And what does that have to do with your answer to the question I posed?" He raised his eyebrows. "Ah, your mother's situation? You are thinking of loyalty to a school above loyalty to House Atreides. It is true, we are placed in service and swear our loyalty when we give our bond— whether Mentat, Swordmaster, Suk doctor . . . or Bene Gesserit."

Paul felt both intrigued and relieved. "Loyalty is an important trait. Do you have an outside loyalty greater than your obligations to House Atreides, Thufir? To the Mentat school, for instance?"

As Paul moved smoothly, so did the warrior Mentat, continuing to place himself with his back to the sunlight that streamed into the room.

"So the answer to my conundrum is that you would choose your father over your mother?" Thufir pressed. "You would exile your mother because she might have a detrimental outside influence? Split obligations? Because her loyalty is not pure, but possibly torn?"

"I didn't say I would exile her permanently. The purpose of your scenario is to see how I might solve an unsolvable problem. I was assembling facts before making a decision."

Thufir seemed amused, and kept pushing. "And your decision?"

"My decision is this: I will keep the decision to myself, which is the right of a Duke."

The Mentat offered a rare smile, then gave him a formal nod. "Very well, young Master. In this mental match, you have fought me to a draw."

"All of life is training, isn't it, Thufir?" Paul grinned as he reminded the old warrior of his own familiar phrase.

"Yes, it is. Yes, it is." The Mentat gave another bow, then left him alone in the harsh sunlight of the training room.

*An opportunity is already a victory, for someone with the proper attitude.
I see victories everywhere.*

— JAXSON ARU, draft manifesto

When he returned to Caladan in secret, Jaxson Aru wore a different face. His cheeks itched, especially under the eyes, and he had an unpleasant numb patch above his left eyebrow. He prodded his features, not because they were uncomfortable, but because he was amazed by what the Tleilaxu had done to him. Even the color of his eyes had changed.

Facial cloning had altered the visible manifestation of his genetics and highlighted familiar memories of Brondon Aru. His hair was still dark with natural tight curls like thick smoke. The underlying bone structure had adjusted so that his eye separation, cheekbones, and jawline made him a different person. Even the most rigorous identity scans, including those used by the Spacing Guild, would not mark him as Jaxson Aru. Sardaukar hunters and Imperial investigators would continue to search in vain even as he walked among them.

He made his way to Caladan, thinking to observe Duke Leto Atreides. He was still sure he could convince the Duke that the true path of honor did not lie with the corrupt Imperium, but with a vibrant and independent Noble Commonwealth. If only he could open the man's eyes, get him to acknowledge the continuing injustices perpetrated by Corrino rule. Leto was a reasonable man, not a fool.

Jaxson enjoyed a challenge.

Since the intense inner circle of rebels could not operate from the Aru family sanctuary on Tupile—his mother would certainly throw him out—Jaxson needed a new base of operations. He had visited the glassy crater of devastation on Otorio and considered the irony of establishing a new headquarters in the ruins of the Imperial Museum, but that would not do.

He'd lived on Otorio with his father, relaxed and at peace. They had gone glide-sailing together and soared across the waters in suspensor racers. Brondon Aru—the man Jaxson was reminded of each time he looked in the mirror now—had been his hero, his mentor. Brondon had given the young man his self-worth after Malina Aru made it abundantly clear that her son did not meet her expectations. Jaxson could have been happy in exile . . . if his father had not suffered a devastating brain hemorrhage. Jaxson had helped ease him into death, an act that put Brondon at peace and had altered the young man forever, turned him into an agent of change.

Yes, there would have been a certain satisfaction in setting up his new base right on Otorio, but that would be too foolish and obvious. Instead, he chose another out-of-the way planet, Nossus—a temperate, bucolic world with a small population that had no interest in Imperial politics. Nossus reminded him of Otorio in many ways, and he could have prospered there, if he'd been willing just to go into hiding.

But that was not Jaxson's interest. He had set the wheels of rebellion in motion, and he would see this through. The shock waves of his first bold act had cracked the foundation of the Corrino Imperium. Now he had to widen those flaws until the whole thing broke apart.

Starting with Caladan.

As Jaxson traveled to the ocean world, he planned another dramatic statement, a follow-up to his first victory. He needed to put the pieces into play and bring Shaddam to his knees.

When he arrived on Caladan, just another passenger with features that no one noted, he was disappointed to learn that Leto Atreides was visiting Kaitain and that his son, Paul, served as the provisional Duke, under the guidance of several respected advisers.

Jaxson was annoyed by this, but didn't press for answers, not wanting to draw attention. So, another meeting with the Duke of Caladan was not feasible, not now. He would have to bide his time. He considered investigating the young heir, but Paul was just a teenager. Instead, Jaxson would hope that once Leto returned from the decadence and corruption in the Imperial Court, he might be more amenable to Jaxson's ideas.

Lurking around Cala City for a day, he watched townspeople repairing the inns and storefronts that his partner Chaen Marek had damaged in his foolish attempt to intimidate the Duke. Being a Tleilaxu, Marek did not understand the nuances of human personality, the subtleties of how to make people cooperate. Among his distributors and users of the dried barra ferns, Marek had imposed a reign of terror that kept them in line. But such tactics only worked with a certain sort of person. Definitely not Leto Atreides.

Well, Jaxson had come all the way to Caladan. If he could not try to seduce Leto to their all-important cause, at least he would make certain his financing and his new drug operations were secure. Jaxson decided to visit Marek's new operations, unmarked growing fields in the steamy jungles on the southern continent. Purchasing his own craft, Jaxson flew himself to the southern continent. No one else would know his movements.

After landing in the cleared jungle field near the sunny coastline of the primitive land, Jaxson emerged from the flyer. The Tleilaxu geneticist came to meet him and regarded Jaxson's appearance with uneasy astonishment. "You are altered, sir. That is not the face God gave you. Are you a . . . Face Dancer?"

Jaxson scoffed. "This is the face the Tleilaxu gave me. Facial cloning makes it possible for me to go wherever I wish. Now let me see your new growing area."

Paid for with Jaxson's dwindling fortune, Chaen Marek's mercenary crew had cleared acreage in the trackless jungle and planted thousands of modified ferns created in Master Arafa's nightmarish greenhouses in Bandalong.

As Jaxson strolled along beside Marek, the air was redolent with vegetation, the humidity so thick it felt like steam. Jungle leaves drooped all around them, tall trees and thick vines. Jaxson heard the whine of crimson dragonflies swooping through the air engaged in insect aerial combat. Rolling white clouds presaged an afternoon thunderstorm.

Viewed from the edge of the first field, the altered Caladan ferns seemed to be growing well, even on a new continent.

"We will have our first major ailar harvest soon, and we have already sent out feelers to our previous distributors," Marek reported. "The drug influx will fund more Noble Commonwealth activities and help liberate the Tleilaxu people from the Corrino fist."

"Not so easily done." Jaxson clucked his tongue, then rolled it in his mouth. He reached up and felt his new face, still growing accustomed to the regrown flesh. "We mean to give all planets in the Imperium the freedom to create their own cultures, make their own commercial treaties." His voice rose as his passion for the subject increased. He loved talking about his dreams. "Each planet can reach its full potential, much as humanity achieved success after the thinking machines were overthrown. Once we no longer relied on computers as a crutch, our species became better, smarter, faster, deeper." When he smiled, his cheeks moved curiously. "More human than human." He regarded the small-statured drug lord. "Our rebel movement is not only for the benefit of the Tleilaxu."

Marek sniffed. "So long as our goals align, you need not be concerned, sir. My people have their own priorities." He studied the rolling lines of speckled ferns, pale green tendrils rising out of the lush jungle soil. "The new strain will result in fewer accidental deaths, but the ailar is just as addictive. Our customers will return, and the secret wealth will pour in." The Tleilaxu man scowled. "Our distribution network is gone, though, thanks to Leto Atreides."

Jaxson felt an instinctive need to defend the Duke, and his expression grew stormy. "It was because you were so blatant and clumsy."

Marek shrank away. "I've already begun to rebuild our trading web, sir. One of my mercenaries is a dissatisfied Caladanian merchant named Lupar. He worked closely with the northern villages around the moonfish operations and has connections out in the Imperium as well. We will soon have a new underground network for spreading ailar."

"I need to know more about it—all of it," Jaxson said.

"No, you don't!" Marek snapped. "You asked me to rebuild, sir, and you told me to be more careful." The small man bent down, uprooted one of the curled ferns, sniffed it, and wrinkled his nose. "I want these operations to succeed as much as you do. The ailar crop will be restored, as will our distribution network. I will provide all the money you need." The smaller man's eyes hardened. "Meanwhile, your job is to tear apart the Imperium, so that my people can break free of Imperial control."

Every predator can become someone else's prey. In order to survive, you must understand which you are.

—CHOAM Ur-Director MALINA ARU,
The Evolutionary Chain of Business

Even as one of the most powerful people in the Imperium, Malina Aru was stalled by obdurate Tleilaxu restrictions. Through CHOAM, she had the power to push, but that was not always the best way to get something from a client. And she had an unusual request.

She headed to Tleilax after her important business on Kaitain, and now she sat in the quarantine station above Tleilax, just like any other commercial visitor. Without Malina's CHOAM connections, Tleilaxu business would wither and starve, and—conversely—Malina understood that without the broad array of Tleilaxu genetic products, CHOAM's profits would drop. It was the best sort of relationship, a push and pull, mutually beneficial. She needed their commodities, and right now she had a special request to make of them.

While she waited in isolation, Malina knew she would not be allowed to go down to the gray-green planet below. The Tleilaxu called her *powindah*, an outsider, "unclean" by definition. While they made some exceptions for male outsiders, she was *female*, and a powerful one at that. She did not waste emotional energy on resenting them, though. This was business.

When the sealed door of her waiting quarters whisked open, Malina saw that Master Arafa had come to meet her himself, accompanied by five other Tleilaxu. She assumed the entourage was meant to demonstrate his own importance, whereas she demonstrated her importance by needing no one but herself.

Beneath his slick hood, Arafa had a high forehead and a heavier brow than most Tleilaxu, with a pale scar over one eye. He offered a deferential bow, but his eyes held no deference. Malina did not let her disdain show. Instead, she pretended to treat this man as her equal.

Motioning for his entourage to wait for him in the corridor, the Tleilaxu man moved closer to her, but kept a discreet distance, as if guarded. "We are honored that you came to us in person, Ur-Director," Arafa said, "rather than sending a representative through traditional channels."

Malina sat down in the lone chair in her waiting suite, visibly relaxing in front of him. "It is because I don't have a traditional request. I wanted to ask you myself."

Arafa's interest was piqued. "The Bene Tleilax create commodities that no one else offers. We have great wealth, but little respect. Without the shackles of the Corrino Imperium, an independent Tleilax could wield true financial strength."

A chill of surprise went down Malina's neck, and she lowered her voice. "You sound as if you support the Noble Commonwealth." Her eyes flitted back and forth. Could it be true? She and her fellow conspirators had expanded their influence throughout the Landsraad, sometimes succeeding, sometimes failing. But the Tleilax were something else entirely.

"Words are words, and anyone can have ideas." Arafa's voice was flat and guarded as if he acknowledged the dangerous subject. "That does not confirm or imply any kind of allegiance to a rebel cause."

Her mind spun with these new ideas. The Bene Tleilax, such outliers . . . She had never imagined. Now that she considered the idea, though, Malina realized they might well be likely candidates to turn against the Imperial power structure. Wheels spun in her mind. The Tleilaxu were known to prefer long-term planning over instant gratification or ill-advised bold actions. She needed to think about this. . . .

Arafa was growing impatient. "Why are you here, Ur-Director?"

She flashed him her most charming smile, aware that it would have little effect on a Tleilaxu Master. "Because of our long-standing business relationship, I have a favor to request of the Tleilaxu. It should not be too difficult."

"Favors often come with hidden costs," Arafa said.

"You created two spinehounds for me, some years ago. The excellent genetic design, their formidable appearance, their personalities—I could not have asked for better companions. Through a properly completed blood-bonding sequence, they became more loyal to me than any CHOAM employee." Her lips drew down in a frown. "More loyal than some of my own family."

Arafa showed genuine pride. "Yes, the spinehounds were a very successful experiment."

"I want two more—a pair of young and healthy specimens, just like Har and Kar."

The Master's face darkened. "Has something happened to your pets? Those were exclusive specimens."

"No, they are in perfect health aboard my private ship, heading home." She crossed her arms over her chest. "Because of other business obligations, though, I would like a second pair . . . as a gift."

Arafa considered. "That would be a deadly gift. The animals are dangerous even under the best of circumstances."

Malina drew her brows together. "They are gifts for a Harkonnen, who is familiar with dangerous things."

Behind him in the corridor, the other Tleilaxu whispered. After a long pause, Master Arafa nodded. "Yes, we have the genetic maps and the tanks to produce them in one of our laboratory domes. We will create them for you."

Smiling, Malina rose to her feet, anxious to be away from this place and back on her own ship, with her own special pets. "Excellent." She would have stepped forward to shake his hand, but she knew the Tleilaxu loathed touching human flesh, especially a woman's.

Arafa studied her intently, as if dissecting her. "We do not have the same long-term relationship with your son Jaxson, but he offers definite opportunities for us. He continues to ask for difficult things and continues to pay handsomely."

Malina tried to cover her shock again. Yet another surprise! They were involved with her renegade son? Jaxson had been here? *Here?* She had not seen him since before his attack on Otorio, and he remained a fugitive. What sort of schemes was he developing with these people?

"When did you meet with my son? Where is he?"

Master Arafa pressed his palms together again and bowed with feigned deference. "He is a customer, Urdir, and our confidentiality rules apply to him as well as to you. I mentioned him because you are highly valued by us, and you are his mother. I cannot, however, reveal the specifics of our dealings."

"I am his mother." Her throat went dry as she wrestled with these surprising revelations. "I could bring the full pressure of the CHOAM Company to bear, and you would reveal what I need to know."

"Your coercion would not be effective," Arafa said. "It is better that you do not know what he is doing. He will tell you himself, if he wishes. Our business here is concluded. We will inform you when the spinehounds are ready for delivery." The Master bowed deeply and retreated from her isolation suite.

The Mother School had two botanical conservatories, a large structure in the gardens on the west side of the ancient complex and another in the walled cloister by the kitchens. When she was a young girl, Jessica had been assigned to work in the smaller private greenhouse and she smiled to see it again.

"I remember this building," she said to Xora as they passed into the humid structure. "Good memories."

Her voice grew wistful as she thought of simpler times, when her life as an Acolyte had been clear and untroubled. "For three years Reverend Mother Mohiam assigned me to tend and harvest the herbs and leafy greens. I often assisted the main chef—what was her name? Oh, yes, Sister Enid." Her green eyes sparkled. "She was quirky, but quite endearing. And she was everywhere! Sometimes I think *she* really ran the Bene Gesserit Sisterhood!" Jessica chuckled. "Is she still here?"

Xora flashed a smile. "Her assistants do almost all of the work now, and Enid just supervises, but she is still pervasive throughout the school. I think she's partaking in a few of the . . . medicinal herbs herself."

"I always liked her." Jessica inhaled the heady scents of all the aromatic plants in the conservatory, sorting and identifying the distinctive signatures of rosemary, lavender, thyme, jarma.

"Everyone likes Enid. Any Sister who leaves the Mother School goes into the Imperium with fond memories of the communal meals she prepared. I certainly did . . ." Xora was one of the only women at the Mother School who did not look on Jessica with suspicion, but Xora sounded sad. "I've been here for so long, I wish they would give me a new assignment. I could prove myself, I know it."

Jessica thought of the continuing resonance of Xora's scandal, her illegitimate child . . . More than seventeen years had passed. "The Sisters have long memories, and very little forgiveness." She felt a deepening fear that they might keep *her* here for that long as punishment, even if she did as they asked. How much more did they need her to pry out of Lethea? She had reported her nighttime conversation, the scattered and deadly warnings, which remained incomprehensible . . . and after what Lethea had done to the poor Acolyte Rinni, Jessica had very little sympathy for the mad and broken crone. Her ranting was unreliable, and all her conclusions were suspect.

Jessica was done here. But the Mother Superior would not release her.

"They're vindictive, and you and I are part of the order," Xora said. "A finger has to do what the rest of the hand does."

Jessica walked down the central aisle and noticed some of the leaves turning brown, the herbs overgrown. The late-morning sun was just beginning to kiss the highest windows of the conservatory, revealing complex patterns of spiderwebs. More than twenty years ago, Jessica remembered being given a long stick and told to clear the webs. Apparently, that chore had not been done in some time. Looking around with a skeptical eye, she noticed that the garden beds were not as neat as they had been, either. Terra-cotta shards from broken pots had been piled in a corner, and some of the plants were drooping from lack of water. Sister Enid would never have put up with that in the old days. She was either preoccupied, or forgetful.

Jessica had few other people to talk to, and she felt increasingly friendly toward Xora, whose situation had so many parallels to her own. The silence stretched out, and the sudden activation of the water misting systems startled them both. Jessica broke the silence. "I am disturbed, deeply disturbed. Lethea suggested that something I do, or Paul does, may harm the Sisterhood."

Xora reacted with surprise. "Is that why she said you have to be separated from your son?"

Jessica had so much more she wanted to confide, but she did not let her caution lapse. "She even suggested I kill him! But she is also angry and vengeful toward the Bene Gesserit."

A dark expression crossed Xora's face. "You know she suffers from dementia, don't you? She is violent, mercurial, senile . . ."

"She has a cacophony of voices inside her head. Which one is her true desire? Is it all part of a twisted plan, or just the ramblings of a twisted mind? Mother Superior keeps her alive for a reason." Jessica couldn't keep the bitterness from her tone. "If Lethea is simply mad, why disrupt my life? Why would they uproot everything I held dear?"

She realized that every word and sound of her late-night conversation with Lethea had been recorded and already reviewed hundreds of times. Mother Superior Harishka and her closest advisers had dissected the entire dialogue, interrogated Jessica. Rinni was still locked in her mental loop, babbling the Litany over and over again.

Beside her in the greenhouse, Xora seemed annoyed. "It would benefit us all if Lethea were to draw her last breath." She clamped her lips together as if regretting that she had said such a harsh thing, but her silence lasted only a moment before she opened up to Jessica. "She is a rampaging animal. I knew one of the Sisters she murdered. At one time, Lethea's powers of prescience may have been vital for the order, but now everything she says is suspect." Xora reached into a pot of dirt and with bare fingers pulled out a small thistle. "Lethea is a noxious weed, and I see no more use for her."

The misting system switched off, and the greenhouse fell quiet again. Jessica closed her eyes, inhaled the sweet scent of a flowering anise, and wished she were back in Caladan.

*Betrayed in such a manner, disgraced by his wife's affair with his own son,
it is amazing that Esmar Tuek did not kill them both.*

—COUNT HASIMIR FENRING, private
conversation with Lady Margot

Whether he was back at the Imperial Court or here on Arrakis again, Count Fenring liked being unpredictable. He found it to be an effective strategy, provided he could react more quickly and fluidly than any opponent. Upon his return to the harsh desert world, he chose to do something especially unanticipated.

He didn't trust Esmar Tuek or his son, Staban. He didn't trust anyone. It was all business.

After making arrangements to meet his handpicked group of sanctioned smugglers, the Count abruptly changed the time and place. He threw them off balance when he declared that the meeting would take place not in their isolated hideout in the caves, and under their control, but in the dusty frontier city of Arrakeen, changing the time twice. Then at the last minute, he announced that they must meet at the Cave of Birds out in the desert, not far from the smuggler base. Esmar Tuek would find the changes capricious and frustrating, but Fenring wanted to keep them disoriented.

He had enemies—he had assassinated too many important people for it to be otherwise—but he was also a survivor. On hostile Arrakis, one could never be too careful.

Accompanied by his peculiar Mentat Grix Dardik from the Arrakeen Residency, he took a contract ornithopter piloted across the sands by a young Fremen woman named Kiafa, who knew the region well. Dardik expressed his displeasure for flying, especially in such a small and fragile aircraft over such a large and imposing desert. He did not like the odds, muttering a long string of numbers that must have had something to do with his calculations. Fenring countermanded his objections.

After flying far from the outskirts of Arrakeen and hundreds of miles into the open desert, the Fremen pilot circled her 'thopter over a rock formation, double-checking her charts. She shouted back over the thrum of the articulated wings. "We're here, sir. The Cave of Birds is in those rocks directly below. You'll have access to the side entrance you specified. From my contacts, I know that Fremen are not likely to be anywhere near."

"If Fremen brigands attacked, I might have to defend you, hmmmm?" Count Fenring said.

She glanced over at him from the cockpit, not releasing the controls. "That will not be necessary, sir." She had pretty, dark eyes and an intense, wild beauty, like a desert flower. "I am perfectly capable of taking care of myself."

"Do you want to know the probability of betrayal, my Count?" Grix Dardik asked from the rear seat, as if he were discussing a change in the weather. "This pilot could have sold us for our water."

"This pilot did not!" she snapped indignantly. The 'thopter lurched in the air.

"Fremen do that, you know," the Mentat said, in a matter-of-fact tone. "Distill water from bodies."

Before the pilot could retort, Fenring said, "Because they are resourceful." He leaned close to a plaz window on his left, looked down at the rock formation. "But we are not at risk. I am the Emperor's Spice Minister. The Harkonnens, the smugglers, and the Fremen would not dare."

"The odds are still not zero," said Dardik, bobbing his head from side to side. "It is not possible to be completely certain of anything,"

"Don't get lost in a mental swamp or I'll let our pilot sell your water to the Fremen," the Count scolded. "Save your energy for what is ahead." Despite his confidence, he never let down his guard. He looked back to see the flawed Mentat sitting with his eyes closed, rocking along with the motion of the aircraft. He wore mismatched clothing and a wrinkled, misshapen hat with a full brim. Fenring was glad he had left the man here on Arrakis, rather than putting up with him at the Imperial Court.

Sometimes Mentat trainees went off track and became useless to their masters, but even with his flaws and eccentricities, Grix Dardik possessed remarkable abilities. The twists and convolutions of his mind enabled him to innovate better than an ordinary Mentat. By keeping the bad traits under control, Fenring could make him function in a useful, if unorthodox, way.

Averting his gaze after the scolding, Dardik surveyed the rock formation through the scratched and dusty window. If he truly needed to control the man's unpredictable behavior, Fenring had more stringent measures he could use. A hidden needle in the gold Imperial ring on his forefinger could impart a powerful sedative, or even a poison, if necessary. Sooner or later, Dardik would become too troublesome, but for now, the man continued to have redeeming value, but if it reached that point, the desert was a good place to dispose of a body. . . .

"Figures down below, motionless and camouflaged." Dardik tapped his finger on the windowplaz. "But I can see them. The shadow patterns are wrong. Camouflage doesn't work against Mentat analysis."

Fenring looked, but could see nothing. The Fremen pilot offered him a pair of high-powered oil lenses, and he focused on the area his Mentat had indicated. "Ahhh, Esmar Tuek and his son waiting to greet us outside the cave entrance." He was impressed that they had managed to arrive already in response to his abrupt change of plans. But given the rush, they would not have had time for greater subtlety. "I see at least a dozen others in hiding."

"Fourteen," Dardik said. "Probability of a trap has increased."

"We knew they would bring others. They have too much to lose if they betray us." He had forced Tuek to sacrifice his own duplicitous wife, but the Count did not expect the man would try for revenge against him. Even though Rulla's transgressions had nothing to do with the mysterious black-market spice operations, sacrificing her had benefited all of them.

Dardik muttered his frustration. "You assume rational behavior." He adjusted his ridiculous hat. "I can foresee several scenarios—"

"Yes I do assume rational behavior. I will ask when I want your projections." The Mentat's eyes opened again. "I cannot put my mind into dormancy and await your commands about when I should think." Before Fenring could lash out at him, he quickly added, "But very well, I will be quiet."

With masterful piloting skills even in the uncertain thermals around the rock formations, Kiafa brought the aircraft down just outside the black vertical fissure that formed the entrance to the Cave of Birds. After she stabilized the landing struts, Fenring sprang down onto the sand and rocks.

As Dardik followed, his odd wardrobe came into full view. He wore his strange hat, an Ecaz-style tunic with a high lace collar, billowing pantaloons, and bull-riding boots. He said the outfit allowed him to think better, and Fenring ignored the eccentricity. Both of them adjusted nose plugs and mouth coverings as they faced the depthless dryness.

The smugglers moved toward them from the rocks at the cliff wall, young Staban Tuek in the lead, but Fenring held up an open palm for them to stop. He needed to make sure his Mentat was in a proper state for the important meeting.

Dardik was still muttering numbers, and Fenring gave him a brisk shake of his shoulders. "Do you see those men over there? The Emperor sent me to talk with them. I briefed you on it."

"Yes, spice. Missing spice."

"That's right."

Because the Mentat had a tendency to stumble around when engrossed in thought, Count Fenring took his arm and led him toward the waiting smugglers. Behind them, the pilot shut down the 'thopter.

Esmar Tuek scowled as he stood with his dusty companions in the shade of the cave opening. They seemed taken aback by the Mentat's strange outfit. Finally, Dardik noticed their curious stares. "Why do they look at me so? Two of them appear to be on the verge of laughter."

Fenring sighed. "Because your brain is so filled with important thoughts, you do not care what fashions might be in vogue. Fashions come and go."

The Mentat considered. "Fashions come and go. Yes, you are right, my Lord. If you like, I could review and summarize stylistic trends from a historical and galactic standpoint."

Fenring cut him off. "You have more important things on which to spend your time and energy."

"I have more important things on which to spend my time and energy."

"Good." He could feel Dardik walking more steadily as his thoughts fit back into a stable, well-worn groove. They approached the cave opening and the waiting smugglers.

"Mind and body, in perfect harmony," Dardik said.

The pilot trotted past them to the smugglers at the cave mouth. "Have you been inside? Is it secure?"

The younger Tuek, Staban, glanced behind him. Two of his companions stood close. "This cave is unfamiliar to us. Count Fenring suggested it at the last minute. Our 'thopter is under the rock overhang that you specified, covered with camouflage netting."

Kiafa gestured to all of them. "Let me lead you inside. I am familiar with the Cave of Birds."

Four of Tuek's smugglers remained outside to keep watch, while Fenring, Esmar, Staban, and the odd Mentat followed the Fremen pilot into the deep shadows. They ignited handlights and moved down a narrow rock passageway into a large meeting chamber.

"This vault has three exit tunnels, and is the safest for your purposes," Kiafa said. "I will wait outside in the tunnel. This is a Fremen place, and you can talk in privacy."

She left with the rest of the smuggler escorts, while the Tueks sat on low stone benches by a sunken pit where illumination or heating crystals could be lit. A natural chimney rose through the ceiling, and Fenring saw a glimmer of daylight a long way up. He chose another bench and signaled Dardik to stay beside him.

As the pilot departed, Esmar Tuek sent a suspicious glance after her, but Fenring said, "She is, ahhhhh, well paid—overpaid, in point of fact. We are perfectly safe."

The smuggler leader still looked around warily, showing his survival instincts. His son sat rigidly beside him, and the tension between them was obvious. Fenring was still surprised that Esmar hadn't killed Staban along with his deceitful wife. But she had fulfilled her necessary purpose.

The Count got down to business. "We executed Rulla and her supposed compatriots, because it was necessary to divert attention. Emperor Shaddam and

Baron Harkonnen are convinced we've put an end to the operations, but we know that spice is still being smuggled from Arrakis through unknown black-market channels. We must find the perpetrators and eliminate them before anyone learns otherwise. We won't have much time."

Staban's shoulders shook. "I wish it had not been necessary to kill Rulla. She was never guilty of stealing spice."

"She was guilty enough," Esmar snapped, and under the elder's withering glare, his son fell instantly silent. "I told you never to speak to me of this, and now you embarrass me in front of our guests?"

"I apologize, Father." Staban seemed to shrink. "I won't betray you."

"You won't betray me *again*. And you won't betray me on anything else either."

Fenring watched the conflict, noting that the father was the clear winner. He interrupted, "The, ahhh, situation with Rulla was most unfortunate, most unfortunate, indeed. Both of you cared deeply about her, in your own way. But we should care more about our mutual survival."

Seated on the rock bench, Esmar gave a slight bow of his head. "You are our honored guest, Count Fenring, and should not have to witness a family squabble."

"Count, you are not a guest," Grix Dardik interjected. "This is not the headquarters of the smuggler band. This is neutral ground. Another term should be used."

Fenring cut him off. "An irrelevant point. Watch and listen. I will ask your opinion when it is appropriate."

Maybe he should have met the smuggler leader alone after all, but he thought Dardik's unique analytical perspective would be useful later. Someone was smuggling large quantities of melange without his knowledge, and the smugglers seemed just as baffled. With his ability to assemble and analyze data, Dardik could identify connections, glean hints, and make intuitive leaps that others would not.

"This is a serious situation to the Emperor, and we could invite severe reprisals," Esmar said. "I know full well that my people would be your next scapegoats, if more sacrifices became necessary. I am grateful that you have condoned my operations for a long time."

Fenring stared intently at the weathered smuggler leader. "And you pay for that forbearance with information—deep information that is beyond the scope of my own sources. We need the eyes and ears of your people more than ever. They must hear the whisper of the sands, see beyond the shadow of every dune. Go and find these black-market sources, so we can shut them down together, before the Emperor finds out."

"I will do my best to solve this," Esmar promised. "Staban and his comrades will scout the great open areas for any hidden operations. They already know all the Harkonnen harvesters and the spice sands they work. They will comb the desert to find any grain of sand out of place."

He and his son locked gazes, agreeing. All the while, Dardik analyzed every movement, every cranny of the cave meeting area. "Grains of sand out of place . . ."

"Hmmm, exactly what I expect." The Count rose to his feet, convinced the smugglers understood the magnitude of their obligations. "You are correct that I could identify you as the next scapegoats, but even that would only delay my own downfall. Find our true enemies, for all our sakes."

ONCE SEALED BACK in the 'thopter, Fenring adjusted his seat straps while Dardik fidgeted in the back seat. Kiafa powered the engines and flexed the articulated wings. She asked no questions about the meeting.

The Count scrutinized his Mentat. "Report. What are your impressions?"

Dardik rattled off a response, seemingly without thinking. "The father does not trust the son. The son is angry with the father, but afraid to openly defy him. Both, though, are struggling to heal the breach. They are united in their priorities."

"Hmmm, interesting. Can I trust them?"

"Trust and competence are different things. Can you trust them to discover the information you require? It might be beyond their abilities, depending on how devious the black-market smugglers are. But if you ask whether you can trust them not to betray you, that answer is yes. They understand that they are permitted to operate only by special sanction—and your advice to the Emperor will determine if they live or die. They will not risk that."

Fenring faced forward again, nodding. The 'thopter flew above the rocks and raced low over the desert. Kiafa worked the controls, studiously ignoring their conversation.

Dardik surprised Fenring by tapping him on the shoulder. "Are we best friends, sir? Am I your best friend?"

Fenring brushed the hand away. "What a ridiculous question, hmmm. Why focus on such frivolous speculation about emotional matters? I want you to be logical."

"My question is logical. I want to be your best friend, because then you will not kill me. You are Count Hasimir Fenring, the deadliest assassin in the Imperium." He narrowed his eyes. "And I think there is more to you."

"What do you mean?"

"Not yet expressible in words. But we are very good friends, aren't we?"

In the few years since Fenring had retrieved this man from the dustbin of Imperial history, Dardik had constantly irritated him, yet he had proven his worth numerous times. That might not always be the case, however.

He decided that his Mentat needed a rest, and he himself needed time away from him. He would leave Dardik behind when he returned to Kaitain.

"I have killed friends before," Fenring said.

The odd Mentat accepted the warning. He leaned back in his seat and, wisely, fell silent.

It is difficult to choose the most enjoyable part—the planning, execution, or fruition of a deliciously intricate scheme.

—PITER DE VRIES, Mentat for House Harkonnen

From the expression on his blunt-featured face, Rabban was wrestling with deep inner thoughts; Piter de Vries could tell. The Baron's thick nephew struggled to express himself, and Piter bided his time in the close, private chamber. As a Mentat, he knew to wait and gather data.

After the Baron went back to the spice-harvesting operations on Arrakis, Rabban stayed behind in Harkonnen headquarters and surprised the twisted Mentat by asking to meet him in private. He chose a secret, stone-walled room that Piter had often used for spying on others. He was surprised that Rabban knew of its existence.

Now, as the big man faced him in the dimness, bunching his fists, he finally came out with what he needed to say. "My uncle says that I should not approach each problem with mere brute force." He drew a breath, and Piter detected that he was actually . . . reluctant? Insecure? The line of his jaw worked as if the words were tough meat to chew. "An intelligent man demonstrates his strength by asking for help if he needs it." Rabban's close-set eyes flicked away.

The Mentat arched his eyebrows. "Rabban—you are asking me for help?" He could already imagine how he might use that as leverage against the other man, hold it over his head.

The light seemed to grow dimmer in the small stone chamber. Piter had spent countless hours here, silent, staring, analyzing, as he observed surreptitious activity, but he had always been alone and safe. He was suddenly aware of how close the Beast was and how dangerous his temper could be. Although Rabban held a cultured title, Count of Lankiveil, he was anything but cultured.

The two were often rivals. At times, the Mentat provoked Rabban, nudged him to the edge, but the other man never followed through on his threats against Piter. Now, however, Piter felt heat rising as Rabban struggled with his own inclinations.

The Baron's nephew managed to calm himself and drew a deep, loud breath, like a panting bull. "You are the Mentat for House Harkonnen, are you not? My uncle challenged me to hurt the Atreides and to prove I'm good at it. You can help me."

Piter tried to keep the surprise from his face. "Why, my dear Rabban, that does sound like something I would enjoy!"

The large man brightened at the response, and he suddenly looked much younger, as if he'd been given a surprise gift.

Piter didn't intend to be entirely cooperative, though. "I was there when the Baron issued his challenge, remember. Did he not expect you to concoct your own scheme? To do it yourself?"

"I am asking you—by myself. We'll keep this our secret." Rabban paced like a caged animal, bounded by the walls of the small chamber. "I could just send in an attack force and smash House Atreides, but that would be too obvious. It's what my uncle expects of me, so I need to prove him wrong." In the dimness, he seemed troubled, even introspective. "He underestimates me. But I am not just a clenched fist. Help me prove that I can be a Baron, too."

The twisted Mentat ran a forefinger along his stained lower lip. He could definitely use this to his advantage. "Oh, I can devise something that will wreak great havoc upon House Atreides, and also have an interesting layer of nuance." He smiled, already pursuing projections in his intricate mind. "Yes, I can do that."

"Good." Impatient to be out of the confined space, Rabban pushed his way into the corridor. "Give me your detailed plan by the end of the day."

RABBAN MIGHT HAVE thought he was rushing Piter de Vries, but for a Mentat, even half a day provided enough time to run through myriad possibilities. Piter considered more than just bloodshed and mayhem.

Looking for ideas, he studied Rabban's holdings on Lankiveil, his whale-fur operations and fishing industry . . . which led Piter's thoughts to consider Caladan's fishing industry, which was enjoying an economic boom due to a species called moonfish. Much wealth had begun to flow in to House Atreides, a real expansion of their exports.

Piter concocted a scheme that would hurt Duke Leto, and now he needed to convince Rabban. Of utmost importance, he had to keep his own involvement secret, so he did not upset the Baron.

But Piter knew exactly what they needed to do. First, he and Rabban would have to go to Lankiveil.

＊

The fighters of House Atreides have proprietary techniques, which remain distinctive even after extensive training in other methods. The Atreides are fast and light on their feet, with unrivaled instincts and a myriad of attack moves. This keeps any opponent off balance.

— Plaque under a painting of Duke Paulus Atreides
teaching young Leto to fight bulls

With so much responsibility while his father was away, Paul had less time to train with Duncan and Gurney. His mother remained completely out of contact at the Bene Gesserit school, and Duke Leto continued his pursuits on Kaitain. Paul had to learn his responsibilities, with many people depending on him. Sparring and conditioning sessions could wait.

The instruction he'd already received, not just in physical skills but in history, leadership, politics, science, and mental acuity, had prepared him to assume this position, yet he knew that it was foolish to act overconfident. He kept his advisers close and met with Thufir Hawat each day in the Duke's office to review security and discuss petitions from the people. He had no intention of taking his father's place, but he wanted to show he was actively learning the business of being a Duke. Leto Atreides left large shoes for him to fill.

All of life is training.

For the afternoon briefing, Paul wore a pale green Atreides military shirt with epaulets and the red hawk insignia on the breast. Leto had advised him to wear formal dress in the office rather than casual clothes, to remind himself that he was doing a job. His green-and-black military jacket hung on a rack nearby, next to one of his father's. Paul expected to grow into it someday. It was only a matter of time.

Paul sat behind the heavy elaccawood desk, while the old Mentat stood at attention in front of him. They'd been discussing a compassionate petition from a woman, begging for her son to be released from prison. Her handwritten plea lay open on the desk surface, and Paul scanned it again.

The woman's son had been convicted of murdering his father, who had lashed his bare back ten times, leaving bloody welts and humiliating him while the neighborhood watched. The young man left in a fit of rage. Hours later, he came back with a club and bludgeoned his father to death. The mother asked for mercy, but the court ruled that murder was not a proportional response to a mere beating. They convicted him.

Looking at the details in the petition, Paul saw that the young man was his own age, but they were in very different circumstances. He mused aloud to Thufir, "The mother is the true victim here. She has already lost her husband and wants her son to live, regardless of what he did. But if the boy has such a streak of uncontrolled violence, and he is only fourteen, will he not become worse as he gets older? We should not set him free, for the safety of others."

The Mentat pursed sapho-stained lips. "Caladan has a well-respected legal system, my Lord, and the court has already sentenced him to life in prison. The mother wants you to overturn their decision, out of mercy. If you intercede now, that could weaken other rulings." He picked up the petition, scanned the words. "Also, it is interesting that the mother filed this plea for clemency only after Duke Leto departed for Kaitain."

"Because she thinks I will be softer?" Paul asked.

"And more, young Master. Her husband was an Atreides officer, and your father had recommended him for a promotion. The Duke was deeply affected by his death. He did not question the decision of the magistrate who put the young man in prison. It is no accident that the mother waited until he was gone."

Paul remained silent as he pondered. "My heart does go out to her and the son, but the crime was terrible, by any measure. The boy could have responded in other ways, simply by running away, or by petitioning the Duke. Yet he chose the course of violence. And if I show leniency in this matter, I will receive a flood of similar requests." He shook his head and set aside the paper. "Her petition seems opportunistic, and I would appear weak. Tell the woman that the matter will remain under consideration, but she will have to wait until the Duke returns."

"Very wise, young Master."

Paul looked at the stack of paperwork, both relieved and intimidated that they had worked through half of the documents since yesterday. He rose from his father's desk. "Gurney is taking me into the village this evening so I can hear what people are saying. Many of them don't know me, and I want to be in touch with them, as my father has always been."

Thufir ran his gaze up and down Paul's shirt with its epaulets and insignia. "If you intend to blend in with the common people in town, I would not wear that shirt or the jacket that goes with it."

Paul nodded.

The Mentat considered. "If you wish to hear unfiltered conversation, dirty yourself up a bit and put on a cap and fisherman's clothes. Best to have Gurney wear old garments as well. He's recognizable enough, but he knows how to become invisible." He gave a rare smile. "It is good for a Duke, even a young heir, to keep his finger on the pulse of the people."

He stepped toward the office door, the limp from his old injury barely noticeable, then he stopped and looked back. "You told me that you consider yourself no better than others, that your noble station is only a matter of happenstance. Go walk among your people and remind yourself of that."

"I FEEL NAKED without my baliset." Gurney plucked at his vest. "And I've never been much of a fisherman, so I'm out of place in these clothes."

Paul took a step ahead, confident and eager as they entered the old section of Cala City. "You're at my side, so you are not out of place."

"That's true, lad." With his rolling gait, Gurney accompanied him. Around them, the streets grew busier with evening traffic, customers heading to taverns and restaurants, while daytime shopkeepers rolled in their wares and closed shutters.

Paul didn't mind Gurney's informal comment, especially under these circumstances. Casual camaraderie between the two, as Paul had with Duncan, was the impression he wanted to give in town. He adjusted a soft cap over his dark hair and looked down at the worn boots he'd borrowed from one of the staff.

They walked along, listening, watching, inhaling the aromas of roasting fish, savory soups, strong ale, fresh-baked bread, and spiced nuts on a grate over open coals. Taverns and bakeries sported colorful signs with imaginative names.

Paul realized they were near the street where he and Duncan had witnessed explosions from bombs planted by Chaen Marek. People here were rebuilding, recovering. A potbellied man sat on a crate in front of a boarded-up storefront, singing a familiar folk melody, and Gurney instinctively hummed along.

A few doors down, coming from an establishment that called itself Song of the Sea, they heard the lively music of men and women singing Caladan chanteys. Glowglobes hung outside, but a warm fire and brighter lights shone from within. Peering in the window, Gurney nodded. "This place will do, lad. Let's have some dinner. You'll never find a more common lot. Get to know these people, and you'll know Caladan."

Paul smiled, remembering Thufir's admonition. "All of life is training, and I'm ready to do some living."

Gurney chose a small corner table, from which they could see the activity in the pub. Paul recalled the Mentat's advice never to sit with his back to a doorway.

A waitress took their order, giving Paul a brief glance, but she did not recognize him through the grime on his face. Moments later, tankards of Caladan brew were set in front of them.

"Don't drink too much, lad," Gurney cautioned. "You're not accustomed to the sort of ale they serve here. Your father would not like to hear that I took you out and let you drink too much!"

Paul nodded. He wanted to keep his wits about him. Paul took his first sip, mostly foam. "Your advice is good. And so is the ale." After a few more swallows, though, he did begin to feel a fuzziness at the back of his mind, which made him realize that he'd hardly eaten anything all day. He rested his elbows on the wooden table. "You drink half of yours, while I only sip mine. Then we'll do a switch."

"A good solution." Gurney looked around the room, always alert.

Paul listened to the drone of conversation in the tavern. He always assumed his father was well liked, and he heard many kind words from the people whenever they came to the castle. Leto was their Duke, and House Atreides had ruled here for centuries. How would these people react if his father expanded his holdings to include other planets to govern?

But the Duke of Caladan had not governed alone. The thought reminded Paul of Jessica, who had gone away so abruptly. "I wonder if I'll ever see my mother again. I have so many unanswered questions."

Gurney's expression grew serious. "Your parents keep their emotions close. It's a private matter between them, and not my place to ask."

"But it affects me, too," Paul said. "My mother was training me in skills that will help me become a better leader." He also missed her, worried about her, but he didn't say that aloud.

Gurney rested a hand on his forearm. "And she is your mother, so you naturally miss her." He took a gulp of the ale and watched two men and a woman take seats at the adjacent table. They were of stocky build, obviously laborers from their soiled clothing, and none of them were smiling.

Gurney was clearly not comfortable talking about the rift between Leto and Jessica, so he changed the subject with a preposterous story about a fishing boat that sank when a giant spiny starfish ripped a hole in its hull. Paul dutifully laughed at the yarn.

When Gurney had nearly finished his ale, Paul swapped tankards with him, beginning to feel relaxed.

Paul sat back and listened, feeling the warm rush of conversation, the camaraderie of so many workers—fisherman and merchants, carpenters, farmers in the city after delivering loads of their produce, shipwrights, clothiers. He rolled the taste of the ale in his mouth and recalled what his father had said about Caladan, that all the people here were like flecks in a kaleidoscopic image, one dizzying and beautiful picture of humanity.

He closed his eyes and listened to the words around him, one man complaining that his wife had gained so much weight while his companion chided him for the size of his own potbelly. A baker and his apprentice played a game of strings and ribbons, forming a web between their fingers as they attempted to entrap each other, while a third person kept score. A man with a stentorian voice promised a great tale for anyone who would buy him a drink, but apparently, the other customers had heard his stories before and didn't consider them worth the investment of another tankard of ale.

Gurney lounged back on his chair, quiet, but alert. While Paul absorbed the details as he taught himself to be a better Duke, he noticed that Gurney's eyes were like targeting crosses, always watching.

One man with red eyes and gaunt unshaven cheeks muttered into his own drink, obviously not his first. He looked angry and miserable while his companions, two muscular men with close-cropped hair and a pair of stocky women dressed in the garments of day laborers, tried to console him.

"She should be with me," the man said. "She gave me her vow, and our children only ever see us fighting . . ."

"This has been a long time coming, Rade," said one of the burly women. "You know she has a wandering eye—it's no surprise to you."

"It's always a surprise," retorted the gaunt man, Rade. "You think I was happy? But a man's promise means something."

One of his friends laughed, but it sounded forced. "I've heard you talk on and on about the women you find pretty in the streets. Don't tell me you weren't looking for an opportunity yourself. Now you'll have a chance to act. Think how much fun you'll have." The supposed friend clapped him on the back, jarring Rade as he hunched over his mug.

Paul looked over at Gurney, who listened intently.

The tavern door opened, and five others came in, all dressed as construction workers. A big man with a long, dark ponytail swaggered in front of the group. They laughed boisterously as they commandeered a large table near the front.

Seeing them, Rade reacted as if someone had fired a weapon in his direction. He rose from his seat like a lion about to spring, but the two stocky women pushed him back down. "Looks like we'll have to go somewhere else," the first one said, but Rade just kept shaking his head.

The cocky man with the ponytail spotted him, hesitated, then let out a loud laugh. "Well, look there! Bartender, another mug of ale for my friend Rade. The least I can do for all the enjoyment I've had recently."

"Where's my wife?" Rade lurched to his feet and pushed the chair back.

Paul noticed that suddenly the mood in the tavern had shifted. The people became more wary and tense. Gurney's hand strayed to his side. He whispered, "Maybe we'd better go, young Master."

"Your wife is home—my home—keeping your children safe." The man with the ponytail glowered. "You're already drunk. If you went to them now, you'd give the boys black eyes again, and I won't abide that."

Unexpectedly, Rade hurled his heavy tankard and struck his rival full in the face, possibly breaking his cheekbone. One of Rade's companions grabbed his arm, tried to wrestle him back down, but the two stocky women threw themselves in among the carpenters. The man with the ponytail bent over, moaning and nursing his swelling face.

Paul had engaged in precise weapons training, carefully choreographed duels, shield fighting with the most skilled practice opponents—but the tavern became a wild brawl faster than he could see people take sides. The patrons of the Song of the Sea already seemed to have tangled alliances. The bartender bellowed for calm, but no one heard him.

Paul sprang to his feet, thinking he should put an end to the fight, but he didn't duck quickly enough when a thrown stool clipped the side of his head. He clapped a hand to his bruised skull. "Gurney, we have to stop this. We have to defend them."

"Defend *who*, lad?" He heard shouts, the smash of crockery, the landing of blows. Gurney grabbed his arm, managing to shield him with his much larger body. "Can you so quickly decide which side is right?" The other man swept him up, began to crash his way to the exit. "To the door as fast as you can."

"Gurney, we can't run. I have to—"

"My job is to keep you safe, and you cannot be involved in this."

Gurney pushed him forward just as one of the stocky women spun backward and her elbow caught him in the eye. With a roar, she spun to land another blow, but Gurney swept her feet out from under her and knocked her flat on her back.

Suddenly, several other fighters were upon them, a whirlwind of clumsy, reckless fists, and Paul had no choice but to fight back. He was small, but an unexpectedly good fighter, and he landed far more blows than he received. But he lost his temper, didn't hear Gurney shouting at him, until finally he was dragged away from the heated brawl by a firm hand around his collar.

"To the door—now!" Gurney dragged Paul off. They burst through the door and staggered out into the relative quiet of the streets, while the noisy brawl continued inside the tavern.

Gurney hurried him along. "We're not supposed to be seen."

Paul's head and eye throbbed from the unexpected, clumsy blows. "A Duke should have handled that differently!"

Gurney kept moving him along. "There's no way we should be involved in a petty squabble like that." He was flushed, a simmering pot of anger and wariness. "You are under my protection, lad. The heir to House Atreides is not going to be killed by some foolish accidental knife to the back."

Paul stopped, brushing his grip aside. "You're Gurney Halleck. You could have single-handedly defeated every person in there."

"Aye. I could have slain every single person in that tavern—and that would have changed everything. Would you be so quick to declare who was right and who was wrong?"

Paul realized the wisdom in his words. They walked at a normal pace now, and Paul touched the sore bruise under his eye.

Gurney continued, "We don't need to get involved in every fight. Oh, they'll have bruises and a few broken bones in the morning. That man and his wife, they'll work it out or they won't. Some people need to solve their own problems, and leave the Duke to handle the big ones."

Secrets, no matter how burdensome, should not be shared with friends. A secret can always turn on you.

—LADY JESSICA, private notes

Jessica looked up from where she knelt in the dirt outside one of the dormitory buildings. Sister Xora came up to her with an open smile, her feline blue eyes sparkling. She wore a simple black robe like Jessica's.

"Would you like some help?"

Jessica paused in her work digging with a small trowel. She had enjoyed their conversation in the greenhouse. "It's nice talking to someone. Someone with . . . shared circumstances." She looked up at the dormitory building. "I lived in this building from the time I was seven until I was around twelve, when Reverend Mother Mohiam moved me into a newer building." She looked down at the trowel in her hand, at the empty flower bed she had dug up. "I planted my own garden here one summer, but the cold weather killed it."

Xora knelt beside her and helped churn the soil now that all the dead plants had been removed. A group of Acolytes hurried past in the courtyard, chattering. Several of the young women turned to stare at Jessica, then moved on as she scooped more dirt aside, excavating a deeper trough. The hole was already up to her elbows.

Xora remained curious. "You're digging deep. Are you looking for something?"

Jessica used her knuckles to brush a strand of bronze hair out of her eyes. "I planted tomatoes here, and I buried something deep under the plant. It's been more than twenty-five years, and seeing this garden plot reminded me . . ."

Xora helped dig. "What was it?"

Jessica felt tense. "A silly project from wood-carving shop, a purlwood sculpture that got me in trouble with my teachers."

Now her companion was more intrigued. "Purlwood is durable. It could still be there." The two women worked shoulder to shoulder, Jessica with the trowel, Xora with her bare hands. When the trowel hit something hard, Jessica prodded with the tip, then dug around with her fingers, found something light-colored. Purlwood?

She pulled it from the soil, brushing dirt away. She remembered working so hard on this, and she had gotten into trouble not for her lack of artistic skill, but for what it represented. The Sisterhood considered the dreams to be dangerous for a loyal Bene Gesserit adept.

As a twelve-year-old girl, she had carved three figures together in a unit—mother and father, with a child enfolded between them. A traditional nuclear family, something young Jessica had only imagined. Holding the figurine now, Jessica felt a wash of nostalgic memories, and the sting of how Mohiam and the other proctors had punished her!

Wiping off the dirt, she held the sculpture up. "A good Acolyte should not be dreaming of a perfect and normal family." She looked down at the crude faces, still preserved in the purlwood. In her mind, she had pictured a little girl—her own face—along with imagined parents. Jessica had been raised here—was she a foundling? Abandoned by her mother? Or the child of some disgraced Sister?

Xora's eyes widened as she realized what it was. "The Sisterhood is our family."

"Reverend Mother Mohiam told me to destroy the carving, but I buried it here instead." She turned it in her hands, remembering how earnest she had been, and how much the punishment had hurt. "I should have done a better job of getting rid of it."

"What are you going to do with it now?" Xora asked, lowering her voice as if part of a conspiracy.

"I'll keep it. They punished me already, and the Sisters have far greater concerns now." She brushed away more of the dirt caked on the lumpy faces. "It makes me think of naïve ambitions, and how things don't always turn out the way you imagine."

Xora scooped the freshly turned soil back into the hole and smoothed over the plot. "You remind me of myself . . . and of things buried away here at the Mother School." The other Sister was trembling as she confided, "They are raising my son here without me. I've caught a glimpse of him a few times with the other young men here. His name is Brom. Because of his bloodlines—something about my own breeding and his Sardaukar father—they think he could be a potential candidate for their Kwisatz Haderach, too. They gamble so much . . ."

Jessica whispered, "We are more alike than I realized."

Preoccupied, Xora didn't seem to hear. "Brom would be seventeen now, and they must be ready to send him out into the Imperium. I'm sure he doesn't know I'm his mother."

Jessica looked down at the dirt-encrusted carving, mother, father, child . . . her, Leto, Paul? "I miss my son, and my Duke just as much. My crime was letting myself have a human heart, and experiencing love. Now, if they listen to Lethea, they'll keep me separated from Paul." *If not kill him. . . .*

Standing, they brushed dirt off their dark robes and walked toward the iron-wood doors of the main congregate building. "We can keep each other company," Xora said.

Jessica had always been a good judge of human nature, and she liked Xora. From the stony looks of her fellow Sisters, she knew that none of the others here could relate to her own inner turmoil. "Mother Superior Harishka has heard Lethea's wild concerns about me and my son, but there is more. Another indicator . . . I . . . I've long thought there was something special about Paul, whether or not the Sisterhood wants to admit it. They both hope and fear what he might be. I'm not sure if I should tell the Mother Superior."

"I'm a willing listener," Xora said, "if you want to tell me."

Jessica carefully considered how much to say. "Paul has been having strange dreams, prescient ones, I think. He sees things that sometimes come true."

Xora was intrigued. "One can easily assign meaning to a vague dream, after the fact."

Jessica shook her head. "It's not a coincidence. Not long ago, he awoke in terror, convinced his father was in great danger—only later did we realize that his dream came exactly at the time of the Otorio attack, which Leto barely escaped. And Paul keeps seeing the same girl in his dreams, in a stark desert. He doesn't know who she is, but he insists that he will know her someday."

Xora was intensely interested, but she tried to disguise it with skepticism. "All teenage boys dream of beautiful girls."

"Yes, he's of that age." Jessica remembered all the young women they had considered as marriage candidates for Paul, how he had reviewed the profiles and said that none of them were right—because of his dreams. Now she shook her head. "Not like this. It's not just a wistful fantasy about an imaginary girl. He's described the scene in detail, and it's always the same young woman, the same desert. He sees rock escarpments, dry canyons, a yellow sky. The girl's face keeps coming to him. The visions will not stop."

Xora considered this. "Shouldn't you reveal this to Mother Superior? She must know!"

Paul's birth had already caused such consternation in the breeding program. *You were told to bear only Atreides daughters!* And the Sisterhood had already done serious meddling in the list of Paul's betrothal candidates—his *breeding* candidates. The thought of what they had done caused a bitter burn in her throat.

"The Sisterhood already knows too much. *Does* too much." Jessica spoke as if to herself. She looked at Xora. "I am not a timid woman, but I do not intend to give Harishka evidence to support Lethea's wild claims. Who knows what they would do to Paul? They operate on fear, while I choose to hope."

"Hoping for what? That your son might actually be the Kwisatz Haderach?" It felt strange, even a little ludicrous, to hear her say it out loud. But the Sisterhood had been quietly working toward that goal for countless generations, and Jessica knew the plans were close.

Taking her silence as an answer, Xora said, "That is all the more reason to explain about his prescient dreams. Let them decide what to do with him."

"I'm his mother. It's not their decision," Jessica said.

Xora leaned closer to Jessica as if speaking a secret. "The Bene Gesserit web of possibilities has thousands of paths that might lead to a Kwisatz Haderach. I am sure they've come close, again and again, but genetics is not an exact science. They are still searching. That's why they are so interested in my son, Brom, too."

Jessica remained keenly aware of what Lethea had said. "If I tell them, will it make Paul seem more important to them? Or will it only frighten the Bene Gesserit more? Will it endanger us all?" She shook her head, answering her own questions. "No, the Sisterhood does not need to know everything. That piece of information is one of the only bits of leverage I still have over them."

"As you wish," Xora said, still troubled. "As his mother, you should have the right to decide what to do."

Walking together across the large central courtyard, Jessica sighed. "I wish I could send a message to Paul, just a note to tell him I still think of him, that I . . . that I still love him."

Xora looked simultaneously alarmed and fascinated. "I never got a chance to tell that to my Sardaukar lover, my dear Runvir . . ." She lowered her voice. "The Mother School uses a messenger service to distribute discreet communiqués to countless noble connections and Sisters assigned to Landsraad Houses." She let the words hang for a moment. "I know where the message cylinders are kept."

Even though Leto had broken from her, Jessica still had a relationship with her son. The Bene Gesserit might be able to force her to come here, to demand that she serve them by threatening to destroy the ones she loved, but they could not erase the bond between mother and son.

It sounded just like what they had done to Xora—which made her even more determined to send a message to Paul.

She looked sharply at Xora. "Could I send one to Caladan?"

Xora seemed light on her feet as she darted off. "Trust me. I'll get you a message cylinder."

Over the course of history, too many Landsraad nobles have evolved into
purely political animals, losing sight of their humanity.

—DUKE LETO ATREIDES, letters to his son

When Leto arranged to have a private dinner with Vikka Londine, his heart did not feel capable of romance. He forced himself to think of it as a political encounter and nothing more, but that didn't make it any less awkward. Count Fenring was due to return soon from Arrakis, possibly even that day, but for now Leto was on his own.

He didn't know what Vikka herself expected from the meeting. Would she be looking for a warm and caring replacement for her husband, Clarton, who had been killed in the Otorio explosion? As far as he could tell, her first marriage had been a loveless business arrangement, like that of Leto's parents, Paulus and Helena. Some such relationships managed to succeed, and Leto had prepared himself when he agreed to marry a few years ago, a merger of Atreides and Ecaz. But he had always expected that his heart would remain with Jessica.

Now he reset his expectations.

After Count Fenring's initial suggestion, he'd researched House Londine, their main planet of Cuarte and other holdings, as well as Vikka's dead husband. Leto had stared at the image of Clarton Londine, trying to recall seeing him among the crowds in the Imperial Monolith before the explosions. So much of that evening was a blur.

More importantly, he studied Vikka's father, Rajiv Londine, a quiet and re-served man, who held an important CHOAM inner-circle Directorship. Some of his Landsraad speeches had upset the Emperor. After Shaddam had branded Fausto Verdun as a traitorous rebel and obliterated his entire House, Rajiv Londine demanded proof, insisting that evidence be presented in open session. Shaddam was incensed. While most other members of the court quickly turned against House Verdun, Lord Londine had stood his ground.

Leto respected him for that, and he felt he might get along well with the older nobleman. But if he married Vikka, he would apparently be expected to keep Rajiv Londine under control, dampen the man's criticisms.

Leto's retainers from Caladan dithered about, getting him ready for the important dinner. They chose an impeccable tunic for him, polished his ducal signet ring, and groomed his dark hair. He braced himself for an evening with the lovely and influential woman whom Count Fenring had suggested.

When Vikka arrived at his suite at the appointed hour, he was surprised to see that she was escorted by the Empress herself. Aricatha glided along with Vikka Londine's arm through her own. Her full lips formed a smile as she waited at the door. "Duke Leto Atreides, I wanted to introduce you personally to my dear friend Vikka."

Leto bowed to the Empress and turned to Vikka Londine. The woman was even prettier than the images, and she seemed a little out of her depth, too. "Thank you for inviting me, Duke Leto." Her voice was deeper than he had expected, almost husky. She disengaged her arm from the Empress. "Majesty, thank you for the honor of escorting me."

Aricatha chuckled. "I'll leave you two now, so you can get to know each other without feeling awkward around me. I expect you'll get along nicely." With a swirl of her shimmering gown, the Empress left.

Leto paused just inside the room, looking at his guest, not sure what to say. "After that, I feel pressured," he finally blurted out.

Vikka glided into the suite. "From what I understand, Duke Leto Atreides is not a man who bends to pressure." She had short, wavy hair the color of dark chocolate, and gold flecked the lids of her brown eyes. Her skin was a rich tan over high cheekbones, and a tiny mole marked her delicate chin. Her loose dress had the intense colors common to Cuarte, bright reds and oranges, adorned with gossamer ribbons that accentuated her slender figure.

After letting the surprised silence drag out too long, he spoke quickly, "Of course, excuse me, Lady Londine. The business of being a Duke, especially trying to impress the Imperial Court, tasks me with activities that I am not entirely comfortable with—although some of them are enjoyable." He gestured her into the main room. "Such as having a private dinner and conversation with a lovely stranger."

When she laughed, he realized Vikka felt as awkward as he did. "Maybe if we get to know each other quickly, then we won't be strangers, and it'll seem less awkward."

Leto felt relief. "That would make the evening pass more pleasantly."

The palace chefs had prepared a fine meal, multiple courses, expansively laid out on a formal table in his suite. He led her to the small table where their meal had been set out. As she took her seat, her voice and expression softened. "Since the death of my husband, these types of overtures are becoming more routine for me. As the heir to a Great House, my father says it is my obligation."

Leto knew what she meant. When he arrived on Kaitain to test the waters of political ambitions, he felt as if he had blundered into one of the swamps on Caladan's southern coast.

She sampled a small meat pastry from a silver appetizer plate. "Tell me about your world, and I'll tell you about Cuarte. I know you've done your research, but this isn't about comparing business ledgers. Let's talk about our homes."

Leto was happy to do so.

She made a few cool responses when he asked her about her dead husband, and she did not ask about Jessica at all. Instead, she wanted to know more about Paul, and Leto was happy to oblige.

Before Vikka had actually arrived, he'd dreaded the encounter, afraid that the other woman's every word and gesture would remind him of Jessica. He felt surprised, a little disappointed, that he did not compare every aspect of the two women. That would have seemed like another trap laid by the Bene Gesserit.

Four hours passed quickly over an unhurried meal, numerous small courses of sweet and savory, and when the conversation wound down, Vikka Londine politely suggested it was time to go. Leto bowed to kiss her hand, then ushered her to the doorway, where two retainers—tall men, also in startlingly bright colors—arrived to escort her.

When Vikka bade him a good evening and departed, Leto had the impression that she had enjoyed herself as well. He realized he didn't dread the prospect of meeting with her again. In matters like this, though, he knew better than to chase after a fluttering heart and giddy emotions.

Afterward, reviewing the evening—since Count Fenring would certainly press him for details—Leto barely remembered the individual topics of discussion. He felt puzzled by the feelings he experienced: apprehension, confusion, curiosity, satisfaction with how well the dinner had gone.

His hard business mind quickly identified an advantage from a political standpoint. He reminded himself why he had come to Kaitain. Joining with House Londine would raise the standing of House Atreides, and Fenring had said that Emperor Shaddam would give his blessing.

If Leto chose to pursue Vikka and it all worked out, he would not need to find an adequate betrothal for Paul, at least for a while. That alone would be a good thing, and he felt he owed it to his son. Leto was not an impetuous man, but after telling Vikka so much about Caladan, he now felt a need to go home.

Maybe his best move was to make a decision and be done with this nonsense. He could accept his victory and create a new life for himself and for Paul. It would make Castle Caladan feel less empty.

Late at night, he was interrupted by a signal at his door, and when he answered, Hasimir Fenring melted out of the palace shadows. Leto stood unbalanced for a moment in surprise. "Count Fenring, you've returned from Arrakis."

The man slipped into the guest suite as if he were a spy. "I only just arrived on Kaitain, but I, ahhhhh, have my priorities." Inside the main room, he turned in slow circles as if scanning Leto's quarters for observation devices. "I am here to turn the next wheel, Duke Leto. Vikka Londine has other suitors, but none are as satisfactory as yourself. We should move quickly to cement this matter."

Leto raised his eyebrows. "You asked her? She left barely an hour ago."

"I mean satisfactory to myself and to Emperor Shaddam. I intend to move the match forward, if you are willing to do what is necessary."

Leto felt uneasy, defensive. "You didn't even ask me if I found her acceptable."

Fenring's expressive lips made his frown seem extreme. "Of course she is acceptable. You know that as well as I. Your decision is obvious."

Leto dropped down onto a padded divan, feeling oddly more relaxed than he had in some time. "Yes, Count, I did enjoy our dinner, and I would be willing to meet with Vikka Londine again. For various reasons, it does seem a good match, from the Landsraad's perspective."

"Hmmm, ahhhh, yes." Fenring's expression became predatory. "And now we have important matters to discuss, such as your obligations for this gift."

"Obligations? What do you mean?"

"The holdings of House Londine are quite valuable, and you've made your ambitions clear. While I may respect you and your potential, Leto Atreides, I do not do this as a simple gesture of friendship."

Leto was instantly on guard. "What are you suggesting?"

"In order to pave the way for House Atreides to absorb Londine, ahhhh, you must first do something that will earn the undying gratitude of the Padishah Emperor. Prove that you have earned this great boon."

He dreaded what Fenring would say. "The Emperor doesn't give his gratitude lightly."

"Nor does the Emperor accept insults or attacks on his rule. Your marriage to Vikka Londine will be swift, sanctioned, and celebrated, but there is a test you must pass, to demonstrate that you have the mettle for the role you want to play."

Leto's voice came out as a growl. "What do you want me to do?"

"Before you can become the head of House Londine, hmmmm, you must ruin Rajiv Londine, destroy the head of that House. Lord Londine has caused many problems, and Shaddam would like him gone. We suspect he is sympathetic to the Noble Commonwealth movement. You will uncover those ties—or manufacture them." Fenring raised his eyebrows and smiled. "Either way, you must bring the old man down. Once he is disgraced, alive or dead—it matters not to me—you will marry Vikka Londine, and all Londine holdings will be transferred to House Atreides. Simple and clear, hmmmm?"

Leto's heart pounded, and he was reminded of how Duke Paulus had been forced to crush House Kolona and take over the planet Borhees. That stain on

Atreides honor had lasted for years before Leto finally relinquished the holding to clear his conscience.

"What you ask goes against my code of honor," Leto said, sitting stiff and formal on the divan.

"It is politics, and a true noble does what he must," Fenring replied. "Are you willing to pay the price to get what you want, Duke Atreides?"

The word blood *can have several meanings. It may imply violence or family ties. When speaking of family, however, more than one meaning may apply.*

—JAXSON ARU, private eulogy for his father

When he secretly went to see his sister on Pliesse, it was not a casual visit, and Jaxson Aru felt it was necessary. He and Jalma had no sibling rivalry, but they had spent much time apart, which created a cool personal distance. Once he understood his sister's ambition to rule House Uchan by getting rid of her doddering old husband, though, Jaxson felt they might have a lot more in common than he had thought. He was anxious to get to know her. More importantly, he wanted her to understand *him*.

In the uproar after the Otorio massacre, no one would expect the infamous Jaxson Aru to come to Pliesse—certainly not the Sardaukar teams searching for him, and certainly not Jalma herself. But with his new-grown face, Jaxson could travel anywhere with impunity. His features were maddeningly familiar, yet different from before. His face evoked warm memories of Brondon Aru, overlaid with hints of Jaxson in ways that no biometric scanner could identify.

After traveling in a roundabout fashion from his quiet hiding place on Nossus, he arrived on Pliesse as part of a group of potential investors in the planet's lucrative hederwood industry. Hederwood was famed for its aromatic properties that imparted euphoric medicinal benefits.

Jaxson had moved finances into several shell accounts to prove that he had the wealth to back up his stated interest in hederwood investment. Under one of his many assumed names, he secured a spot on a private walking tour through a large hederwood grove near the capital city, after which the visitors were scheduled to be addressed by Lady Jalma herself.

The group consisted of twenty men and women. One man giggled often, and he and his wife seemed like vapid buffoons, but Jaxson saw through the act and knew that they were the most likely potential investors.

The showpiece grove was dense and dark, the trunks shaggy as the bark naturally peeled into a hairlike mass before sloughing off to the forest floor, though the special tourist path had been raked clean. The tour was led by Jalma's designated majordomo, Orney, an officious man with bristly gray hair.

The majordomo guided them through the thick grove, giving a compelling, well-practiced description of the hederwood industry. Jaxson remained in the back of the group, calling no attention to himself while enjoying the heady scent of the exotic trees.

Orney stopped at a low-hanging bough that sparkled with tiny white flowers. "These flowers are remarkable because they are so transient. We cannot ship them or distill their essence. One can only experience the blossoms here in the actual grove."

With a small sharp knife, he nipped the white hederwood flowers from the bough and dispersed them among the group members. They sniffed the blossoms and sighed with pleasure. "You'll feel a sense of well-being, which we all need in these turbulent times."

Along with the others, Jaxson relished the bite of the perfume and the low comforting effect, but the calm happiness seemed to blunt his edge. He didn't like it, wanted his thoughts to be bright and sharp.

Orney resumed his rehearsed speech as the group strolled on. "Hederwood lumber, however, is a much more stable commodity. When the wood is used for decorative accents inside homes and buildings, the aroma persists for years. Smaller chips can be used in conventional fireplaces or as incense."

He led them toward the end of the showpiece grove. "The expansion of markets presents numerous opportunities for investment on Pliesse. Lady Jalma will entertain suggestions. She'll meet us at the gathering point just outside the holding house."

The men and women made appropriate noises of interest as they emerged from the trees and out to the open air again. Jaxson inhaled deeply, glad to clear his lungs. The majordomo moved among the participants taking names, answering specific questions.

As they stood in the waiting area, with the large buildings of the town and the Uchan holding house rising high behind them, Lady Jalma came forward from where she had been waiting, doing her expected duty to smile at potential investors.

Jaxson remained a step back, disguised by the crowd so he could have a look at her, after all this time. His sister met the group with a firm, professional grace that bore the marks of their mother. She wore a prim high-collared dress with long sleeves and a low hem. Jaxson watched his sister, studying her. She had a trim figure and her short brown hair was accented with a single white ribbon, according to Pliesse fashion. Her face was objectively beautiful, but hard, and he also saw echoes of their father, the clear bloodline of Brondon Aru . . . much like the features he himself saw in a mirror now.

"Thank you for traveling to Pliesse, and for your interest in our planet's commodities. Majordomo Orney has done a good job enticing you, I am sure." Her smile was thin and brittle, and she seemed to be making a visible effort. "We have all the supplementary information you might need. For those who wish to make an offer, I am available for further discussion." She ducked her head, more a nod than a bow, and Jaxson could tell she wanted to be done with this duty dance and back to matters she considered important. Perhaps, the Noble Commonwealth movement. . . .

Observing her, Jaxson was reminded of his last argument with their mother on Tupile. He and Malina—and, he hoped, his brother and sister—agreed that the Corrino Imperium must be shattered in order to expand commercial markets across the known universe, but they disagreed on tactics. While sitting at the bedside of his dying father, Jaxson had been sharply reminded of the shortness of life, and he did not intend to live a short, pointless life, so he decided to take action—necessary action. Jaxson Aru had learned impatience, and he hoped his sister might think the same way.

Now he needed to speak to her. In private.

His sister turned around, and for the first time, her gaze caught on his face. He met her eyes with his own and knew what she was seeing. Her brow furrowed as if she were searching for a name. Jaxson held her gaze as he slowly walked toward her, like a snake locking a rodent in its gaze. But he was not a predator to Jalma. They were equals.

She said, "You look . . . familiar, something about you. Do we know each other?"

Jaxson did not blink, boring his gaze into hers. "Yes, very well." He didn't explain further.

A light came to her eyes, and he thought she was on the verge of guessing, if she didn't already know. Before she could speak, he said, "I would prefer a conversation with you in private, Lady Jalma. I have many ideas to share, if you dare. Are you brave enough?"

"Accompany me to the holding house." She whirled as if she were spring-loaded. "Mr. Orney, I have a meeting."

The majordomo was taken aback. "Who is this man, my Lady?"

"I am about to find out."

Jaxson followed her as other members of the group stared after him, clearly wanting to know who he was to receive such special treatment. Moving with an angry urgency that might just have been her normal intensity, Jalma led him into the holding house, down wood-walled corridors that smelled strongly of hederwood, and to her private office, saying nothing until she had closed the door.

In the hearth burned the low orange coals of a hederwood fire, and the smoke in the air was velvety, calming, distracting. With the door sealed, Jaxson went immediately to the large window and opened it to let in fresh air. "I prefer clear thoughts."

Jalma placed her hands on her hips, her entire stance a demand. "You remind me of my father. Your voice, your mannerisms . . . What is your game? Who are you?"

He waited a second, then said, "You should know your own brother."

She responded with intense curiosity rather than alarm, stepping closer. "Jaxson . . . What is it, a skin graft? It looks perfect." Her mood shifted abruptly. "Why do you think you can come here and endanger me, even with a perfect disguise?"

"I wanted to see my sister. The Tleilaxu have a process that makes me unidentifiable to genetic or facial scanners. It's safe for me to be here."

Jalma lashed out. "No one is safe around you! All those innocent people on Otorio! We don't support what you did—"

Jaxson laughed. "Innocents? You know better, dear sister. They were all sycophants at Shaddam Corrino's grand gala, although if one of the casualties was your husband, I apologize for killing him."

"If?" Jalma asked.

Jaxson watched her expression. "I've studied records, and no one seems to recall seeing the old fool there. He may in fact have died elsewhere, and the ruins of Otorio merely provided a convenient cover-up."

"No one can say he didn't die on Otorio," Jalma said with faux innocence, then her expression turned bland. "My old husband needed to be removed, and your actions presented an opportunity to clear the deadwood out of the Landsraad. Even our mother recognizes certain advantages to the disruption you caused. She said so specifically."

Jaxson chuckled. "Ha, but she disowned me in that tearful speech in the Landsraad Hall!"

"What did you expect? As Ur-Director of CHOAM, she clearly knows what she needs to say and do, but don't make the mistake of thinking that her speech reflects her innermost thoughts."

Jaxson leaned against her ornate desk, intently watching her. His sister paced the floor in front of the glowing hearth, looking uncomfortable, yet glad to have him there. He said, "Jalma, we're all tired of slowly whittling away the Corrino influence. So, I used an ax. Other members of the Noble Commonwealth are just as impatient for results as I. Our mother would be surprised to know how many people have quietly expressed their support for my more vigorous actions."

"They'll never admit it publicly, or to our mother."

"Not until it is time. But a few more blows of the ax should topple the giant Corrino tree." He softened his voice. "I would like to know you support me."

"You're drawing on family ties now?" Jalma asked. "I barely know you, brother . . . though I understand you."

"Understanding is the most important part. I have clear plans and a compressed timeline. I want to see a free Commonwealth prosper in our lifetimes, not in some vague and misty future."

His sister sighed. "So do I, Jaxson, but you must be careful. Even with your disguise, the Sardaukar hunt down anyone who even hints at sympathy for the rebellion. Shaddam would like nothing more than to execute you in the most appalling fashion."

"No one will find me, sister. I rather enjoy the infamy."

The door to Jalma's office suddenly burst open, and the officious majordomo stepped in and stood quaking, his mouth open, his eyes wide. He must have been eavesdropping through the window Jaxson had opened. "My Lady! That is Jaxson Aru, the butcher of Otorio! You're not safe. I'll call the guards."

He spun toward the corridor and sucked in a great breath of air to shout, but Jaxson was already there. He grabbed the man's throat and squeezed with a viselike grip, turning Orney's outcry into a gasp and a wheeze. The majordomo clutched at Jaxson's hand, struggling. His eyes rolled in panic—and suddenly bulged.

Jaxson saw his sister there right behind the other man, and she thrust harder, jammed her personal dagger deep into the man's back, twisted it a second time. She yanked it out and rammed the blade into his kidneys. Orney went limp.

Jaxson released his grip on the throat, and the dead man crumpled to the floor of the office.

His sister stood holding her dagger, biting her lower lip in concern. "Orney was a fool and prone to overreaction. Efficient but small-minded. If he'd considered for even two seconds, he would have realized that revealing your presence here would destroy my standing in the Landsraad. Even if you escaped, the Sardaukar would come and wipe out Pliesse, just like House Verdun."

She gave the corpse a look of annoyance and addressed her brother. "I don't want you to stay for much longer. That would be too risky, but perhaps you could serve as my new majordomo for a while? So we can get to know each other?"

"Let's not tell Mother," Jaxson said.

Jalma considered. "Agreed. For now, she stays in the dark."

A s she pondered the wording for her secret message, Jessica felt more alive than at any time since she had returned to Wallach IX. This might be the most important letter she ever wrote.

After nearly two decades as Leto's lover, close companion, and intimate adviser, Jessica believed she could resolve this tangled wreck of a misunderstanding. But to do that, she needed the right words, needed to apologize, needed to make a connection. . . .

Her greatest regret about her abrupt, forced departure from Caladan was that she'd been unable to explain to Paul what she had done and what the Sisterhood was forcing her to do.

Now Xora had given her this unexpected chance.

In her private quarters under the light of a single glowglobe, she hunched over the small writing desk, consumed with the idea of what she had to say. On the desk beside her rested an unmarked, burnished-metal message cylinder, which Xora had smuggled to her along with whispered instructions. Jessica wondered if the other Sister had ever used this scheme to sneak secret letters to her lost Sardaukar lover . . . or if Xora had been cut off entirely during her seventeen years of punishment here. Was she helping Jessica now, perhaps as a vicarious way to do what she wished she had done?

Jessica wrote quickly with her stylus in the neat handwriting that Reverend Mother Mohiam had insisted she learn. She felt like a student again, controlled by the Bene Gesserit at every turn. Not much had changed since she was a child here at the Mother School. . . .

She made use of one of the coded languages used only by the Atreides—a simple but obvious precaution. She wrote the letter primarily to Paul, her most important overture, and she felt he might be more open to her words. What she needed to say to Leto could not be conveyed with mere words on paper. She would have to use this message, hope Paul would understand, and possibly say something to his father.

When her vision blurred, she closed her eyes and drew a breath, feeling the weight of responsibility on her shoulders.

She couldn't explain to them what Mother Superior Harishka wanted, couldn't reveal the complex manipulations of the Bene Gesserit or the bizarre warning—or vendetta?—that Lethea had raised, but she could tell Paul that she loved him, and she knew he would believe it.

Jessica had already done what the Mother Superior asked, had faced the senile and vindictive old Kwisatz Mother to learn what she wanted. Harishka and the others had heard Lethea's garbled predictions of Paul's terrible purpose and how Jessica herself might be the first tipping point in a long chain of events that would ultimately ruin the Sisterhood. To Jessica, it was obvious madness.

But even though she had done as they commanded, Harishka and the others would already be suspicious of her, and she doubted they would simply let her go back to her normal life. But she had to hope that at least Paul wasn't in danger. The Bene Gesserit would be watching him, she was sure, with whatever subtle operatives they could slip into Caladan. If they ever learned of his prescient dreams, their interest would be sharpened to a razor's edge. That revelation would add even more weight to Lethea's warnings.

At least Jessica had kept that a secret.

She looked up from her letter. On the back of the desk sat her purlwood carving, crudely done, but with a certain power of longing and ambition. She had cleaned away the dirt and kept it here. Looking at it, she drew inspiration.

She began writing again. In the letter, she opened her heart, promised to find a way to return to Caladan, return to her son, and make the situation right with his father. After considering for long moments, she also asked Paul to tell "the Duke" that she still loved him and how sorry she was.

She stared at her words under the soft light of the glowglobe. Now that she knew how to slip a message cylinder away from Wallach IX, with Xora's help, perhaps she could send out other letters, maintain a dangerous but vital line of communication.

She began to roll the instroy paper so she could seal away her letter, when the door to her quarters burst open. Jessica rose and spun, trying to block the view of her writing desk. Mother Superior Harishka stood in the hall next to Sister Jiara and the bitter-faced Reverend Mother Ruthine. They looked like a pair of executioners.

Jessica feigned indignation. "What is this? Am I not entitled to—"

From behind them Xora stepped forward, flushed with excitement. "You see, Mother Superior! Not only did Jessica hide her son's prescient dreams from you, she's also trying to smuggle out a secret message."

Knowing she was caught, Jessica felt anger flare inside her. "You provided the message cylinder. You were the cause of this, Xora."

But the Sister looked triumphant. "I gave you the rope to hang yourself, and you've done so admirably." She lifted her chin, looking like a complete stranger. "I am loyal, Mother Superior—I am skilled, and I am important. It is time for you to send me on another mission. I will not disappoint you or the Sisterhood."

"We'll discuss that later," Harishka said in a brusque voice that immediately silenced Xora.

Ruthine and Jiara came forward, and for just an instant, Jessica considered fighting them all. She had superior combat skills, but these other Bene Gesserit could be just as well trained. And what would that accomplish?

While Jiara and Xora stood next to the Mother Superior like bodyguards, Ruthine swept to Jessica's writing desk. She snatched up the purlwood carving. "You have many dangerous thorns, Jessica of Caladan! If left unchecked, your poison could spread everywhere."

With unexpected strength, Ruthine squeezed the purlwood carving. She snapped and splintered the piece, breaking the figures apart. She glanced at Harishka. "Lethea was right to bring her here, if only to curtail any further damage she might cause."

Harishka's voice was like a storm brewing over the sea. "A breach of protocol, Jessica, and a demonstration of where your loyalties lie. You must be reminded that you are a Bene Gesserit, and everything else is irrelevant."

"I am a Bene Gesserit," Jessica said. "And look at the harm it's caused me."

Ruthine smiled. "We know how to remind you of the fact!"

Jessica, though, directed her anger toward Xora, feeling betrayed. "I am a Sister. I can never forget that. But I also know that even Sisters cannot be trusted."

*For any important job, one must choose the proper tool, whether it is a
simple wrench or a mercenary army.*

> —BARON DMITRI HARKONNEN, notes on taking
> siridar-governorship of Arrakis

On Giedi Prime, an unmarked shuttle arrived on the private landing balcony, and the twisted Swordmaster emerged into the smoky light. Feyd-
Rautha refrained from showing that he was impressed by the look of the man,
since open admiration would not put him in an effective negotiating position.

Feyd sauntered forward in his leotard and tight tunic. He had a well-sculpted
form, but he didn't intend to fight this man, merely to hire him for a job. The
deadly Swordmaster had been extremely hard to find, and Feyd had plans. . . .

Egan Saar was a panther of a man with a mop of black hair on his head, but
shaved at the temples. His eyes were like obsidian chips broken off by a hammer
blow. His loose, bulky clothes gave him complete freedom of movement, while
hiding his physique. Saar wore a long sword, covered by a drab brown cape which
showed signs of frequent mending. Feyd decided it was an affectation.

Without a glance behind him, Saar came within killing distance in three
alarmingly swift steps. "M'Lord Harkonnen, I offer you my services, if we can
come to terms."

"That depends on whether or not you impress me."

"There's no doubt I will."

Feyd couldn't decide if this man rubbed him the wrong way. "I see that you
do not lack confidence."

The Swordmaster narrowed his black eyes. "Truth is different from empty
bravado, my Lord. I do not rely on credentials or references, and I can demonstrate my capabilities in any way you wish."

"Good, because the job I have in mind will require flexibility, innovation,
and an array of deadly skills. I don't care about your methods, only the results."
He continued assessing the man. "Follow me to the arena. There is a blood sport
exhibition today, and it will be a good place for us to exchange ideas."

Saar nodded. "The mood will be right."

Feyd's personal guards cleared the way, moving through the Harkonnen headquarters down lifts and into the crowded streets. The Harko City

structures were surrounded by manufactories and towering metal-and-stone cubes—administrative buildings, prisons, warehouses, and secure research laboratories. At street level, Feyd's retainers had prepared a vehicle so that he and the Swordmaster could ride in comfort and privacy. The open passenger compartment was surrounded by a silence screen, and their conversations would not be overheard.

While his uncle returned to oversee spice operations on Arrakis, and Rabban went to the family holdings on Lankiveil, Feyd remained on Giedi Prime to observe Harkonnen business. He had to prove he would be a worthy na-Baron. It should have been obvious that he deserved to be the heir designate, yet his uncle's recent challenge would make Feyd prove himself. Demonstrating superiority over his brother had never been much of a challenge.

But while Rabban was concocting some crude scheme—he had refused to provide details—Feyd wanted to do something much more personal, much more intimate. The Baron would appreciate that, especially since he claimed to have his own plan afoot, something to do with the Suk doctor. Feyd would make him proud.

Now with the vehicle rolling through the streets, the young man mused, "I have read your dossier. You claim to be a Swordmaster, yet you never completed your training on Ginaz."

Saar sat next to him as they cruised toward the prominent coliseum, where the gladiatorial combats took place. "The school there collapsed about fifteen years ago, my Lord. House Moritani broke apart the Ginaz School, killed many of the training masters. I barely survived, myself." Saar stared ahead, then added, "The ordeal strengthened me."

"If your training was incomplete, how can you claim to be a Swordmaster?"

"I am resourceful. I found other sources of knowledge, unorthodox instructors, harder training—more ruthless training." He didn't look at Feyd's expression, but continued, "I excelled in methods that the Ginaz training masters refused to teach."

Feyd chuckled. "That sounds appropriate. Where does one go to become a . . . twisted Swordmaster? Is that what you called it?"

"It doesn't matter what I call it, my Lord. What matters is what *is*."

Feyd stroked his own chin. "If your bluster has any merit, perhaps I should hire an entire army of twisted Swordmasters. Then House Harkonnen would be invincible."

Saar's face darkened. "Such an army would not be provided, even to the head of an important House Major." Feyd felt incensed, until the other man continued, "But if you hire the correct twisted Swordmaster, you would not need an army to make yourself invincible."

"Bold words, sir."

Egan Saar merely shrugged.

The vehicle arrived at the tall pillars that held up the arches of the exhibition arena. The sound of so many people filing into the giant forum produced a thunderous buzz in the air. Griffin statues towered like guardian monsters on either side of the entrance. Orange pennants flew from high windows and rooftop parapets.

Feeling the energy of anticipation and bloodlust, Feyd made up his mind. "Today our champion fights. Codo has been undefeated for four months. Last week, he fought a Salusan bull bare-handed."

"Impressive," said the Swordmaster without sounding impressed at all.

Feyd remembered the enormous creature with its branched horns and fiery eyes, the patches of dark fur as well as reptilian scales on its hide. Codo had faced the bull, a beast the size of a small spacecraft, as it thundered forward. The champion was a mountain of muscles and scars, but despite his size, he was quite nimble. As the Salusan bull charged past, the champion sprang away and hammered the side of the beast's head with a fist like a boulder.

Feyd could still hear the crack of that blow, which had nearly felled the bull right then, but the Salusan monster turned and charged back. Codo fought it, evaded it, danced around in circles, which enraged the monster and built the frenzy of the crowd to a fever pitch. Then, the champion had planted his booted feet and braced himself on legs like anchored tree trunks. He met the bull head-on, grasped its curved horns, and held it back. As the bull pawed the ground, snorted, roared, Codo twisted and pushed until he drove the bull down onto its forelegs. With a tremendous crack, he had wrenched the head sideways and snapped the beast's neck.

"I want to see you fight Codo," Feyd said. He watched to see if the Swordmaster flinched.

Saar shrugged. "So long as you don't mind losing your champion, my Lord."

Feyd's nostrils flared. "You are an arrogant one!"

Saar merely touched the sword at his side. "I am ready."

WHEN FEYD-RAUTHA HARKONNEN was installed in his observation box several levels up from the bloodied sand of the arena, he watched the spectacle with avid eyes. The crowd grew louder when Codo, the champion, emerged from the shadowed tunnels into the hazy sunlight and stalked onto the combat field.

The oppressed people of Giedi Prime had dark, downtrodden lives, but they reveled in blood sport exhibitions. Baron Harkonnen understood how to release pressure and dissent among the populace. Not only did frequent public executions maintain a level of fear, respect, and meek cooperation, but such entertainments channeled the anger of the masses. Let them see others suffer the punishments that they feared might happen to them. And in the champion who had slain so many for their enjoyment, they saw a hero who was different from the harsh overlords they dreaded.

Codo had a bullet-shaped head shaved clean so that an opponent would have no hair to grasp. His torso was like an inverted triangle with shoulders broad enough to accommodate his massively muscled arms. To a rush of cheers, Codo raised his arms, displaying skin that was a tapestry of ropy scars, healed gashes, and ornamental implanted rings and hooks.

Feyd knew the man added one such adornment to commemorate each victory in the arena. The young man pursed his lips with interest. The champion already seemed to be taking a victory walk, but he might be in for a surprise. On the other hand, if Egan Saar was not as skilled as his brash claims indicated, Feyd would gladly waste no more time.

From the opposite side of the arena, the twisted Swordmaster emerged, wearing his patched cape over loose and rumpled clothes. As he stepped onto the sand, he drew his sword.

The crowd gasped as they saw him. Some booed; all were intrigued. They watched intently, but not with the singular focus that Feyd did.

Codo's challenging growl built to a roar that was echoed by the audience. Egan Saar raised his sword in a mock salute to his opponent, then turned to look up at the Harkonnen box and called out. "M'Lord Feyd-Rautha, would you prefer that I kill him, or just cripple him?"

The crowd laughed and hissed.

Codo bunched his muscles and gripped a long sword in one hand and a barbed trident in the other. The crowd noise dropped to a murmur as they waited for Feyd's answer.

He shouted back, "Bring me his head—if you can."

The twisted Swordmaster nodded and went to work.

THE DUEL LASTED for half an hour, but it became readily apparent not only to Feyd but to everyone in the coliseum that Egan Saar was merely toying with his rival. The Swordmaster demonstrated elaborate techniques, yet he pulled his strike at the last moment each time. He inflicted dozens of what could easily have become mortal blows, but he intentionally left only bleeding cuts, so that Codo grew increasingly frustrated. The blood on his oiled body and scarred skin made him look like a walking charnel house.

The brutish champion, though incredibly strong, was not quick-witted. Saar fought him steadily, until even the champion realized that he was doomed. When the look on Codo's face melted to one of disbelief and then despair, the twisted Swordmaster ended the combat.

He struck Codo's sword, then slipped his own blade around to catch the deadly trident, which he yanked out of the champion's hand. In his opponent's instant of surprise, Saar followed through, swinging with a blow that chopped off the man's forearm, then he drove his long sword through the champion's heart.

When the corpse dropped to the bloodied sands, Saar listened to the re-sounding silence in the arena. He raised his blade and struck off Codo's head.

The Swordmaster carried the gory object to the edge of the stands, lifting it high until a slow rumble of applause and stomping echoed throughout the coliseum. Saar looked up at the Harkonnen box and said, "I trust I have demon-strated my qualifications for the job, m'Lord."

Then he dropped the bloody head to the sand.

In the box above, Feyd tapped his fingertips together and nodded. He realized he was grinning. "Indeed you have."

When does boyhood end and manhood begin? For Paul Atreides, thrust into a position of responsibility at a young age, it came sooner than expected.

—PRINCESS IRULAN, *The Journey of Muad'Dib*

Paul once again spent hours in his father's office, still feeling out of place. As he studied reports to discuss with Thufir Hawat, he expected Dr. Yueh at any moment. The Suk doctor wanted to reexamine the bruises and scrapes from the tavern brawl the night before.

Hearing a voice in the courtyard outside, he went to a large, open window and looked out. In the garden below, he saw a young falconer with a large red-tailed hawk perched on his gloved hands. Duke Leto had hired the man to work with the hawk, the symbol of House Atreides.

Leaning out, Paul smiled and watched as the falconer flung the bird into the air, and it beat its wings, gaining height. Years ago, Paul's great-grandfather had kept several of the magnificent raptors, training them himself. Duke Leto wanted to revive the tradition, maybe even have a trained hawk appear at public events. As he watched the soaring bird, Paul decided he liked the idea.

His left eye throbbed. The bruises had darkened, but he knew they would gradually look worse. His knuckles were sore, too, as well as the ball of his foot, for some reason. He knew that his opponents must be in far worse shape, but he was glad that he and Gurney had managed to slip away without being identified. He felt both excited and disappointed by the incident. He was glad his father wasn't here.

After years of training with his mother, Paul rarely lost his temper, and he usually felt guilty about it when he did, wishing he'd shown more self-control. Leto would have called it conduct unbecoming a Duke. A young nobleman, particularly the heir to the fief of Caladan, should behave in a dignified fashion.

Once, when Paul was nine, he'd gotten into a tussle with the son of a minor noble who came calling at Castle Caladan. The Duke and the other noble had assumed their boys would get along, but they didn't. And the commotion had resulted in a severe scolding when the visitors were gone.

"A Duke and his family must always think of consequences," Leto had lectured him, pacing back and forth in this very office. "Especially what your behavior might look like to others." Only now, as Paul recalled the lecture, did he appreciate that his father had spoken to him as if he were an adult, rather than a nine-year-old boy.

Paul had retorted, "The boy insulted Gurney, called him ugly because of the scar on his face!"

"I'm sure Gurney values your loyalty, but he is quite capable of ignoring a verbal slight."

Paul hung his head. "I hit the boy first."

"So an insult turned into violence. Let it be a lesson to you. Rather than lashing out, you could have sent him to a waiting room, or you could have left the chamber yourself."

"Isn't it good to fight my own battles?"

Leto had leaned over the elaccawood desk to look into his son's eyes. "Pick your battles, Paul, and pick them carefully. A few unpleasant words were not worth a physical altercation, and you made my trade negotiations more difficult as a result. His father was insulted and embarrassed, and he was put into a position of having to side with his own son, as was I. You see how foolish things like that could escalate into a full kanly feud?"

Those words had resonated with Paul, and he had not forgotten them.

"It's about maturity, son. Each situation is different, and you have to think quickly. Choosing your battles is tied to understanding the consequences of your actions. Fight a battle only after you've analyzed the options."

Paul wished he had remembered as much at the Song of the Sea. He heard footsteps in the corridor and thought he recognized the cadence of Dr. Yueh, but there was something different in the gait . . . a little slower, more halting?

Dressed in rumpled black garments, the doctor entered the office bearing his medkit. His squarish face wore a dark expression, and his eyes darted around. Like a cloud clearing from the sun, his demeanor changed, and he shifted his attention to Paul. He ran his eyes over the young man. "Are you feeling any better, sir? The aches will no doubt be worse on the second day, and I can provide relief, if you need it."

Paul felt a flush come to his cheeks. "Are you here to lecture me, since my father is away?"

The Suk doctor seemed unflappable. "Do you want me to scold you?"

"I should have listened to Gurney and left the tavern the moment trouble started." When he smiled, he suddenly felt the soreness of his bruised lip.

Yueh's dark lips formed the slightest smile, framed by his mustaches. "Or don't go into taverns at all."

Now it was Paul's turn to express concern. "Is something wrong, Dr. Yueh? I see it all over your face."

"You are the patient, not the doctor. It is not my place to discuss this with you." His brow furrowed, and he bent to his medkit, suddenly busy.

Paul drew himself up and faced Yueh. "If I am to act in the role of Duke, I need you to tell me truthfully if something is wrong."

Yueh stepped back and gave him a deep bow, gathering his thoughts. "It is a train of thought, young Master. I was . . . reminded of my wife."

Paul was puzzled. Yueh had always been alone during his years of service to House Atreides. He rarely spoke of his wife. "How so?" Paul asked. "What is the connection?"

"Seeing you alone reminds me that your mother has gone away, and that in turn reminds me of the Bene Gesserit. My own wife has been on Sisterhood assignments for many years. I hope that the Lady Jessica is not forced to remain apart from your father for so long." He lowered his head, uneasy. "I apologize that my worries are so apparent. I bear the burden of confidentiality, and I should be better at it."

Paul was alarmed to hear this as well. He had not truly allowed himself to believe the Sisterhood would keep his mother away. For years? What if she never came back? "What sort of hold does the Sisterhood have over them?"

"We cannot say," Yueh answered, "nor can we understand."

As if embarrassed to be opening himself to his emotions, the doctor busied himself inspecting Paul's bruises and tending his wounds. The young man wondered what his mother was doing now, far away on Wallach IX, and what the Bene Gesserit might ask of her.

The Sisterhood was like an octopus, with tentacles reaching throughout the Imperium. And all that secrecy! Jessica had taught him a fraction of what she knew, fighting and breathing exercises, analytical techniques, the beginnings of using Voice to command certain reactions. She had also warned him that she was technically proscribed from teaching him these things, but she had made the choice on her own.

Was she being punished now? Recalled to the Mother School as a reprimand? Had the Bene Gesserit learned how she was training her own son? Or did it have something to do with Duke Leto?

Paul had been very close with his mother, and he was aware of her complex feelings about the Sisterhood: a combination of love and hate, admiration and loathing, duty and defiance. He wondered if they would ever let her come home to Caladan. That gave him something in common with Dr. Yueh. . . .

The Bene Gesserit Sisterhood specialized in the study of humanity, in improving the condition of being human. He wondered if they remembered their own humanity in what they asked their Sisters to do.

As Dr. Yueh finished putting an ointment around the eye and med-pads on the other injuries, Paul admitted, "I feel that my mother's absence weakens our family, and it weakens House Atreides. I . . . I'm sorry that you're feeling sad, too."

A squall of worry flickered across the doctor's face, but he quickly controlled it. "Thank you, young Master. We have to hope that they are in good hands, my wife and your mother." He bowed, gathered the materials from his medkit, and hastily departed as if he didn't trust himself to continue the conversation.

Paul looked after the doctor, seeing only the empty corridor for a long moment. Duke Leto was gone, and Lady Jessica as well. In the past, Yueh had performed his job with great efficiency, yet now he seemed distant. Though he and the Suk doctor were close in a way, Paul didn't think Yueh would ever truly be his friend, like Duncan, Gurney, and even the formal Thufir Hawat.

Paul heard the falconer shout from the garden, and in a great flutter of wings, the trained red-tailed hawk flew in through the open window. The raptor landed on the desk and tucked its wings neatly, without scattering the petitions and other documents there.

The bird looked him askance, while the handler down in the garden continued to shout. Paul held his breath, admiring the magnificent creature. Keeping its golden eyes fixed on Paul, the hawk cocked its head this way and that.

Finally, Paul sighed. "All right, all right. I'll get back to work."

The hawk fluttered its wings, sprang up from the desk, circled the office once, and swooped back out the window.

Too often, people are at cross-purposes. It should be the other way around.
People should pull together, rather than pull apart.

—LADY JESSICA, private journals

Sealed in her dark isolation cell, Jessica thought of her carved figurine, mother, father, child, broken asunder by the vindictive Ruthine. She had needed to communicate with her son, to make contact—which any mother should have been able to understand.

But Jessica had defied the Sisterhood, gone against their orders, and that was reason enough for them to lock her away in this cold, stone-walled chamber. She was trapped in an outbuilding connected to the huge ancient complex with a sealed metal door as the only entrance. Up against the ceiling, narrow windows let in gray light, but she was not tall enough to see through them. The damp air smelled of mildew. It was a miserable place, calculatedly so.

Mother Superior Harishka would probably keep her locked away here for an extended time. She had not yet used the privy in the corner, but it reeked. The cell had no running water, no basin, only a bowl with a little water and a soiled washcloth folded next to it. It was all meant to demean her.

Jessica was supposed to remember that she was a Bene Gesserit. As she sat alone, silently concentrating, she knew that the most significant reason for her punishment was not that she had tried to send a message to Paul, but that she *felt* something for him. She missed her son terribly, wanted to be in touch with him, but the Sisters tried to cauterize those feelings—like Xora, taken away from Brom and expected to function as if nothing had changed.

Maybe this isolation was meant to impose unthinking obedience, but it was a damned foolish way to instill loyalty to the order. She preferred Lethea's bitter company to this—at least the old crone was open in her hostility.

Jessica looked around in the shadows, saw the pale frost of her breath, but she had endured far worse. Her instinct was to try to escape, to shout out and demand justice, to explain herself, to plead for mercy, but then she remembered her Sisterhood training. She calmed her pulse, her breathing, adjusted her mindset so that she no longer felt the discomfort of the cell. Bene Gesserit techniques.

Ironically, she would have to rely on the skills she learned here at the Mother School to survive their punishment.

Maybe that was what they wanted her to realize. In the end, all Sisters would fall back on the foundation of their special instruction.

The cell was large enough that she could pace from one corner to the other, a small comfort, but the broad emptiness gave her nowhere to go. She sat on the hard wooden bench, shivering, then forced herself to feel warm again, shifting her body temperature.

She wondered how many had inhabited this dismal place over the centuries, how many had died here. Was that what they wanted her to think? Did they want her to worry so much that she slipped into panic and became pliable? Or would they see that as a weakness, too? Another failure?

Her questions were going around in circles.

As the reinforced door had sealed shut, the Mother Superior called, "You defied us, not just by trying to send a message to your son. The boy himself is a defiance. Your decision to bear a male child triggered a cascade of terrible problems—Lethea can see things that we cannot." She clucked her tongue. "That's probably what drove her mad!"

That was the last contact she'd had for more than a day. Identical, interminable hours passed. In extremis, Jessica could place herself into a silent bindu suspension, a trance that made her metabolism drop to almost nothing, and time would pass much more swiftly. That was a way she could endure.

The Mother School wanted her to be a pawn in their plans, mindlessly cooperative. Maybe Lethea would be her "salvation." Would the Sisters release her if the old crone lashed out again and demanded to see her? "Bring me Jessica, Jessica of Caladan!"

Well, she was no longer Jessica of Caladan. She was a Bene Gesserit to her core, but she resented *not* believing in the order, and the Sisterhood would never compromise. The Bene Gesserit believed they had superior knowledge, an unprecedented perspective on history and the human race. But they had forgotten small yet vital bits of humanity, such as love.

She took a deep breath, listened to her heartbeat. Maybe she should have waited for Harishka to determine that she had finished her usefulness, and then she could have gone back to Paul, her Duke.

Or maybe the Sisterhood would find a new assignment for her, just to prove that they could move their women around like game pieces, use her in some other way—and she would never see her family again.

All those years ago, holding Leto and loving him, she had not been able to forsake the Sisterhood in the way she knew he wanted. In his devastating grief after the loss of his son Victor, Jessica had chosen to give him another male heir—a power that, ironically, the Sisterhood had given to her. If offered the chance to do it over, she would do the same thing.

She shivered again, despite her efforts to ignore the cold. In the bleak shadows, a small amount of light came through the high cell windows. She felt confusion, frustration, and more—all emotions that the Sisterhood wanted to keep under lock and key.

When the Sisters had burst into her room that night, Harishka had been angry. Jessica found it ironic in a way. Apparently, *anger* was permitted on behalf of the Sisterhood, but love was forbidden? What could be more important than love, for the preservation of humanity's future?

Jessica still heard the sharp edge of the Mother Superior's words and the echoing clang of the isolation cell door. She felt very alone, far from her family, and all she had left of Leto and Paul were her memories.

STANDING JUST INSIDE Lethea's room, Mother Superior Harishka glared at the sticklike crone, who had somehow managed to sit up on the medical bed. The two women locked eyes, and neither looked away.

Harishka ignored the foul odors, concentrated on this clash with her opponent, her friend . . . this enigma. "We brought Jessica to you, as you demanded. We separated her from her son, and now I demand your cooperation. Explain! What do you know? What does the Sisterhood need to know? What have you *seen*, and how can we fix it?"

The ancient woman cackled to herself. She finally broke the Mother Superior's gaze when her eyes rolled up, showing only the whites. Whisper words rattled out of her mouth. "You ask for a rational conversation, when I see death and chaos in our future? The near future is impacted, as is the distant future. Jessica is the trigger, the prime mover. What she did will bring . . ." Her words trailed off into a long, wet sigh like the last trickles after a flash flood.

"What?" Harishka shouted the word tinged with Voice, even though the old Kwisatz Mother was immune. "What will she bring?"

Lethea snapped her head back, like a snake striking. "Jessica will bring exactly what you deserve! I should never have warned you." She slumped back as if deflating. A maddening smile hung on her withered lips.

Harishka remained poised at the doorway but ready to evacuate into the hall if necessary. "I am the Mother Superior, but I cannot make good decisions unless you give me the information I need. What use are you to me? We did what you asked, yet you destroyed other innocent Sisters." She took a cautious step closer, remembering all too clearly how Rinni was locked in an obsessive insanity, repeating the Litany over and over, or the other victims who bashed their heads against walls, clawed out their eyes, leaped from high windows. "What is it about Jessica's son? We know about his prescient dreams now. Is it possible he is the

Kwisatz Haderach, a generation sooner than we expected? What does your pre-science tell you?"

Lethea's laugh was a deep cachinnation that rolled on and on. "There are many possible futures, not a single predetermined one. And because of your failure, you are doomed in most of them."

"Does that mean there could be more than one possible Kwisatz Haderach? We have tried so many alternate paths to reach our goal. One of them has to work!"

Lethea refused to answer. Something was welling up inside her, and her gaze seemed to go straight through the Mother Superior before her eyes rolled again and went unfocused. She sank deeper into her open-eyed silence and finally said, "You cannot begin to understand what I see. Where I must go, you cannot follow. And I'll kill anyone who tries to enter my memories! You can't have them!"

The ancient woman sagged in her medical bed as if she had tumbled down an endless slope. Her eyes fell closed, her mouth grew slack. Her breathing sounded desperate and labored. Fearing some trick, Harishka summoned medical technicians to tend the distressed patient.

The old crone reeked of death as if she were rotting away, cell by cell. What little remained of her physical self was disintegrating.

Forcing out a croak, Lethea said, "The Sisterhood can't recover from this. Blood, terrible pain, and disaster!" She slumped back, glaring at the ceiling and seething with helplessness.

Every nobleman has his role to play. We can make lofty speeches, we can grasp for glory, we can profess all manner of virtue. But a person's essential core is as immutable as diamond, even if it remains hidden from outside eyes.

—DUKE PAULUS ATREIDES, *Fundamentals of Honor*

*W*ho am I?

Leto did not need to speak the question aloud because he was asking himself. No one else could give him the answer he needed.

At night, the capital city exploded with colors, noise, and grandeur, but he sat alone in his guest suite. He had tuned the glowglobes to a dim setting. Neither light nor shadows gave him comfort.

Who am I?

He was Leto Atreides, Duke of Caladan, father of Paul. He had defined himself by honor and determination. He had ruled his people with a steady hand because he didn't doubt what he was doing. They called him Leto the Just.

But in just the past few months, his heart and his core had been rocked as if by an asteroid impact. The spread of ailar, the "Caladan drug," had soiled his reputation, even though Leto had learned of it only after the drug was thriving. He'd wiped out the scourge, obliterated Chaen Marek's fern forests in the northern wilderness, but that had not been enough.

People still believed the ailar distribution network was some black-market scheme that he had concocted. Lord Atikk had declared kanly over the loss of his son, and Leto defended his honor. It surprised him that the members of the Imperial Court could believe that he had underhandedly poisoned his rival to avoid facing him in a duel. Leto would have fought to the death rather than let anyone think he was such a deceitful worm.

He guessed that Count Fenring or one of his henchmen had slipped the poison into Lord Atikk's drink in a misguided attempt to "help" him. If so, the Count had done him no favors.

And now this unconscionable requirement Fenring had laid down. Did he consider Leto beholden to him?

Was ruining a man of integrity the price to increase the standing of House Atreides?

Through the window, he watched a firefountain that shot a sparkling pillar into the sky, perhaps as a memorial to some fallen nobleman or to celebrate a pivotal event, or merely to announce a garment sale at one of Kaitain's markets.

Wealth and energy shimmered throughout the capital world. Leto had come here to seek political influence for his family, but maybe it was a misplaced ambition that would not benefit his House after all.

Immersed in the room's shadows, he stood at the plaz window and stared across the hive-like panorama. He had been fooled into thinking he should grasp at unnecessary wealth, a poisonous obsession with acquiring influence and resources. To what end? Such wealth and clout did not lead to good deeds, but merely to a hunger for more wealth, more power. It was a serpent that ate its own tail.

Who am I?

Duke Leto Atreides ruled Caladan well, and he'd raised his son to follow his model, to become a genuine leader and an honorable man. Was one planet not enough? Should he have kept the Kolona holdings after all, even if his father had seized them in an unconscionable way? Leto clenched his fists and stared until the city lights and colors made him dizzy.

Political machinations and misplaced loyalties had ultimately taken Jessica from him. The Sisterhood was no better than the worst political operative in the Landsraad or the Imperial Court. Out of spite, did he need to stoop as low?

Count Fenring wanted him to destroy Rajiv Londine, a man he barely knew. Leto went back to his shigawire spools, activated a reader, and called up more records of House Londine. He studied images of their home planet, looked at the histories and the family trees of the noble bloodline.

Leto's dinner with Vikka had been one of the more pleasant evenings he'd spent on Kaitain. She was intelligent and pleasant company, certainly a more than tolerable partner. But would he have noticed her at all if Count Fenring hadn't arranged for the two of them to meet?

He could only imagine what Duke Paulus had endured during the long vetting and betrothal process when he had finally married Lady Helena of House Richese.

He thought of the heated rumors, the quiet snickers, and the disrespect for disgraced Baron Molay, who was either defiant or oblivious to the ridicule. But Leto was just as incensed by how Molay had discarded several Bene Gesserit concubines, out of spite for the way Sister Xora had embarrassed him. Leto didn't want to be like that either, to think of whatever woman he brought into his bed as a mere political alliance or business transaction, whether it was a formal wife or just another concubine. What sort of example was he setting for his son?

He rearranged the shigawire spools and played more recordings of old Rajiv Londine. The well-spoken nobleman had strong opinions, many of them critical of House Corrino or the bureaucracy of the Imperium. His arguments against the Emperor's overreach were well laid out, articulate rather than abrasive. Londine was no ranting rebel, but rather a man who hoped to use his power and station to implement legitimate change.

Fenring had said, *You must ruin Rajiv Londine, destroy the head of that House.*

Shaddam IV refused to tolerate criticism, but the fact that Rajiv Londine spoke criticism did not make him a bloodthirsty terrorist like Jaxson Aru.

For House Atreides, the business, political, and financial advantages of marrying into House Londine were myriad and obvious, but none of them added up to the price Fenring had asked him to pay.

Leto thought of Paul again, then removed the shigawire spool.

Who am I? What legacy will I leave?

He knew the answer to both questions.

AN ENTIRE WING of the palace was designated as the Padishah Emperor's personal residence. Others might have felt intimidated by the sheer grandeur. Leto simply felt out of place, reminded again that he preferred Caladan.

He had requested a private audience with Fenring and the Emperor, and the chamberlain directed him to the wing at an appointed time. He wore the formal garments that the protocol minister chose for him and carried his ceremonial sword, which had been bonded to his belt so it could not be used as a weapon. His retainers followed him through the vaulted palace hallways, fanning out to clear a way through the crowd, inflating the Duke's importance.

After today, Leto would be finished with such things.

Sardaukar guards blocked the entrance to the Emperor's wing, and the Atreides retainers formed ranks and waited formally, while Leto presented himself. The rest of his company were forced to remain behind outside the private wing, and a sub-chamberlain directed the Duke through a gallery to a high-ceilinged gaming chamber.

There, Fenring and Shaddam occupied themselves with controls connected to a round table. Projected above, spheres circled around targets and left rainbow paths in the air behind them, and the two played their games, smiling as if they were boys again. Fenring's score was presently higher. With a flick of his dark, close-set eyes, the Count noticed Leto, turned back to the game, intentionally fumbled with the game controls, and surrendered the last two points to Shaddam.

The Emperor straightened, laughing. "You let me win again, Hasimir."

"I am no fool, Sire." Fenring backed away from the controls. "Ahhh, Duke Leto, we've been expecting you. I already explained to Shaddam our plans for joining your holdings with House Londine."

When Shaddam looked at Leto, his expression was mixed. "Hasimir tells me that you are our best hope of solving our problems with Rajiv Londine. For that,

I would be more than pleased to reward you with their wealth, as well as a lovely wife. Everything you could want. I have always respected you, cousin, and this will bind us more closely together."

Leto felt cold inside, knowing what he had to do, yet he was resolved. "Sire, you will recall that years ago I experienced conflicting emotions about the way House Atreides received the wealth of House Kolona."

Shaddam frowned. "You must have regretted surrendering so much wealth and influence."

Leto blinked his gray eyes. "On the contrary, I am satisfied with what I did. It was the only course that kept my honor intact."

"And your treasury much smaller than it might be," Fenring added. "Hmmm?"

"That is not the only measure of a person's worth," Leto said. "I admit, the Londine holdings would be excellent assets for my family and a strong legacy for my son when he becomes Duke." Leto squeezed his fist, felt the ducal signet ring on his finger. "And on a personal note, I find Vikka Londine to be pleasant and attractive. But if the condition for this marriage is that I must ruin a fellow nobleman, then I refuse. If this is a test you set for me, then I've failed." He looked up. "Or I passed, depending on your criteria. I will not sell myself out for material gain or political influence."

The Emperor's face pinched. "We've studied Rajiv Londine, particularly his public and private statements. I am certain he is an active member of the Noble Commonwealth! At the very least he sympathizes with the rebel movement. He needs to be punished."

"That must first be proved in a court of Imperial law, Sire," Leto said. "I had no great love for Duke Fausto Verdun, but I would make the same statement on his behalf."

Shaddam turned cold. "I am the final arbiter of Imperial law, and we must do everything possible to crush this destructive movement. You were on Otorio yourself. You saw how violent and ruthless they are."

"I witnessed what Jaxson Aru did," Leto admitted. "But I don't see the same thing with Rajiv Londine. You may disagree with some of the man's criticisms, but if a disagreeable statement carries a death sentence, this Imperium is not what I always believed it to be."

Fenring's hands fidgeted. "Hmmm, I beg you to reconsider, Duke Leto. There is much at stake. The rebel movement must be found and extinguished."

"You can see shadows under any bed, if you wish to," Leto said, then lowered his voice. "I've had enough of politics. I made a mistake in coming to Kaitain. I let myself chase after the wrong goal." He paused as memories of Jessica welled up within him. She had been his close companion for so many years. But her true loyalty remained with the Bene Gesserit. Politics! He also resolved to write a polite letter to Vikka Londine, thanking her for the pleasure of her company, and wishing her the best. He could not pursue a relationship at this time.

"I am going back to Caladan. I have my own people to rule, and I need to set a good example for my son." He bowed formally, then turned to depart.

Shaddam and Fenring were so astonished they didn't call after him when he left without being dismissed.

FROM HER COVERT observation alcove above, Empress Aricatha listened to the conversation with great interest. She found Duke Leto Atreides fascinating, and had been attentive to his adventures and interactions ever since his arrival at court. She could see the hurt inside him, surely because he had lost his lady love.

Caladan was not an overly important world in the annals of the Landsraad, but Aricatha had duties and obligations. After Leto exited the Imperial wing, she wrote up a report and dispatched it through secret channels to the Silver Needle, where it would be forwarded to CHOAM Ur-Director Malina Aru.

I hear your arguments and justifications, but they pale in comparison with the debate raging inside my own mind.

—MOTHER SUPERIOR HARISHKA, remarks at
Bene Gesserit council session

Although Lethea drifted in and out of consciousness, the Mother Superior no longer considered her useful. And Jessica was locked away in her isolation cell because of her intractability, and the danger she might pose to the order—if anything Lethea said could be believed.

Harishka marched across the courtyard to the expanded and refurbished Chapterhouse Building, funded a decade ago by an endowment from House Tull. As Mother Superior, she knew she should retain a better grasp on her emotions, but frustration boiled off of her like a fever. She paused and half closed her eyes to force a moment of calm, seeing the pale steam of her breath in the chill air. Resolute again, she lifted her chin and entered the impressive stone building.

The main level was large enough to hold Sisterhood convocations, but more often, Harishka met with only a small group of counselors in a modest, round room on the top level—Harishka's special, secure chamber. She needed the conflicting, but ultimately balanced, advice of Ruthine and Cordana, the two Reverend Mothers who had taken Mohiam's place as her most important sounding boards.

She made her way to the upper level and past a complex of private offices to the council chamber. Inside, a warm fire burned in a metal-framed fireplace, adding an orange glow to the austere room. Wide triangular skylights in the high ceiling illuminated the room using an amplifier that enhanced Wallach IX's weak sun.

The special room contained sophisticated projectors so that in council session the attendees could observe activities around the entire Mother School complex. As Harishka entered, one of the wall projectors showed three uniformed young men working downstairs to clean the large Assembly Chamber. A more relevant projection showed a live view of the medical chamber where Lethea lay like a figure sculpted entirely out of bones and wrinkles, her face slack, eyes closed.

Harishka sealed the door. Ruthine and Cordana were seated in their customary places at a round table, and the Mother Superior went to the tallest chair. "If

Lethea dies, we have no more need for Jessica. We brought her here, but learned little that was useful. The gamble did not pay off."

"We learned that she is potentially dangerous. As is her son." Reverend Mother Ruthine was of average height and build, with a brilliant mind, full lips, and a sharp tongue.

"And also potentially beneficial," the Mother Superior pointed out. "You do not throw away a sharp knife just because you might cut yourself with it."

Beside her, Reverend Mother Cordana had piercing eyes, tight features, and a twisted spine. Born into the Sisterhood, Cordana was the product of a failed genetic path, and even advanced surgery had failed to correct the severely damaged vertebrae. Her shoulders were rounded and bent, and Cordana had carried that failure with her throughout childhood. Sometimes, the Sisterhood euthanized such physical disappointments, but at other times, they found uses for such women. Cordana's mental brilliance soon vaulted her to prominence. She was tough, resilient, patient, and compassionate. Harishka did not need her high advisers to be beautiful, just remarkably competent.

Cordana often consumed small amounts of melange, which increased her vigor and diminished her bodily aches, but Ruthine hated the smell of the stuff. She seemed to draw her energy from criticizing others. Now, with a sniff, Ruthine said, "Mother Superior, I asked her not to consume spice before being near me. She reeks of it now."

Cordana rolled her shoulders, trying to make herself more comfortable. "I consume spice in moderation. My last dose was many hours ago."

To make a point, Ruthine rose from her chair and moved to a seat farther away.

Familiar with their tiresome bickering, Harishka directed her advisers back to the vital matter at hand. "Sister Xora revealed that Jessica's son has prescient dreams, which is an important indicator. I find that both interesting and troubling."

"As is the fact that Jessica chose not to reveal such an important thing to us," Ruthine said.

"She was protecting her son," Cordana said, rubbing her shoulder. "And Xora is always trying to get into our good graces. She has her own tainted past, as well as desperate ambitions. It makes me suspicious of anything she says to us, especially if it benefits her—at Jessica's expense."

"A few dreams do not make an illegitimate boy into the Kwisatz Haderach," Harishka pointed out.

Ruthine huffed. "We looked at the breeding index and reviewed the possible bloodlines. By having a son with Leto Atreides, Jessica squandered generations of planning."

"That matter has been exhaustively reviewed," Cordana said with exaggerated patience. "And the breeding index is not an exact science, as we all know. The obvious solution is just to send Jessica back to Caladan with orders to get pregnant again, with a daughter this time. The boy Paul doesn't matter. He isn't the one we want."

Harishka let out a long, patient sigh. "Anirul was Kwisatz Mother at the time the boy was born. She wrote a thorough report shortly before her death. As the next Kwisatz Mother, Lethea expressed both interest and concern about Paul Atreides throughout his childhood, evaluating that he might be the best of our numerous possibilities, but her mind is now so fragmented that I find her warnings unreliable." Her brow furrowed.

"Or maybe she's had an epiphany—we can't just ignore her warnings," Ruthine said. "Everything about Jessica and her son are disruptive to our plans. What more damage will they cause?"

The Mother Superior's expression twisted. "Lethea may be working at cross-purposes to the Sisterhood. I'm not sure I can trust anything she says. I will demand to hear more from Jessica."

Cordana, deep in thought, finally added her opinion. "Sister Jessica is in a difficult position—because of us—and if you ask her to bear another daughter by Leto, we have damaged her chances. We interfered with her life, broke her relationship with her son, with the man she loves . . ."

"Love," Ruthine snapped, "is the root of her many problems!"

Cordana leaned forward on the heavy table. "Jessica is human, as we all are."

Ruthine sniffed and her nose twitched as if she could still smell melange. "Her vulnerability to emotions is the root cause of our problems. As the former Kwisatz Mother, Lethea knew more about the breeding plan than any of us. Jessica's daughter—by Leto Atreides—should have been matched with a Harkonnen, according to the genetic index. A son does nothing for us. And Lethea says he is dangerous."

"There are always alternate paths," Cordana said, "a tapestry of fallback positions that were established just as long ago. Our breeding calculations depend on controlling human decisions—which is not always possible."

"Jessica has a wild streak, foolish and lovestruck," Harishka admitted. "But it is pointless to rail against a decision she made fifteen years ago. I must decide how we respond now. What if Paul Atreides can become what we sought for thousands of years? The Sisterhood should at least investigate."

"If Fate has thrown this into our lap, who are we to waste the opportunity?" Cordana agreed.

Ruthine's bland face flushed, demonstrating an alarming lack of control. "It is not an opportunity, but the opposite. A rogue male with great power could ruin the Bene Gesserit, exactly as Lethea warned. We dare not take any chances." She huffed. "I say, put them to death and don't waste any time about it."

As the dispute grew more heated, Harishka leaned back in her tall chair. "I seek counsel from both of you because you hold such differing views, but I must make my own decision."

"He is just another failed Kwisatz Haderach," Ruthine insisted. "We should put all of them to death."

"We do not simply kill all unexpected failures. Sometimes they prove invaluable in their own ways." Harishka looked at Cordana's twisted spine, and the small-statured Reverend Mother straightened with evident pride.

Cordana added, "Hasimir Fenring was another failed Kwisatz Haderach, and he still serves our purposes, at times."

"He is a killer without conscience," Ruthine said.

"And sometimes that is useful," Cordana retorted.

"Only under controlled circumstances . . . and Lady Margot can control him," Harishka said. "This Paul Atreides is not like that, though. At the moment, he is unguided, his training is incomplete—and we have taken his mother away."

"That can cause havoc," Ruthine interjected. "Lethea foresaw this! We should heed her warnings."

"Perhaps." Harishka looked down at her hands resting on the tabletop, noting the deep creases and age spots. It made her think of a lifetime of wise decisions as well as disastrous ones. "And perhaps not."

Cordana asked in a calm voice, "Should you consult with the new Kwisatz Mother? She replaced Lethea—should we not rely on her advice, rather than incoherent ramblings." She seemed to be pressing for more information. Only Harishka knew the woman's identity.

"You do not need to know about my discussions with the Kwisatz Mother."

"The safest course would be to kill them, before they get out of hand," Ruthine repeated. "As Cordana admitted, there are alternate paths we can follow. Reverend Mother Wanna has supervised several possible candidates, sired by specific noblemen. We have other Kwisatz Haderach possibilities, even one here in the Mother School. The boy Brom, for instance. I say they are safer than letting Paul Atreides remain alive, outside of our control."

"Sister Xora would agree with you, because it helps with her ambitions," Harishka said. She had scrutinized the bloodlines, the branch points, the possible paths to the one they had sought for so long. Genetics offered many suggestions but no firm answers. "Brom has no idea of his own potential, but he does fit our criteria so far, and he has been raised here at the Mother School, so we know how to control him." She pursed her lips. "We don't necessarily need Paul Atreides."

"Jessica's current actions are only the tip of the iceberg," Ruthine said. "When we left her alone and unmonitored on Caladan, what Bene Gesserit secrets did she teach her son?" With a sound of disgust, she shook her head.

"Caladan is far away," Cordana said as if that were an answer. "She had to do her best."

Harishka recalled the objectionable figurine the young girl had made long ago, which was now smashed. "Jessica's defiance did manifest early, I remember. She caused Mohiam no end of grief."

Cordana said, "When we finally assigned her as concubine to Duke Leto Atreides, she did her job too well. He was fooled for all these years."

The Mother Superior pushed back. "Not fooled—*convinced*. Jessica formed a true bond with the Duke of Caladan, and with her son."

"We should not have trusted her in the first place," Ruthine muttered.

"That was my mistake, and Mohiam's," Harishka admitted. "But we considered it worth the risk."

Cordana shifted, tried to find a comfortable position for her back. Reaching into a hidden pocket, she withdrew a small container of spice powder and put a pinch on her tongue. She closed her eyes.

Ruthine moved even farther away. "And what do we do about her now? We must control the damage. We can't trust Jessica to follow orders, and her son could be dangerous. Best to cut our losses, for the good of the order."

"Jessica is a strong woman, I agree," Cordana said, "but we can still use her, if we find the appropriate purpose . . . and that may be far from Caladan."

Harishka looked up at the wall monitor showing Lethea strapped down and drugged in her medical chamber. "Maybe Jessica can be reeducated . . . at least unless we have better answers about what Lethea wanted."

"Regardless, Jessica must face consequences for her defiance." Ruthine's dark eyes narrowed. They had always reminded Harishka of Tleilaxu eyes.

Harishka got to her feet, moved slowly toward the door. "Oh, there will be consequences."

In this life, we make many acquaintances. We share time with them until economic, familial, or other circumstances push us apart. But a truly good friend does not move on when circumstances change.

—LADY MARGOT FENRING, love letters

Whenever Shaddam Corrino was disturbed, he liked to sit on his great throne in the Imperial audience chamber with no one present except for his Truthsayer. The Reverend Mother Mohiam was a creature of the shadows, preferring not to be noticed, and her unobtrusiveness didn't bother him.

When he entered the chamber, Count Fenring knew what his friend would be thinking. The thin-faced Emperor brooded on the blue-green block of Hagal crystal, and the black-robed Bene Gesserit stood off to one side near the empty throne of the Empress. Aricatha kept herself busy with other court activities, wisely leaving Shaddam alone.

But Fenring still wanted to clear the air. He had been right to leave Grix Dardik on Arrakis, since the odd Mentat always managed to annoy the Emperor. That would only have made the situation worse.

Leto Atreides had departed from Kaitain that morning, taking his retinue and his damnable honor with him—while unraveling Fenring's plans to quash the gadfly Londine. Disappointed, Shaddam would blame his friend.

The Count removed his gilded hat and bowed before the magnificent quartz throne, taking a formal approach, since the Emperor had chosen this ostentatious setting. The gilded hat, a gift from his wife, was of an antiquated cavalier style, black with a silver band, which she said made him look like a dashing historic figure.

Shaddam let out a long sigh. "Duke Leto came here, and we granted him our favor. He came here explicitly seeking to improve and empower his House. Why would he make such a request if he's not willing to accept an offer to do exactly that?" It seemed a rhetorical question. "He must know that there are costs to advancement. Why did he waste my time?" Fenring noticed that the Emperor's gold-trimmed white robe did not look as crisp as usual.

Nearby, Mohiam registered every word in her mind. She served as more than a Truthsayer, but also an adviser, someone who could whisper schemes in his ear, or unravel them. Fenring did not like to be the subject of her scrutiny, and he knew that everything she witnessed would also be reported to the Bene Gesserit order.

"Ahhh, he wasted my time as well, Sire," Fenring said, threading his fingers together in front of him. "I expended a significant amount of time and influence to make him a potential protégé. I expected him to be, ahhhh, more flexible. And more malleable." His close-set eyes shone, and he changed the tone of his voice. "But it was not a useless effort. Leto Atreides is a fascinating and contradictory man with an inconvenient conscience. He does indeed wish to advance himself and his House, ahhh, but only on his terms."

Shaddam's cold eyes flashed. "On *his* terms? I cannot have every nobleman setting his own terms! Leto might cause them to question too much. Then I would no longer be Emperor."

"You're right, Sire."

"Now, however frustrating it may be at times, Leto's core of honor makes him predictable and reliable. He did save my life at Otorio, and yours as well, and I am deeply grateful for that. But his moral straitjacket makes him look too independent in the eyes of others. Doesn't he realize that I am the one to set the rules?"

"I'm sure he does."

"I wonder." Shaddam drummed his fingertips on the arm of his crystal throne. "When nobles pay me the spice surtax, it is as much to prove their fealty as to fill Imperial coffers. They all understand that. It is not a matter for negotiation. That's why I intend to make a grand public demonstration soon, to show everyone how the people, and especially my nobles, have jointly contributed to the betterment of the Imperium. Maybe Leto should be there . . ."

Fenring frowned. He had never been convinced the heavy burden of the surtax was the best way to pay for the damage done on Otorio, and it had only agitated the Landsraad. Upon the Count's return from Arrakis, Shaddam had giddily told him of his new plan to make some kind of procession to flaunt all the tax income. The Emperor was enchanted with his idea, but to Fenring, the plan seemed tone-deaf, more of a provocation than a celebration, but the Emperor would not be convinced otherwise. Fenring had known him much of his life, and he understood which subjects he could push, and when.

For now, he hoped for a different consideration regarding Duke Atreides. "Hmmm-ah, many important things are subject to negotiation, Sire. Sometimes it is easier to get what you want if you let the other party feel satisfied as well. Our own friendship, yours and mine, is a result of a lifetime of subtle negotiations and concessions." He paced at the base of the throne dais, pondering. "I am not willing to give up on the Duke of Caladan yet. Perhaps I can make this right with him. He has no interest in spice or the surtax, but what makes him tick? Maybe I can find a way to obligate him, yet stay within his terms."

It was the right thing to say, to remind the Emperor of their friendship. He was rewarded with a thin smile, and the disappointed expression eased. "So, in addition to everything else you do for me, you are my Imperial philosopher? Philosophize and negotiate all you want, Hasimir, but remember there is a time for the knife as well."

Fenring bowed, smiling craftily. "I might have to use it against this Atreides Duke, but first I hope to gather more information. And that, ahhhh, may require me to visit his holdings, see Leto in his own element." He locked gazes with the Emperor. "It is the best way to understand what he's up to."

"Yes, study him closely. At times Leto can be an enigma, and I do not trust a man I don't understand." Shaddam nodded, obviously intrigued. "I'm not sure I believe in my cousin's stalwart nature and his utter adherence to honor. It seems like hubris to me. He likes to appear more pure than others." He ran his palm over his slicked reddish hair. "I am starting to suspect that it's all for show. What if he really sympathizes with the Noble Commonwealth."

Since Jaxson Aru's terrorist strike on Otorio, the Emperor attributed every slight to the rebellion, although many in the Landsraad had disapproved of various actions and decisions throughout Shaddam's entire reign. Fenring had not personally seen any compelling evidence against Viscount Tull on Elegy, or Lord Rajiv Londine (despite his outspoken criticisms of the throne), or even the recently obliterated Duke Fausto Verdun.

Certainly not Leto Atreides.

"Hmmm, I believe the Duke of Caladan has more depth and complexity than people give him credit for. Atreides honor is no mere affectation, not for Leto, nor for his predecessors."

The Emperor snorted. "If he is so wise and deep, then why does he have only one planet? Why did he surrender the wealth of House Kolona, an act that did not benefit him at all? No one asked him to do that. And why did he turn down a marriage alliance with House Londine? Is he truly just a naïve fool, or is he up to something?" He drummed his fingers on the crystal armrest again. "Yes, Hasimir, I need you to find out what is happening on Caladan. Continue to observe Leto Atreides, learn what you can—build him up and make him an ally, or we will have to take other actions. I must be certain of those around me!"

Fenring had many of the same questions, though he was convinced that Leto Atreides saw himself as a heroic figure, building his own legacy. The Duke just needed guidance in the reality of Imperial politics so he could work around the limitations of his intrusive conscience.

"Very well, I will go to Caladan, Sire. I'll spend time with the Duke on his home planet, learn his interests and weaknesses, and strengthen the bond we had begun to form. In fact, I already suggested that I might like to invest in his moonfish operations. While there, I can turn over a few stones and see what crawls out." He would follow his gut instincts. They had always served him well.

Shifting on his throne, the Emperor said, "Your insights are as sharp as razors, Hasimir." He leaned forward. "What do you sense in me?"

Fenring rocked back on his heels, giving himself a moment. "You are a dangerous person, Sire, as am I. But we are the closest of allies, with common interests. And we are friends." He did not want Shaddam to get off track, though. "And if we can bring this Atreides Duke into our circle and make him share our goals, it could realign the power structure in the Imperium and greatly strengthen you."

The Emperor scoffed. "Duke Leto Atreides? Ruler of one world that's mostly oceans? You set your sights too low, my friend."

"Leto is well admired in the Landsraad, known to be a man of his word. I have heard him speak of the traditions of the Imperium and the strength of past Corrino Emperors. He is not the sort of man to join this rebellion, no matter his independent nature."

Mohiam surprised them by speaking up. "He saved my life as well. The Bene Gesserit have had a Sister at his side for many years, but we recently withdrew her to Wallach IX for other obligations." Her wrinkled lips drew together. "Leto rebuffed my initial offer to send another concubine to keep him company, so at present, we do not have eyes on Caladan. The Sisterhood may have to try harder."

Shaddam chuckled. "It seems he is not Baron Molay, to jump at any fresh concubine you dangle in front of him."

The Truthsayer seemed offended. "We Bene Gesserit have skills and experience in selecting a proper companion. We would have given the Duke a new partner fully suitable to his needs and tastes, but he brushed the idea aside. We will try again."

Fenring listened with great interest, although he already knew what had happened with Leto and his lady, Jessica. "Perhaps, hmmm, you chose too well in the first place?"

Anyone who crosses paths with me runs the risk of being killed. Displease me, and the odds are high that you will not survive.

—BEAST RABBAN

After receiving his uncle's challenge, Glossu Rabban departed from Giedi Prime and went to his own primary holding on Lankiveil. His home-world . . . which he loathed. Piter de Vries accompanied him.

Rabban stood on the frosty terrace of his dacha at the mouth of one of the deepest, coldest fjords. He left his thick coat open at the front, and the bracing air energized his senses. He liked to test his physical limits, from a frigid place like this to the desert heat of Arrakis. It was all about survival, and he was good at it.

He glanced at his chronometer, annoyed that his smuggling contact from Caladan was late. De Vries had arranged the meeting, but the twisted Mentat was busy with final preparations at the coastal laboratory. Rabban decided to receive the contact alone, and set him up with the plan to ruin House Atreides.

Though he ruled this secondary Harkonnen holding, Rabban had unpleasant memories of the time he had spent here in his youth. He despised his parents, especially his worm of a father, Abulurd, who had renounced the Harkonnen name and all rights to the title. Both of them were dead now, thankfully. Under his administration, the Lankiveil whale-fur operations and fishing industry had become commercially successful. Still, he didn't like to be here.

As he waited for the arrival of Lupar, an important drug merchant, he squeezed his cold fingers into fists. Rabban refused to accept excuses for tardiness or other forms of failure. He gazed up at the gray cloud-encased sky, then out to the stone-colored waters of the fjord. It wasn't mating season for the fur whales that roamed the seas, but they could still be hunted for sport.

And he was stuck here, waiting for the man from Caladan. But Piter de Vries insisted he was necessary for the plan. "The delivery system, Rabban," the Mentat had said. "The delivery system."

Once they implemented the scheme to wreak havoc on the Atreides moon-fish industry, Rabban would feel very satisfied. He was Count of Lankiveil, but that was only a stepping-stone to something greater. *I am a Harkonnen, the Bar-*

on's oldest nephew. I intend to claim the title that is rightfully mine. With Piter's secret assistance, he would prove himself the best choice to become the na-Baron.

I am not stupid, as my uncle will see. The Baron had deprecating names for him, but he knew his nephew was not lacking in imagination or abilities. His insults were meant to motivate Rabban. It was irritating as well as crafty, and this complex, ambitious plan would prove his worth. The Baron would never expect a scheme of such depth.

If only that smuggler would get here!

Finally, a suspensor-boat skimmed toward him from the orbital landing field. The boat glided in and docked at the private jetty below the dacha. A small, silver-haired man stepped out onto the dock and hurried up the frost-covered stairs to the terrace. Lupar was a merchant who moved the Caladan drug on the Atreides world as well as out among the Imperium, but he moved more like a beetle than a businessman.

Folding his arms across his chest, Rabban didn't move toward the man at all, and made Lupar cross the terrace. Despite the frosty air, Lupar was sweating profusely. "I apologize for my tardiness, my Lord Rabban. The shuttle from orbit was delayed by turbulence in the atmosphere."

I am Beast Rabban. I could kill you in an instant, and you know it. "I only know that you are late, and my time is valuable."

Pale and nervous, Lupar bowed. "I will make it up to you in carrying out your wishes. By way of apology, I have also brought the first load of new ailar from Caladan, for your own private use or disposition. I have a special contact in the new fields. That should please you."

Rabban grumbled, refusing to accept the apology, but he knew the value of the Caladan drug was significant, and he had ways to sell the ailar through his own connections . . . maybe even give some to Piter de Vries, to acknowledge the twisted Mentat's help in the intricate planning. His thick lips formed a smile, and Lupar relaxed.

"And does Duke Leto Atreides grow and distribute this Caladan drug himself?" Rabban asked. "He pretends to be charming while picking peoples' pockets."

Lupar's head snapped up, mussing his neat silver hair. "The Duke producing ailar? By the wind and sea, he is the greatest thorn in our sides! A fool who refuses to let his own people soothe their misery with ailar! He hates the drug. He burned all the barra fern fields, practically incited a civil war." Lupar's face darkened.

Rabban's smile widened as he imagined the unrest on Caladan. "But you managed to bring a shipment here anyway?"

The smuggler spoke rapidly. "The operations recovered. New fern fields have been planted, and a fresh harvest just took place. I made sure you got some of the first batch, my Lord. Before long, we will be back to normal levels of drug distribution."

Rabban exhaled cold, curling plumes of vapor. "I'm pleased that this black market harms the Atreides, but I brought you here to help me on something far more destructive. I want to ruin the Duke of Caladan. We will devastate the Atreides financially, make them beggars among the Landsraad." He chuckled to himself. Piter had described each detail to him and enumerated the consequences.

The smuggler nodded, though he looked uneasy. "How can I help?"

"You can make a delivery for me. If you are already working ailar customers among the Caladan fisheries, you can easily introduce something new."

Lupar blinked in confusion. "A new drug, m'Lord?"

"No, simpler than that. I want you to empty sample vials into the canals and holding pools wherever you go. Nature will take care of the rest." Rabban turned, gestured impatiently. "Follow me."

He crossed the terrace to an icy stone path that led to a separate building behind the dacha. The outbuilding looked like a rustic wood-paneled guest cottage with a sloped roof, but it housed his secure laboratory. Both of them had to pass through a perimeter field and then secure doors to reach a clean, well-lit interior with sealed brick walls. "We have been gathering samples from the isolated mountain tarns, and we chose a very nasty native specimen. You'll bring it to Caladan."

Inside, several pale, hard-bitten workers busied themselves at a polished metal table near tanks and cylinders filled with murky water. They wore gloves and polymer aprons as they drew fluid from the tanks and transferred it to transparent vials. Working with great care as if handling explosives, the laborers sealed the vials. They glanced up nervously as Rabban arrived, then turned back to work even harder.

Piter de Vries, the Harkonnen Mentat, pranced among them, supervising while also interfering. Like lashing a whip, he waved a hand at Rabban and Lupar as they entered. "Ah, our delivery system—the key to implementing this beautifully simple destruction of an entire industry."

"It's a nice plan," Rabban said. "Everyone will think so."

He marched across the floor to a large aquarium on a rack of shelves against the wall. Inside the tank were four large fish with coppery scales and a drumhead membrane above their bulging eyes. Two fish swam aimlessly, mouths agape, gills pumping. They were obviously dying. The other two already floated belly-up.

Rabban placed his hands on his hips. "Excellent progress." The workers looked up but seemed to fear the compliment.

Lupar came forward, curious. "Those are moonfish from Caladan."

Piter was there, jittery but smiling. "Yes, and they will be wiped out. One simple step." He glanced up at Rabban and added quickly, "One very complicated plan." The Mentat led Rabban and the smuggler to the packaged vials. "In Lankiveil's harsh tundra tarns lives a particularly pernicious mite, you see. When the mite gets into free water, it spreads rapidly and wipes out any fish it encounters. Many of the mountain lakes are dead."

Lupar leaned close to the aquarium, saw the suffering moonfish. "It also kills the Caladan species?"

"Look in the tank!" Rabban said. "The mites particularly like moonfish."

Piter lifted the small rack. "Each of these sample vials contains the Lankiveil mite. When you go to the Atreides moonfish operations, empty a vial into the fishery ponds. Go to as many of them as you can. The mites will spread and take care of everything else."

"This is going to be good," Rabban said. "They won't be able to stop it."

The smuggler picked up one of the small, sealed vials on the table. "You want me to introduce an invasive species into the waters of Caladan?"

"That is why I'm paying you so much. It should wipe out the moonfish industry in a week!" Despite the chill inside the laboratory building, Rabban felt warm with excitement. His uncle would be impressed when everything started to unravel on Caladan.

Lupar replaced the vial into the small rack and wiped his hand on his trousers. He glanced around at the fidgety workers, who wore thick gloves and turned to the twisted Mentat. "Is it dangerous to humans?"

"Not very," Piter said.

Rabban directed the workers to package the rest of the samples so the smuggler could take them. "No one here has died, yet."

Lupar seemed reluctant to accept the package until Rabban glared at him. Then he swallowed, bowed, and stashed the vials in the folds of his bulky jacket.

"I will do as you ask, m'Lord Rabban. And I hope this translates into a continuing lucrative arrangement for the distribution of ailar offworld. I can arrange to sell you more. Perhaps the people of Lankiveil might become a new market?"

Rabban considered, and beside him, Piter seemed to be running through calculations in his mind. "They certainly have wretched enough lives," Rabban said. "That makes them a good market." He himself had been miserable here as a young man, embarrassed by his worthless parents. He was eager to return to Arrakis on the next outbound Heighliner.

"First, we have to make our mark on House Atreides."

The only true loyalty I've experienced is in my animals. They do not know how to be deceitful.

—CHOAM Ur-Director MALINA ARU

The two young spinehounds whined on the deck of the small transport ship. Smoke and thermals buffeted the craft during its descent to Harko City, but Malina's CHOAM pilot deftly stabilized them and glided toward the industrial buildings, smokestacks, and hazard beacons.

"Send a message to Harkonnen headquarters," Malina said. "Inform Feyd-Rautha that I have a gift for him. Have him meet me at the private landing zone." She peered out at the grimy city. "I do not intend to stay long."

Keeping her balance against the vibrating descent, Malina knelt near the two young spinehounds in their anchored cages. The animals made her miss Har and Kar, who were waiting for her back at the Tupile residence. With accelerated growth, these two specimens were more than pups, young and sleek, made of coiled muscles. Their sharp ears were pointed like knives, their muzzles long and narrow, and their needlelike fur was swirled and spotted with dark colors, whereas her own pets looked like burnished metal. Their eyes were a reddish gold that made her think of molten copper.

Upon delivering the two creatures to her in the station above Tleilax, Master Arafa had assured her that the animals were from the same genetic stock as her own pets, though with some cellular variances. These young males, as yet unnamed because that would be the purview of their new owner, were skittish during the flight, startled by every noise. Though in separate cages, they pressed against the adjoining bars, taking comfort in nearness to each other. Malina extended her hand to let them sniff her, but the animals responded like spring-loaded weapons, cringing back but ready to rip her to pieces.

Har and Kar would never act like this to her. Her animals had her personal scent and blood keyed to them, but these two had not yet been bonded to a master. She sat back on her bench and smiled from a safe distance as the spinehounds continued to glare at her with feral fire in their eyes.

She said to them in a soothing voice, "From what the Baron has told me, Feyd-Rautha will like you very much."

The aloof young Harkonnen met her as soon as the transport ship set down in the private landing hub. He was joined by an entourage of guards who kept a respectful distance, but he allowed one attendant at his side, a well-built man with a mop of dark hair on top of his head and shaved temples. A tattered brown cape half covered a sword.

Feyd-Rautha sauntered up to meet her. She remembered him from her previous visit to Giedi Prime, when the Baron had presented his proposal for an ultrasecret spice-distribution channel. Feyd had struck her as moody, even surly, although his uncle claimed to have high hopes for the young man. What she remembered most was how he'd been fascinated with Har and Kar.

Feyd raised his chin. "I've never been visited by the CHOAM Ur-Director before. The message said you have a gift?" He glanced at his bodyguard, who remained stock-still, his hand resting on the sword hilt. "It must be impressive."

She gave him a smile of anticipation now. "You'll have to judge for yourself. I chose this with you in mind."

Feyd crossed his arms over his chest. "Why?"

Malina saw he was trying to be provocative, as if he wanted to test her reactions. Compared to her, this boy was a rank amateur at such manipulative games. "Your uncle is an important business ally of mine. Any goodwill I earn from this gesture will be well worth the expense."

Feyd was suspicious, but eager, though he tried not to show it. Malina called back into the transport, "Bring out the cages."

Two CHOAM attendants used suspensors and safeguarded poles to carry the cages down the ramp and set the animals in front of a delighted Feyd-Rautha. "They're just like your spinehounds! Only more magnificent."

Malina hardened her expression, but let him have his joy. "They are unique animals, specially bred for you from rare genetic stock."

With wide eyes, Feyd bent close to the cages. "Wonderful!" The beasts snapped and snarled, but that did not seem to intimidate him. He looked up at her. "Yours were so tame."

Malina shook her head. "Not tame—*controlled*." She removed a metal disc from the pocket of her business jacket and placed it on the side of the cage. "A sonic imprinter. Complete the process properly, and they are yours forever." She activated the device, and a low hum vibrated through the air and resonated with the bars of the cages. The young spinehounds shifted uneasily, but the tone swiftly put them into a faint hypnotic state.

"Both are now imprintable." Malina reached forward. "Give me your hand."

Focused on the animals, Feyd extended his left hand without giving it a thought. Malina grabbed his fingers and slashed his palm with a sharp knife in her other hand. The young man yelped, and the bodyguard—a Swordmaster?—lunged in, ready to defend him.

Feyd waved him away, though, and stared down at the blood welling up in his hand. The red liquid seemed to fascinate him. "Why did you do that?"

"It is part of the process. You need to be blood-bonded." She released him, and he turned his hand to watch the scarlet droplets drip down. "Now, let the two spinehounds taste your blood."

Feyd reached toward the first cage. The suspicious beast sniffed the blood, then licked as the sonic imprinter continued to thrum. The young man flexed and squeezed his hand, made more blood ooze from the wound, and then moved to the second cage.

As the other spinehound licked at the gash, though, a lumbering cargo ship roared over the Harko City hub, overwhelming the thrumming sound. Proximity alarms and landing horns blatted out a deafening blast as the imprinter device continued to throb. Feyd yanked back his hand, looked at the cut.

Malina smiled and nodded, remembering when she had done the same thing for Har and Kar. "They have your blood in them now. The spinehounds are part of you. You own them, and they will be utterly obedient. Command them, train with them." She smiled. "Do with them as you wish. I will leave the detailed instructions that the Tleilaxu provided."

"My spinehounds," Feyd said. He touched the cages, and the two animals were utterly calm in his presence.

The brain is a powerful organ with tremendous untapped capabilities. It is the core of each human being, yet remains as mysterious as a distant cosmic realm. Doctors, psychologists, and researchers have barely begun to tap into its potential.

—A teaching of the Suk School

I solated, deprived, alone. *Emptiness is a punishment.*

But I am not empty.

Jessica floated supine on a suspensor mechanism in her solitary confinement cell. Earlier that morning, her jailers had placed her in the field and injected drugs that sent her into a trance, depriving her of sensory impulses. She knew what they were trying to do, understood the manipulation techniques, and she applied her analytical mind. They were punishing her, softening her.

With her intense training on how to control her metabolism and her biochemistry, she could detect and resist some poisons, some drugs, but not a deluge of them. A Reverend Mother might be able to resist and convert all these chemicals pouring into her body, but it was beyond Jessica's abilities.

Still, she was not defenseless. While the drugs were being administered and the suspensor placed her in a hellish limbo, Jessica had prepared herself, using the Sisterhood's techniques against them. She took quick breaths and performed precise muscular exercises, seeking the relaxed poise and perfect balance of prana-bindu suspension. She visualized herself in the flow of time and reminded herself, "My mind controls my reality." Years ago, Reverend Mother Mohiam had taught her to do that in this very school.

Now her best defense against the Bene Gesserit was to *be* a Bene Gesserit. Surely they knew her abilities, but maybe they could not be certain how well she had maintained her skills in the years since leaving Wallach IX. Jessica was stronger now, more independent, more confident—and she had more at stake. Just teaching Paul some of these techniques had honed her own abilities.

No, she was not defenseless.

When training her son in prana and bindu, the fiber and the nerve, the unspoken competition had strengthened both mother and son. While she was away from Caladan, she hoped Paul was still working on his skills. And now, by herself, she had to call on everything she knew.

Emptiness is a punishment.

As she hovered in the void of her own self, detached from the universe, Jessica felt two competing Bene Gesserit energies working at her—internal and external—pushing in opposite directions. She wrestled with them and finally reached a stasis-point, so each system operated, but neither dominated.

She reached a semiconscious state on her own terms, and only partially what her jailers sought. She was much more aware of her surroundings than they wanted her to be, hyperalert to even the smallest detail, even if she couldn't resist and alter the flow of drugs. In a personal limbo, she stared upward, not moving her eyes, and focused on the rock ceiling of her cell, identifying the tiniest blemishes in the natural stone. Dancing around that reality, she saw black-robed Sisters and white-robed Acolytes, shouting at her, scolding her, threatening her. But they hardly penetrated. She didn't even know if they were real.

Jessica tried to hold on against the onslaught, wasn't sure how successful she was, because she felt herself slipping, slipping away to another place. She went into a halcyon vision, one in which she was free, on Caladan with her family. Leto and Paul were smiling at her, and she felt no disharmony. She clung to that sweet memory, that wish. And she endured.

Emptiness is strength. Emptiness is a shield.

After an endless instant, Jessica found herself lying on her simple hard pallet. The suspensor mechanism was gone, as were the drug infusers, and her own state of self-induced reverie.

A voice spoke, close to her. "Sister Jessica." A *male* voice.

Startled, she opened her eyes. Her reality and her surroundings rushed back around her like a winter avalanche. She blinked, breathed, and looked up to see a handsome young man standing beside her bed with a tray of food.

"You haven't eaten in two days. The Sisters told me to bring your evening meal." He set the tray on her small table, which he pulled closer to the bedside. He was a blond-haired teenager, a year or two older than Paul, and moved with poise and grace like a dancer. He gave her a shy smile. "I am Brom."

Jessica sat up, wary now, wondering what the Sisterhood intended by sending the young man here. Xora's son. As she studied his features, she detected hints of the other Sister in the shape of the face, the eyes, and the chin. Xora herself said that she had barely seen the young man after he was born. Brom had no idea who he was . . . but Jessica did.

A million questions rushed through her mind, but she didn't speak them. Others were surely listening.

Brom removed a covering from a plate to display a sandwich roll stuffed with white cheese, bright green leaves, and sliced vegetables. Realizing how hungry she was, she picked up the meal, but controlled herself.

Brom stood politely aside. She needed information, wanted to keep him here. "Tell me about yourself. I have not seen you before."

As she ate, he explained, "I live in the men's compound, performing whatever services the Sisters call upon us to do. Not much else to tell. I've never been allowed to leave Wallach IX." He stepped toward the door of her cell. "Now I have to attend to my other duties."

"Will you come see me again, Brom?"

"If that is what the Sisters ask me to do."

He walked away in a graceful, poised manner as if he had been trained in athletics and balance. She sensed something eerie about him.

After he sealed the cell door, leaving her isolated again, Jessica let it sink in. *Mother Superior sent him here as a message. Are they showing me they have their own potential Kwisatz Haderach already? To point out they can get rid of me, and Paul?*

REVEREND MOTHER RUTHINE grew increasingly agitated at Lethea's prescient warnings, about Jessica and her son.

Shortly before noon, she hurried through a third-floor corridor, ready to seize an opportunity but also knowing that she didn't have much time. Sister Jiara had dismissed her assistants for their communal lunch, and this was Ruthine's chance to get answers of her own . . . answers that Harishka apparently didn't want to hear.

As Ruthine rushed forward, the younger Jiara saw her coming and deactivated the monitoring devices. Giving the Reverend Mother a knowing smile, she turned off the surveillance cameras on this level and inserted old recorded footage, then gave a quick acknowledgment. No one would see Ruthine slip into Lethea's medical chamber.

Ruthine drew a deep breath and reminded herself of why she was here. The Mother Superior needed her wise advice, and therefore Ruthine needed to collect vital, objective information from the former Kwisatz Mother—*if* she could wrest answers from the fragmented and irrational crone. She already knew how she would justify herself to Harishka, if necessary. Sometimes, considering all the options, the truth was the best defense.

Jiara stood at the sealed door. "This is dangerous. Are you certain?"

"I can be dangerous, too. I don't trust the answers Lethea gave Jessica, and we need the whole story. The Mother Superior needs to know." She braced herself. "The Sisterhood needs to know, and I will take the risk. Guard the door, and . . . be ready."

Jiara allowed her companion into the rank-smelling room. Ruthine glided inside, her muscles tense as spring wires, her mind hyperalert and ready to defend herself against whatever the dying Kwisatz Mother intended to do.

"Reverend Mother Ruthine," Lethea said, though she lay on the bed under restraint, staring at the ceiling. "I've been expecting you."

She was taken aback. "You knew I was coming?"

"I have seen you look at me through the observation plaz with the most sympathetic expression. I thought you might actually be brave enough."

"I am," Ruthine said, "because I need to know what you are doing. What are these fears that plague you? What are the dangers posed by Jessica and her son? I would hear the reasons from your own lips . . . and only then can I decide what I must do."

Lethea cackled. "Are you here to release my restraints and let me go?" She struggled against the bindings, but could not break free.

"No, I am here to talk with you. Objectively." She glanced back at the plaz wall, knew Jiara was out there. "The recorders are off. No one is watching. It's just you and me—so you can say what you need to say. What do you *see*?"

Lethea struggled to sit up, fighting against her restraints. "How nice, just two girls talking. Shall we order tea and sweets?"

Ruthine smiled, something she did not often do. "I'd like to help you, provided you explain to me. What is your deepest concern? How would you resolve the matter? Is Jessica's son the Kwisatz Haderach?"

Lethea's cloudy eyes suddenly grew brighter, and she sounded lucid for a change. "He could be. I have seen Atreides banners flying above a wave of bloodshed. I have seen the Sisterhood crippled, diminished . . . for centuries. I have seen . . . a little mouse, and a giant worm." Ruthine backed away, seeing the other woman's thoughts broken, nonsensical. "Harishka refuses to take the obvious course of action. She sees too many possibilities, but she doesn't *see*. She should know what she has to do."

Ruthine knew what she meant, but she spoke the words anyway. "To kill Jessica and Paul?"

"You speak so easily of killing! Of killing so easily . . ." Lethea chuckled at her wordplay. "Paul Atreides is only fourteen."

Ruthine's brow furrowed. "Does that mean we should watch him closely and give him a chance . . . or should we take a chance now and eliminate him before he causes irreparable harm?"

"Chance! A chance . . . If I am wrong, then two will die. If I am right, then *billions* will perish!" Lethea seemed to fold back into her wrinkles. "What answer do you want? What answer do *I* want? What answer does the Sisterhood deserve?" She began to cough uncontrollably, barely choked out the words. "After what they've done."

Ruthine listened, flicking her eyes back and forth, knowing her time was short. What did old Lethea mean? Should she go tell Mother Superior Harishka? But what could she say? What *should* she tell her?

She came to an important realization that old Lethea was not the crazy, irrational one. Perhaps it was Harishka for blinding herself to the terrible threat.

If I am wrong, then two will die. If I am right, then billions *will perish!*

"I'm here without the Mother Superior's permission," Ruthine said, stepping closer to the restrained woman. She touched the gnarled hand. "I will see that it's taken care of."

Lethea's rheumy eyes brightened. "So you will cast the die? Or is it a wrecking ball?"

The old crone closed her eyes and fell back into herself, weariness and unspeakable age folding into wrinkles and weakness—still alive, but no longer present. Ruthine immediately sensed the change. The medical readings also shifted.

Jiara came running in. "What happened? What did you say to her?"

"It's what she said to me," Ruthine answered, wrestling with decisions.

Sweating now, moving with quick urgency, Jiara checked the readouts on the equipment, then touched Lethea's forehead, checked her eyes, felt the pulse on her neck. "She is in a coma."

"It's what she wanted." Ruthine moved toward the door. "I was never here."

There are certain watershed moments in the life of a young noble as he grows into the responsibilities of his birth. Muad'Dib himself had to be strong enough to overcome the depths of his despair.

—PRINCESS IRULAN, *Manual of Muad'Dib*

At local dawn—though he had become accustomed to Kaitain time—Duke Leto stepped off the shuttle in the Cala City Spaceport. He adjusted to the familiar gravity, the cool dampness in the air, the vibrancy of *home*. The rest of his entourage would disembark soon with all the pomp and paraphernalia from the Imperial capital, but Leto had no patience for all that. Gurney Halleck and Duncan Idaho would manage the full disembarkation and unloading.

He strode down the ramp, looking around the crowds that had gathered. He drank in the familiar scenery, the Cala City Spaceport, the town streets, the road leading up to the castle on the high cliffs above the sea. He smiled. He just wanted to see his son.

In the past, when he came home from necessary business offworld, Jessica had always come to greet him, dutifully debriefing the Duke on what had occurred in his absence. Now, she wasn't there.

His gaze locked on the black-haired young man who stood wearing a formal green-and-black Atreides jacket with the hawk crest on the lapel. The jacket looked a little too large for him, but it matched the one Leto wore. The reunion was formal enough, as Paul seemed so serious in his role acting as Duke in his father's absence, but he seemed to be fighting back a grin. "It's good to be home, Paul."

"Yes, sir. I'm glad to have you back." The boy's voice sounded stiff. "I managed as best I could while you were gone."

Cracks showed in his own formality, and Leto was the one who stepped toward Paul and scooped him up in a hug. "I'm certain you did a fine job." His son appeared to be both grateful and sad. Leto drew in a deep breath, let it out in a contented sigh. "It'll be good to go back to a normal life."

A NORMAL LIFE. The words sent a flash of pain through Paul, because he knew this was not a normal life, not with Jessica far away. As they returned to the castle in a blur of businesslike greetings and quick conversations, Paul acutely felt his mother's absence. He wished he knew what had torn them apart, why she'd gone away.

When they finally arrived at the weatherworn stone edifice that had been the home of House Atreides for many generations, Paul's father led him into the main courtyard gardens inside the tall gate, where they could relax and be alone. Leto seemed to be drinking in the atmosphere like a plant absorbing fresh rain after a drought. In the shade of a great tree, they paused at one of the smaller sparkling fountains.

Leto turned to him, and his gray eyes contained a universe of emotion and experience. "I know the task I left with you wasn't easy, but I'm confident you will be a fine Duke someday." He looked down at the signet ring on his own hand.

Paul felt both proud and embarrassed. "I appreciate that, Father."

Looking at him again, Leto leaned back and smiled. "I do believe you've grown in my absence. I've been expecting a growth spurt."

"If not in stature, then I hope I've grown in other ways. You were gone only a month, but we did so much." He would judiciously not tell his father about the tavern brawl he and Gurney had barely escaped.

The Duke nodded and looked as if he wanted to say something more, but didn't know how. Paul loved his father and knew the man often had trouble expressing warm emotions, while Jessica had been more open. But Paul could feel his father's palpable pride in him, and he was thankful for it.

Leto looked away to the sparkling water of the fountain. A trio of sea sparrows clung precariously to the edge of the bowl and bent down to drink from it. Finally, his father said, "You haven't asked me about your mother."

Paul felt a lump in his throat. "I—I didn't think it was my place to ask about her. I haven't received any message, any word at all from her. But I assumed you would tell me."

As they watched, the sparrows flew away.

Leto looked up at the sky and finally explained what Paul had wanted to know for so long. "You're aware that your mother was helping screen betrothal candidates for you. She and Thufir studied possibilities, vetted them, made their recommendations to me."

Paul nodded. "Like Junu Verdun."

Leto's expression darkened. "Yes, the Verdun girl and others. But I discovered that your mother had secretly altered the list on orders from the Bene Gesserit witches. She tried to hide it from me."

Paul remembered finding his mother in the Duke's office, doing something with the dossier of names. "Why would she do that? You would have listened if she'd just told you."

"I cannot explain her actions, son. I asked whether her true loyalty lay with me, with us, or with the Bene Gesserit. I . . . I wanted her to stay, but when the witches pulled her puppet strings and ordered her back to the Mother School, she left. I've thought about it until my head and my heart were ready to explode."

Paul was acutely aware that his mother was not there to defend herself, or to explain. "I know she was thinking about my welfare and my future."

Leto shook his head. "No, this wasn't done for your benefit, Paul. As I said, she was following commands from the Sisterhood. When I confronted her with it, she did not deny what she was trying to do . . . or where her loyalties truly are." The weight and bitterness was plain in his words.

Paul didn't know what to say. His mother must have had some reason, but she hadn't voiced it to him, or to his father. Would she really have chosen the Sisterhood over the man she had been with for so many years? Over her own son?

Leto closed his eyes, trapped in the situation and unable to solve it. He held his emotions inside with a visible effort. "She did show me, though, that I must keep the interests of House Atreides foremost in my mind." He forced the words out in a wooden voice. "As the head of a Great House of the Landsraad, I cannot be sidetracked by the loss of a . . . mere concubine."

A mere concubine.

The three words did not describe his mother. Not even close.

Paul's feelings were raw. As the heir of House Atreides, he had to live in a web of rules and connections. "Don't I have a say in it? No one asked me."

Leto smiled ruefully. "Oh? Now I have two of you to contend with?"

"Father, I must respect your final judgment in the matter, but . . . can't you contact Wallach IX? Maybe if we had a chance to talk to her? We all make mistakes."

Leto walked to the fountain, dipped his hands in the water, and swirled them as if to wash away his concerns. He stared at the sparkling spray of water, then straightening, he shook the water from his hands and brushed them on his jacket. "What's done is done. It is you and me, Paul. And Caladan."

Paul felt stunned. It sounded so final. He refused to cry, and had always tried to model himself after his father. But now a gaping hole had opened up in his life.

I hear your public denials, I see the stance you feel forced to take, but I know what is in your hearts. I know you agree with our cause. Perhaps I understand you better than you will admit to yourself.

—JAXSON ARU, open letter to CHOAM (censored)

When he traveled to Kaitain, Jaxson knew he was entering the lion's den—the golden Corrino lion. For him, this was the most dangerous place in the Imperium, yet he reveled in it.

He had no doubt that he was completely safe. His confidence might look like arrogance, but he knew the Emperor was even more arrogant. The skittish and paranoid Shaddam would never dream that his greatest enemy might voluntarily come here. Jaxson's boldness was as effective a disguise as his facial cloning.

Arriving at the Silver Needle, he flowed in with the daily bureaucratic traffic. The bustling corporate headquarters was filled with countless administrators, delegates, trade ministers, commercial negotiators, patent experts, accountants, inventory specialists, and Spacing Guild ambassadors. Many of the clerks were Mentats, able to provide complex insights on galactic trade.

Jaxson knew that a Noble Commonwealth of free, independent planets would create the biggest economic boom in human history, but first the main impediment had to be removed. House Corrino.

Jaxson had spent weeks with his sister on Pliesse and had found her company refreshing. Jalma was much more like he was than he had expected. While Jaxson's siblings had been raised by their mother and destined for great things, he himself had always felt left out—the black sheep of the family, rather than a golden child.

During the recent weeks serving as Jalma's temporary majordomo, he learned the depth of her plans. She had locked down her rule of House Uchan and also supported the Noble Commonwealth movement. When he pressed her, she agreed with Jaxson that the movement's pace over the past century was too slow, too passive. Many of Malina Aru's supporters felt the same way, although they remained in lockstep with her slow dabbling. When he left Pliesse, Jaxson felt optimistic and energized that maybe they could change the timetable.

Now if he could only convince his brother, Frankos.

The CHOAM President was fifteen years older than Jaxson, much more closely aligned with their mother, and he had more to lose. Frankos had always known that his role was a mere public face, an avatar for the true workings of the great company. Now it was time for Jaxson to see what his brother really thought.

Since he held the position as Jalma's majordomo, in name at least, he traveled with proper CHOAM credentials and House Uchan papers. He wore a conservative Pliesse jacket and slacks. His curly, dark hair had been trimmed tight and short so that he looked less like himself or their father.

The base of the Silver Needle was a hive of activity, and he moved through the crowded lobby level. Security increased as he worked his way higher, one level after another, and his formal access could only take him so far.

Jaxson reserved a private chamber ostensibly for reviewing classified commercial documents, claiming he needed to work on sensitive hederwood export data. None of the CHOAM guards gave him a second thought.

Once alone, he used the confidential access code his sister had given him and sent a direct message to the CHOAM President. When his brother appeared on the secure comm screen, his neat dark hair had more threads of silver than Jaxson had remembered, but his tanned skin was smooth and tight, likely from melange consumption. Frankos narrowed his blue-gray eyes and scrutinized this stranger who had used Jalma's exclusive code. "You say you're Jalma's new majordomo, but you look . . ." He couldn't find the words.

"I need to see you, brother," Jaxson said. "Alone, obviously."

Startled, the CHOAM President leaned closer to the screen, making his image very large. His response was like the slash of a serrated knife. "I should seal you in that room and gas you to death! That would earn us the Emperor's gratitude, and then CHOAM could do our own work more effectively." He paused, and his expression remained stony. "Convince me that isn't the most rational decision."

Jaxson just smiled at the other man's face. "Brother, I believe you have the capability to do that, but you won't."

"And why won't I?"

"Because despite all your public outrage at what I did on Otorio, you know how effective it was. Come, grant me access to the top of the Needle so we can speak in person." His smile became broader. "Jalma sends her regards. Hear me out."

Frankos stared at him for a long moment. "For her sake, I will see you. I'm transmitting a code. Go to the security lift."

Jaxson left the secure reviewing chamber and followed the instructions. He had been to the upper levels before, attending tedious meetings of the inner-circle CHOAM Directors. All he remembered were the endlessly banal voices and the drone of discussions about commercial operations.

After Brondon Aru died, Malina had tried to bring Jaxson into the family business, but he was far more active and impatient than either his brother or sister. He had fidgeted in the top boardroom as he listened to discussions that were as interesting as studying dirt.

But he had remained silent, attended the meetings, read the reports, and learned from them. Finally, he had been eased into more important conversations. His brother and sister also appeared, as did Duke Fausto Verdun, Lord Rajiv Londine, old Viscount Alfred Tull, who died not long afterward, and more—an assortment of Landsraad Houses, some vastly wealthier than others. These were the people who dreamed about the collapse of the Corrino Imperium and a free Noble Commonwealth. But they were in no hurry to accomplish it.

Jaxson had embraced that goal and formulated a more direct path.

Now, the private secure lift swept him to the top of the Silver Needle as if he were a projectile fired from ancient artillery. When the metal door slid aside at the topmost level, he stood face-to-face with his brother for the first time in nearly two years.

"Frankos, have you missed me?" He flashed a smile and knew it was just like the smile his father had worn when they went windsailing on Otorio's Inland Sea.

A troubled look crossed Frankos's face. "Your appearance is off-putting, even eerie, Jaxson. I feel as if I'm seeing a ghost."

"I am more effective than a ghost. We should haunt the Imperium together."

Unsettled, the CHOAM President led him into the isolated penthouse. The offices were empty and sealed, but the great boardroom was open for just the two of them. Frankos had sent away all possible observers.

He shook his head. "Such audacity in coming here. You must have a death wish. But that much was apparent when you attacked Otorio."

Jaxson chuckled, taking unexpected delight in his brother's comment. "Oh, that was not a death wish. It was a call to arms! A blow that rang out across the stagnant Imperium, waking everyone. And even as you decry my tactics, you can still whisper to supporters of the Noble Commonwealth. Be the voice of reason, while urging forward movement and more decisive action."

Jaxson went to a panoramic window to stare out at the vista. From this vantage, all the grand museums and monuments looked small.

The President dropped into one of the suspensor chairs at the boardroom table. "You know it doesn't matter what I say. Mother makes the important decisions, and she has issued many public statements about what you did. Her opinions are a matter of record."

"Her *statements* are a matter of record," Jaxson said, "and we both know why she had to say those things. But I think she secretly celebrates the fire igniting our rebellion at last. Jalma certainly does."

Frankos turned in his floating chair as he pondered. "Mother has made comments that we might use what you've done to our advantage."

"I suspected as much." Jaxson took another chair and tapped his fingers on the quicksilver tabletop. "I may be keeping a low profile now, but I do have my ear to the ground and I know what the people are saying. Despite condemnations from every House in the Landsraad, more and more families realize that the Corrino stranglehold has to be weakened. You know it as well as I."

"It is all talk," Frankos said.

"Talk can become action. Emperor Shaddam continues to flaunt his corruption, as if the Landsraad can't see what he's doing. The nobles are drained and starved from his spice surtax. They know it is unjust, and Shaddam uses it to finance an even tighter grip on their freedoms."

Now, Frankos leaned forward on the table as if suddenly exhausted. "The Emperor is oblivious. Have you heard? Shaddam announced a demonstration of the spice surtax, showing us all the 'benefits' of what he's done." Frankos closed his eyes as if the weight were too much to bear. "He wants to bring a treasury ship filled with actual solari coins, just so he can show everyone how much wealth his nobles have contributed." His normally placid face tightened in a sour expression. "Flaunting the money he's taken from the pockets of CHOAM and the Landsraad!"

Jaxson knew full well about the plan. "It is clumsy and ham-handed, but he doesn't even seem to realize it."

His brother sighed again. "Exactly what one would expect of Shaddam's character."

"Another example of his aloof and callous lack of understanding. The Imperial Court ruins those who participate in this blatant corruption. No one remains pure."

Jaxson spun in the suspensor chair and rose to his feet. The seat bobbed and swayed behind him. His face was flushed. "I always thought Duke Leto Atreides of Caladan would be an excellent recruit for our movement. He's a man of dignity and character, and by now, he has seen the damage Shaddam does to all those who are close to him."

"Duke Atreides was recently here on Kaitain," Frankos said.

"Oh, I know." Jaxson grinned. "I followed his activities very closely. Leto believed he could fit in and use Imperial politics to his benefit. Instead, he left feeling soiled." His eyes sparkled. "That was exactly what I needed to happen."

The CHOAM President joined his brother at the high window, and they looked over at the immense Imperial Palace. "What do you mean?"

"I spoke with Leto once before, just after Otorio, trying to make him understand. He refused to join us, of course, but at the time, the shock of Otorio was still too raw."

"He did almost die there," Frankos pointed out. "That wouldn't make someone feel gracious to you."

Jaxson ran a finger along his chin. "Ah, but after his eye-opening experiences at court, perhaps he'll reconsider who his friends are, and what the future of the Imperium should be. I will try again, soon."

Frankos nodded. "Leto Atreides would indeed be a good addition to the Noble Commonwealth cause. Our mother would approve."

Jaxson looked intently at his brother, wishing they had more memories together, but the bond of blood and a shared goal would have to be enough for now. "We are on the same side, Frankos."

Hesitant, Frankos stared, and stared, at Jaxson. "You look a lot like . . ." He shook his head, then stepped forward, surprising him by awkwardly slipping an arm around him in a brief hug, more than a pat on the back. Jaxson returned the embrace.

"Watch out for yourself, brother," Frankos said. "I don't want us to be at odds."

"Neither do I. That's why I am here. I want to succeed—for the Noble Commonwealth and for the future of humanity."

Even asleep, some people are dangerous enough to cause nightmares in others.

—Bene Gesserit teaching

M other Superior Harishka had designed the small council chamber herself, making rough drawings and then tasking her architects and builders to accomplish what was in her mind. This room was an intimate enclosure to discuss matters of utmost importance and secrecy.

In her medical chamber, Lethea lay near death in a vegetative stupor, yet also like a coiled viper. Her coma was not feigned, and even the Medical Sisters could not rouse her. The old woman was locked inside herself. Even so, the Mother Superior did not feel safe. Lethea had hurled mocking revelations like bombs, and then retreated from the resulting damage without explaining herself.

There also remained the matter of what to do with the rebellious Jessica and even more mundane crises such as the recalcitrant new Viscount Tull, who had terminated his connection with—and funding for—the Bene Gesserit.

Harishka decided she needed to call a special meeting of the Sisterhood. For certain difficult decisions, she had to rely on more than just Ruthine and Cordana. Her two closest advisers provided a balanced perspective, if only because their opinions were at opposite poles, with herself as the pivot at the center.

But now she wanted more input and had called a core group of Reverend Mothers, all women who had undergone the Agony and raised themselves to a higher state of mental being, who had access to the whispered voices and remembered experiences of ancestors through Other Memory. Fifty Reverend Mothers gathered in the large, sealed discussion hall beneath Harishka's secure council chamber.

Preparing to face them, Harishka sat with Ruthine and Cordana in the smaller, secure chamber above and observed the gathered women below through the high-resolution screens that illuminated the floor. In the inner-circle convocation below, a murmuring of voices filled the sealed and shielded discussion hall.

Harishka looked to her two advisers and could feel the silent, invisible push-and-pull of their opinions, their recommendations, and she braced herself for the larger discussion. She would raise at least one core issue—Xora's new assignment, her reward—to the inner-circle Reverend Mothers. "We want to decide this now," she said. "In a few days, the Emperor's Truthsayer will be coming to Wallach IX. I look forward to seeing my old friend."

"I miss having Mohiam in these sessions with you," said Cordana, sounding warm and conciliatory. "Ruthine and I try to fill her role, but our discussions were much more productive with her input." Her gaze darted to Ruthine, but the normally energetic Reverend Mother just sniffed, not taking the bait. Harishka wished these two got along better.

Harishka said, "Xora is ready. We need Mohiam's counsel for the Jessica matter."

Through the floor images, she could see that the Reverend Mothers had taken their seats in concentric circles around a large empty space, like ripples in water. And Harishka's special chamber would be the pebble in the pond. Below, two male attendants closed the single entrance door and sealed it behind them.

When she was ready, Harishka chose to make a dramatic entrance, to emphasize to these Reverend Mothers the unusual and critical nature of this meeting. She waved her hand and activated the mechanism she had designed. With a gentle hum of suspensors, the Mother Superior's enclosed room descended through the ceiling and down into the larger discussion hall.

From their seats, the Reverend Mothers watched the chamber come to a smooth stop in the center of the hall, then the walls and ceiling of the sphere slid downward and away, leaving Harishka and her two top aides looking out at half of the audience. The women fell silent, respectful and waiting. The dais slowly began to rotate so she could view all the women in the circular rows of seats.

Harishka's voice filled the hall. "Today's business will focus on certain challenges the Sisterhood faces. You will help me address the matter."

"First, we continue to face resistance from House Tull. Following the death of the old Viscount Alfred, one of our greatest supporters, his heir immediately cut off their financial contributions. Giandro Tull sent away his father's long-established concubine with an abrupt and rude dismissal." She paused, then admitted, "Zoanna made an error in attempting to seduce the son. It was not . . . elegantly done. I think the incident has poisoned the Viscount against us."

Around the room, the Reverend Mothers murmured. Beside her, like supporting members of a tribunal, Ruthine and Cordana remained silent.

"We currently have no Bene Gesserit representative on Elegy, an important planet controlled by a wealthy noble house. This is a very serious matter. The regular financial endowment from old Viscount Alfred greatly benefited the Mother School. Several major buildings, including the annex to this Chapterhouse, were funded by such gifts. Now that assistance is gone."

Damn that Zoanna! How could she have made such a blunder?

The Reverend Mothers grumbled quietly.

As Harishka spoke, the central dais continued to rotate. "But it is more than just the financial loss. Without a Sister in House Tull, we are blinded to their activities—and we strongly suspect the new Viscount is doing something important behind the scenes that he does not want outsiders to see."

Cordana rose to interject, though her bent back kept her in a half crouch. "The money that should have gone into Sisterhood coffers is being spent on something else, possibly corrupt or dangerous. We must learn what it is."

The Mother Superior steadied herself on the back of her chair and regarded the discussion hall for one full revolution of the dais. "We must also discuss the matter of Lethea's warnings and Sister Jessica." A chill seemed to go through the room. "We withdrew Jessica as concubine for the Duke of Caladan and brought her here because Lethea demanded it. She insisted that we keep Jessica from her son." Her own frown deepened. "Jessica did as she was told. She faced Lethea, tried to draw out information, but the revelations were contradictory, unreliable. Now Lethea is in a coma and unable to clarify her warnings."

"She should never have given birth to a son in the first place," Ruthine muttered, but loudly enough for everyone to hear.

"Lethea is too great a risk, even in a coma," said Cordana, working her way back into her seat. "She will kill other Sisters, or drive them mad. Who knows how she dredged up the name Jessica of Caladan. Jessica did what we asked. We should end her punishment and make her useful again."

Ruthine grimaced with angry disbelief. "She concealed crucial information from us about her son's prescient dreams. He is a greater danger than she is."

Harishka silenced the bickering and spoke to the rest of the gathered Reverend Mothers. "No matter what else, Jessica's defiance and intractability requires some form of punishment, adjustment."

"Complete reeducation," Ruthine said. "She has been too long away from us, too distant and unsupervised on Caladan, taking risks with her own son . . ."

"Jessica's situation must be fundamentally changed, or we will never be sure of her loyalty." Amplifiers carried the Mother Superior's voice around the sealed hall. "Send in Sister Xora."

The hall doors swung wide, and a tall woman entered wearing the robes of a Sister, not yet a Reverend Mother. Her blue eyes were bright, and her expression reflected both excitement and fear.

Harishka halted the dais so she could face the once-disgraced Sister. Since her scandal, Xora had worked at the Mother School and never been released back into the Imperium. Xora had smoothly completed her task of getting close to Jessica, revealed the intrinsic weakness in her loyalty. Jessica was still attached—far too attached—to the Duke and to her son, and that love made her vulnerable and unreliable. It would have to be fundamentally changed if Jessica were ever to be trusted in the Sisterhood again.

As for Xora, Harishka concluded that after seventeen years she finally deserved another chance. Now she faced the younger woman. "Sister Xora, do you know why you're here?"

The woman's feline blue eyes shone bright with optimism and ambition. "I know the Sisterhood's needs, and I know my abilities. I hope you will give me the opportunity to use the skills I have mastered. I will not disappoint you!"

"Again . . . ," Ruthine muttered.

Xora flushed, then pressed ahead. "I know of our great needs with House Tull, Mother Superior. I implore you, send me to Elegy. Let me get close to the new Viscount. I believe I am the perfect alternative to suit him, a concubine tailored to his tastes rather than his father's. I am nearly his age, and I am exactly the type of woman who would catch his attention. Unlike Zoanna." She dropped her gaze, but continued to speak in a rush. "I have always been adept in the Sisterhood's seductive arts. Baron Molay never had any complaints." She lowered her voice.

Harishka almost smiled, but remained rigid and expressionless as a stone. "You have earned the right, yes. With the agreement of the other Reverend Mothers in this convocation, we will end your punishment here and send you on another assignment."

Xora beamed, then managed to control her expression again.

"The assignment of a new concubine for House Tull is an exceptionally important position, and we are still considering who will fill that role. We have a different challenge for you." Harishka glanced at Ruthine and Cordana on the dais, then back at the tall Sister. "The Duke of Caladan needs a new concubine. You will go there to replace Jessica."

Xora swayed, taken by surprise, then straightened. "Yes, Mother Superior. I will do it."

Even Cordana smiled, as did the other Reverend Mothers in the chamber. Ruthine nodded. "Yes, I like that idea. We will send the Atreides Duke another woman who has a penchant for falling in love."

Pleased just to be given another chance, Xora bowed, partly to hide her broad smile. "I've had a long time to think about what I did wrong. I will take the time to prepare, and then prove myself anew."

I have a recurring nightmare in which I am surrounded by faceless women. One holds a poison needle at my neck and threatens me if I don't do the right thing. I feel the cold point against my skin, and I cannot move, knowing that a single prick will cause my death. The image fades, and I am vaulted into a universe of excruciating pain.

—COUNT HASIMIR FENRING, verbatim note taken by his wife

Duke Leto was surprised and suspicious when he received word of his unexpected visitors, a most unusual pair who waited for him in the guest parlor of the castle.

For Count Hasimir Fenring to come all the way to Caladan, he must have elaborate schemes, and Leto wasn't sure he wanted to be involved in them, or expose his people to their perils. He had already learned what kind of demands the Count might make of him in return for a favor. He had not ruined Lord Londine, and he wanted nothing more to do with that kind of politics.

Wearing crisp but informal attire, Leto strode into the room, leaving Thufir Hawat and two escort guards at the door. The warrior Mentat insisted on the security, ever alert to the safety of the Atreides family. Though Leto did not fear direct violence from the Count, despite the man's reputation, he remained on guard for convoluted scheming.

At least Paul was far away and safe. When he'd learned that the Count was coming to Caladan, Leto had not wanted to let his son be drawn into the web of politics. He insisted on keeping the young man apart. If Fenring met Paul and learned too much about him, would he find a way to use that knowledge as leverage? Perhaps try to lure his son into some scheme? Leto, still unsettled by his experiences at the Imperial Court, wanted to shield the young man, at least for now.

Only hours before Count Fenring arrived in a shuttle from the Heighliner in orbit, Duke Leto had dispatched Paul, along with Duncan and Gurney, on an expedition to the northern pundi rice paddies. Paul would be the Duke's representative to the Muadh Archvicar, Torono, helping to smooth over the strained relations there after the debacle of the "Caladan drug." Gurney Halleck was all too ready to verify that the Muadh people had stopped gathering the barra ferns, and Paul was happy to be given the responsibility of the expedition.

That left Duke Leto to face Fenring alone in the room, waiting to see why the ferret-like man was here.

Careful to keep up appearances, Leto spoke as soon as he entered. "Count

Fenring, I did not expect to see you again so soon, and certainly not here on humble Caladan."

He looked at the two men—the elegantly dressed Spice Minister as well as his adviser, an odd failed Mentat, introduced as Grix Dardik. Fenring and his companion stood by the reefstone-billiards table, apparently quarreling over something the Mentat held in his hand. As soon as Leto entered, they both froze, then quickly stepped apart.

Fenring had overlarge eyes that absorbed his surroundings, filing details into the recesses of his mind. He wore a dark jacket and a frilly white shirt with a lace collar, jeweled cuffs, and gold and platinum rings on his fingers.

His companion was strikingly different, and even stranger. Grix Dardik wore clothing similar to the Count's, though with less flair. His jacket was pale yellow, and unadorned, except for a prominent gold ring he wore on one finger of a defensively clenched fist. His jittery gaze wandered around the guest parlor as if searching for something, or seeking a way to escape. Fenring gripped one of his companion's spindly arms, to keep him under control.

Fenring made a quick move, took Dardik's finger, and yanked the gold ring from it. "He's not supposed to have this, ahhh."

The failed Mentat looked indignant. "I didn't steal the ring. I was only using it." He frowned at his knuckles. "In point of fact . . . in point of *precise* fact, I used its hidden needle to inject myself. The drugs are quite beneficial."

Fenring slid the ring onto his own finger. "You are fortunate I did not load it with poison today."

Dardik was focused on one subject as if he felt obligated to explain in great detail. "Count Hasimir Fenring's ring! His ring has a concealed needle, but it has drugs set up for me—sapho, verite, and the elacca drug, a precise formulation set to my metabolism."

Fenring shook his head, embarrassed. "Apologies, Duke Leto. Obviously, my companion needs a little more medication." With another quick move, he swept his hand aside and stabbed Dardik on the side of the neck.

Thufir Hawat slipped into the room and stood by Leto, ready to protect him, but the Count made no move closer to him. The odd Dardik calmed with the additional dose.

"Forgive him, please," Fenring said. "My Mentat is really quite brilliant, although his thoughts are often elsewhere, as he searches the deep reservoirs of his mind for data."

"A failed Mentat," Hawat said, his voice carefully neutral, but with clearly implied disapproval.

"Still able to make innovative and unorthodox mental connections," Fenring retorted with a frown.

Leto straightened his jacket. "I am more interested in why you have come here, Count."

Fenring bowed slightly and tried to form a smile on his narrow face. "You left Kaitain so abruptly, my dear Duke, that I did not have a chance to discuss further options with you. Honestly, you captured my interest with your, ahhhh, potential, and I thought it might be better to discuss, hmmm, in person."

Leto straightened. "I did not mean it as a rebuff. I had made my decision, and I didn't want to waste any more of your time, or the Emperor's." Feeling a heaviness at the pit of his stomach, he wondered if Fenring had found someone else to destroy Rajiv Londine as the price for marrying the daughter.

The Count stepped away from the billiard table. "Ahhh, but we have so much more to discuss, and I can think of other opportunities for us . . . and opportunities for *me*, as we discussed a bit at our dinner, hmmm? Emperor Shaddam sent me to inform you that he holds no ill will about your decision to leave court politics. He, ahhh, fully understands your reasoning and he respects your commitment to honor. He thinks of you almost as the son he never had, rather than a mere cousin."

The Duke bowed his head, just a little, in return. "I've only been home myself for a few days. I am honored by your visit, but what does Caladan have to offer that would make such a journey worthwhile for you?"

As Dardik stood beside the billiards table, his muscles relaxed, and his skin took on a dull cast, while his eyes became bright and sharp.

Fenring strolled forward. "Why, ahhh, because you impressed me, Duke Leto Atreides. I understand your ambitions, and I respect the boundaries you established. So many, hmmm, other nobles have no compunctions against harming another House so long as it benefits them. True, the Emperor is still annoyed at Lord Londine, but by standing your ground, you proved something to *me*, my dear Duke."

"And what is that?"

"That you would be a steadfast ally and an excellent business partner." He smiled. "Perhaps we could enter into an arrangement that would benefit us both, and would be acceptable to your own moral code?"

Leto glanced at Hawat, saw that his own Mentat was listening closely. The Duke replied, "I think I've had enough of power games and Landsraad squabbles." Leto scratched the side of his face, felt a little stubble of beard that he'd missed when shaving. "Here on Caladan, I am focused on helping my own people."

"Ahhh, but my idea is something that would benefit your lovely world! And it would not be any endeavor of the Emperor's, but my personal investment, for my own profit. For *our* profit."

Leto was wary, but felt obligated to listen. "And for Caladan's?"

"Yes, ahhhh, of course." The Count glided up to him. "I am intrigued by your moonfish industry. You spoke of it with such great pride, and I would like to help expand your operations. With my finances and connections, we could greatly increase the profits of House Atreides." He raised his eyebrows, wrinkling his broad forehead. "Which would thereby increase your standing among the other nobles, without compromising your code of honor. That is what you seek, correct? And, hmmm, it would be under your own terms."

Leto was surprised by the suggestion. "You want to invest in our moonfish operations?"

"I want to expand them, my dear Duke. Grow your market, increase your exports, and then Caladan would become justifiably famous across the Imperium. Moonfish from Caladan, just like spice from Arrakis."

Leto met Hawat's gaze, saw a quick flicker of a nod. "I would be wise to listen, Count Fenring." He led them to a more relaxed setting outside, and they sat at two tables on the western terrace overlooking the ocean. Small, puffy clouds sailed through the sky, and colorful fishing boats plied the waves.

As the men drank bitter lichen tea and nibbled on little sandwiches, Fenring asked business questions about the current state of the moonfish industry, most of which Leto was able to answer. As the discussion became more detailed—tonnage of the harvests, annual revenues, number of satellite fisheries, distribution facilities—the Duke deferred to Hawat, and Grix Dardik at the adjacent table became energized again. After the failed Mentat gathered and organized the data, he rattled off reasons that the operations would be a good investment for Count Fenring.

Leto didn't let the peculiar man distract him, but instead concentrated on Fenring, trying to assess his real reason for coming. Finally, he said, "Even if the numbers are compelling, Count, I am certain that you have numerous other investment opportunities. Why are you so interested in me?"

"Hmmm, ahhh," he said, then snapped up a small fish samosa in a single bite. "Because it is you, my dear Leto. I do not have other investment opportunities with *the Duke of Caladan*. At present, you are what interests me. You asked for my help the moment you arrived at the Imperial Palace. You did want me to take an interest in you, did you not?"

Because of Jessica and the Bene Gesserit, Leto had been in a volatile state when he went to Kaitain. He did not want to admit that he had changed his mind.

Into the pause, Fenring continued, "I would like us to be friends." His overlarge eyes looked innocent and sincere now, but Leto knew not to trust him. Still, he would rather be on the man's good side than his bad side. Even so, he was glad Paul wasn't here.

At their table, Thufir Hawat and Grix Dardik were engaged in a complex conversation about numbers and trends. They spoke rapidly, as if in a foreign language, and the conversation seemed amiable. He knew that later Hawat would give him his full assessment.

Gazing out to sea, Count Fenring seemed fascinated. A strange expression filled his face as he stared at the ocean. "Incredible to see so much water in one place . . . such a sharp contrast to Arrakis, where I spend much of my time at the Residency in Arrakeen."

"The desert planet must have its own beauty," Leto said, hiding his grimace to think of the place that had been under vile Harkonnen rule for so many years.

"Indeed it does," Fenring said. "And my Lady Margot is there."

AFTER THE CASTLE steward provided adjacent quarters for Count Fenring and his Mentat companion, Leto arranged a trip for the following day to the fisheries in the Atreides ceremonial frigate. They would depart first thing in the morning.

Granted privacy to rest, Fenring faced Dardik, guiding the easily distracted man into a quiet conversation. "I see that my second dose from the needle worked well. You were more focused."

"I am always focused. Not always focused on your focus." The Mentat's expression shifted to a curious frown. "But you cannot be certain that it was only my second injection of the drug. False assumptions lead to false conclusions."

Fenring leaned closer to whisper, "How much of the drug did you take?" He was worried about an overdose, though the ring's reservoir did not contain enough to be dangerous.

"One," Dardik said with a shrug. "I just didn't want you to assume."

A flash of annoyance crossed Fenring's mind. "The dosage must be under my control. Don't ever get into my things again, or I will have you killed."

The failed Mentat did not look at all nervous. "I ran the odds that you would say that. I even ran a projection on what your exact words might be—"

Fenring cut him off. "What are the odds that I will simply poison you to death right now?"

"I cannot calculate the specific numerical value, but I estimate they are rather high."

"And getting higher, I assure you." The Count paced the room, ignoring the rustic finery. "Continue to observe and collect data. By the time we leave here, I will have your full assessment."

Dardik blinked his large eyes, waiting.

"Tell me if you believe Duke Leto Atreides is involved in the Noble Commonwealth rebellion. If so, we will take action."

I am the Duke. I see with the eyes of Caladan, and my people see through my eyes.

— DUKE LETO ATREIDES, letters to his son

Though Paul wanted to spend as much time as possible with his father now that he was home from Kaitain, the young man was happy to travel to the pundi rice fields and the Muadh villages. Gurney Halleck and Duncan Idaho accompanied the heir of Caladan. As they flew to the fertile wetlands, Duncan let Paul pilot the personnel 'thopter that carried the three of them.

Paul knew how important it was to meet personally with Archvicar Torono, especially to reinforce their united stance against the insidious spread of the drug ailar. The previous misunderstanding had caused unintended friction between the peaceful Muadh and their beloved Duke. Paul did his best to adapt and grow. He could never guess when his life would really go back to the way it was—if ever. With Lady Jessica gone, gloom seemed to hover over Castle Caladan.

After spending a month in the dark political morass of the Imperial capital, Duke Leto had come home changed. Paul felt more distant from his father now, but in some ways they were tied more closely. After Paul had served well in the role as acting Duke, Leto relied on him more. It was just the two of them.

As the 'thopter flew to the expansive wilderness, Paul concentrated on the mission ahead. He was aware of the secondary reason for this impromptu expedition, because Leto wanted to keep him separated from Count Fenring, out of an abundance of caution. In the meantime, Paul set his mind to fulfilling his new duties and making his father proud.

"It's good to visit even these outlying villages, lad," Gurney said from the rear seat of the aircraft. "The people will grow accustomed to seeing you as the next Duke."

Paul forced a laugh. "Not for quite a while, Gurney! Besides, didn't you tell me there was an advantage to observing the people surreptitiously?"

Gurney snorted. "I don't think I'll ever enter the Song of the Sea again, thanks to our last adventure!"

Duncan glanced over at Paul in the adjacent seat. "No hiding this time, young Master. To these people, your identity will be fully known, so make a good show of it."

The young man nodded to himself as he looked at the terrain below. "All of life is training."

He flew a circuitous route that passed over green fields threaded with the silver ribbons of irrigation tributaries. Villages were dotted throughout the paddies, where the hardworking people planted, tended, and harvested one of Caladan's primary export crops. These isolated pundi rice farmers had their own culture, and they were always loyal to their Duke.

Reaching the striking landmark of the Arondi Cliffs, Paul circled over the giant rock formation, knowing their destination lay at its base. With a quick grin at Duncan, he accelerated the aircraft high, then came down in a swift dive, flurrying the articulated wings and then looping in an aerial show that evoked laughter from Duncan and an astonished groan from Gurney in the back. Paul trimmed the wings, cut back on the thrusters, and dropped down in a pinpoint landing right in front of the main Muadh village they had visited before.

"These people need to see the skills of their future Duke," Paul explained as he powered down the engines and peered through the windowplaz of the aircraft. He saw hundreds of Muadh villagers approaching, cautious but fascinated.

Gurney muttered as he exited the craft on shaky legs, "Duke Leto would never show off like that."

"But the Old Duke would!" Paul laughed. "My grandfather would have hosted a bullfight for them."

Duncan clapped a hand on Paul's shoulder. "Remember, these pundi rice farmers have quiet lives. We don't want to scare them."

Their visit was scheduled to last several days, and Paul made up his mind to be thorough. He would enjoy his time here—unlike his swift and unsatisfying trip with Duncan to the sand dunes and the experimental grass plantings. On this visit, he would truly represent the Duke of Caladan.

Leading the group of Muadh people, Archvicar Torono came forward dressed in green-trimmed brown robes. He wore a cap embroidered with a fern symbol—a barra fern. Paul recognized the symbol of the Muadh religion, although now the fern held darker connotations because of its connection to the ailar drug trade.

The bearded religious leader had a placid face, wrinkles around his eyes, and a warm smile. He bowed, recognizing Paul. "Blessings to you, young Master." He touched his fingertips together, then drew his hands apart as if stretching invisible lines in the air.

"I come to you on my father's behalf," Paul said, "to strengthen our ties of friendship and loyalty with all pundi rice farmers, his Muadh subjects."

The Archvicar smiled again. "The Duke is our friend and will always be our friend. His people will strengthen Caladan."

With Gurney and Duncan following, Paul strode into the village, smiling and nodding to people. Many workers his age came out, waving and clapping politely. Paul greeted them all, remembering several faces from the purification and centering ceremony he had attended not long ago with his parents.

Not long ago. . . .

Back when he had taken so much of "normal" for granted.

In front of the Muadh temple, the Archvicar stood by the door and gestured to a rock garden, where the pale green curls of several barra ferns grew prominently among lichen roses.

Gurney made an angry sound low in his throat. "Barra ferns! Your Duke eradicated the drug fields. You should know better! Are you flaunting—"

Torono's eyes were suddenly urgent, and he shook his head. "These are sanctioned by Duke Leto, special ferns that we use only at precise times. Our people found and marked all of the naturally growing barra ferns in the forests, but we do not harvest them. We watch them. We will never let this mistake happen again. We promise."

Gurney looked skeptical, and Duncan's expression was stern, but Paul was more tolerant. "We know the sacred meaning that your people attach to the barra ferns. Purification and centering. For countless generations, the Muadh rituals caused no harm, but with your help, we must keep watch and defend against the people who would abuse this cherished sacrament."

"Yes, young Master." The Archvicar bowed, placed his fingertips together again. "Your blessing means as much to us as our Duke's would."

PAUL AND HIS companions spent the next three days among these quiet people, learning their observances, attending their prayers and rituals, and understanding how dutiful, loyal, and peaceful the Muadh people were.

They toured the impressive, steeply terraced rice paddies. Paul waded knee-deep in the slurry of mud and warm water as he helped plant seedlings, and on other terraces, he joined the work crews threshing the long stalks and carrying rice grains in woven baskets. Gurney and Duncan stood guard, always alert, but they avoided getting muddy with the work. Paul took seriously that he was standing in the stead of his father, and he was pleased with what he accomplished.

The last evening, they ate a farewell feast while they prepared to depart for Castle Caladan the following day, Archvicar Torono came to Paul. With a sad expression, the religious leader touched the embroidered fern symbol on his brown cap. "I promised that my people would not allow the scourge of ailar to spread again, young Master. We watch and listen, and we ask our people to report any sign of that terrible drug coming back. The Muadh do not wish to be tarnished again by any association with ailar."

"Thank you, Archvicar," Paul said, sensing the man had more to say. "I believe you."

Torono's brow furrowed. "Even though we have nothing to do with it, we hear rumors, whispered offers of ailar for sale. It has come back."

Astonished, Paul glanced over to where Duncan and Gurney were running a safety check on the aircraft. He lowered his voice and leaned closer to the Archvicar. "But all the fields were destroyed!"

"Someone planted new ones, but I do not know where. Not in the northern wilderness, at least not close, but somewhere," Torono said. "Someone is trying to start the distribution again, and Caladan is the only world where they can grow the special ferns profitably." He bowed his head, so that his thick beard was buried in his collar. "The Muadh do not want more blood on our hands. Please take this report back to our Duke."

Paul squared his shoulders. "I will tell him. You are our eyes and ears here. Please inform us of anything else you learn." He drew a breath. "And I'll make sure my father knows that you are not involved, except to help us protect Caladan."

Even predators have rules, if you can survive long enough to learn them.

— BARON VLADIMIR HARKONNEN,
discussion with his Mentat, Piter de Vries

In industrial tunnels beneath the metropolis, Feyd ran with his lean young hounds. The passageways were lit by harsh glowstrips. Forced-air circulation roared through ventilation shafts, filling the tunnels with a low moan, but the yips and howls of his two pets were the only sound that interested him.

As the animals bounded ahead, Feyd followed, sweating and exhilarated. The beasts made him feel the joy of the hunt, the liberation of pursuit, stretching muscles, searching for something to kill. He had named the two spinehounds Blood and Bone, and he already adored them.

In the past, his brother had hunted prisoners down here, turning them loose in the tunnels and giving them false promises of freedom if they survived. With a whole crew of guards and hunters, Rabban would run after the desperate wretches—men, women, even spunky children. Although some managed to survive the actual hunts, none of them ever escaped.

The CHOAM Ur-Director had given Feyd instruction manuals and additional information about his new pets, and he had studied the crystal sheets. He read about techniques, training suggestions, and advanced imprinting for the two beasts.

Once, Blood and Bone had mistakenly torn apart a trembling servant who came to deliver Feyd's meal in his living suite. Afterward, the two spinehounds had licked his hands, whimpering, knowing they had done something wrong. Of course, he forgave them and let them feed on the servant they had killed.

From then on, he praised them more when they recognized and obeyed commands. They could still be distractible, but they were improving. Blood and Bone followed him, loyal, calm, but cagey. They were energetic and more than a little skittish; loud noises made them distraught. Late one night two days earlier, Bone had awakened from a canine nightmare, lashing out and then whining, cowed as soon as he recognized Feyd.

The young man often took the two pets with him in the open car as he traveled through the Harko City streets or when he appeared at the fighting arena to watch the day's spectacle. Egan Saar remained on Giedi Prime for the time being, waiting to be dispatched on his mission.

For now, he trained the pair of beasts down in the tunnels. The spinehounds didn't know where they were going, but simply bounded after imaginary prey. He ran behind them, listening to their panting breaths, their clicking nails on the polished tunnel floor.

Ahead, the lights brightened at a juncture with the levitating tube trains that rushed beneath the city bearing materials, equipment, and work crews. Feyd noticed a maintenance team, a man and a woman in drab jumpsuits, repairing some malfunction in the tube-train substation.

Seeing them, the spinehounds howled and ran faster. Feyd saw their eyes lock on the two workers, who stood up from the substation, startled. They held tools in their hands but were too surprised to do anything.

Feyd could tell what was going to happen, and knew he couldn't stop it. He shouted anyway. "Hold!"

Blood skittered at the sound of his master's voice, turning, but Bone launched himself into the female maintenance worker. The spinehound drove her to the ground and ripped out her throat before she even hit the floor.

The man flailed at Bone with the tool in his hands, but the second spine-hound lunged forward to defend his companion. Blood killed the other worker.

Feyd caught up to them in seconds, but the animals had already ripped their prey to pieces. Disappointed, he chastised the creatures. "I said *hold!*"

Blood and Bone immediately sat on their haunches, pricking up their ears and looking at him with rapt attention. Their muzzles dripped with gore. The workers' bodies lay mangled next to their equipment.

Feyd decided to refer to the Tleilaxu instruction document again and deepen their training. So far, the most important thing he had learned about them was that, because of their blood-bonding with him, they would never attack their new master. It gave him some comfort, but not enough. He didn't want them attacking the wrong people.

I t was her tenth day of solitary confinement, as far as she could tell. Jessica lay
on her hard mattress, staring up at a corner where an arachnid was building
a web in the shadows, going back and forth with meticulous care as it wove a
beautiful, intricate tapestry—a deadly trap for its prey.

She was trapped in the Sisterhood's web. What were they waiting for? Had
Lethea said anything else? The ancient woman's mind was twisted and tangled
by the fearful confusion of prescience and also her spiteful hatred of the Bene
Gesserit. Would the Sisters keep her in this cell forever, put her to death, or
devise some other punishment?

She longed to see Paul again, and she wanted to face Leto, to explain everything, to appeal to his sense of justice, to pour out all the secrets that she had
kept . . . even the huge revelation of how she had conceived a son—for him. She
vowed to do anything to get back to them, whatever it took to convince the
Sisterhood.

Leto and Paul. . . .

Interminably alone, in silence, Jessica envisioned their faces, every detail of
her son's dark hair and green-tinted eyes, the rugged line of Leto's jaw, his gray
gaze. But with the numbing passage of days, she had more difficulty visualizing
them, and she fought to keep the reality from fading to a jumbled blur. With
dogged effort, she called on the discipline of her Bene Gesserit training. Sum-
moning their images, she painstakingly reassembled the memories and focused,
focused until every detail of Paul and Leto became sharp again, and their presence strengthened her. It was like exercising a muscle, she told herself—a mental
muscle. Virtually, she traveled back to Caladan to be with them.

A lilting voice interrupted her memories. "I've come to see you, Sister Jessica."
A woman's voice, all too familiar.

Opening her eyes, she saw Xora standing at the doorway. Jessica emerged
from her trance, sharpening her focus on the here and now as the other woman
entered. Xora resembled her in height, hair, and facial structure.

Resentment made Jessica grimace. Xora had lured her with warm conversation, playing upon the things they had in common, only to betray her. She thought of her purlwood carving, the three idealized figures smashed by bitter Ruthine.

"Have you come to do more damage?" Jessica asked. "You already made sure I was locked away and forgotten in here."

Xora kept her distance. "Bene Gesserit punishments don't last forever, although the Sisterhood's influence does."

"It already feels like forever." Jessica sat on the edge of her narrow sleeping pallet. "Were you always a spy, or did you just see an opportunity?"

The other Sister became stony. "It was my obligation to report what you revealed about your son's prescient dreams. Such vital information! If you had told them yourself, you wouldn't be here."

"You entrapped me." Jessica realized how pointless it was to make such accusations. Xora was impenetrable.

"I am free to make suggestions, even bad ones." The other woman moved closer, though Jessica had not invited her. "Your crime was in *taking* the suggestion to thwart the Sisterhood." A light floral scent wafted from the other woman, reminding Jessica of how she herself must smell after this extended captivity without the opportunity to tend to her own hygiene.

"I needed to send a message to my son."

Xora merely shrugged. "There is another way to get the message to him. I can deliver it myself."

Jessica grew intensely alert. Was this some further deception to test her in isolation? "What do you mean?"

Xora gave a faint smile, seemed uncertain. "Not that, but many things are happening. Reverend Mother Gaius Helen Mohiam will be coming to the Mother School soon. I think she wants to see you. She intends to see me . . . before my new assignment."

Jessica's tension increased. "She's a stern one. You'll have a hard time finding the warmth within her." Her former teacher knew exactly how to hurt her, how to think like her. "What did you mean, your new assignment?"

Xora brightened as if sharing good news. "I'm finally being allowed off Wallach IX and granted a special undertaking to prove myself."

Jessica inhaled, then exhaled, a relaxation routine. "At least you can cause no further damage here, or to me."

Xora's expression shone like a polished steel blade. "I am being sent to Caladan, assigned as a replacement concubine to Leto Atreides." Jessica lurched to her feet, but Xora added in a maddeningly sweet voice, "I am only following the Sisterhood's orders. I'll serve the Duke to the best of my ability."

Jessica felt an almost physical pain, as if struck by an assassin's dagger, but she instantly realized that this was exactly the kind of thing the Sisterhood would do to break her, to remind her that they controlled every aspect of her life. "Leto will never have you. He is the father of our son. I am his bound concubine."

"That agreement has been rescinded, as you know full well," Xora said, and now her true ambitions seeped through into her tone. "I only do what is best for the Bene Gesserit. We must serve in whatever manner we are commanded. Both of us." She was not very good at concealing the truth. "The Mother Superior will find some other use for you, I am sure."

Acid dripped from Jessica's voice. "I don't need a Truthsayer to see that you are lying."

Now, Xora seemed much less formal. "I've worked seventeen years to atone for my indiscretion! This is my chance." Xora looked oddly flustered, in spite of her pride. "I promise to do my best for our order and for your—for the Duke, for his sake. As his new concubine, I'll make him believe that I actually love him, a skill you mastered so well."

Jessica felt the wound deepen. Because she had shared her secrets with a Sister she had believed was a friend, Xora knew her vulnerabilities and exploited them. Coldly, biting off each word, Jessica said, "Is love only a game for you now? Did you ever truly love your Sardaukar officer, Brom's father?"

"I was weak then." Xora looked away. "But I am strong now. I will do my best to fulfill my new assignment, employing all the training I have."

Jessica warned, "Bene Gesserit techniques are different from true love between two people."

Xora flushed. She said in a small voice, "I so wanted us to be friends."

"You came here to revel in your victory. I was foolish to let down my guard. I made a mistake in telling you that I love Leto and Paul, because I thought you, of all people, would understand." Tears burned in Jessica's eyes. "But I made no mistake in loving him. No matter what happens, Leto will not forget that he loved me, too."

Xora crossed her arms over her dark robe. "But I must make him forget. That is my assignment."

Jessica knew this woman well enough now, and she pitched her words, her tone, in a very subtle application of Voice. "Don't think you can take my place so easily. Leto will not be fooled by you, and neither will Paul. You will never be what I was to them, not even close."

Xora backed toward the cell door, and the power of Jessica's words made her sway. Abruptly, she turned and fled, her confidence shaken. She sealed the door and vanished down the corridor.

Jessica felt torn, disturbed that she had manipulated Xora with Voice. It was something that Lethea might have tried. . . .

Now that she was alone again, thoughts and questions swarmed through her mind. It seemed obvious that the Mother Superior had given Xora this assignment to crush Jessica's spirit, to demonstrate that the Sisterhood made every decision, issued every command.

Were they so foolish—was *Xora* so foolish—as to think that proud Leto Atreides would simply accept whatever new concubine they dealt him from a deck of seductresses, as if they were interchangeable? Not even Xora could be that skilled at personal manipulation.

But even if she was right that the Sisterhood wanted to break her spirit and her will, there had to be another objective. The Bene Gesserit were clearly afraid of what Paul might become, and they had shown her Brom as if to flaunt that they already had their own schemes for creating a Kwisatz Haderach.

In a secret ultimatum that forced Jessica to return to the Mother School, Reverend Mother Mohiam had threatened to destroy Leto and Paul if she disobeyed. What if the Sisterhood had decided to eliminate the risk of her son anyway? In their conversations, the other woman had boasted that she was a high-level Bene Gesserit fighter. Jessica felt her eyes burn. What if Xora was being dispatched to Caladan not only to seduce Leto, but to eliminate Paul? Alarm jolted through her.

Jessica could not prevent it from happening, not from here.

Though trapped in her cell, she altered her mindset and made a deep, invisible change. Somehow, she *had* to convince the Sisterhood to release her. She knew what they were looking for. Jessica had gotten into trouble because she'd dared to fall in love, but she would now become the exact opposite. Jessica would learn to be what the Bene Gesserit had always wanted her to be: willing, responsive, pliant, devoted. And that would be her power over her situation.

She would make Mother Superior Harishka listen to her. She would offer new promises, ask for forgiveness and a chance for redemption, all to do what she needed to do. No matter the cost, no matter the lies she had to tell.

They had offered Xora a path to redemption. They could do the same for Jessica. She would be cold and calculating, but not against any hapless nobleman. Instead, she would focus this skill on the Sisterhood, and use it as a weapon against *them*.

I will beat them at their own game.

To do a thing, or not to do a thing—each path involves risk.
　　　　　　　　　　　　—Conclusion of the Guild Bank

W *e do not need to be friends.*
　　　As he and Count Fenring went to tour the moonfish operations, Leto
kept reminding himself that this was an important business matter. Their dealings would be open, above board, and completely legal, even if it did tie Atreides
business with the Count. He could not deny that a sizable investment could
modernize and expand the fishery equipment and facilities, as well as improve
the lives of all those working under the hard conditions in the marshy lands.

Knowing Fenring's dubious reputation, he was sure the man had ulterior
motivations, maybe to spy for the Emperor. But to what end? What was Leto
suspected of? He wasn't easily fooled, but he was professional. The Count could
observe all he wanted, but House Atreides had nothing to hide, no quiet sedition against the Imperium. Maybe it would even earn him grudging respect from
Shaddam IV.

He knew it was better to keep a man like Fenring on his side, rather than
allowing doubt to spread about House Atreides. Was it possible that they were
trying to bring him down, as they were doing to Rajiv Londine? Leto had to be
cautious.

He had contacted the administrator of the main fishery, Condu Natok, to
arrange for a tour. Natok had replaced the disgraced former operations supervisor
who had been entangled in illegal ailar use throughout the fishery complex and
nearby villages. Natok had been brought in from the administrative side in Cala
City, a merchant who had managed large agricultural operations, and he was
familiar with moonfish raising and processing.

Still new in his position and wanting to impress his Duke, the man had
agreed to let Count Fenring and his Mentat companion tour the fishery. Since
he was also a businessman, Natok was pleased to hear about the possibility of a
significant investment.

Now, led by a loquacious administrator, Leto and Fenring walked together
from the landing platform along the connecting paths above the holding ponds.

Although the Count wore a slicker over his fine garments, he was still inappropriately dressed for the fog and mud. He dismissed Leto's concern, "Ahhh, my dear Duke, I have been dirty before." His words seemed to suggest a secondary meaning.

Their boots rang on the metal grid above the trickling brown water of the canals. Spawning ponds were ringed with throbbing membranes that added a low vibration to the air, a tone that had been proven to induce spawning. Patchwork dwellings sat on stilts above the wet ground. On the far side of the holding pools, an open processing deck held long tables under sloped awnings, where workers would clean and fillet the moonfish in an amazingly swift flow. The air smelled fishy and dank. Fortunately, the offal was taken away to a deeper part of the marshes or the odor might have been unbearable.

Fenring showed intense interest as Leto and the fishery manager explained the breeding pools, transfer canals, processing huts, and packaging lines.

"And there are seven other major moonfish operations in this vicinity," Natok said. "This one produces the most product for export, but these northern marshlands are extensive, and Caladan has room for many more breeding pools and processing ponds." The administrator smiled at Fenring. "Now that we may have the financial resources to do so. This would be a wise investment for you, sir."

Intent on their own inspection, Thufir Hawat and his thin Mentat counterpart conversed near a warehouse building on the other side of the waterway. Their interchange was a back-and-forth flow of data, since they shared a propensity to speak a language of facts and numbers, of probabilities and projections—in this case about the economics of the moonfish industry.

Leto knew that Hawat would not reveal any inappropriate information, and would try to use his Mentat skills to discern the Count's real purpose in engaging with the Duke. Thufir Hawat was normally inscrutable, but Leto could tell from his strained expression that he was growing frustrated with Grix Dardik. Obviously, Fenring's Mentat was not entirely the eccentric fool he appeared to be.

Leaning over the edge of the dock to peer into the sluggish water, Fenring mused, "Strange-looking creatures, but a fine delicacy, hmmmm. We could greatly increase exports by modernizing operations and streamlining systems." He looked around at the breeding pools that thrummed with the sonic membranes. "You said there are seven other major fisheries, Mr. Natok? We could double that number, hmmm."

The administrator bobbed his head. "I agree. This is a wonderful opportunity, sir." He looked at Leto, then quickly averted his eyes. "If my Duke agrees, of course."

Leto nodded slightly and made a noncommittal sound.

As he walked beside Count Fenring, he remained alert. Out of mutual caution, both men wore personal shields, and Leto tried to imagine dueling with Fenring here on the metal walkway, blades dancing, shields thrumming. Though Fenring glided through the Imperial Court dressed in finery, and was Shaddam's Spice Minister on Arrakis, Leto had heard rumors about this man's speed afoot and vicious fighting ability.

Right now, though, Fenring seemed to have another target in mind. He wanted something—perhaps it was a genuine investment opportunity. Perhaps something much more. . . .

Hawat and the other Mentat joined them at the edge of the platform looking down at the sluggish fish. "Is it true they are drawn to music?" Dardik asked. "Shall I sing?"

"Don't do that," Fenring said.

"We intend to conduct more thorough studies of moonfish habits," Leto said, "but we do have indications that music draws them." He allowed himself a smile, recalling his last expedition with Paul, Gurney, and Yueh. "One of my men, Gurney Halleck, is well known for playing the baliset. When we were camping, he would strum his instrument, which attracted the fish and mesmerized them, so they were easy to catch in a net."

Fenring mused. "Interesting, ahhh, but not very sporting."

"We were hungry," Leto said. "Out in the wild, the moonfish grow larger, but these have a more delicate flavor." He indicated the rippled surface of the pond. Copper-scaled fish swam about below, surfacing and then disappearing back into the water.

"And, ahhhh, is it true that the meat of a spawning female is poisonous?"

Leto felt a chill. How could Fenring know that? Was he aware that Paul had nearly died from eating such a fish when they were out in the wilderness? That fact was not at all widely known.

"So I've heard," Leto said, then gestured toward the processing huts with his chin. "We never harvest the females when they are filled with eggs. It's curious you would have heard such a fact."

"I am considering a substantial investment, Duke Leto. I like to do my research," Fenring answered. Grix Dardik nodded vigorously as if his head were coming loose on his stalk of a neck.

Leto was even more convinced that the Count's reason for coming here must be for more than investment purposes. Fenring was on a fishing expedition in a different sense of the word.

Dardik suddenly chuckled and pointed at the murky water. "See those fish dancing around, almost like a ballet in the water . . . but it looks deadly. Is it two males facing off?"

"The males of many species do that," Hawat said. He shot a quick glance at the Duke. The Atreides Mentat understood there was much subtext here, too.

Count Fenring smiled, glanced at his odd companion, and then abruptly terminated the tour. "I have seen enough to be reassured in all respects. My Mentat will summarize his analysis on our journey back to Kaitain, but I have made up my mind." His darting eyes sparkled as they locked on Leto's, ignoring everyone and everything else around him. "This is a fine industry, with great potential. I spoke with my Guild Bank representative before leaving Kaitain, and I've set aside a substantial sum of solaris in my personal account, which I can transfer immediately." He sniffed. "Our respective Mentats can work out the details. And you'll undoubtedly get the better of that exchange."

"I'm not so sure about that," Leto said with a glance at Dardik twitching and shifting on his feet.

ONLY A DAY after the party returned to Castle Caladan, a final agreement was signed and Fenring committed an extensive investment to be used immediately for a significant upgrade of the largest fishery operations.

Once he had seen what he needed to see, however, the Count was eager to get back to Kaitain. Leto had no doubt that he would submit some kind of report to Emperor Shaddam, but what had the man seen? Leto felt no real anxiety, because Caladan was an open book.

Shortly after Count Fenring left for the Cala City Spaceport, Paul returned from the pundi rice paddies with Duncan and Gurney. Leto was glad to have his son back, and they had much to talk about. Proud of his work, Paul spoke quickly, reporting on what they had seen and done—and most importantly what the Archvicar had told him about the possible return of illegal ailar distribution. Leto vowed to have Thufir Hawat immediately step up his investigations and crack down.

But Leto didn't let the dire news diminish his happiness to have Paul home. The two stood together on the castle terrace, watching ships take off from the spaceport. Paul belonged there with him.

When it launched, Fenring's shuttle was a bright streak in the cloudy sky heading toward the orbiting Heighliner. Watching it, Leto said to Paul, "I'm glad you were not here. Count Fenring has always made me uneasy, and I've been torn about whether or not to trust him."

"I wish I could have met him. You and I together, Father, make a formidable pair." Paul looked suddenly more mature in his eyes.

Leto sighed. "If Fenring and I remain business partners, you will undoubtedly see him another time. But there's a shadow around him, and I wanted to keep you . . . untainted. He invested a great deal of money in our moonfish industry, and we will immediately put it to good use. I still wonder what he really wanted."

Paul's brow furrowed. "Sometimes it's good to keep a potential enemy close, where we can observe him."

Leto chuckled as the ascending shuttle dwindled to only a bright spark. "I was just thinking the same thing! Who taught you that? Thufir Hawat? Duncan?"

"You did, sir. And I took your words to heart."

Camouflage is a critical survival skill, not only for exotic animals, but for astute business leaders.

—CHOAM Directors' meeting notes

When the hot tropical sunlight struck the neat rows of barra ferns, a pungent aroma filled the air. Inhaling the intense fragrance, Chaen Marek could comprehend the enticement of the Caladan drug, somewhat, but he was not tempted to use it.

No Tleilaxu would partake of the ailar. They were God's special people, and needed no crutches to live their lives.

On the other hand, the Tleilaxu had no qualms about using the weaknesses of outsiders for their own profit. Spreading the drug didn't require deviousness or even much difficulty. So many people were eager for addictive diversions, all of which sapped them of strength.

Marek had planted Master Arafa's fast-growing fern varieties and watched them thrive on Caladan. His work crews already grew and processed tons of the specially adapted ferns. Something about the planet's atmosphere, the precise color of its sunlight, or the chemical composition of its soils made the barra ferns flourish here unlike any other growing place. Master Arafa could keep specimens alive under carefully controlled conditions in Bandalong, but that was not a commercially viable operation. Here, Marek could cultivate drug fields, and he had already reestablished most operations . . . after Leto Atreides destroyed his northern fields.

Camouflage nets projected a hologram of thick jungles, disguising the new fern fields. Marek admitted that his operations had been easier with Leto Atreides away at the Imperial Court, but the Duke had returned to Caladan, which could pose problems. Still, the man would not think to look here in the southern continent. Marek felt he was safe for the time being.

The Tleilaxu man walked along the rows, noting the different types of modified ferns. Some were the palest green, while others were so dark that the black mottling was nearly invisible. The ailar concentrations also varied in the dried fern nubs, and he had tried different processing techniques to find the most profitable strains. Some were still deadly, despite their best efforts.

He and Jaxson Aru had already found an ambitious distributor, a smuggler named Lupar, to reintroduce ailar to users in the northern continent near the fisheries, and the man also had offworld connections. But Jaxson's instructions had been very firm that they must be exceedingly careful this time. Duke Leto Atreides could not know. Some of the ailar was still deadly.

Chaen Marek balanced the need for restored profits—for the Noble Commonwealth movement—with his need for caution. The liberation of the Tleilaxu people was at stake, freeing them from the Corrino yoke, and he didn't dare let the operations be exposed again.

He had tested Master Arafa's new strains to verify that the narcotic effect was not so unstable or deadly. For the most part that was true. Previously, both he and Jaxson had been too eager to unleash a dangerous product, and the sheer number of accidental overdoses drew the angry attention of Duke Leto Atreides. Their operations had nearly been ruined.

To reassure himself about the new ailar, that it would not leave a trail of casualties, he had needed test subjects. He wouldn't risk his own workforce, since trusted laborers were precious. After searching the thick jungles of the southern continent, his scouts had found remote villages inhabited by shaggy Caladan Muadh primitives. No one would miss them.

Marek had rounded up the primitives and brought them back to the growing fields, where he forced them to consume the new ailar. The Muadh savages easily became addicted, euphoric, listless. He fed them increasing doses and ran medical tests, pleased to see that very few of them died. He finally managed to kill more with overdoses, but the amount required to do that was so extreme that it would never happen to a normal user, certainly not by accident. The lethal specimens were rare anomalies. Satisfied with his test results, he had poisoned the remaining savages and dumped their bodies into the churning surf around the nearby reefs.

Jaxson Aru had not been to Caladan in more than a month. In the meantime, Marek had provided a significant batch of the new product to Lupar and instructed him to expand distribution again, imploring him to use the greatest discretion. The people of Caladan were good customers, but they were not wealthy; in order to fund the rebellion, he would need to expand ailar distribution out into the Imperium again with as few deaths as possible. Lupar had delivered a shipment to a key contact on Lankiveil, but Chaen Marek had other distributors as well.

That afternoon, an unmarked flyer set down on the cleared landing field just up from the beach. It was a private craft, the sort a wealthy businessman might take for a joyride to the islands. The visiting flyer shut down its suspensor engines and tucked its wings against the fuselage. Marek had been expecting it, and he called to his work supervisors. "Prepare the packages—a complete shipment. It has already been paid in full." Chaen Marek smiled with anticipation. "This customer does good work for the Noble Commonwealth."

The man who emerged from the landed flyer had a high forehead and narrow features, a well-trimmed gray beard, and carefully tailored hair. His garments shouted with color, scarlet and yellow in a celebration-of-life style common on the planet Cuarte. The visitor was accompanied by his chief administrator, bland of face but also dressed in brilliant colors. Marek sensed something distinctly different about the new man.

The Tleilaxu came forward, formally bowed to both of them. "Lord Rajiv Londine, I am pleased to greet you in person, but I am surprised. I expected you to be a bit more discreet." He frowned.

"I have a legitimate excuse to be here. I came to Caladan to pick up a shipment of moonfish fillets. In the past few days, Count Hasimir Fenring made a substantial investment in the industry here, and I will quietly follow his lead. Duke Leto was too busy showing Fenring around, so I was able to slip in quietly, but my presence on Caladan is a matter of record. I have nothing to hide."

"Nothing to hide?" Marek raised his eyebrows. "Yes, you do, sir."

Rajiv Londine chuckled as he looked around the growing areas. "Well, a few things, but no one will notice them. Before long, Duke Leto Atreides may have a close personal alliance with my House, which will necessitate more frequent visits here. Another reason I have decided I'm fond of moonfish. It could make our operations smoother."

Marek was confused. "How so?"

"My daughter is a prime candidate as a wife for the Duke of Caladan. With the departure of his bound concubine, Leto is considering a political marriage again—at least, that is the rumor around Kaitain. He left the palace with the situation regarding Vikka unresolved, though—and we have not been notified of any outright rejection. I do hope he didn't find her lacking."

Chaen Marek kept his expression stony. The natural mating rituals of humanity made him ill. He preferred Tleilaxu ways, scientific ways.

The lord continued, "Such a marriage alliance could certainly help our movement. I know Jaxson has his eyes on Duke Leto as a potential recruit." Londine's expression hardened as he shifted the subject. "Can you get a message to Jaxson? My compatriots and I are growing impatient. He is like a ghost, and we need guidance."

"Jaxson Aru is wanted by the entire Imperium," Marek pointed out.

"And for good reason! But I heard he went to ground on a new planet. His inner circle needs to meet, especially if he is planning another one of his spectacular gestures. Is that true?"

Marek frowned, wondering what Jaxson had in mind now. "I know nothing of this, and I am trying not to draw attention to myself. These ailar operations keep me fully occupied. I am doing my part."

"The Noble Commonwealth is bigger than just Caladan," Londine said. "And if Jaxson is planning some other heinous attack, I need to know ahead of time so

I can prepare. I was able to send my abusive son-in-law to die at Otorio, and that turned out well. How can we use this new scheme to our advantage?"

"I do not know any of his plans," Marek insisted. "I merely do my part—as should you."

The chief administrator at Londine's side said nothing, but a quick glance reminded the nobleman of his business. The lord nodded. "Very well, that is a matter for later discussion. I wanted to come personally to retrieve our first shipment of the new ailar. My accounts grow empty."

"You should have alternative sources of income," Marek said, refusing to address the man with his noble title, because the Tleilaxu did not recognize noble blood.

"Oh, I do." Rajiv Londine was well respected in the Landsraad, although he had not been shy about criticizing the Emperor. For a long time, this man had been part of the slow, quiet dissidence fostered by Malina Aru, but he also worked secretly with Jaxson's more extreme faction. He wanted to see dramatic change in his own lifetime.

Londine's administrator shifted, catching the nobleman's attention. The lord smiled. "Ah, let me introduce my chief administrator, Rodundi. He attended the Mentat school for several years and received careful instruction. Though he did not complete the full course of training. He is still an invaluable asset to House Londine."

Marek bowed to the bland-faced administrator, but he felt a thrill go down his spine, recognizing exactly who—or what—Rodundi was. Hiding his surprise, he gestured toward the rows of green ferns poking out of the fertile soil. "Let me show you our new fields. These altered barra ferns produce a pure ailar with a greatly diminished risk to the user. The modified drug is flawless."

"Good." Frowning, Londine scratched his neat gray beard. "When Lord Atikk's son died of an overdose, my distribution operations in his court were very nearly exposed." He paused. "And, of course, I am sad over the death of Atikk's miserable wretch of a son."

"A real tragedy," said Rodundi, the first words he had spoken.

The three men walked along the rows of ferns. High above, a shimmering camouflage net blocked them from outside view.

"My workers are loading a full shipment onto your craft, Lord Londine," Marek said. "When you return to Cala City, these crates can be hidden among your moonfish purchases, and sent off to Cuarte with no one the wiser."

The chief administrator said, "Lord Londine, let me handle the details with Master Marek. You mentioned that you wanted to look at the reefs? Take a moment for yourself."

Londine gave a wistful smile. "Yes, I would like to stand on the Caladan shore and just enjoy the waves. My base on Cuarte is far inland." Humming to himself, the nobleman walked off, satisfied, though Marek guessed that his brilliant clothing might scare off any fish in the tide pools.

As soon as Londine was gone, Rodundi's features shifted, flattened, grew duller. By altering his facial muscles, skin, and expressions with the subtlest of movements, a Face Dancer mimic could take on the appearance and manner-isms of any chosen subject. Marek did not know how long ago the Face Dancer had subsumed the real Rodundi, no doubt killing the man and disposing of his body, but he was convinced that Rajiv Londine did not know the difference.

Now that they were alone, the Face Dancer could communicate plainly, in the private language of the Tleilaxu. Marek picked up the distinctive scent of the creature, but only because he was attuned to the differences. No one else would have detected it.

"I will smuggle a report to Bandalong," said the Face Dancer. "The Bene Tleilax eagerly observe your activities here."

Marek looked along the rows of ferns, inhaled deeply, finding a calm in the potent smell of drug-laden oils that evaporated into the humid air. "I will not fail. This is God's plan. All Tleilaxu know the plan, and Jaxson Aru is our pawn."

The Face Dancer nodded. Marek pressed his fingertips together in acknowl-edgment, relieved just to be in contact with a representative from his own race. He was all alone here on Caladan and wished he could go back to sacred Band-along.

But he could not return until his work was done. Until the Tleilaxu people were free.

The Face Dancer shifted his features back, became Rodundi again, and smiled. "I will see that the shipment is loaded. We expect to do frequent business together from now on." He walked off to the private aircraft.

Even if we gouge out our eyes, we cannot unsee the truth. Even if we cut out our tongues, we cannot unspeak the truth. The truth is permanent.

—Fremen aphorism

tray gusts of wind, sand, and grit swirled in the high-walled canyon that hid the Orgiz spice refinery. The heat and dust made Rabban's mouth go dry and his eyes burn, but he was glad to be back on Arrakis from miserable Lankiveil. Rough conditions like the desert made him feel more alive, and out here he was in command.

At the end of the box canyon, the spice silos were filled with powdery rust-colored melange. A mere handful of the substance was equivalent to a year's wages for the lower classes on Giedi Prime. His desert workers were hard-bitten veterans, their faces weathered, wiry bodies encased in stillsuits. They were chosen from the regular spice crews and reassigned to the secret operations at Orgiz. The brooding shift supervisors were Harkonnen loyalists brought in from Giedi Prime. Every person here had been conditioned to absolute loyalty, whether through indoctrination, bribes, or blackmail.

Once transferred to Orgiz, though, no one was allowed to leave, and the workers were beginning to realize it. Supplies were delivered, and their accounts were full, but they received no furlough—Rabban couldn't risk it. Even though they grumbled, there was no place to which they could escape. Setting out across the desert would mean certain death, as they well knew.

He looked up, hearing the thrum of a carryall, and he saw its underside shift as its electronic camouflage began to fade. The sound vibrated against the rock walls as another load came in, but the lumbering craft barely cleared the jagged mountain peaks. The loss of the original refinery here had been an embarrassment to House Harkonnen, when a rogue sandworm destroyed everything. But now the outer canyon opening was blocked off by a cascade of detonated rock, and the restored operations were proving to be highly profitable.

With sunlight slashing down into the canyon, Rabban strutted through the complex. By letting the crew see him, he could make them work harder, produce more melange. He wore protective armor, high boots, and a personal shield belt, which he would never use out in the open sands, but he disdained a confining stillsuit like his workers wore. He could feel the sweat pouring off of him and evaporating into the air, and it felt liberating. He was Glossu Rabban, the Count of Lankiveil, and he could purchase as much water as he needed.

After his uncle's recent challenge to demonstrate his skills, Rabban was sure he would be the next Baron Harkonnen instead of his brother. He had received confirmation from Lupar that the deadly invasive mite had been released on Caladan, and in a few weeks, it would spread throughout the fishery operations. Soon, all the moonfish would die off, and the entire Atreides industry would collapse. Surely it was enough to impress the Baron.

Before leaving Giedi Prime, his uncle had told them he had an even more devious plan in motion, something to do with the Bene Gesserit wife of an Atreides Suk doctor, but Rabban couldn't imagine what it was. Nevertheless, he would never underestimate the Baron's abilities. Destroying the moonfish industry would have to be his own triumph.

Meanwhile, he was in charge of maintaining this secret channel of spice to be sold to wealthy CHOAM customers. Everything hinged on their operations remaining undiscovered. His uncle had given Rabban that responsibility.

One of his underlings trotted up, holding an imager and a crystal projector. "M'Lord Rabban, one of our patrol flights captured something interesting, and we thought you would like to see." The man's blue-stained eyes widened as he grinned beneath his breathing mask. "These images have not been altered in any way." He projected a holo-image: one of the titanic sandworms cruising like a battleship across the open dunes, rolling and roaring along.

Rabban squinted, watched the movement. "Yes, I've seen the monsters up close, even killed one, though it took enough explosives to level a city." His eyebrows drew together. "Worms don't normally run on the open sand in broad daylight."

"Look closer—this is what I wanted you to see!" The scout enlarged the image. "Note the figures on the upper ridges of the worm."

Rabban could discern black spots, silhouettes. "Some kind of parasites?"

"More than that!" He enlarged the view even further. The figures looked like humans wearing cloaks . . . similar to the ones worn by the desert rabble.

Rabban burst out laughing. "This is ridiculous!"

"And yet . . ." The scout shrugged. "We've heard that the Fremen can summon and ride sandworms. They worship the monsters like some kind of collective god."

"Someone is playing a joke on you." Rabban's voice became harsher. "And also attempting to make a fool out of me! Go away."

He strode off to watch the battered and often-repaired carryall descend into the canyon with its heavy load of spice. Moving with practiced speed, his gritty workers transferred melange into the spice silos, from which it would soon be emptied into unmarked ships for distribution to CHOAM. When the carryall finished dumping its loose spice powder into the silo and sealed the lower hatches, Rabban inhaled the sweet-potent fragrance of melange.

All of the official harvesters and spice factories on the open sands were plainly marked with the Harkonnen griffin and flew House colors, every piece of equipment documented on inventory records and transportation logs. Emperor Shaddam could track the wealth being generated under the loyal administration of House Harkonnen.

Here in Orgiz, though, nothing could be traced to the Harkonnens. There were no symbols, no banners, no uniforms. All admin records had been rigged with flash points and acids that would immediately wipe damning evidence, should the refinery complex be discovered. Other contingency plans were in place to deal with the work crews in a worst-case scenario.

But the best solution was for Orgiz to remain hidden.

Just as the thought crossed his mind, perimeter alarms activated. A mottled scout flyer cruised overhead above the top of the canyon. Surveillance parties rushed out, running among the rocks and cliffs and using suspensor-assists to climb the canyon walls.

One of his lieutenants in an unmarked jumpsuit rushed up to him. Rabban never kept track of their names. "Movement spotted, m'Lord!"

"A spy?" He watched search parties rush down the canyon and climb to high outcroppings to hunt down the intruder.

Another scout transmitted on the scrambled comm, "Could be a Fremen. They're the only ones who can move out here like that."

"Find him. Capture him!" Rabban roared back as if his people didn't already know their orders. "If he's seen this place, he can't be allowed to leave."

The refinery operations came to a standstill as Rabban summoned all workers to help with the hunt. He listened to the reports of other sightings, saw his teams closing in on the spy.

Before long, they found him, and a dust-covered man in a stillsuit was dragged before Rabban. He had been beaten during capture. His left eye was swollen nearly shut; his face mask and nose plugs had been ripped out. Blood leaked from a nostril, and more spilled from the corner of his mouth.

"We caught him in a cleft in the rock above, my Lord. He was watching us. He surrendered."

Rabban saw how badly the man had been pounded and wondered how swift the "surrender" had been. He leaned close to the wounded intruder. "I will have your name. Who are you? Where are you from?"

The man mumbled, forming words through damaged lips and broken teeth. "I am called Corvir Dur. I am from the desert."

Rabban put his hands on his hips. "Are you one of the dirty Fremen?"

The man shook his head. "I know Fremen." He looked up with his good eye. "And I know you, Beast Rabban. I am a smuggler, and you're well aware of our activities. Your own hunting parties attacked our hidden bases, but our group has an understanding with Count Hasimir Fenring." A flicker of defiance came to his features. "The Imperial Observer has given us protection. You were told to leave us alone. But has he sanctioned these operations? I don't think so."

Rabban growled deep in his throat. Yes, Fenring had imposed the rule that they had to leave Tuek and his smugglers alone, and Baron Harkonnen resented it. But not even sanctioned smugglers could be allowed to know about the Orgiz refinery. "We know you act as the Count's spies, but now you've seen something you should not have seen."

Corvir Dur looked resigned rather than terrified. "I was exploring the desert. I spotted an unmarked flyer and the carryall in these mountains, where they should not have been. I followed them here. You were careless."

"As were you," Rabban said. "But I will not die from my carelessness. You, on the other hand . . ." He pressed his thick lips together and paced. Corvir Dur did not plead for his life, did not snarl or shout defiance. Rabban said, "Throw him into the spice silo."

The prisoner twitched as he realized what Rabban had just said. Two guards seized his muscular arms and dragged the spy over to the nearest cylindrical structure. Rabban followed as they hauled the man up the metal steps to the top of the open container. From the platform, he looked down into the dry red-brown quicksand of spice, the flaky powder so painstakingly harvested from the sands. Rabban inhaled again, felt the euphoria and energy ring through his mind and his ears.

He announced, "Now you'll have as much spice as the wealthiest man in the Imperium." He nodded to his guards.

Though the two were troubled by the orders, they heaved the thrashing captive over the lip of the silo and into the soft powder. Corvir Dur flailed, swirled, but the powder engulfed him. He coughed and choked, and his open mouth filled with thick red dust. The man clawed for his life, but the spice gave him no purchase. It swallowed him up like a well of powder sand out in the open bled.

Rabban wondered how far down the spy would sink . . . or what the CHOAM customers would say when they found his melange-infused body at some end point in the commercial chain.

He chuckled, "I guess spice does not always prolong life."

His men dutifully laughed.

IN THE CLIFFS above, wedged into a narrow crack in the volcanic rock, another figure stirred. Dirt and pebbles sloughed off to reveal a protective cloak. The second man, Benak, scraped his way out of the hiding place.

His heart still pounded, and his mouth was dry from fear. He sipped a mouthful of lukewarm water from one of the catchpockets in his stillsuit and brushed dust from his face and cloak. He had evaded capture, had survived.

He and his companion, Corvir Dur, had scouted these mountains following reports of hidden spice activities. Working for Esmar Tuek, they were determined to track down the illicit thieves who sold melange outside of normal commercial channels, circumventing the Emperor's taxes and control. It was not the way power worked on Arrakis.

Count Fenring had demanded that Esmar and Staban Tuek find and stop this piracy, and now Benak and Corvir had discovered their secret base of operations. The two comrades had been so careful, creeping along the top of the canyon and blending in with the rocks. Together, they had captured images as a new unmarked carryall arrived. Spotter ships flew overhead, keeping watch for intruders, and the two spies must have let some small detail slip.

The brigands swarmed out in an overwhelming search party. As the hunters closed in, he and Corvir Dur had seen the small hiding place in the rock, only big enough for one person, and they formulated a desperate plan. They cast throwing sticks quickly onto the rocks, and Benak's marker scored highest. As the winner, he tucked himself into that narrow crack in the rocks, and his companion had covered him with dust, dirt, and flakes of rock. Corvir Dur then slipped off, trying to hide, but they both knew he would be captured. His friend sacrificed himself so that Benak could get away with the vital intelligence.

Now, after he emerged from the tiny cleft, Benak looked down at the crowded operations, saw a burly man interrogating Corvir and then dumping him into a spice silo. Benak could not tear his gaze away as his companion died, but his anger and determination flared brighter. He knew he had to leave.

From this vantage, Benak could not determine exactly who ran this hidden refinery. He saw no company or family markers, could not identify any of the people below. All the equipment looked old, battered, salvaged, but still seemed to function at high capacity. Without a doubt, this was the source of the black-market spice. These operations were why Emperor Shaddam was so outraged, why Rulla had been executed as a scapegoat to buy Count Fenring time, to give the Tueks room to solve the problem before they, too, were exterminated.

Benak absorbed the details, recorded more surreptitious images as proof. He hid in shadows throughout the day, waiting until full nightfall. Then he slipped off, using all of his skills to remain in the shadows, unseen.

It would be a long and exhausting desert crossing to get home, but he understood his responsibility. Benak vowed to deliver his accurate report to Esmar Tuek. His friend had died for the information.

Every day as we go about our lives, an unknown awaits us, only moments away from revealing itself, for good or ill. We swim in a universe of unknowns.

—LADY JESSICA, Wallach IX journals

Jessica slept, but did not rest. She suffered through a nightmare in which Leto and Paul fought countless enemies in the midst of a massive conflagration. The Imperium was awash in red, some kind of civil war, and the Atreides fought in it, not just Leto and Paul, but Gurney and Duncan back-to-back in a city square, swords bloody, shields shimmering.

In Lethea's dementia-addled brain, she would probably have considered a simple nightmare like that to be *prescience*. . . .

Inside her isolation cell, she shivered during the night on her hard pallet, with nothing but a thin blanket to keep her warm. Periodically, she woke enough to adjust her metabolism, but each time, she drifted back to sleep to the same nightmare and the same violent conflagration—it unnerved her so much that she woke again, alternately shivering and sweating.

Jessica told herself this was not one of the visions that Paul sometimes experienced, the special dreams that so terrified yet fascinated the Bene Gesserit. Her subconscious must be manifesting the stress and doubt in her own mind, rather than picking up paranormal communication.

This was all that Lethea had imagined. Her warnings weren't real—Mother Superior Harishka had to see that.

Still, Jessica did have her maternal instinct, and perhaps she could sense danger to her son, even far away. She hoped Paul was all right, and Leto. Her heart felt heavy to know that Xora would be departing for Caladan soon. *Leto's assigned new concubine.* . . .

Surely he would turn her away. Or would he? How much did he feel for Jessica anymore? Worse, she feared the Bene Gesserit might pose some threat to her son.

As Jessica drifted back into the nightmare again, she saw Leto, Paul, and their companions fighting on. The attacking enemies wore the uniforms of Sardaukar, who were considered invincible. Leto and his companions slew waves of the Emperor's elite troops, but an endless number flooded back against them and finally broke through the defenses.

Her dream-self was just an invisible observer, and she could do nothing to help. Leto was killed first, followed by Duncan and Gurney. In the horrific nightmare, Paul was the last to die, and Jessica could not save him, could not save any of them. Flowing red blood turned into the blackest void in the galaxy. All four were gone. From a vast distance she heard her own voice, screaming their names, but her anguished cries grew fainter and fainter, until she found herself alone in the quiet of a tomb. They were doomed, and so was she.

Just a nightmare.

Jessica awoke to a real sound, a faint rustle of fabric—the stirring of a robe? She sensed something, *someone*, nearby. Instantly alert, she sat up on her pallet, listened into the darkness outside her cell and heard jagged breathing, then an unfamiliar voice . . . an altered voice. "Jessica!"

She spun around in the dark, trying to identify the source.

"Jessica!" The voice was behind her now. Inside the cell.

Breathing, convincing herself she was awake, Jessica struggled to gain control of her awareness. Her fighting spirit, her will to live, roused her like a hard, icy slap across her face.

She lurched off the pallet and backed away, pressed against the wall. With hyperawareness, her eyes adjusted, and she saw a shadowy form standing before her—a woman in a robe of the deepest black, but different from the usual garments of a Sister or Reverend Mother. Her face was masked with a veil of black threads, and the mesh moved in and out as she breathed with rasping, wheezing sounds.

Jessica suddenly remembered the hooded woman outside of Lethea's medical chamber on the very day she arrived at the Mother School. "Who are you?"

"I pose the questions! And I require acceptable answers. Why did Lethea place such importance on you—an unremarkable Sister, a Duke's concubine from a small holding?" Judging by the voice, the strange woman must be quite old. "Is your son the Kwisatz Haderach? I have looked at the bloodlines, the breeding possibilities."

Jessica said, "Ask Lethea—maybe she'll give you a coherent answer. Then I can be released from here."

"I have already heard the answers," rasped the veiled woman. "I need to sift the worthy ones from the foolish ones. We must watch you, Lady Jessica of Caladan."

A wave of bitterness drenched her. "I am no longer a lady, nor am I of Caladan, thanks to the meddling of the Sisterhood." She faced the mysterious woman, close enough now to see details even in the dim light. The stranger seemed lean within the billowing folds of her black garment. The threads that masked her face moved with each breath she took.

The visitor clucked her tongue. "Truly, you don't look like much to me at all, girl. Yet Lethea singled you out. Why? What do you know that you aren't telling us?"

Jessica folded her arms over her chest. "I do not answer to strangers. Why do you hide behind that veil?"

"Because I am the Kwisatz Mother."

Jessica caught her breath.

The old woman lifted a wrinkled, age-spotted hand to her veil. "I succeeded Lethea, and she succeeded Empress Anirul, back when your son was born. Anirul saw something, too . . ."

Jessica felt the puzzle pieces slide into place. It made sense that Harishka would send the Kwisatz Mother here to interrogate her. "Because you are in charge of the breeding program, you're afraid of me, or Paul, or both of us."

"Lethea was afraid, perhaps confused, yet we cannot completely disregard her. I was appointed out of necessity, because her dementia caused so much turmoil." She turned her veiled face away. "We could not leave her in control of the breeding program, but we could not discard her."

Jessica stood up for herself, not afraid or intimidated. "Her irrational demands and murderous actions caused turmoil for me as well." She drew a long breath. "And now you can't even tell me why? That you yourself don't know? You're the Kwisatz Mother."

The old woman laughed, a grating noise. "I have many answers, but they are not necessarily true. Lethea is untrustworthy and mad. The other Sisters fear her, and fear what she says. Even the Mother Superior doesn't know what to do . . . but Harishka is too fond of her. Our own Mother Superior has fallen to the softness of her own emotions."

Jessica stood firm. "I was brought to the Mother School against my will. The Sisterhood threatened my family if I did not cooperate. I was forced to break my word to my Duke, and the Bene Gesserit still demand that I prove my subservience. I faced Lethea as commanded, like a sacrifice thrown to the wolves, but she didn't kill me as she killed others." She raised her voice, but controlled her anger. "What more do you need me to do? Shall I face Lethea again? Then get on with it—take me to her."

The comment elicited a dry chuckle from behind the veil. "Lethea is beyond answering questions."

Jessica was instantly on her guard, sensing danger. "What do you mean?"

"She has fallen into a coma—she may even have brought it on herself. We will be rid of her before long."

The news left Jessica's mind swimming.

The Kwisatz Mother continued with unexpected vitriol, "Lethea had unique capabilities, but having a capability does not mean she has value. Now she can best serve the Sisterhood by dying."

The veiled woman retreated to the door and left. After the dark form glided away, the illumination in the cell glowed brighter as if she had taken her darkness with her.

━━━━━━

When a life form knows it is dying, a remarkable phenomenon can occur. Some plants burst into glorious foliage and flowers, then wither and die. It is their final, satisfying moment of beauty in the ever-challenging life cycle. Animals can feel a final, frenetic energy. This is the way with humans as well, if they have the internal strength to accomplish it.

—Scientific study from Old Earth,
found in Bene Gesserit archives

L ethea encompassed her own universe, dreaming of long ago: a young and beautiful breeding mistress sent to seduce an important nobleman so the Sisterhood could control the offspring. Deep in her shattered-mirror mind, she was in the palais again, stepping onto a terrace in her gossamer nightgown, feeling the cool night air. Aware of every fiber of her body, she knew instinctively that she was with child—as ordered. Looking up, she saw the flag of the Great House illuminated and fluttering in the breeze, a seashell with a rising sun. She couldn't even remember the name of the noble family. . . .

Lethea had found ways to conceal her pregnancy from her nobleman and his attendants—just as she had done on other occasions. When it came time, she would find an excuse to return to Wallach IX, never to see her noble lover again. She had what she, and the Sisterhood, needed.

But they kept taking and taking. . . .

Lethea had already conceived five children this way, and such successes had been instrumental in her advancement in the order, which led to her becoming a Reverend Mother, then ultimately the Kwisatz Mother—for all the good it had done her.

In her marvelous dream, Lethea stood on that distant memory-terrace, remembering the successful mission. It had been a heady time for her, and she allowed herself to swell with a pride that she would always conceal from her superiors. She had known she would never forget those happy times. Now, an eternity later, she nestled into that warm recollection as if it were a comfortable blanket. She didn't ever want it to end. If only she could lose herself here, never return to the awful, treacherous reality, and the disrespectful way she had been treated by the Sisterhood. . . .

But drugs coursed through her, the sadistic Medical Sisters prodded her, the persistent torturers who tried to wring more, more, *more!* from her, even though Lethea had already ruined her life for them . . . ruined many lives. They deserved whatever happened to them in the future. Why should she try to change it?

Lethea felt herself awakening, leaving the beautiful memory-dream, and despite all her efforts found herself back in the harsh reality of confinement, restrained to the bed and surrounded by viewing windows, tubes, chemicals, and monitors. She lay on her back watching a play of colored lights high on one wall, reflections of the firefly monitors blinking, blinking.

They think I am still in a coma, but I am not. They know my brain has hemorrhaged, but I have repaired it.

In recent days, with Lethea seemingly lost to the world and posing no threat, the Medical Sisters had grown bold and lax. They came and went to her bedside, certain that she would not awaken and harm them. They thought her weak, impotent.

At any moment, she could have snapped awake and lashed out with her implacable Voice. They had no idea how close they all were to a sudden and violent death. It was what they deserved. . . .

Faking the coma and sending false data to the monitoring equipment had not been a simple task, despite her own gifts in adjusting and balancing her own internal chemistry. Even a strong person could not fight forever against the inevitable, and Death beckoned.

Lethea had tried to warn them, tried to avert the looming crisis, even tried to help Jessica, in her own way. She was done. *Done!* She would achieve one more victory against the Bene Gesserit, for what they had done . . . and what they refused to do. So many variables, so many perils.

Losing all track of time, she resolved to give up the effort and slip away, intending to be gone by morning. She wanted to retreat forever into that comfortable, welcoming dream shared by others in the order, a place where she could be at peace, satisfied with her accomplishments. She had not gone unnoticed through this life.

Turning her head ever so slightly and opening her eyes just a crack, she saw only one Sister in the main viewing window, distracted, almost nodding off. *Sister Jiara.* If Lethea's vital signs worsened, automatic medical alarms would awaken the guard, but she used her mental and bodily control to maintain her vital signs. The readings showed that she had suffered brain damage, that she clung to life by a thread, deep in a coma.

Some people lived their normal lives as if in a coma, oblivious to the universe around them. Like Jiara out there . . . Feeling far superior to anyone she'd ever met, Lethea preferred her own company. It had enabled her to be gruff, to push others away from her. She could retreat to her inner self and be just fine. She could go far, far down and never come back. From a great gulf of thought, Lethea wondered if she would miss herself. It was like a Zensunni question within a question.

A heavy sadness came over her at what she was about to do, despite all of her rationalization leading up to this point.

She could easily kill more people, punish more Sisters, leave a more permanent scar. It would be simple. She could pretend to die, which would set off the terminal alarms. When frantic Sisters rushed into the room, Lethea would roar out in Voice, command them to use their own fingers to gouge out their eyes, and then claw out their brains through the bloody sockets.

I am the mind-killer!

Maybe she could lure Mother Superior Harishka in here and have her do the same.

Yes, she could do that.

While maintaining the monitors with a steady, hypnotic throb, Lethea summoned a sudden burst of strength and ripped through her restraints without moving a single unnecessary muscle.

But she couldn't hold everything steady. Medical bells chimed, rising to an urgent volume. Outside the window, Sister Jiara jumped to her feet, looked into the confinement room.

Lethea had only moments before other Sisters came rushing in. She knew now with her waning abilities that she could not accomplish the grand final gesture she had envisioned.

I am tired of games, Lethea thought. *Just this last one will suffice.*

As if she were young again, using the strength in her dream-body more than her actual withered husk, she swung out of bed. She twisted a metal flange on the corner of a monitoring machine to create a sharp edge. She cut both wrists, ripping open her flesh so that blood gushed out.

The alarms grew louder. The monitoring Sister at the window was calling for help. Figures scurried down the corridor, gathered at the door, worked the codes and seals.

With a cadaverous smile, Lethea pressed her bloody wrists against the inside of the plaz observation window, and she wrote her message, two ominous words—backward but clearly legible from the other side.

JESSICA
DANGER

Satisfied with her life, Lethea slipped to the floor in her own pools of blood. She was gone before the other Sisters managed to open the door.

Understand the depth of hatred our enemy holds for us. They may attack from any direction, and not always with military force. They can strike through bureaucracy or commerce, through the air we breathe or the food we eat.

—DUKE PAULUS ATREIDES, from a letter to his son

After Count Fenring's money had been invested in the moonfish operations, Duke Leto settled back in to his normal duties and tried to remember normal times.

Thufir Hawat had run projections on how rapidly the fisheries could be rebuilt and expanded with the substantial influx of funds. Materials had been ordered, commitments made. Scientific research would be conducted to fine-tune the sonic membranes that lulled the fish into breeding more frequently. Dr. Yueh had expressed his interest in following the research.

Leto called for a fine dinner to be prepared, moonfish of course, accompanied by seasoned pundi rice. Paul joined him for the hearty feast, and together they made the castle seem less empty. At the long banquet table, the young man took the chair adjacent to his father's.

Leto attempted to enjoy the food and casual conversation, but Paul was quiet, as if a shadow hung over him. He glanced at Jessica's empty seat. "When will my mother come back? Will she ever continue my training?"

Leto knew he could never explain adequately, because he didn't understand it all himself. For years, Jessica had softened him with her love. He had always believed that their relationship made him a stronger man, but now he realized it was also a vulnerability.

"I won't pretend that everything is the same, Paul, or that it ever will be," he said. "This is not our old normal, but it is . . . the new normal. It was not my choice, but now we have to make the best of it."

Paul took a bite of his thick fish fillet and chewed silently before saying, "Dr. Yueh says that all creatures must adapt to survive."

"And so we will." Leto wished he could just ask Jessica the thousands of questions in his mind, ones that she probably could not answer. "This is what we have now," he muttered, more to himself than to Paul, then fell to his dinner. He looked up. "Does it taste better now that we're so well funded? Moonfish will be more popular throughout the Imperium, could even make Caladan famous."

This would help to accomplish his original aim of building up the foundation of House Atreides, to make them more prominent and influential in the Landsraad. Count Fenring's investment would do that in part . . . and without costing Leto his honor.

Paul picked at his food, then looked up with a wan smile. "Moonfish always tastes delicious, especially when we catch them ourselves." The young man's sigh reminded him of their recent expedition to the northern wilderness, where Paul had almost died from moonfish poisoning. "But it won't seem as special anymore if every merchant and Landsraad lord can have a meal like this."

Leto sat back and looked at Paul, feeling a swell of pride. "No one will have a meal like this, because I am having it with my son."

DISASTER STRUCK THE following day.

Leto was in his private study going through administrative reports, assessments of commercial operations and agricultural activities compiled by the Atreides Mentat. Then the new manager of the largest fishery sent an urgent communiqué directly to the castle. "Our moonfish are dying, my lord Duke!" Natok transmitted. "A plague is sweeping through them. We don't know the cause or how to stop it. Thousands of fish are floating belly-up in the canals and holding pools. And the smell is unspeakable."

Before long, Leto received desperate messages from five other fisheries experiencing the same die-off. He immediately called for Thufir Hawat and handed him the messages. Dr. Yueh also hurried in.

Leto asked, "Sabotage? Some kind of poison spread throughout the operations? It has to be intentional."

"A mere poison would eventually be diluted, unless it were constantly replenished," Yueh pointed out.

The Mentat reviewed the messages, shaking his head. "Unless a saboteur had a large amount of a toxin and widespread access. I do not have enough data for projections, my Lord. I need to see for myself. I can be there in hours."

Leto paced the office, looking at the Mentat and the Suk doctor. "Prepare the ducal frigate for immediate departure to the north. Gather a team of experts. We will go up and review in person." With his instructions, Hawat nodded and turned to the study door, but Leto called after him, "And Paul. Paul will go with us."

Within two hours, the swift Atreides frigate was ready, but this was no showy formal procession. When everyone was aboard, the vessel sped toward to the coastal fishery operations in the north. Leto didn't know for certain, but he sensed they were somehow under attack. During the flight, Hawat sat next to him in the padded seat, deep in Mentat computations.

Both disturbed and excited by the crisis, Paul looked over at his father, then at Dr. Yueh. "Has a plague like this ever happened before?"

Yueh scribed notes on a pad that he rested on his lap, jotting questions as well as possible causes of the problem. "There's so much we don't know about moonfish."

"I've never heard of anything like this. We still have to investigate in every way." Leto wrestled with his unease. "We harvested moonfish for so long, but mostly in a natural environment, and then our exports increased after my father expanded the market. Caladan is on the verge of a substantial increase, thanks to Count Fenring's investment." He closed his eyes. "But not if all the moonfish die off."

Hawat gave a grim assessment. "The timing is suspicious, my Lord. Such a dramatic die-off, right after Fenring gets involved? If these reports are accurate, the entire industry could collapse. You told me you questioned the Count's motivations since you refused his demand to ruin Lord Londine. Could he be doing this to ruin House Atreides finances? Some kind of elaborate retribution?" He paused. "I do not entirely trust his Mentat."

Paul spoke up. "I know you sent me up to the Muadh villages so I wouldn't be involved with Count Fenring. Do you think he might have targeted me if I hadn't gone away?"

"That was just a precaution, Paul," Leto said. "I can't imagine there's any connection here."

Hawat's brow furrowed. "Is it possible the Count means to obligate you somehow? He extends the gift with one hand, while stabbing you with the other? Fenring may not actually be your friend."

"Nor is the Emperor, Thufir. I am not naïve. But while Shaddam has been capricious in the past, I know of nothing that would have brought this sort of retaliation. Why would they do this to us? It makes no sense."

Paul watched out the windowport as the frigate streaked over the dense trees to the marshlands and fisheries. "Fenring poured so much money into the operations that he stands to lose a fortune if the industry collapses." He looked up as an idea occurred to him. "Could somebody be striking at *him*? An enemy using our moonfish operations as a way to financially harm Fenring?"

Leto's eyebrows rose as he considered the possibility. "The Count surely has many enemies. This might be about him and not us . . ."

The frigate pilot signaled their arrival at the main fishery complex and directed them all to strap in as the craft descended sharply. Leto sat back in the hard seat. "We will see what is happening for ourselves."

A cold, weak drizzle hung in the air as they emerged from the ornate craft onto the raised landing grid. Paul stayed close to his father and stood at his side, the Duke and his heir. Thufir Hawat and Dr. Yueh followed. The stink in the air made them all cringe.

The fishery complex sprawled through the wetlands, and now the transfer canals were clogged with floating fish. Some of the scaly creatures had thrown themselves into the grassy marshes, where they died. Workers in polymer protective suits used rakes and nets to haul hundreds of dead fish out of the foul water and dump them into disposal bins.

Atreides soldiers wearing cloth coverings over their mouths and noses were stationed through the operations, previously assigned there to keep watch for insidious ailar smuggling. They had been especially alert since Paul's recent report from Archvicar Torono. The gray-faced soldiers looked at the dying fish in dismay, not knowing what to do.

Condu Natok popped his head out of a patched-up hut, climbed down steps to a walkway, and scuttled over to where the frigate had landed. When assigning him to replace his disgraced predecessor, Leto had been confident the new fishery manager would learn the ropes and become a competent administrator, but this crisis was over his head. The plague, whatever it was, had thrown everything into a total disaster.

Marching along the metal grid, the Duke looked down at the many, many dying fish clogging the murky brown water. Their gills fluttered, gasping, and their round eyes were wide and staring. The coin-size scales were tarnished, discolored.

Leto met the manager at an intersection of walkways. "Have you discovered the cause?"

Natok looked queasy from the stench in the air. He still wore out-of-place city clothing, and he had wrapped a cloth over his lower face to muffle the smell. "We tested the water in the canals and pools, my Lord. It's the same in the neighboring complexes, too." He raised his hands in a helpless gesture and hurried them along. "Come with me to the processing line, and I'll show you what we found."

Only a few workers stood at the processing table under the sloped coverings that shielded them from the drizzle. Wearing gloves and goggles, they spread out dead moonfish on the planks and gutted them, not for processing, but to study them.

"It's very bad, my Lord," Natok reported. "All of the meat will have to be discarded. Inedible. Possibly toxic."

"But what killed them?" Leto demanded.

"It's worse than a poison—a biological scourge, a small creature." Natok stepped up to where one of the dead moonfish had been mounted like a murder victim on an autopsy table. Natok swung a viewer into place, activated the field, and expanded the magnification. "A voracious invasive mite. It's killing them all."

The holo-image in the magnifier showed a tiny crablike creature, monstrous looking with eight sharp legs, fangs, multiple eyes, and an egg sac on its back. "I've never seen this species before, not like anything on Caladan. They devour the sensitive gill lining so that the fish can't extract oxygen from the water."

Natok leaned closer, pointing into the image. "And see the egg sac. It's filled with hundreds of mites. The mites seem to be hermaphroditic, and all they do is eat and reproduce. They infest moonfish, breed inside their gills, create more mites, and then spread."

"How could we not have known of this species before?" Leto asked.

Dr. Yueh studied the image and then prodded the dissected fish, deep in thought. "I researched everything known about moonfish after young Master Paul nearly died from poisoning. I have no record of these mites in my volumes."

Hawat sounded angry and skeptical. "Surely some naturalist has recorded the life cycle of moonfish and the predators that afflict them?"

Paul examined the magnified mite, fascinated, but Leto was disgusted by the thing.

Natok stepped away from the magnifier. "Many of my crew have worked in the fisheries all their lives, as have their parents and grandparents before them. No one has heard of any creature like this. It's a new scourge, an invasive species. I have no idea where it came from."

Hawat frowned. "How could these deadly mites appear here and at multiple fisheries, all at the same time?"

Paul joined Dr. Yueh, and both peered down at the dissected fish on the wooden table. The Suk doctor glanced up at him, then at the Duke. "It cannot be natural. All the ponds at the same time?"

"No, it does not seem natural." Leto felt bile rising in his throat, caused by more than just the stench of dying fish. "Hawat, I want a full investigative team. Trace the spread of the mites. Find out how we can eliminate them." He paused, then added in a harder voice, "Track down where they came from—and who did this to House Atreides."

Plans within plans within plans. Is anything the way it seems?
—Bene Gesserit teaching, introduction to Acolytes

Reverend Mother Ruthine sat in near-darkness in her bungalow on a shrub-covered slope just above the noise and bustle of the dormitories. Leading Sisters were sometimes given such bungalows for privacy. In the darkness, she looked out on the security lights of the Mother School complex, and all the orange-gold foliage looked like a low fire in the night. A heater glowed in one corner, but the bungalow room remained in shadows.

Jessica. Danger. How could Harishka not see it?

In the early days of the Sisterhood, when the first Mother Superior lay dying, two main factions had vied for control, each with radically different views of the order's future. The group led by Reverend Mother Valya Harkonnen had won the dispute, but the schism was not healed without a great deal of blood-shed. The Bene Gesserit Sisterhood had been founded on violence.

Ruthine realized that Lethea might have created another fundamental schism . . . and even though people might die over this, Ruthine would not be deterred. The risk to the future was painfully clear. In that, at least, Lethea's prescience had left no doubt.

If I am wrong, then two will die. If I am right, then billions *will perish!*

The bungalow door opened, letting in a chill night draft as well as a group of furtive robed figures. They closed the door and waited in shadows. Even though Ruthine had been expecting them, she was immediately alert, ready to fight. Confirming who they were, she called them over to empty seats she had arranged by the window. She did not activate the glowglobes.

The Sisters moved like oiled darkness as they joined her, each of them knowing not to risk discovery. The tallest of the four sat on one side of Ruthine—Xora herself. Sister Jiara sat on her other side, while the remaining pair sat across from her, with a low table in between.

"Why did you call us here?" asked the heavier of the pair across the table, Sister Taula. Sister Aislan, the one beside her, just stared at Ruthine, waiting, her eyes glittering. She was thin, wiry, and she was just as dedicated. The two women were among the best Bene Gesserit fighters Ruthine knew.

Jiara snorted. "You saw what Lethea wrote in blood! She died to give us that message. Are we brave enough to listen to it?"

Ruthine regarded them all. They sat wrapped in tension, though she knew they agreed with her thinking, or she wouldn't have called them here in the first place. "You four would do anything I asked you to do, wouldn't you?"

"For the good of the Sisterhood," Xora said. She, in particular, had avid eyes. She seemed excited to be included in their private discussions . . . their conspiracy.

"Mother Superior Harishka is letting the Sisterhood falter," Taula said. "She's more interested in constructing new school buildings than in our breeding program, the Missionaria Protectiva, the creation of more Truthsayers, the—"

Ruthine cut her off. "We'll be here all night making the list." Edgy laughter passed around the group. "We have serious matters to discuss."

"You should be Mother Superior, not Harishka. She doesn't appreciate you," Jiara said.

"Oh, Harishka appreciates me," Ruthine said, "but not enough. When the time comes, perhaps I will be her replacement. But that is not the vital matter we need to discuss tonight." She measured her words carefully, building up to the demand she was going to make. "I know you are all loyal to me. But would you kill for me?" She paused during their quick intake of breath. "For the Sisterhood? Would you heed the warning right in front of you?"

Without hesitation they said, one after the other, "We would kill for you, and for the Bene Gesserit." Xora seemed eager to agree, to prove herself.

Aislan said boldly, "You want us to assassinate Harishka? Is that it?"

Taula swallowed. "Has it come to that already?"

Grimacing, Ruthine shook her head. "No, that would put a permanent stain on your lives and legacies, as well as my own." She did not add that if the crisis ever reached such a point, she would do it herself. "It would be the wrong thing to do, at least at the moment. No, it is not that."

"Is it Sister Jessica, then?" Xora asked. "Lethea's warning? I am going to Caladan, as the Duke's new concubine."

Ruthine pursed her lips. "At present, Jessica is secure and not in any position to harm us . . . and we have many potential options for dealing with her. She is only part of the problem. Lethea identified another threat that could bring about the downfall of our entire Sisterhood." The room fell silent, and Ruthine let the anticipation mount. "I want you to kill a child."

Murmurs rippled around her quiet followers.

Aislan asked, "Which child?"

"A fourteen-year-old boy, almost a man. But we cannot let him become a man."

"You're talking about Paul Atreides," Xora said. "Duke Leto's son."

"Jessica's son." Now Ruthine began to lay out her plan. "Lethea's premonitions may be cryptic, but we know the veracity of some of them. Can we afford to ignore them? Her mind might have been twisted and changed with her extreme age and distress, but the circumstances could also have unlocked bright revelations previously denied her. Her warning to me was absolute before she fell into her coma. Billions of lives are at stake. In her last moments, Lethea found the strength to send us another message—in her own blood."

Ruthine looked at the shadowy faces of the other conspirators. "Jessica's son born out of rebellion poses an existential threat to the Bene Gesserit. We must remove him, because Mother Superior Harishka will not make the necessary decision. While Jiara and I remain here and look for our opportunity to control, or more likely eliminate, Sister Jessica, Taula and Aislan, you will slip away to Caladan on the next Heighliner, ostensibly on a recruiting mission to find young women to become Acolytes. But you will disguise yourselves in common clothes—with nothing to identify you as Bene Gesserit—and find a way to eliminate this dangerous boy."

Taula nodded, her smile plain even in the dim light. "That should not be difficult."

Xora stiffened, obviously upset. "But I have just been assigned as the Duke's concubine! I will be going there myself. Why do you need to send them? Am I not in a better position to do it?"

Now Ruthine was even more calculating. "We can't have the Duke's new concubine kill his own son, now can we? Then what chance would you have to win his heart?" She sniffed. "*Think,* Xora! Think of the history of Duke Leto Atreides."

Xora fidgeted, mulling over her complicated thoughts. She lifted her head as she remembered. "Ah, he already had one young son who was killed. After that tragedy, Jessica came to him in his time of grief, made him fall in love with her . . . and that's when she conceived her own son." She paused. "I see now."

Ruthine nodded. "Reverend Mother Mohiam is coming here soon, and she will want to brief Xora about Duke Leto Atreides before she is dispatched on her assignment. Taula and Aislan, you must be gone before then, set the wheels in motion. Jiara and I will watch over matters here, in case something needs to be done with Mother Superior Harishka. Lethea is dead, but the repercussions are just beginning."

The pair agreed and fell silent as they contemplated the details. Xora, though, could not contain her excitement. "I'm pleased about this! Yes, Paul Atreides is a ticking bomb." Ruthine knew she was merely thinking to increase the chances of her own illicit son, who did have the markers, the potential. . . .

Ruthine was impatient. "One matter at a time. This is about eliminating a very large problem, a potentially dangerous individual. The unexpected birth of

Paul Atreides has thrown the breeding calculations and projections into chaos. We must uproot the noxious weed before it spreads."

Taula and Aislan both stood, looking eager. "We will take care of it."

Xora was breathing hard, her excitement apparent. Ruthine spoke guardedly, not sure whether her words would quell or increase the excitement. "And Xora, if these other two Sisters fail in their mission, then it *will* fall to you to eliminate Paul Atreides."

"That is not going to be necessary," Aislan said, sounding offended.

"I will accept any opportunities provided to me," Xora said. "I can be both a lover and a killer."

〜☙〜

*Do not let political grandstanding interfere with profits. Business is far
more stable than any government.*

—CHOAM Directors' briefing

The asteroid supply cluster was located on the fringe of the Bendine system, a single white star with two habitable but uninteresting planets. The Spacing Guild serviced Bendine far more often than should have been necessary, but CHOAM classified it as a valuable market, so that Malina Aru had an excuse to maintain private operations out in the asteroids, far from prying eyes.

After the Heighliner arrived at the first Bendine planet for off-loading operations, which would take a day or so, Malina took a fast, unmarked CHOAM hauler, outbound. The ship accelerated away from the planetary orbits to reach the cluster of drifting rocks out in the frigid darkness. Composed of rock and ice with only trace amounts of metals, this worthless debris drew no attention for their resources; therefore, the asteroids were a perfect hiding place.

Relaxed in the passenger compartment, the Ur-Director trusted her pilot to navigate around the shadowy, dangerous asteroids. When first planning this brief inspection trip, Malina had invited her daughter to accompany her. She wanted Jalma to see the growth of their plans, a visible manifestation of the enormous hoard that CHOAM had recently gathered. Their melange stockpile appeared on no ledger sheets or Imperial tax records.

It was meant to be a private show of wealth for her daughter, so they could plan—very different from the imminent spectacle at which Shaddam intended to display mountains of actual coins at the palace just to flaunt his power. She remembered from ancient Earth history how the powerful elite would host banquets where the food was dusted with flakes of real gold, just because they could. Malina found such displays to be ill advised and counterproductive, and the restless peasants at the time had felt the same. Subtle wealth was much more important than a flashy show. The Urdir had not felt the need to brag about her own accomplishments here.

Unfortunately, her daughter had declined the invitation. Jalma was busy expanding her hederwood exports on Pliesse and locking down her power over

House Uchan. She was among CHOAM's wisest and most powerful Directors, one of the heirs to the Aru dynasty.

The company's influence would continue for generations more, but occasionally Malina regretted the fact that she had faltered in her role as mother. No matter. The Ur-Director would revel in the stockpile herself.

"Arriving at the primary storage asteroid, Urdir," her pilot transmitted. "There's breathable atmosphere inside the complex, though I believe the temperature is less than comfortable. Dress warmly."

Malina added an outer wrap over her comfortable business suit, then donned a pair of thick gloves and insulated slippers. As the hauler approached the hollowed asteroid, she looked down at a pockmarked gray expanse, a tumbling rock among many similar rocks. It wasn't a vacation resort, just a vault.

The asteroid's interior was honeycombed with passages and grotto chambers. All the rocky debris had been spewed out into space during the construction process, and now Malina heard the patter of pelting rubble as her ship matched orbits with the big asteroid.

The transport hauler docked, and CHOAM workers paired the air locks, engaged the seals, then opened the hatch. Suited cargo handlers swiftly transferred hundreds of neat rectangular packages filled with compressed spice—the current haul, adding to the stockpile. Malina followed them into the rock-walled chamber. Steam curled out of her nostrils in the frigid air, but the rich tingle of melange permeated each breath and warmed her heart.

If Jalma had joined her, the two of them—mother and daughter—could have walked the corridors together, reveling in the vast fortune of spice. Baron Harkonnen had certainly delivered on his promise. This off-books melange had been extremely expensive to obtain, but it was an unencumbered resource worth far more than its monetary value. Emperor Shaddam's spice surtax had made the melange market unstable, and now his upcoming grandiose event . . . Empress Aricatha had reported all the details to her, describing what Shaddam wanted to do with his shipload of solari coins, but she also claimed she would try to put a different spin on the event, to salvage what she could.

Malina shook her head. Such a tone-deaf spectacle would earn the Corrinos no friends, but at least it would give the Noble Commonwealth movement another crowbar to help destroy the stagnant old Imperium.

As she moved alone through the asteroid's spice-filled chambers, her pilot sent her a message. "Urdir, the Heighliner is now moving to the second Bendine planet. They expect cargo off-loading operations to last another five hours. We will need to return and be back aboard by then."

She touched her comm. "Let me enjoy my surroundings for a few moments longer." She reached one of the largest vaults, where packaged melange was stacked to the curved rock ceiling. This room alone contained a planet's ransom.

House Corrino had immense strategic reserves of spice, and Malina was certain that the Spacing Guild also had its own world-size coffers, filled over the centuries. Baron Harkonnen surely kept a large stockpile himself in case his family fortunes should ever collapse, though the Ur-Director couldn't imagine how the Harkonnens would ever be ousted from their Arrakis governorship.

What would Jalma or Frankos have done with so much wealth? She frowned as the next natural thought occurred to her. What would *Jaxson* have done with it? Likely used the money to finance more violence! She had cut her rebel son off from all CHOAM funding and terminated his access to the family accounts, but he still thrived.

Secretly, she applauded him. She loved her youngest child despite his actions. She knew, too, that he wasn't finished.

Jalma had sent a carefully worded message to Malina's offices, explaining in code that Jaxson had come to see her on Pliesse. Frankos sent a similar message, and Malina was appalled that her son would flaunt his presence, and endanger his siblings, but Jaxson seemed convinced that he was invulnerable. He had promised both his brother and sister that he intended to make yet another bold statement, throwing more ice water into the faces of the listless nobles. Her other two children felt unsettled, perhaps even threatened.

Malina was sure she would once again have to decry Jaxson and express her sympathy for the victims. But Jalma and Frankos had attended important Noble Commonwealth strategy meetings, and they knew the groundwork their predecessors had done for more than a century. Trying to be the voice of reason, Malina laid out the unraveling of the Corrino Imperium as a long-term battle strategy, a thousand dots to connect.

But even she was growing impatient. Shaddam Corrino's obvious mismanagement, his corruption, his provocation of the Landsraad—each thing hastened his downfall. The Ur-Director had spent her life orchestrating slow nudges, while Jaxson struck with a club. More and more people were listening to his fringe of the movement.

She missed Jaxson. Oh, they'd often argued, but it was merely philosophical sparring, a clash of ideas, an energetic debate. Was she so set in her ways that she couldn't hear another opinion? Wouldn't she love to have Corrino rule ended—and right now?

Malina closed her eyes inside the large storage chamber, and inhaled deeply. The redolence of cinnamon was so thick and furry that she nearly coughed, but a rush went through her mind.

Maybe she and Jaxson weren't so far apart. Malina checked her chronometer, then made her way through the chilly tunnels, drifting along in the negligible gravity, until she returned to her ship.

No, maybe they weren't so far apart after all.

When we are wronged, we must find those responsible. But in seeking the guilty, is one person enough? I will not be satisfied until I have followed the line to its bitter end.

—DUKE PAULUS ATREIDES, *The Responsibilities of a Duke*

Working in close analysis with Dr. Yueh, Thufir Hawat sent teams of experts through the devastated moonfish operations, interrogating workers and witnesses, conducting thorough searches. Technicians took samples from the water in all the connected fisheries, so that teams of scientists could try to trace the origin of the pernicious mite.

From his previous investigations about Chaen Marek's black market in the ailar drug, the Atreides Mentat had a framework of informants in place among the fishery villages, and he began digging deeper because of the recent disturbing news from Archvicar Torono. But this moonfish tragedy was something much more disastrous.

Hawat unraveled the mystery in less than a week. Duke Leto was impressed when the warrior Mentat came to his office to submit a verbal report. "The two problems are connected, my Lord—the ailar and the deadly mite." He paused to select his words carefully. "This is far more personal than you imagine."

Behind his elaccawood desk, Leto listened to the trickling music of a fountain that poured over a slab of rough rock, but it did not have its usual calming effect on him. He braced himself, fearing the worst. "What is this connection, Thufir?" Anger had simmered inside him for so long, yet the fires intensified with each dark activity exposed right here on Caladan. He was glad Paul wasn't in the room, because he feared his own reaction.

The Mentat reached into his pocket and withdrew a shriveled bit of barra fern. "The ailar black market is back, my Lord." Hawat held up the dried brown curl of fern. "Archvicar Torono was right."

Leto stood up from behind his desk. Goose bumps crawled on his flesh as he touched the dried fern as if he were poking a spider. "But we burned the barra fields, all of them. We destroyed Chaen Marek's operations."

Hawat nodded. "But he got away, no doubt to grow more drugs." He held up the dried fern. "This ailar was being distributed among fishery workers and also showed up in the isolated towns around fisheries. At least there have been no new deaths reported. Apparently, these barra ferns are a modified species."

"I don't care if they're different!" Feeling soiled, Leto wiped his hands on his trouser leg.

Dr. Yueh entered and stood solemnly, watching the dark flush on Leto's face. "I will run a chemical analysis on the new ferns and compare them with previous samples. I believe they are grown in a different region of Caladan, then smuggled up here."

"Thufir, you assured me you had crushed all of the distributors," Leto said.

"Yet, like a noxious weed, it grows back. The people of Caladan lead good lives, but it is a flaw in human nature. Weak people seek their addictive drugs, and Chaen Marek was more than happy to provide them."

Leto stewed. The problem wasn't just weak or hopeless people. "I know." He thought of how many other ailar users had been discovered around the Landsraad, including Lord Atikk's unfortunate son.

Then another thought swept through his mind like a pendulum completing an arc. "But you were investigating the mite infestation in the moonfish operations. What does that have to do with drug smuggling?"

"Both are attacks on House Atreides, Sire." The Mentat delivered his report in a crisp voice. "After thorough interrogations and following up many leads, we apprehended the man who runs the primary ailar network and smuggles the drug. He is also the one responsible for spreading the invasive mite. He released it in all the fisheries where he distributed his new ailar. His name is Lupar." He smiled stiffly. "And I have him in custody."

A red haze glowed around Leto's vision. Why would anyone do that? "Is he still alive?"

"Still clinging to life, my Lord. We had to encourage him to speak using certain extreme measures. Fortunately, with Dr. Yueh's pharmaceuticals and my own Mentat techniques, the more barbaric parts of physical interrogation were kept to a minimum."

Yueh nodded as if embarrassed. "The Suk medical school has a special branch of training that is useful in intense interrogations. Although I've rarely been called upon to employ such methods, it was part of my necessary instruction. If, for example, an assassination plot were discovered against the Emperor, we Suk doctors would need to use every technique available to produce answers."

Hawat explained, "But the man was more terrified of Chaen Marek than of us. It seems that something was implanted in him to keep him from talking. He can't tell us where the new barra fields are grown. It is permanently blocked."

Dr. Yueh looked somber. "I will continue to work on him, Sire, but the block is severe. He may not produce the answer."

At some later point when he calmed down, Leto knew he would appreciate such restraint, but right now, he didn't care if this dealer had been broken into dozens of pieces, so long as he talked.

Even though he was furious about the return of the so-called Caladan drug, Leto had another mystery to solve. "What about all the dying moonfish? Did Chaen Marek destroy my fisheries, too? To what purpose?"

"The mites, the moonfish—that wasn't Chaen Marek," the Mentat explained. "That was just to hurt House Atreides."

"Losing those fisheries is a huge blow to House Atreides," Leto said. He tried to imagine who his competitors were. What other noble house would be so ruthless as to release an invasive parasite throughout the moonfish ecosystem? "Is it another CHOAM Director?"

Yueh looked at Hawat, then at the Duke. "The mite is not a species native to Caladan. Biologically, we traced its planet of origin. It comes from Lankiveil, Sire."

House Harkonnen!

Hawat explained further. "Apparently, Lupar had already worked with Beast Rabban to distribute ailar to some planets in the Imperium. Because of their connection, Rabban hired this man to release mites into our fisheries, just to cause damage." The Mentat's eyes hardened. "Just to hurt *you*, my Lord."

Leto breathed slowly, trying to calm himself. He felt as if a hundred razor fish were nipping at his body, drawing blood, attacking from all sides. "Rabban . . . The Harkonnens . . ." He looked up at Hawat. "Send all of your evidence and documentation to Count Fenring immediately. He has been attacked as well."

Leto began to think of the many ways he could respond, how House Atreides could strike back at their mortal enemies.

You take pride in your Landsraad decrees, CHOAM Directorships, and family alliances as ways to flaunt your wealth and exert influence. I prefer to use fang and claw as a measure of power.

—FEYD-RAUTHA HARKONNEN, response to Landsraad
invitation to the Introductory Spring Ball

He knew there was nothing natural about his pets, Blood and Bone. Feyd-Rautha could see the irony in his idea to take them into the wild, since the spinehounds had been genetically designed by the Tleilaxu, bred in tanks, and accelerated to maturity inside laboratory domes. They had been fed a perfect diet, held in cages, and transported to Giedi Prime, where they were sonically imprinted to recognize Feyd's blood and obey his commands.

By no measure were the spinehounds wild animals, yet he relished the idea of seeing them in a primal state. Feyd wanted to watch them run and hunt and kill in the rugged forest, tearing the flesh and fur of any prey they found.

On the outskirts of loud, dirty Harko City, a large hunting preserve had been blocked off, used primarily by his brother, Rabban. Forest Guard Station was a slice of unruly landscape with dense pines, stark rock outcroppings, sheer cliffs, and streams that poured through canyons. Rabban made sure the area was well stocked with predators. His brother sometimes turned human victims loose and hunted them as they struggled to survive.

But right now, with Rabban preoccupied on Arrakis, this wilderness preserve was ignored, left on its own. The seasoned hunt captains were bored, fat, and lazy, and Feyd decided to put them to work. The lead hunter, Dimos, had a round and sweaty face and dark stubble on his chin. How surprised he had been when Feyd sauntered up to him in his cluttered office with Blood and Bone behind him.

Dimos stepped forward and regarded the spinehounds with great interest. "M'Lord Feyd," he said.

"I need your services." He gestured with his hand, and the laboratory-bred beasts flared their silver spines and growled.

The hunter looked impressed rather than terrified. He rocked back on his heels. "Excellent animals. Have they hunted?"

"Not yet. That's what I want you to arrange."

Dimos inspected Blood and Bone from a distance, not coming within reach of their snapping jaws. "Take them out for a killing run? Will you be joining us, my Lord?"

"Of course I will be joining you! I want to see my pets hunt, and they are blood-bonded to me. How would you control them?" At first Feyd felt insulted by the man's question, until realizing that he rarely left the city. Feyd kept his body well tuned through killing, but preferred combat with actual humans to hunting. He honed his skills and finesse with swords and daggers, kindjals and slip-tips, sharp pikes and poisoned needles. He had trained himself to put on a grand show in the arena against designated opponents. He did not like the dirt or the uncivilized nature of the wilderness.

Though only fifteen, Feyd had already killed two of his training masters in combat exercises—one by defeating him with a blade, and the other by trickery, a spring-loaded hook in his armor with a poisoned point. Feyd hadn't disliked either of the instructors; he simply felt that if he could best them, kill them, then they had nothing more to teach him.

"Are you prepared for a hunt yourself, m'Lord?" Dimos asked again.

Feyd realized his own thoughts had wandered. He ground his teeth together. "Of course I am. Shall I have my pets hunt *you?*" The two spinehounds picked up on his annoyance and growled again.

The round-faced man paled. "I'll make preparations. I have two tawny bucks ready to go. We can turn them loose, one by one." He smiled wistfully. "It'll be good to see the preserve again, to hear the baying of predators, and smell the blood scent myself."

Feyd reached down to pat the two animals. "I'll also bring my Swordmaster to inspire him for a different kind of hunt." He led Blood and Bone away.

TWO DAYS LATER, when they loaded the transport craft in the late afternoon, Feyd arrived at the rendezvous flanked by the two animals. He sported a fine hunting outfit, a new tunic and trousers of supple schlag leather, mesh-reinforced boots. He armed himself with a ceremonial dagger and a lightweight short sword. Even on an isolated hunt, Feyd-Rautha Harkonnen, one of the Baron's presumed heirs, never dismissed the possibility of assassins.

Egan Saar stood on the boarding ramp of the transport ship, his long sword slung beneath his tattered cape. He looked no different for the hunt than when he'd engaged in gladiatorial combat in the arena.

While Dimos finished the final preparations on board the transport craft, Saar reported, "Two tawny bucks are already loaded, my Lord. The hunt captain says the meat will make for a delicious feast, if your spinehounds don't tear apart the carcasses too badly."

"If Blood and Bone make the kill, they can have their own feast," Feyd said.

His pulse raced with excitement, and the hounds picked up on it. They fidgeted restlessly, sniffing, pacing. When Bone inadvertently bumped into his brother, they snarled and slashed at each other until Feyd commanded them to break apart. He waited for his pets to calm down before he led them aboard the transport. Feyd took a seat beside the Swordmaster, who stared ahead, hands wrapped around the hilt of his sword.

Blood and Bone lay on the deck at Feyd's feet, their pointed ears pricked as the thrum of suspensors increased. Dimos yelled from the cockpit that they were ready to depart for Forest Guard Station.

Feyd leaned closer to Egan Saar as the craft rose up and headed out of the city into the gathering dusk. "When you go to Caladan, the Atreides prey will be different from tawny bucks in a forest."

"I'm always in the mood for a hunt of any sort." Saar looked up with his intense eyes. "But you hired me for a subtle blow, not just a bludgeon. I shall make it painful, have no fear of that."

The swift craft left the garish lights of Harko City far behind, as full night fell. The sun had set in a bloody, smoky sky, and the light began thickening into darkness. The best time for a hunt, according to Dimos.

Saar called up to the piloting compartment. "Hunt captain, you said there are other animals in Forest Guard Preserve? Gaze hounds, striped panthers, and the like?"

"Those, and other breeds, sir," said Dimos. "All vicious and deadly."

Feyd looked out the windowport, saw thick stands of dark pines, rugged sandstone outcroppings like rotten teeth protruding from hillsides. He was dismayed to see no roads, not even any paths. Forest Guard Station was simply a blot of uncharted terrain.

Saar called out, "Good, then I will take time for a hunt of my own. Drop me in the wilderness while you let Feyd-Rautha's pets kill a couple of helpless bucks. I need some exercise myself."

Feyd chuckled at the idea, then saw that the twisted Swordmaster was serious. He shrugged. "Whatever inspires you."

Egan Saar stepped past the spinehounds, who paid no further attention to him, and stood by the craft's side door. He touched the hilt of his sword, secured the belt in place. "Swing down and hover low over that bluff so I can jump out."

Dimos was surprised. "But why? There's a meadow up ahead that we like to use as our starting point. You can leave from there."

"I will find my own way, either to you or back to the city," said the Swordmaster. "When I am ready." The forest darkness loomed across the landscape below, like a shadow that had swallowed up the world.

"Do as he says," Feyd called.

The side hatch opened to the whistling wind and the rush of pine boughs.

Saar sprang out, dropping several meters to a broad shelf of tan rock, where he landed neatly. He was intent on his own killing.

Moments later, easing the controls, the hunt captain settled the transport craft down on the open meadow, and Feyd walked down the extended ramp to stand in the dew-moist grasses. Shading his eyes from the glare of the landing lights, he surveyed the tall trees and the shadow-pocked cliffs. He heard a rustle of winds, the drone of night insects, but no sounds indicating human presence except for the humming of the suspensor engines as they powered down.

Dimos first unloaded a pair of small skeletal vehicles that were little more than one-person rider frames equipped with suspensors and propulsion engines. "These flitters will let us follow the hunt, my Lord," he said, powering up the systems. "When the tawny bucks run, they streak like lightning." He glanced at Blood and Bone. "I assume your spinehounds will be able to keep up?"

"Don't worry about that," Feyd promised. "Let's get on with it." His two animals panted, their coppery eyes gleaming as they waited to be set loose.

The slender vehicles bobbed in the air just off the ground, flyer-bikes waiting for riders. Feyd was amused to think of the round-faced lead hunter mounted on such a precarious craft. The young man inspected the controls.

Back at the landed transport, Dimos opened the lower hold and maneuvered a large cage that held an antelope-like creature, all ropy muscle and long graceful legs, eyes too large for its oblong head, and branched antlers like extended, sharp thorns.

Saliva drooled from the spinehounds' sharp fangs. The tawny buck made a keening sound of terror when it saw the beasts.

"Keep them under control, my Lord," the hunt captain warned. "We want this to be a sporting hunt."

"In the wilderness, is it always sporting?" Feyd sneered.

Dimos flushed, but Feyd gestured to his blood-bonded pets. He had practiced using the Tleilaxu instruction document, and the spinehounds were trained in their commands. While Feyd held the animals in check, Dimos opened the cage and released the first buck. The prey bounded out like a projectile, burning the chemical energy stored in its muscles. Even Feyd was astonished by how fast the animal ran.

Blood and Bone coiled, ready to launch themselves, but the invisible bonds of Feyd's command kept them frozen. The tawny buck had already vanished into the thick woods, but the hunt master gazed off in that direction, silently counting. "Wait . . . wait."

Feyd squirmed, as anxious as his pets to be on the chase. Finally, Dimos made a twitch that might have been a nod, and Feyd released the spinehounds. They streaked off after the prey, silvery weapons that disappeared into the trees.

Feyd and Dimos mounted the flitters, turned up the suspensors and propulsion, and raced off, rising higher above the meadow. In the forest, the tawny buck crashed through the underbrush, and the hounds raced after it, eerily silent, though Feyd could hear their panting, their paws tearing up the fallen pine needles and debris.

The pines were too dense for the flitters to arrow between them, so Feyd and Dimos had to fly above the treetops, where they caught only glimpses of the hounds rushing along like targeted missiles. The tawny buck put on a burst of speed, dove over a deadfall, crashed into broken branches below, stumbled, and then ran over leaf-strewn rocks.

Cruising overhead, Feyd looked down, so excited that he cheered Blood and Bone, shouting to encourage them. The spinehounds didn't flinch or look up at him as they surged forward in unison. Strangely coordinated, they leaped in a graceful arc over the deadfall and lunged.

Together, they struck the tawny buck hard and knocked it to the ground, where it was impaled on an upthrust branch from the fallen tree. The doomed animal gave a wild, sickening cry as it struggled. Then the spinehounds ripped its neck and underbelly. By the time Feyd and Dimos swooped down to land their flitters next to it, the buck was mangled beyond recognition.

Blood and Bone tore at their prey as they fed. They looked up at their master with dripping muzzles and coppery eyes hot with bloodlust.

"Come!" Feyd called. "To me."

The animals snarled, looked at each other, then growled at him.

"To *me*!"

Bone snapped at the other hound, and Blood lashed back, but the two pets sullenly came to stand beside him.

"That was over too quickly," he told the hunt captain, energized but disappointed. "It was just practice. We'll draw out the second chase a little longer."

Dimos left a marker by the dead buck so the meat could be retrieved later, though he warned that other scavengers in Forest Guard Station would find it soon enough.

Blood and Bone, spattered with gore, panted hard, their eyes shining with eagerness for another hunt. They followed Feyd's slow flitter back to the meadow, then sat attentively on their haunches, intense and waiting.

The hunt captain reentered the transport craft's lower hold and returned with a second cage that contained another skittish tawny buck. The trapped animal bleated, clattered its horns against the bars of the cage. The spinehounds yipped and growled, shuddering with anticipation.

"Stay!" Feyd snapped. His pets coiled, trembling.

Dimos fumbled with the cage. "We will let the buck run longer this time, my Lord—range farther so we have a more satisfying hunt." He worked the latch, and the tawny buck charged out.

But in a flash, Blood exploded away from Feyd's side and raced after it.

Feyd yelled, as did the hunt captain who bolted forward, waving his arms as if to call back the tawny buck. Startled by the noise and movement, Bone broke from Feyd's command and lunged, but not after the fleeing animal. His target was Dimos.

Before the hunt captain had taken two steps from the cage, the spinehound crashed into him, knocking him back onto the transport craft's boarding ramp. The man's screams rapidly turned into wet gurgles as Bone ripped out his throat and shook the wads of flesh back and forth.

Feyd yelled, remembering how the spinehounds had killed the maintenance workers in the tunnels beneath Harko City and his own attendant in his chambers. "No!"

Blood brought down the second tawny buck even before it reached the trees at the edge of the meadow. The two animals crashed and rolled across the tall grasses, and the spinehound snarled as he eviscerated the prey.

"Stop!" Feyd used his command voice, angry that his pets wouldn't heel. He wondered if something had gone wrong with the original sonic imprinting at the spaceport. "Come! *Now!*" He put all the threat he could into his voice.

The pair of silvery predators looked up from their feeding. Scarlet blood drooled from their muzzles and fangs. They came.

They came at him, fast and hard.

Feyd shouted one more time, but he knew it was useless. He had seen the eyes of countless opponents who wanted to kill him, and in the molten-metal gaze of these predators, he realized that Blood and Bone saw him only as more prey, another victim. They had reverted to their intrinsic nature, somehow breaking their conditioning.

Feyd saw that he could never make it to the safety of the transport craft. He had his dagger and short sword, and he could fight, but as the spiny beasts charged toward him, he sprang onto his flitter and activated the suspensors. The flyer-bike lurched a meter into the air, and Feyd swerved just as one of the spinehounds leaped high and snapped its jaws shut right where Feyd had been.

He wheeled, then accelerated, adding energy to the propulsion engines so that he shot toward the trees. Blood and Bone raced after him, eerily silent again.

Feyd hunched over the lightweight craft, rushing into the thick trees where he hoped to lose them. The black pines were like grabbing claws, extending branches to stop him. He increased the suspensors to lift him out of reach of the treacherous spinehounds. He felt a flash of anger as he glared down at his beloved pets bounding after him. . . .

A thick pine bough struck him in the head like a club, knocking him from the flyer-bike. Feyd cried out as he tumbled, grabbing at branches, snatching for clumps of needles. He heard a crash as the unmanned flitter rammed into more branches and became hung up high above the ground.

He landed hard on the forest floor, stunned. He shook his head and jumped to his feet, looking around. He heard the spinehounds racing toward him through the forest, and he began to run.

Feyd looked frantically for a shelter where he could hole up, some sort of defensible position. During the fall from the skimmer he had dropped his short sword, and now he had only his dagger. He looked up at the trees, wondering if he could climb high enough off the ground, but the branches were mockingly far overhead. He kept running.

The spinehounds bounded after him, panting hard, hunting.

He reached a sandstone outcropping with a fallen tree in front of it. This was the best he could do. Making a stand, Feyd stood behind the tree trunk with his back against the rock wall, pulled out his dagger, and bared his teeth as if to match the predatory snarls of his pets.

Blood and Bone galloped forward, slavering for the kill, and Feyd faced them, ready to die. He had fought in the arena many times, but never before had the fear of dying been so real and visceral. He raised his dagger.

Suddenly, Bone yelped and tumbled to the ground. Feyd saw a shadow emerge from the trees, a human figure moving with incredible speed. A blade flashed, and blood sprayed from the animal's back as its spine was severed.

The second spinehound whirled, sensing an attack.

Feyd still held his dagger to defend himself.

Egan Saar leaped in, swinging his blade even as Bone slumped on the forest floor. Blood lunged at the Swordmaster, but Saar met the animal. He struck hard, slashing open the hound's chest, then pulled away and thrust again through Blood's heart.

Paralyzed nearby, Bone snarled and groaned.

Feyd sprang toward the spinehound. He slit the treacherous beast's throat, putting Bone out of his misery, though he felt angry and disappointed at having to do so.

Saar stood in front of Feyd, barely panting.

As the sweat evaporated, Feyd felt a chill in the afterwash of terror, then incredulous, then outraged. "They turned on *me!*"

"It is the way of things," said the Swordmaster. "You're a Harkonnen. You know that such things can happen." Saar looked down at the two dead animals. "I couldn't find any of the other prey that the hunt master promised, but I'm glad I was here for the most important kills of the day." He planted his bloody sword tip into the forest soil and met Feyd's gaze. "Do you need to test me any further, my Lord, or are you ready to turn me loose to do my real mission? On Caladan."

Feyd was incapable of forming words, so he only nodded.

Jessica heard movement outside her cell. The door unsealed, and Brom stood there, looking worried. "Did they tell you? Do you hear any news in here?" He did not look like he was on an assignment given to him by the Sisters. This young man was either an unwitting tool, or a possible ally.

"I know nothing in here," she said. Jessica had tried to count how many hours or days she had been isolated, and now she weighed her decisions. "Has Reverend Mother Mohiam arrived? I know she is coming sometime soon." She braced herself, wondering what the powerful woman wanted from her. "Has she asked to see me?"

Brom looked confused for a moment. "The Emperor's Truthsayer? No, she is not due for another day." He stepped into the cell, full of nervous energy. "It's about Lethea!"

Jessica knew before he said any more. "She is dead?"

"Yes, and more than that!" He seemed eager to share secrets. "Just before she died, Lethea scrawled a last message in her own blood! It said, 'Jessica. Danger.'"

Her mind intensely alert, Jessica realized that Lethea's last message could be interpreted in two ways, either that she was *in* danger, or that she herself *posed* a danger. If the Bene Gesserit interpreted it as the latter, then her own life might be in peril. They could even murder Paul, for good measure.

Lethea had done this on purpose, Jessica was certain, a last twist of the knife, to throw the Sisterhood into an uproar.

Looking anxious and hunted, Brom darted back to the door. "That's all I have time for." He hurried away, but his words reverberated in Jessica's brain. Lethea's chaotic prescience had given her tremendous responsibility and influence, but her predictions and warnings had been so unreliable as to be worthless.

Jessica. Danger. What would Mother Superior Harishka do with that?

HARISHKA AND HER two top counselors debated the implications, but she knew one thing for certain. "Lethea knew exactly what she was doing. Damn her! She meant to cause turmoil—her last malicious act."

Ruthine appeared more determined than ever, and she sounded . . . smug. "One more reason why we should dispose of Jessica and take no further risks. With or without Lethea's warning, we know what to do. She is a danger! Her son is a danger."

Cordana stood warming herself by the fireplace, her twisted back profiled against the flickering light.

Harishka sighed. "When Reverend Mother Mohiam arrives soon, she will tell us what an intractable student Jessica was."

Cordana returned to her seat at the table. "Jessica is here, completely under our control. We can watch her, teach her, help her. And Xora is due to depart for Caladan, where she can be our eyes on young Paul Atreides." She wrapped both hands around a hot cup of tea that sat on the table in front of her. She gave Ruthine a pointed look. "Some Sisters insisted on killing *me* as a baby. Even so, I've risen above those difficulties and served the order." She sipped her tea, maddeningly drawing out the pause. "We should not condemn a valuable Sister just because a vindictive madwoman left a cryptic last message."

Harishka felt as if she sat near a throbbing hornet's nest. In a low voice, she said, "Lethea was not like this when I met her, but the disappointments of a long life made her cruel and unstable. I don't think even Lethea could interpret her visions, and the paradox broke her mind." She rubbed her temples. Her head throbbed. "With her last breath, did Lethea intend to help the Sisterhood, or hurt us?"

"We can't take the risk. Jessica and the boy should be eliminated, two lives for the sake of billions."

"It must be convenient to have only one solution to every problem!" Cordana snapped. "As for Jessica, I still vote no. We should be cautious, but this might be the opportunity we've sought for hundreds of generations. Let's do some testing, to make sure."

Ruthine turned away from the warm fire. "There were other candidates who might have been the Kwisatz Haderach. There still are. We do not need Paul Atreides."

Harishka faced them. "Right now, I do not need either of you. Go. As the Mother Superior, the final decision rests with me."

Ruthine offered a strange smile. "We try to advise, but that doesn't make your answers clear and simple."

"By logic, I accept the possible risk Jessica poses to the order, but my emotional side sees a glimmer of hope and wants to show some compassion for this woman and her son."

"We are taught to be wary of emotions," Ruthine warned.

"And we are taught to be experts on humanity," Cordana countered.

"If we dispose of Jessica, our decision is irrevocable," Harishka said. "We still have the option of sending her back to Duke Leto with instructions to get pregnant, with a daughter this time. Then the conditions of our breeding program projections will be satisfied."

Cordana squirmed, pressed her hand against her back. "If you send Xora to Caladan, you may permanently close that door."

"We shall see. I would not underestimate Jessica's abilities—if that is what she has to do." She shook her head. "My instincts tell me to give her another chance to prove herself useful to us."

As the two advisers left the council chamber, Ruthine stopped at the door and turned. Her bland face looked frightening. "I hope we are not too late."

To the uninitiated outsider, a vendetta between rivals may seem inconsequential, but to my eyes the price owed by my enemies is writ large and bold.

—DUKE LETO ATREIDES, war council notes

e will not wait for Shaddam's response to this catastrophe." Leto's voice simmered like a cauldron coming to a boil. "We will retaliate on our own terms." He pounded his fist on the war room table, and the loud thump made his son flinch.

Paul was intent as he looked across the table at his trainers, Hawat, Halleck, and Idaho. "The Emperor will surely dismiss this attack on House Atreides as some inter-House spat. He does not like to get involved. He will watch with detached amusement and do nothing."

The flicker of intelligence and hyperawareness in Paul's eyes reminded Leto of the subtle Bene Gesserit training that Jessica had given the young man. Leto had resented her actions at first when he learned what she was doing, because he disliked the scheming Sisterhood, but he did want Paul to be prepared for every conceivable circumstance. Thufir Hawat had also been surreptitiously priming the young man with Mentat training, and even Paul didn't know the extent of his abilities. Yes, someday, he would be a remarkable Duke.

Gurney spoke up, gruff and angry. "Are you so certain Shaddam won't respond, m'Lord? Count Fenring lost a fortune, too. Surely the Emperor will be outraged by what happened to his friend?"

Leto tapped his fingers on the tabletop. Outside, a brief storm had whipped up at sea, and even through the thick castle walls, the Duke was attuned enough to sense the turmoil out there. This planet, Caladan, where he had been born, reflected his moods.

Paul had more to say. "Is it possible that we could work with Count Fenring to strike back at the Harkonnens? If we unite our response with his, that would ensure we'd garner no Imperial reprisals."

Leto allowed himself a thin smile. "A good strategic suggestion, Paul, but Fenring himself is problematic for me. His allegiances are conditional rather than absolute. I am still not certain why he invested here, and he's likely to be very angry."

"The lad is right. He's certainly taken an interest in you, my Lord Duke," said Duncan. "We might leverage that."

"He took an interest in trying to get me to like him," Leto said, still surprised by the very idea. "He felt he could mold me into something different than I am . . . and I even considered it, to further the goals of House Atreides. It would have changed our fortunes dramatically." His chest tightened as he considered the repercussions of the devil's bargain that had been presented to him. He could have married Vikka Londine, but only on the condition that he destroy her father . . . "When I felt myself wallowing in the swamp of political schemes, I realized I had to leave. I would not become one of his cronies."

At the far end of the table, Hawat removed a half-full vial of sapho juice and downed it in a single gulp. He wiped a hand over his lips, closed his eyes as he drew a breath, then opened them. "It is not clear whether Glossu Rabban took this destructive action against us on his own, or whether it was with the Baron's cooperation. Because we so easily caught Lupar and unraveled the plan, it does not seem likely that Baron Harkonnen developed the scheme. But it seems too complex for Rabban to have concocted on his own."

Duncan's expression darkened. "And are there other Harkonnen plots in process right now?"

Gurney spoke up. "Sire, if we brought our accusations before the Landsraad Council, the Baron would deny any knowledge, but he might use his nephew as a scapegoat." The troubadour warrior rolled his shoulders. "Aye, I would be amenable to that. It would get rid of one of them."

"No matter who originated the plan, this action was done to hurt *me*," said Leto. "Even if Emperor Shaddam considers it a trivial squabble, Rabban damaged one of Caladan's booming industries." He once again spotted Paul sitting attentively, absorbing everything he could.

He remembered when he had sat in war councils with his father, listening to the old Duke's voice as he shouted out orders. The man had made a tremendous impression on Leto, and now he tried to do the same for his own son.

"Our moonfish operations have been crippled. Mitigation first," Leto said, "then revenge, at such time as is appropriate and can be plotted with great care. Has the invasive mite been halted and sterilized in the waterways and holding pools? We must eradicate it."

Hawat and Gurney looked at each other. Gurney said, "The fisheries have been purged and sterilized, thousands of tainted moonfish killed and burned in great smoky fires in the marshes to prevent further spread of the mites. We had to decontaminate every pond, channel, and processing line. Most of the buildings were so rickety that we had already decided to raze them to the ground and build new facilities with the additional funding."

Hawat cleared his throat. "Just getting back to our previous production levels will require more than Count Fenring's entire investment."

Leto felt sick in his stomach. "So much waste . . ."

Paul sat straight and determined. "House Atreides will survive." He looked so slight in stature compared to his father's larger frame. "And to do that, we need to set up safeguards against contamination in our waterways by segregating operations so that a hazard in one area cannot spread to another."

"That's quite a mouthful," Hawat said, "but the boy is right."

"It means more cost," Paul said, "but will save us in the long run."

Leto felt love swell within him. "Yes, we will make the extra effort, Paul, and I promise I'll leave a solid legacy for you."

The session went on for hours, and the Duke no longer knew what time it was. He looked up as servants entered with cups of bitter tea made from a special forest lichen. The Caladan drink was an acquired taste, and Leto appreciated the rush of flavor and energy. The kitchen staff also delivered bowls of pundi rice caramelized with honey, accompanied by cubes of paradan melon, which they claimed was a treat for the young Master, although Duncan Idaho was known to be particularly fond of the dessert.

The Duke took a spoonful of his caramelized rice, and Paul followed his father's example. Leto said, "I think better when I'm not distracted by hunger pangs."

Showing little restraint, Duncan took his bowl, added paradan melon, and ate with great enjoyment.

"For myself, I plot revenge better when I'm hungry." Gurney pushed his rice away. "Hunger goads my creativity. I was always hungry as a young man on Giedi Prime, and I found creative ways to survive." He rubbed his thumb along the inkvine scar on his cheek. "What that monster Rabban did to my parents, to my sister . . ."

"We all have enough hatred for Rabban," Duncan said. "He hunted me in Forest Guard Station when I was a child—but I got away." He grinned. "If an eight-year-old boy could outsmart that brute, then the best of House Atreides can certainly do better."

Hawat measured out his words as if he were a chef combining ingredients for a special recipe. "We can prove that Rabban illegally attacked House Atreides. The origin of the deadly mite is Lankiveil. The smuggler in our prison cell admitted his involvement. We could submit an appeal to the Emperor or the Landsraad—maybe to both. We are within our rights to demand a monetary judgment for both punitive and compensatory damages well as a larger penalty to recoup our financial losses. Imperial authorities would be forced to take action against House Harkonnen. Imperial penalties come in many forms."

Duncan nearly spat out some of his rice. "Whine and complain in a Landsraad meeting? We would also look weak if we begged the Imperium to slap Harkonnen wrists after what they did to us! Rabban *attacked* Caladan. He targeted our moonfish industries, and he hurt us where we live, my Lord." His face turned ruddy. "He harmed the people of Caladan."

"I agree with you," Leto conceded. "We will do both. I will file a bill of particulars and present my evidence against Rabban. House Harkonnen, or at the very least the Count of Lankiveil, will pay handsomely for what they have done. But we will not ask others to do what we must do ourselves—there are other parts of a vendetta that must be satisfied." He gave Paul a wolfish grin and fixed his gaze on Gurney and Duncan. "We at House Atreides will take matters into our own hands. There are rules. We will make them pay, and we will make them *hurt*. This is the way kanly works."

He looked up, reaching a decision. "Thufir, I want you to make a very careful accounting of whatever enemy assets we destroy in our retaliation. So long as we can justify that it is equivalent to what Rabban did to us, then the Harkonnens cannot file a grievance. If need be, we can deduct the amount from the fines we impose."

Gurney was delighted by the prospect. "Oh ho! The Baron will rage and curse!"

"Let him do so. If we act with precision, the Harkonnens cannot cry foul. And then we will file our bill of particulars and squeeze recompense from Rabban."

Paul finished his sweetened rice and took a sip of the bitter tea. It was an adult beverage, but he followed his father's example. "Will House Atreides claim to be taking revenge on behalf of Count Fenring as well?"

"I'd rather not involve him any more than necessary, although that might be a good point to include in our documentation, should these matters take that route," Leto said. "The Count doesn't need to know what we are doing, but he won't be in a position to complain either."

The Duke felt a warm satisfaction replacing his anger. In the past, before making such a big decision, he would have spoken with Jessica, and together they would have discussed consequences and alternatives. She would have been a voice of reason . . . but she was no longer his adviser. She had sent no word whatsoever from the Mother School, either to him or to Paul. She had gone entirely silent. Leto didn't think that convoluted advice inspired by Bene Gesserits was what he needed now anyway.

"Put together a swift and decisive assault," he ordered, rising to his feet. "Duncan and Gurney, I want you to go together. Take our best commandos and strike at the heart of Rabban's operations on Lankiveil—hit their industry, any shipping warehouses, military garrisons, but not a population center." His mind filled again with thoughts of the moonfish operations, the pyres of dead fish, the black smoke and the stink in the air that even a brisk wind could not drive away. "Rabban will suffer, and I intend to make his wounds deep."

Whenever Count Fenring was on Kaitain, he and the Lady Margot lived in a very old building on the palace grounds. Under the reign of Fondil III, the structure had been a coach house, but Emperor Elrood had enlarged and converted it to luxurious guest quarters. Shaddam IV had changed the layout of the grounds, rerouting the main entrance roadway to enhance the security of the Emperor and the Empress.

The stone-walled guest quarters, constructed in a crenelated baronial style with two small towers and a higher turret rising above it, was modest by Kaitain's standards, but the Count preferred it to the larger buildings that had no soul or character. His dear Lady Margot had been responsible for redesigning the guesthouse interior in recent years, adding tapestries, comfortable upholstered furniture, warm colors, and three new fireplaces. She much preferred this place to the Residency on planet Arrakis, in the bleak frontier settlement of Arrakeen.

Fenring had added security-minded suggestions to the upgrades. Because of him, the top level of an adjacent guardhouse was connected by a bridging corridor to the turret, in order to protect the entryway from the palace grounds. It felt a bit medieval, but very safe.

That morning, Fenring breakfasted with his wife on a terrace overlooking their walled garden. It could not have been a more perfect meal, prepared to her specifications by their private chef. But the Count was distracted as well as annoyed, and even this special time with the Lady Margot did little to improve his disposition. He was restless, and irritated that Grix Dardik had not arrived to give him the vital final report as instructed.

Dressed all in black except for a silver band around his cavalier hat, Fenring left his wife with an apologetic smile and strode across the covered, fortified bridge that connected his residence to the guardhouse. Two rugged palace guards on the opposite side saluted him. He brusquely saluted back as he marched past.

He and his Mentat had returned from their investment expedition to Caladan two weeks earlier, and Dardik should have presented a full assessment of

Duke Leto Atreides. But Fenring had seen no sign of the man at the appointed time.

With an exasperated sigh, the Count decided his eccentric companion must be lost in another Mentat dream. He would have to pull him out of it as usual and extract his answers by whatever means necessary.

Fenring wanted his odd Mentat close, but not too close, so Dardik was billeted with the soldiers in the guardhouse, where they could keep an eye on him. As the Count descended a stairway to the main level, mulling over a necessary confrontation with Dardik, he was surprised to find Shaddam and Empress Aricatha there, talking earnestly with one of their Imperial Mentat accountants as well as Fenring's captain of the guard.

Irritation was plain on the Emperor's face. "Hasimir, your recalcitrant Mentat has been causing a commotion."

Fenring shot a quick glare at the guard captain. "Why wasn't I notified?" He turned to Shaddam. "I could have handled the matter quickly, without bothering you, Sire."

"The palace guards report to me," Shaddam reminded him.

"We came to deliver some news," Aricatha said, her beautiful face forming a frown. "But Grix Dardik is saying unsettling things."

Fenring wasn't the least bit surprised. "He always does that."

"Perhaps you should just get rid of him," Shaddam said. "There are better Mentats available." He glanced at his own accountant, who waited nearby, looking professional and perhaps a bit smug.

With a quick motion to his friend, the Emperor turned and led them down a corridor to Dardik's quarters. Fenring saw guards at the door and heard the Mentat's agitated voice demanding to be set free.

Grix Dardik was a small man, but strong for his size, and it took two large soldiers to pin him to the floor and keep him there. The Mentat's white tunic was torn and bloody, and there was an open wound on the side of his neck.

Having grown tired of controlling Dardik with drugs whenever he acted up, a week ago, Fenring had ordered an implant to administer the mixture of medications that would keep his adviser calm and focused. It seemed to have been working. But now with a darting glance, Fenring spotted the implant on the floor near Dardik, ripped out of his neck. A table and chairs were turned over, and broken glass and pottery covered the floor.

Fenring assessed the details in an instant and had no doubt who had done it. He glowered at Dardik, who finally caught his gaze. The Mentat instantly went limp, like a child caught misbehaving.

Shaddam nodded to the soldiers with an impatient sigh, and they released their hold on the man. Dardik immediately sprang to his feet, his eyes darting around. If he'd been a bird, he would have flown away. He spun to stare fiercely at the Count, his eyes smoldering. "I refuse to be medicated any longer! I cannot tolerate having limitations on my marvelous mind!" He touched the bleeding wound on his neck. "Finally, I broke free!"

"He ripped it out some time ago," the guard captain said. "That's when he started raving."

Fenring muttered, "Hmmm, while I was enjoying breakfast with my lovely wife." He looked at Shaddam and the Empress. The conventional Mentat accountant beside them showed clear disapproval. Fenring tried to bring the situation back under control. "But why were you here in the first place, Sire? Empress Aricatha mentioned you, ahhhh, have some news? You should not have been troubled with a matter such as this."

Aricatha extended a message scroll and some attached documents to Fenring. "We were coming to see you, my dear Count. We intercepted an urgent message sent to you from Duke Leto Atreides. I'm afraid it's bad news."

"Most unfortunate," Shaddam said.

Fenring accepted the message, feeling a flush rise in his skin. "The Duke sent the message to me, but you've read it?" He flicked his eyes from her to the Emperor. "Have I somehow fallen under suspicion, Sire, that you intercept private communiqués intended for me?"

Shaddam waved a hand, aloof, dismissing the accusation. "Not suspicious of you, Hasimir. But the whole reason you went to Caladan was because of our possible concerns about Duke Leto, to keep your eyes open, to get involved. I was . . . interested to find out what my cousin had to say, and whether he mentioned the Noble Commonwealth at all." He pursed his lips and ran a palm over his smooth, pomaded hair. "Fortunately, he said nothing incriminating. Still, my friend, the news is most unfortunate, for you."

Curious and concerned, Fenring read the message and the accompanying documentation. Struggling to maintain his composure, he scanned the report on the devastating infestation that had struck the fisheries—where he had just invested significant capital. The summary report about the introduction of a deadly invasive species that massacred the moonfish had been prepared by Thufir Hawat.

Had Leto somehow sabotaged his own operations, just to harm Fenring? The timing of this disaster could not be a coincidence. Such an incredible loss would be a significant blow to his finances.

Then he saw that the mite was not native to Caladan, but had come from Lankiveil. Someone had transported it to Caladan and introduced it as a biological scourge. Lankiveil . . . Rabban . . . Harkonnens.

Fenring felt his cheeks burn. "I will want Grix Dardik to assess and verify these findings—as soon as he is functional again." Looking at the bloody wreck of his failed Mentat, he tried to control his anger, but grew even more incensed when he saw that the Emperor seemed uninterested in the ecological catastrophe, or Fenring's stinging financial losses.

"If this is true, Sire, we must bring Imperial justice to bear against House Harkonnen. Count Glossu Rabban unleashed rampant destruction on a vital Caladan industry—"

Shaddam clucked his tongue. "Come now, Hasimir! I cannot involve myself in every little prank or squabble among Houses. Tiny mites and fish? I am the Emperor of the Known Universe."

"A prank? Hmmm, Sire, I invested heavily in the moonfish industry—at your suggestion."

"*Implied* suggestion, and I did not tell you how much to invest. Now I'm afraid you've lost it all, if this infestation is truly as bad as the reports show. I'm glad I never grew fond of moonfish." He seemed irritatingly calm. "I will not go wading into the feud between House Atreides and House Harkonnen. They've been fighting for ten thousand years. It will never end. You know that as well as I do."

The Imperial Mentat accountant spoke for the first time. He sounded professorial. "It is always wise to diversify your financial affairs."

Fenring glared at Dardik, who did not seem to grasp the magnitude of what had happened. He kept dabbing his fingers against the coagulating wound on his neck, then looking at the sticky red on his fingers. The Count said, "Dardik, you ran your analysis after studying the fisheries, and you said that nothing could go wrong."

"I did not use those words, my Lord. But now that I've removed that troublesome implant and drugs are no longer flowing into me—as they were even before the implant, thanks to your ever-present needles—I am beginning to see a nonzero likelihood of some outside adversary attacking that vulnerable industry." He frowned. "I should have resisted your drugs sooner. I am a sensitive mental organism, not to be tampered with in such a cavalier fashion." He stared at Fenring's cavalier hat, as if making a bon mot.

"I'm tired of hearing about Landsraad feuds," Shaddam said. "We will take no position on this matter. Let the Houses resolve their own dispute. We have a more important spectacle to plan here. My treasury ship promenade!" His lips quirked in a smile. "It will demonstrate the bounty we've received from the spice surtax. Empress Aricatha is helping me."

Fenring was still upset. He had never thought the Emperor's scheme to dazzle the masses with his wealth was a good idea. Now, though, he had his own diminished fortunes to worry about.

Fenring shook his head in dismay as he mulled over Duke Leto's damning message. He knew Glossu Rabban from his work on Arrakis, and he was surprised that the blunt man had developed a scheme like this. He suspected Baron Harkonnen had put him up to it, and maybe their twisted Mentat had helped. Rabban would never have harmed Fenring intentionally though. He could not be that stupid.

Whatever the intent, the result had cost Count Fenring dearly, and he would not let it stand. Maybe Rabban needed to blunder into some fatal accident on Arrakis . . . He grabbed Dardik by one scrawny arm and began to lead him away. "My Mentat and I will discuss the ramifications of this disaster."

Still dabbing at the blood on his neck, Grix Dardik said, "I have growing suspicions about some of the Baron's operations, especially those on Arrakis." He looked at the floor and kept his voice down as if contrite.

"A Mentat should never voice mere suspicions," the Imperial accountant interrupted in a scolding tone. He looked haughty and in charge as if trying to impress Shaddam by taking another Mentat to the woodshed. He moved into a confrontational position in front of his rival. "A true Mentat assembles and analyzes facts, sifts through them, and discards extraneous details while focusing on what is important. Then he makes projections, not accusations. Are you ready to make a Mentat projection, Grix Dardik?"

The other man dithered. "I was merely going through possibilities with Count Fenring. My thoughts were not intended for an audience."

"No wonder this one was removed from the Mentat school," the accountant said, sneering at Fenring's companion. "Baron Vladimir Harkonnen is a loyal ally of his Imperial Majesty."

Dardik glared at him, and Fenring added his own glare.

Shaddam, though, seemed amused. "It appears that our Mentats are feuding as much as the Great Houses." He turned about and began to walk away with the Empress, followed by their haughty Imperial accountant.

Fenring heard Aricatha say to her husband in an upset tone, "House versus House, Mentat versus Mentat. It goes on and on. This Imperium needs peace, not unending quarrels. You really should allow me to get involved in more diplomatic work."

"You are right, my dear," Shaddam said. Then he spoke over his shoulder to Fenring, "No more diversions with moonfish and investments. You should stay here and watch the glorious procession with my treasury ship."

Fenring fought down a conflagration in his mind. "Perhaps I should return to Arrakis instead, to keep watch over the spice operations—as is my priority."

Oblivious to the Count's stewing indignation, Shaddam and his Empress strolled out of the guardhouse. Their Mentat accountant paused as if to say something more to Dardik, then hurried after them.

Like a schoolteacher taking an unruly child by the ear, Count Fenring pulled Grix Dardik away. Already, the strange man's mind was somewhere else and he rambled about his memories of the Mentat school, years ago.

Tired of moonfish, House feuds, and Imperial politics, Fenring wanted to get back to his own schemes on Arrakis.

What is more valuable, loyalty or morality?
—DUKE PAULUS ATREIDES,
letters to his son

Y ou are a difficult man to see, Duke Leto Atreides." The man's deep voice sounded casually threatening.

Leto didn't react with immediate suspicion. Other locals had spoken with him as he walked through the crowded reef market. Around him, vendors had set up kiosks, tables under fabric awnings, and rickety shelves to display their wares. Merchants and craftsmen haggled with customers, seeking a good price and enjoying the bargaining process. Mothers with energetic children set up crates, buckets, and pots to display shells and urchins they had harvested from nearby tide pools.

One boy proudly held up a fat silverfish he had caught himself, trying to get a few coins for it. At the water's edge nearby, boat crews off-loaded nets and barrels of their catch, while fishmongers displayed the seafood in the cool morning. The sounds and voices combined in a loud happy hum, and even though the Duke was visiting, the reef market conducted business as usual.

Leto paused to look at the man who had interrupted him. He had heavy eyebrows and dark, curly hair trimmed close to his head, and he wore common Caladan clothes, a fishing vest with many pockets, loose trousers, a belt. A wide-brimmed hat was secured by a strap around his stubbly chin so that it wouldn't blow away in a brisk breeze.

The stranger's features looked familiar, yet different, like a sibling to someone Leto had known but not well. The Duke responded with an automatic smile, but he felt that something was off with this man. "If you have a matter to discuss, sir, I receive my people twice weekly up at the castle. I'm always open to hearing their concerns."

"Oh, I have concerns, Leto." The man flashed him an intense smile, and his lack of formality raised the Duke's caution. His brown eyes were hard and deep, like wounds burned into his skull by a lasbeam, and he flashed white teeth, as if waiting for something.

Leto's skin crawled. He asked in low voice, "Do I know you?"

The man laughed. "Yes, you do—you do indeed! But you know even more *about* me."

Leto subconsciously slipped his hand to the hilt of his short sword near the button on his shield belt. The Atreides Dukes were well loved on Caladan, and they felt safe moving among the people. Leto was often accompanied by Duncan or Gurney, but they had already departed for their quick, private strike against Rabban's holdings on Lankiveil.

Thufir Hawat had objected to Leto walking through the reef market without a full guard escort, but the Duke had not heeded him. After being accompanied on Kaitain by his colorful and unnecessary retainers as a show of prestige like peacock feathers, Leto wanted none of that flamboyance here at home. His people did not need such displays from their Duke. Grumbling, the old Mentat had stayed behind in Castle Caladan where he continued Paul's education.

But now that Leto was in a crowd, facing an unsettling stranger, Leto suddenly felt he might want an army surrounding him after all. "Who are you?"

Close by, a woman emptied a basket of fresh-scrubbed shells onto a plank table, yelling out, "Shells! Everyone needs shells!" Two teens wearing gloves sat on low stools in front of saltwater buckets. "Coral gems," one said. "Shuck them yourselves. They stay in the water until you buy them, so they don't burst into flames."

The intense man leaned closer to Leto. He had confidence and a hint of violence about him. Although his facial features had changed significantly, the identity clicked into place for Leto. He froze, then breathed the name. "Jaxson Aru . . ."

The man reached up to touch his own cheeks, his chin, as if to adjust his skin, and his expression brightened. "I've always been proud of you, Leto Atreides! You're an intelligent man, capable of seeing the breadth of the Imperium as well as your own world's potential."

Jaxson's eyes hooded over, and he leaned even closer. Leto flinched, but didn't dare move, knowing all too well the hateful things this man had done, the bloody terrorist acts to support the cause of his violent rebellion. "You are also smart enough not to call for security without knowing what I might do if you did. I need to talk with you."

Leto kept his words icy. "Have you planted more bombs here to destroy the reef market? To murder all these innocent people, as you threatened last time?"

Jaxson looked oddly disappointed. "Would I need to do that just to have a word with the Duke of Caladan? I don't enjoy harming innocents, Leto, and any victims are unintended collateral damage . . . but at Otorio, they did choose to be too close to guilty parties."

Jaxson strolled through the crowds, even jokingly haggled for the fat silverfish the boy was trying to sell. He turned back to Leto. "But you and I are wise and civilized, are we not? Join me for a cup of paradan juice."

Leto felt like a hooked fish, drawn along by an invisible line. The last time

Jaxson Aru had come here trying to recruit him, he said he had hidden explosive devices around Cala City and threatened to kill thousands if Leto didn't hear him out. Later, Thufir Hawat had found the bombs to be inert, mere props to paralyze Caladan's security forces.

"I found out that you were bluffing last time," Leto said.

"Not bluffing." Jaxson sounded sharp and sincere. "I knew your character, Leto Atreides, and that was the lever I required to move you. I also knew you would eventually discover that the bombs were not real, so you might want to consider whether or not I would show up today without backup."

"You did not move me. I refused to join your bloody rebellion."

"But you *listened*." Jaxson handed coins to a vendor, who ladled up fresh, pulped juice. He took a sip and sighed. "One of my favorite rustic treats every time I come to Caladan!" He handed a cup to Leto. "You have had more time to think about the things I explained to you."

Leto pushed back. "There hasn't been enough time for me to forget the carnage you caused on Otorio. Do you forget that I was there?"

The other man dismissed the suggestion and kept walking. "But you've had time to put that in context. I understand that the Bene Gesserit Sisterhood snatched away your concubine, the mother of your son . . . a woman who supposedly loved you." Now his grin was simply cruel. "Never-ending Bene Gesserit schemes! The Sisterhood works hand in hand with the Corrino Emperors, although both have their own insidious goals."

Leto hardened his heart. "I don't need to call security. I can just kill you here."

Jaxson continued to make his case as if he had all the time in the world. "And because of that hurt, you traveled to Kaitain. I follow your movements, Duke Leto. Because you still have some influence and because Shaddam Corrino holds a bit of temporary gratitude, you imagined you could buy more influence at the Imperial Court. But you saw the corruption there, didn't you? You witnessed what the stagnant Imperium is really like."

Leto attempted to respond, but the words caught in his throat.

"You saw the rot and dishonor inside the palace court. You saw the Landsraad squabble over holdings left vacant because of the nobles who died at Otorio. Is that who the Duke of Caladan is?" He slurped his paradan juice. "I understand that you even tried to play the marriage game, but that fell apart." He raised his thick eyebrows. "But I don't understand why. Certainly not because you found Vikka Londine unacceptable?"

"The Emperor's terms were unacceptable," Leto said in a low voice.

"Just one more example of Corrino corruption! I know that your rivals, the Harkonnens, ruined the moonfish operations here, and the Padishah Emperor will likely brush it aside as a joke. Does it feel like a joke to you, Leto? Is this true justice for how you were wronged? Will the Imperium ever grant you the justice you deserve?"

"House Atreides will get its own justice," Leto said.

Jaxson continued, relentless. "On Kaitain, I hear Lord Atikk disparaged Atreides honor and challenged you to a duel . . . and was conveniently killed before you could face him. Everyone believes you secretly poisoned him so you would not have to face him in an open fight. Is it true, Leto?"

Leto felt hot. "Of course not."

Jaxson chuckled. "Of course not, because you are a man of honor. You don't play the game of Imperial bribery and blackmail, and yet your beloved Caladan is caught in the muck like a shining jewel in a cesspool. When will it be enough for you to see that a truer, better path lies in a different direction, one that involves more than this solitary world?"

Shouts erupted nearby, and Leto saw a crowd standing around a pen where fishermen had tossed a spiny starfish to battle a tusked crustacean. The crowd whistled and cheered. Bets were placed. The starfish and the crustacean grappled, sharp joints flailing, claws snapping. The crustacean snipped off one of the starfish arms, but the other creature caught it in a powerful grip and wrapped around its shell, applying implacable force until the bony exoskeleton began to crack.

Jaxson Aru mused as he watched. "That is the way of the Corrino Imperium. The strong tear apart the weak and feast upon the remains."

"It is the natural order of things," Leto said in a whisper. His voice was flat, and felt dead.

"It is the way of animals, not civilized human beings. Under the Noble Commonwealth, once the Imperium is dissolved, every world can set its own rules, its own standards of behavior, its own methods of commerce. Each planet can make whatever alliances it likes and not be beholden to an archaic political structure that was established millennia ago, so that the rich could get richer."

Leto lashed out, "You talk about civilized behavior, yet you hurled cargo vessels into a city, killing tens of thousands!"

"A carefully chosen target, and look at what we gained. The rebellion is burgeoning, and I have more followers than ever. Now many nobles are willing to join our cause, because I shocked them awake." He finished his juice, although Leto had barely touched his. "I want you to join us in the Noble Commonwealth. Caladan is a perfect candidate, and you know it—if you'd just let yourself think outside of your constraints."

"I am loyal to the Landsraad. House Atreides serves the Emperor."

"You can continue to say that, but I know what is really in your heart, even if you don't." He paused. "The human race is ripe for change, Leto. You know it, and I know it. The Imperium is unraveling before your eyes. Shaddam Corrino doesn't even have a designated heir. You know what is best for our future."

Jaxson reached into one of the pockets on his loose vest and withdrew a small spool of shigawire. "These are instructions on how you will find us to discuss the

Noble Commonwealth with forward-thinking individuals. Let them help you to see, if my own words have not yet convinced you."

Leto reluctantly pocketed the spool. Groans and cheers came from the small pen where the spiny starfish had dismantled the tusked crustacean. Gamblers paid off their wagers, while the wranglers snatched both combatants and tossed them into a pot of boiling seawater to be served for lunch.

"I will not be convinced," Leto said.

Jaxson chuckled. "Don't promise anything."

"No promises." Leto felt soiled, his thoughts in turmoil, but he knew he would never change or question his loyalty.

Jaxson flitted away and melted into the reef-market crowd.

Now Leto was free to summon Thufir Hawat and all his security teams to sweep through Cala City and lock down the spaceport, but that could invite dangerous repercussions against his people, because undoubtedly Jaxson Aru would still find a way to evade the search.

Working the situation through his mind, the Duke of Caladan decided to fight in a different manner.

Some deaths pose more danger to others than to the person dying. The loss
of a single Sister, and her essential talents, can be devastating.

—MOTHER SUPERIOR HARISHKA

For once, the high windows of Jessica's cell let in afternoon sunlight, in contrast to the usual gloom. The glow reminded her of what it was like outside, the freedoms she had lost, the people she missed so terribly. Reverend Mother Mohiam was due to arrive today.

Even after Brom had informed her of Lethea's death, she had been left here as if buried in a tomb. Her situation hadn't changed. Mohiam would likely be a catalyst, and Jessica braced herself to face whatever the Sisters would now throw at her.

Brom arrived again with a food tray, and she wondered why he was the one assigned to such a menial task. Maybe Harishka wanted to prevent other Sisters from interacting with her, not just to keep her isolated, but all the others as well. Did they now consider Jessica as dangerous as Lethea?

The young man looked at her with a faintly conspiratorial expression. He lowered his voice as he set the tray on a small table. "There is much excitement at the Mother School. I've never heard so many whispers! Of course, they don't tell me anything—but I know they are anticipating the arrival of the Emperor's Truthsayer. Is it true she was once your proctor here at the Mother School?"

"That is true . . . and she was a hard and heartless teacher." Jessica didn't know if that was cause for hope or dread. Who better to force her to conform than the teacher who knew her better than anyone else? Mohiam was the one who had known exactly how to blackmail Jessica, how to force her into leaving Caladan. No one else could have done that. The old Reverend Mother understood exactly the right sore spots and old wounds to press.

For her own part, Mohiam undoubtedly felt betrayed by her prime student, and she was not one to forgive.

Jessica was careful not to reveal these deeper thoughts to Brom, though. The young man looked innocent, seemingly pleased to have found a secret friend, but he could well be a spy, or involved in a trap. After Xora, she was not open to casual trust, and Brom was her son, raised and sheltered here at the Mother School.

Her heart went heavy and cold, knowing that soon Xora would go off with her orders, present herself to Leto, try to become the next Lady of Caladan. The very idea felt like a knife twisting inside her.

After arranging her meal tray on the small table, Brom was obviously lingering. "Aren't you going to eat?"

Knowing that she needed to keep up her energy for whatever may come, she wolfed down the food. First order of survival. "Thank you for bringing my meal."

He looked at her expectantly as if awaiting her next command. How did Brom fit into their overall breeding program, and what were the Sisterhood's plans for him? The Bene Gesserit seemed to think he might be a potential Kwisatz Haderach. Like Paul. . . .

Did they fear he was as dangerous?

Jessica took a chance, skirting what she knew about him. "You remind me of my son, and I miss him."

"Yes, your son." Brom's eyes flicked away. "I'm sorry you had to return to the Mother School and leave him behind. It would have been nice if you'd brought him here . . . to be with me. We might have a lot in common." She remembered that he didn't know Xora was his mother, and Jessica doubted he'd been told he was the son of a Sardaukar officer.

In his facial expression, especially his eyes, she could see his longing for companionship, and she understood Brom a little more. "It was not my choice."

Then Brom did something she didn't expect. He sat on the hard stone floor in front of her, cross-legged, as if it were a training exercise. He looked up. "The Sisters can't keep everything secret from me. I've heard about you, and seeing you like this, I want to give you some comfort."

She stiffened, alarmed by what he was saying, what he was doing. She observed his expression, his movements, the subtle undertones in his voice, but she detected none of the luring markers, no increased pheromones, no sexuality whatsoever. Still, she needed to be sure. "Were you sent to 'comfort' me? Do you think I can be seduced?"

He looked at her with innocent confusion. "Nothing of the kind! I was instructed to deliver food. I thought you might like to talk." He started to rise. "Do you want me to leave?"

Jessica looked around her cell. By now she would have known about any listening or observation devices, but she could never be sure. She was not naïve. Lethea was dead, and the Sisterhood still considered her a threat. What other possible reason would they have sent him here? "Are you here to kill me, then?"

Brom sprang to his feet, confused and alarmed by her reaction. "I would never think of harming you. I am sorry if I have offended." He looked so young. "You are trapped like I am in a different way."

Something in his words and demeanor rang with authenticity. She felt an unbidden desperation and decided she had nothing to lose by talking with him. "Mohiam is my old teacher. I think they are deciding what to do with me, whether to let me live or not. And Paul, too. They are sending your . . . Xora to take my place on Caladan." A sharp pain went through her again. Xora did resemble Jessica. Would Leto accept her? She doubted it, but she didn't know. The Duke had been deeply hurt. Was his heart broken, or simply hardened?

With obvious trepidation, Brom said, "But you've done nothing wrong, Sister Jessica, and they know that. You tried to send a message to your son, and you didn't choose to reveal some personal things about him. So what? They don't like it when someone breaks their rules, and that's why they threw you in this cell."

"To make me contemplate," she said.

"To teach you a lesson." Brom seemed to be familiar with Bene Gesserit punishments. "They'll let you out when they believe you've fit yourself back into their mold."

Jessica summoned a terse smile, but her mood was dark. "We'll see what Mohiam has to say." She assimilated information, grappling with the problem like a Mentat. She knew the Mother School was in strange turmoil, and the old crone's death would force them to act . . . one way or another. "Thank you for . . . for telling me things I needed to know, for comforting me in a very generous, human way. It makes me feel less isolated."

Brom activated the cell door. "I will provide whatever assistance I can." He paused, his expression open and honest.

Suddenly, two Sisters pushed past him into the isolation chamber as if Brom were mere detritus. Drawing upon her reserves of energy, Jessica sprang to her feet, recognizing the unsettling Reverend Mother Ruthine and the much younger Sister Jiara. She detected a tension in their movements, and knew this was no mere visit.

So, this was the Sisterhood's response at last.

Neither woman spoke, and Jessica's self-preservation kicked in, sensing what was coming. Ruthine and Jiara spread out and approached, not even trying to hide their fighting stances. They had narrow, dark-eyed gazes, very primal.

Jessica had been waiting for this.

STANDING AT NIGHT on the perimeter of the landing zone's paved surface, the Mother Superior watched Mohiam's shuttle land with an uncharacteristically loud thrum of suspensors, generating more wind turbulence than usual. It was a heavy, ornate craft provided by the Imperial Court. Sisters lined up to greet the Emperor's Truthsayer on the illuminated field. As the shuttle's ramp extended and the double-hatch thrummed open, they faced the visitor. Measured by outside political criteria, Mohiam was the highest-placed Sister in the Imperium.

The Reverend Mother emerged, gliding down the slanted metal pathway to the pavement, looking like a cowled black bird. Harishka stepped forward to greet her, feeling uncharacteristic warmth toward her. "It is good to see you, old friend."

Mohiam seemed out of sorts. "I was not surprised to learn of Lethea's death, nor is it particularly unpleasant news. But I had hoped for clear answers before she died—did she say anything important? Why am I here?" She paused, narrowed her eyes. "Is it Jessica?"

Harishka assessed Mohiam's impatience and answered with careful formality. "There is great turmoil at the Mother School. Lethea's last message, scrawled in her own blood, was 'Jessica Danger.'"

Mohiam considered. "Do you know what she meant?"

"We are torn about what to do with your—" She caught herself, almost saying "your daughter," but these others did not know; no one knew. Instead, she said, "Your former student."

Mohiam hurried off with the Mother Superior. "Jessica has caused more than her share of consternation. I no longer find it charming."

RUTHINE DARTED TOWARD Jessica like a nimble spider, while Jiara cut off any escape toward the cell door. Jessica pressed her back toward a corner, her best defensible position. She had expected Reverend Mother Mohiam—were these two using that distraction to make their move? Was Brom part of the plot? Or were they the executioners the Sisterhood had assigned?

"I thought the Mother Superior would have the courage to do her own dirty work," Jessica muttered.

"Loyalty to the Sisterhood sent us," Ruthine said. With deceptive suppleness, she bent into a killing stance, ready to fling herself forward.

A blur flashed behind the attackers, and Brom vaulted over Jiara, kicking her shoulder. He landed in front of her and dropped into a fighting stance, blocking her attack.

Undeterred, Ruthine lunged toward Jessica, whipping and thrashing with liquid agility. Jessica bent sharply, went low, then lashed out with her feet. Avoiding the counterattack, Ruthine dodged and launched herself again like a deadly projectile. She and Jessica slammed hard together.

No words were spoken, no challenge issued. It was merely an attempted execution, but Jessica would not go quietly.

Thrown off balance when Brom sprang in front of her, Jiara struck at the young man, but he startled her with a streak of his own training. After a lifetime of being fashioned and manipulated by the Sisterhood, now he used their skills against them.

Jessica spared only a stray thought to observe and file away for later. Hyperaware, Jessica watched Ruthine's eyes, saw Brom clashing with Jiara. The two attackers had not counted on fighting anyone other than their intended victim. With a practiced thrust of her fingers, Jessica struck Ruthine's neck, aiming for her main artery. The blow would have killed others, but the Reverend Mother deflected part of the deadly strength. But in the instant of her distraction, Jessica darted into Ruthine's defensive perimeter, and slammed her fist into Ruthine's torso.

Silent, Ruthine stumbled, her ringlets of hair waving like seaweed in the air. At the same moment, as if in a coordinated move, Brom collided with Jiara and drove her into Ruthine, just as Jessica struck the Reverend Mother again. Ruthine's and Jiara's skulls banged with a sickening crack, and both women slumped to the floor. Bleeding badly from her forehead, Jiara tried to get up, then slithered back to the hard floor of the isolation cell.

When Ruthine moaned and stirred, Brom kicked her in the temple, a precise blow to knock her unconscious. Jessica knew the strike points on a human body, as did this young man. Both attackers were defeated, unconscious. But not dead, and not mortally wounded.

He stood, barely panting, and assessed the two would-be assassins. "Should we kill them?" He looked up at Jessica, his face strangely innocent, waiting for instructions.

"We could justify it because they came to kill me," Jessica said, forming her disbelief into a statement of fact. She had predicted this, and now she knew it to be absolutely true. "But there are enough consequences already. We don't know if Mother Superior Harishka sent them here, or if they acted independently."

Brom ran to the open doorway, motioned for Jessica. "Then shouldn't we get away from here? Others will be coming. And they will try to finish the job."

She realized the idea rang true, but she had nowhere to go. Nevertheless, she was done with being manipulated by the Sisterhood.

"I can get us to safety, at least for now."

She didn't have time to second-guess the opportunity. After Brom sealed the two unconscious Sisters into Jessica's cell, he led her down the silent corridor to an alcove, where he lifted a decorative statuette. Part of the stone wall slid aside, revealing a hidden passageway. "I know every corner of the Mother School, even parts lost in architectural archives." The young man led the way through a narrow, dimly lit tunnel. "Sometimes it's good to be considered beneath notice."

Jessica didn't ask why he was helping her, didn't wonder if this might be part of an elaborate trap. She had studied him, read him, and she didn't believe he was being deceitful. Besides, she had little choice right now.

Jessica and Brom ran. Whether or not they were acting alone, Ruthine and Jiara had broken any last threads of trust she might have held in the Bene Gesserit. She knew she had to escape.

REACHING THE CHAPTERHOUSE, Mohiam and Harishka met in the Mother Superior's private chambers, sipping fresh, potent spice coffee. The two women had many deep matters to discuss. Mohiam asked to review the records of every word Lethea had uttered since calling for Jessica, and every nebulous answer Jessica had extracted from her.

Mohiam pondered, tried to enter the mindset of her former student. "We brought Jessica here against her will, tore her from the things she cared most about, but I'm convinced that she is still a Bene Gesserit, through and through."

Harishka frowned. "She has divided loyalties, as she demonstrated several times."

Mohiam said, "She is independent and believes she is her own woman. And that makes her . . . *less* of a Bene Gesserit. I tried to adjust her thinking many times. She has been too long away from Wallach IX. We were right to bring her back here, where she can be reminded of her duties and obligations. We can still use her."

Suddenly, a flushed, frantic Acolyte rushed to her chambers, so astonished and breathless she could barely blurt out her report that Ruthine and Jiara had been found beaten in the isolation cell. And Jessica had escaped.

To Harishka, the news sank in from multiple directions.

Jessica had broken out of her confinement and escaped. She had overcome two powerful Sisters.

Then heavier thoughts cascaded into her mind. Why had Ruthine gone to Jessica's cell? And accompanied by Jiara? The two must have had some dark purpose—certainly nothing that Harishka had authorized. She felt a cold dread press down on her heart.

"Jessica is not the type to brawl and batter two of her fellow Sisters and then break free of a cell," Mohiam said. "Except in extremis."

The Mother Superior was astounded as she grasped what must have happened. She, too, had been betrayed. "Ruthine has always insisted on killing Jessica, and Jiara is one of her followers. They acted against my orders! They had no reason to go to that cell. They must have intended to assassinate Jessica."

Mohiam pressed her lips together. "Jessica was just defending herself. And now she has no reason to trust anyone at the Mother School."

The Mother Superior shouted as other Sisters rushed to her office. "Confine Ruthine and Jiara. I want them questioned."

Mohiam looked deeply disturbed, hardened from her time at the Emperor's court. "Dear Harishka, you miss the most time-sensitive point. Jessica has escaped. Where could she possibly go?" Her eyes flicked back and forth. "We must think like she does."

The life of a planetary ruler is a lonely one, no matter how many people serve and advise him.

—PRINCESS IRULAN, *In My Father's House*

His mother's room seemed so empty. Not in a sinister or frightening way, just a hollowness, like an echo where she had once been.

Jessica and Leto had their own private rooms, their own separate spaces, but Paul had never before viewed it as a way for them to keep apart. The Lady Jessica had spent as much time with her Duke as she spent away from him, but they had their own responsibilities, their own interests, and their own boundaries.

Now, though, Jessica's quarters were like a missing tooth, and Paul was drawn there.

He was startled when he stopped at the door to see a tall figure standing in shadow and silence. It seemed like a specter in the untouched chamber, but then Paul recognized his father's profile. Leto was staring at the pillows on her padded chair, the bookshelves, the keepsakes. Paul held his breath, reluctant to disturb him, but Leto spoke aloud. "I miss her, too. It seems . . . unnatural not to have her here."

He sighed and turned around. "I suppose eventually we'll have to repurpose these rooms."

Paul swallowed hard. "Not yet."

Leto nodded. "Not yet."

Paul entered the chamber, and he was sure he could still smell the lingering scent of his mother. It might have been his imagination, or simply more memories. Most of her garments were still here, because she had taken very little with her to the Mother School on Wallach IX. A hairbrush rested in front of one of her mirrors. In a vase by the windowsill, old, dried flowers clung to a few hints of their color, but the servants hadn't come in here to refresh them, as they usually did. They avoided Lady Jessica's rooms, as Paul had. As Leto had.

So many times, the young man remembered coming in here just to talk with his mother, to discuss politics and philosophy, to remark on some nuances of Atreides history or Imperial legends, or even just to discuss an unusual fish that Gurney had caught out at the end of one of the docks.

Leto took a seat on Jessica's divan. The Duke wore his formal working jacket, tunic, slacks, and low-top boots. "This is a good place to talk, Paul. Join me for a while."

Paul felt uneasy. "Are you certain, sir? We could go to your office or one of the other meeting rooms."

Leto leaned back and closed his eyes. "No, this will be just fine."

Paul took the seat next to him, and felt a mixture of awkwardness as well as comfort. His father remained quiet for a moment, then said, "You did a fine job running Atreides affairs while I was away on Kaitain." He had expressed similar confidence before, but Paul wondered if he was expressing something more this time. After a long pause, Leto added, "I . . . I am proud that you're my son."

Paul felt a rush of warmth. This man was not one to dole out easy praise. He wore a worried expression on his face from burdens that weighed heavily on him, especially after the major moonfish setback.

Paul said, "I'm always ready to do what I can to help, even if it's just to give you a friendly sounding board."

Leto smiled. "That's exactly what I need right now, to help me sort some of these contradictory thoughts."

Paul was impressed that his father treated the staff so well. Leto had also taken time to learn all their names. In stories the Duke had told since coming home from the Imperial Palace, most of the haughty nobles at court barely even noticed their retainers. Paul realized this caring, benevolent nature toward the people of Caladan was another reason they loved their Duke. The boy realized that was the kind of leader he wanted to be.

It seemed incongruous that Duke Leto Atreides could also be so cool at times to those closest to him. Paul thought of his mother, gone now for almost two months without sending any word at all. . . .

Paul could see that his father was distant and preoccupied. The Duke stared at a tapestry on the wall, an evocative weaving that was like breakers on the coast. He realized that his father looked thinner than usual, his face all angles.

Leto finally spoke. "Jaxson Aru came to me again. He's courting me to join his rebellion."

Paul sat back in alarm, thinking of all the bloodshed the rebel leader had caused. "Here on Caladan? Have you told Thufir?"

Leto tapped his fingers on the arm of the divan. "He found me in the reef market two days ago, but he is long gone by now."

His father had seemed under a cloud recently, preoccupied and uncommunicative. Now Paul knew the reason. "Did he threaten you?" He remembered too vividly the sharp dream he'd had months ago, awakening with the certainty that his father was in terrible danger—which turned out to be during the Otorio attack, far across the galaxy.

"Jaxson won't hurt me. He has his own dark moral code." Leto let out a sigh. "He wants me to understand him, and he wants me to agree with him, to become part of the Noble Commonwealth movement."

Paul felt as if his father's honor had been insulted. "That's ridiculous."

"Oh, his underlying logic and the rationale for his actions are convincing, from a certain point of view. He desperately wants to win me over, thinks that I—and Caladan—would thrive if the Corrino Imperium were fragmented."

Paul had a dismal, sinking feeling. "You're not thinking of joining him? He would be even worse than Count Fenring. I don't trust either of them."

"Wise words." Leto sat forward with hunched shoulders. Just speaking about his weighty problem did not seem to be lifting the burden from him. "I assure you, I'm treading a careful path. Emperor Shaddam has indeed accumulated vast wealth through arbitrary taxes, and his honor is . . . somewhat flexible. Spending more time at the Imperial Court convinced me it is a cesspool filled with the lowest forms of life, grabbing for any scrap of wealth or influence. House Atreides has no such twisted ambition. The people of Caladan are not like that." He shook his head. "But the corruption of the ancient Imperial government is why the Noble Commonwealth movement is gathering strength as they convince more and more nobles—like me."

Troubled, Paul descended into the concepts as if he'd been given one of Thufir Hawat's intense mental exercises. He asked again in a quieter voice, "Are you actually considering it? You aren't like that, sir. Do you agree with Jaxson Aru, now that you know so much about the corruption on Kaitain?"

"No. But as long as he thinks I *might*, then I am like a ripe fruit hanging just out of reach, and that keeps Caladan—and you—safe." He rested his hand on Paul's forearm. "As a leader you'll be required to make such decisions someday."

Paul decided to push back. "But Jaxson Aru murdered thousands of people on Otorio!"

Instead of looking horrified, Leto just sighed. "Shaddam has killed many more than that. I can think of numerous instances."

Paul lowered his head. "I'm having trouble processing this."

Leto responded with a bitter laugh. "Good! That means you are going through the steps of the decision in your own mind. You're my son, Paul. I ask you this: How much loyalty do we owe to a corrupt Emperor? He comes from a long line of Corrino emperors, some as bad as or worse than he is, but others truly tried to serve their people."

Dropping into silence, Paul followed his thoughts around in circles, knowing his father's previous interactions with Shaddam IV, scandals and crises that had occurred even before he was born . . . and what his grandfather had done to House Kolona, supposedly at the behest of Emperor Elrood IX.

He came to a clear, sharp conclusion. "There have been more than two dozen Atreides Dukes, and our service goes far longer and far deeper than your dislike for one man, however corrupt he might be." He stood from the divan, paced his mother's room. "Our loyalty is to the *Imperium*, not to any one Emperor."

Leto surprised him by letting out a bark of laughter. "Yes, Paul! No matter how flawed Emperor Shaddam may be, it is the *Imperium* I honor with my continued allegiance. I am faithful to the throne, not to the man. The Imperium has lasted ten thousand years, and apart from a few minor disruptions over the course of history, House Corrino has ruled for all that time." His gray eyes intensified. "I can't let it all fall because of recent unpopular decisions. Sometimes I wonder if it takes a bad person, or at least a hard person, to rule in a system that is designed to reward corruption. But there's a much bigger picture, and I believe in it. I believe in the overall arc of history, that the Imperium is beneficial to humankind on a very large scale. One day, Shaddam Corrino will be gone and another Emperor will take his place. It is a stable system going back for millennia. Even with its flaws it is better than the wild dreams of a fanatic like Jaxson Aru."

Paul felt a great sense of relief. "Then your answer to this rebel madman must be no."

"For now, my answer must be *silence*. I may disagree with Shaddam in my thoughts, but not in my actions. As Duke of Caladan and a loyal member of the Landsraad, I must preserve the Imperial throne for future generations to occupy. Never forget what I'm saying to you. I can't even consider accepting the bloody anarchy the Noble Commonwealth wants."

Paul went to the window, looked out at the vast sea. "It seems that a person in ultimate power has to do many distasteful things."

"My son, you are beginning to understand, but not the scale of it all." He rose and began to walk to the door. "Thanks for offering your advice."

Paul joined him, and the two stepped out into the corridor, surprised to see Duncan Idaho and Gurney Halleck strolling toward them. Both men looked pleased with themselves and full of news.

Paul grinned with delight. "You're back from Lankiveil—and *safe!*"

The big troubadour warrior straightened and gave a formal acknowledgment to the Duke, but Duncan seemed cockier. "Not just safe, young Master, but victorious. Ah, we have so many stories to tell! It was spectacular!"

Gurney cleared his throat, straightened his tunic as the two men presented themselves in the quiet corridor. "We have our official report, my Lord. Rabban's operations on Lankiveil are damaged, casualties kept to a minimum, but the deepest wound will be to the Beast's treasury."

"Rabban will be stinging from these wounds a long time," Duncan said. He pulled an imager from his pocket and activated it, showing images of the unmarked raiding ships that destroyed Rabban's military hangar at the edge of a deep fjord, flattened warehouse buildings, and sank waterborne seafood-processing plants tied up to docks, while workers frantically evacuated.

Duncan's grin grew even wider. "And during the mayhem, we even took the opportunity to scatter some passive spy-eyes around the Lankiveil holdings. We'll now get intermittent reports of what Rabban's doing there."

"I am pleased to report that we suffered no casualties, my Lord," Gurney said.

Duncan smirked. "Well, Tanley did sprain his ankle leaping off a roof, firing his weapon all the way down . . ." He and Gurney chuckled.

"He'll be mentioned in one of my heroic ballads," Gurney said. "I've been composing it on our journey home."

The Duke looked as if a great burden had lifted from him. "I'm glad to receive good news. Get cleaned up and join us for dinner in a couple of hours. You can give us a full report while we eat." He patted each man on his back. "And don't come into my dining hall drunk."

Duncan said, "We don't promise not to *leave* the dining hall a little drunk."

Finally reaching a dim chamber, Brom stopped, panting as much from fear as from exertion. He glanced at his wristchron and spread his hands. "I've imagined this often, but I never really made a plan."

Jessica remembered when she had landed here more than a month ago after being torn away from her family. She whispered, "Why are you doing this?"

The young man looked befuddled. "It was instinctive. My entire life, I've been trained to make split-second decisions, and when I saw those two Sisters trying to kill you, I couldn't just look the other way. I . . . I don't like what was done to you in the isolation cell, and that was the final straw."

He reminded her of Paul, with his valiant instinct to help. Her thoughts began turning faster. "There wasn't time to plan. Now we must react, and adapt." She could almost smell freedom, but knew there were still obstacles to overcome. Were Ruthine and Jiara acting on the Mother Superior's orders, or were they rogues? Had her death sentence already been determined?

"I've always wanted to leave Wallach IX," Brom said. "The Sisterhood insisted they had plans for me, but I'm already seventeen. If we get out of here, I can start fresh . . ."

"Yes, we will get out of here," Jessica said, reassuring herself as much as him. The obstacle seemed impossible, but she would not give up. She knew the Sisters would be looking for them as soon as they discovered the battered Ruthine and Jiara in the cell. She had to hope that the young man truly did know ancient hiding places that were unknown to their Bene Gesserit pursuers.

"We *will* get out of here," Brom agreed.

AT DAWN, UNDER the cold, cloudy skies, Reverend Mother Gaius Helen Mohiam stood outside at the base of a bronze statue considered the foundation of the entire Mother School. The statue honored Raquella Berto-Anirul, the first

Mother Superior and founder of the order, ten millennia ago. The graceful, mysterious monument stood in front of a replica of Raquella's ancient residence built after the end of Serena Butler's Jihad, a comparatively small tile-roofed structure that was now a museum. Harishka had commissioned the reconstruction a few years ago, based upon original architectural drawings. It stood in stark contrast to the large, modern structures funded by grants from the late Viscount Alfred Tull.

Mohiam gazed up at Raquella's benign face as if looking for answers. First as an Acolyte ages ago, then a Sister, and finally a Reverend Mother, Mohiam had devoted her entire life to the order. She had accomplished everything, and sacrificed everything. She had borne several daughters as directed, always careful to eschew love. She hoped she had honored the traditions that the first Mother Superior had established. She was one of Harishka's closest, most reliable confidantes, and the other woman certainly needed her.

The Mother Superior approached, accompanied by her adviser Cordana, who walked awkwardly, wrapped in a thick cloak against the chill. Her expression, though, looked both unsettled and pleased. Mohiam knew that Cordana, along with Reverend Mother Ruthine, had taken her former place as Harishka's high adviser after Mohiam went to serve as the Emperor's Truthsayer. Disgraced now, Ruthine had been taken into custody along with her fellow schemer Jiara until such time as they explained their actions.

Mohiam had seen Ruthine's bruised, scraped form, and she actually allowed herself a moment of hidden pride, because she had taught Jessica the fighting skills she had used to survive, to escape. Many people had underestimated Jessica. . . .

The three robed women met in front of the statue of Raquella. Harishka said, "For many years, I relied on you for advice. Now I need your wisdom and clearheaded thinking again."

"It seems you have been getting terrible advice." Mohiam glanced at Cordana, thinking of the battered Ruthine. "And Jessica is still missing."

Cordana said, "Obviously, Ruthine was no longer satisfied with merely giving advice."

Harishka's expression darkened. "She defied my explicit orders, but she and Jiara are in custody now. No doubt, Ruthine believes she serves the best interests of the Bene Gesserit, even as she goes against my clear commands."

Cordana was angry. "You are the Mother Superior! You and the Sisterhood are one and the same."

"Are they?" Harishka muttered. "Ruthine would likely say otherwise." She shook her head. "I keep an open mind when I ask my top people for advice, and some of the advice I receive is wrong." She moved closer to Mohiam at the base of the tall statue. "I seek the advice of my old adviser again . . . my old friend."

"You want me to tell you what to do with Jessica," Mohiam responded, not as a question. "How to punish her for her escape? And what choice did she have if two Sisters came to kill her? Of course she fought back. Of course she fled when she saw the opportunity. She would have assumed the attack was ordered by the Mother Superior." She clucked her tongue and shook her head slowly. "Oh, Jessica has pressed and rebelled in her own ways, but I cannot salve your conscience in this, Harishka."

The Mother Superior's lips formed a tight line. "I want your clarity. When we find Jessica—and we will—how should we respond? She is with the young man, Brom. We think he helped her." They walked slowly away from the looming statue of Raquella to a set of stone benches. "I need your counsel, but considering your background with Jessica, I wonder if you can truly be objective?"

Mohiam and the Mother Superior both knew that Jessica was her own natural daughter. "She was my student. I care for all my students."

Cordana interjected, "The Mother School raised her. She is one of us."

"And therefore subject to our rules," Harishka said.

"And obligations," Mohiam said. "That is what Jessica needs to remember. I taught her well. I made her strong. She has formidable combat skills, but she was not the aggressor. She was right to respond in every way available to her." She locked gazes with Harishka as if Cordana were not there. "Jessica is a Bene Gesserit in her heart, in her blood, in her bones. Rather than kill her, let her prove herself. Find a way for her to demonstrate what she truly is—one of us." She took a deep breath. "And if she fails in that, we discard her. I would do it myself."

They looked up as another Sister approached with a light step, an energy of anticipation. Xora wore a black day-robe with a white collar. "Mother Superior, I am ready to leave for Caladan tomorrow on the Heighliner." She stood before the women, bowed, but was unable to cover her satisfied smile. "I am grateful for the second chance you gave me, Mother Superior. I won't let you down. I will present myself to Duke Leto Atreides and be what he needs me to be. I can shape myself into what this nobleman desires."

Mohiam deflated some of her enthusiasm. "Do not assume your task will be easy. I know Leto Atreides, and he can put up a hard wall if he decides to. He already expressed no interest in a new concubine."

Xora merely squared her shoulders. "He is soured by Jessica leaving him, but he hasn't met me yet. I will make him forget her."

After the Mother Superior dismissed her, Mohiam considered just how much Xora looked like Jessica, except for those feline blue eyes . . . like her father's. None of Mohiam's secret daughters for the Sisterhood knew who their mother was.

Following her gaze, Harishka seemed to know what her old friend was thinking. "No one can say you were unwilling to do your duty for the order."

Mohiam kept her voice low. "At least that one's father wasn't as loathsome as Jessica's." She hardened her expression. "Xora has great potential, accepts her new assignment. Once Jessica is found, it is only fair to give her another opportunity. She can still do much for the Sisterhood. We went to such horrific lengths to get her bloodline in the first place."

"Jessica is still fertile," Cordana pointed out. "She could bear a daughter for us, as she was originally instructed to do. We should send her back to Leto, rather than sending Xora."

"I am not anxious to do away with a Sister as talented as Jessica," Harishka agreed. "But before we send her back to her happy home and her Duke, we need to be certain of her loyalty. And in order to do that, we must test her."

"Her great and obvious flaw is her abiding love for Leto," Mohiam said. "That is her strongest motivation—matched only, perhaps, by love for her son. She would do anything for them."

"Jessica's in a desperate situation now," Cordana said. "She thinks the Sisterhood is trying to kill her. She is hiding, and most certainly afraid. She may be close to giving up hope."

The Mother Superior seemed pleased. "Remember the Bene Gesserit axiom: the surest way to coerce a desperate person is to offer them hope. And her hope would be an emotion that *we* control."

Mohiam smiled with her wrinkled lips. "Dangle the hope that we will let her go back to Leto—but only if she accomplishes an impossible task for us."

Mother Superior Harishka paused, then slowly nodded. Mohiam felt an unaccountable sense of relief. "But first we must find her, flush her out." She rose from the cold stone bench. "Now then, we must prepare my shuttle for departure tomorrow. Make sure its cargo hold is loaded with any materials bound for offplanet. In fact, spread the word that Xora is to accompany me up to the Heighliner. We will go our separate ways, but we can leave here together."

The two other women gave her a puzzled look.

Mohiam said, "Give me the benefit of the doubt. I know something important."

JESSICA AND BROM waited for more than a day, watching, listening. He led her through a maze of passageways, first between walls and then underground, where they were now. Overhead, Jessica saw a narrow corona of light encircling what looked like a hatch, as if in an eclipse. Escape seemed impossible, which meant that somehow they had to do the impossible.

"We're beneath the spaceport outside the Mother School complex," he whispered. "Whoever set up this escape route wanted a direct channel from the main Chapterhouse to transport off-planet. At some point we may be able to slip aboard a supply ship or shuttle that's about to depart."

Jessica felt her pulse race. If she could get off-planet, maybe she could go renegade and slip away into the shadows of the vast Imperium . . . and maybe someday she could find her way back to Caladan. Someday. But she could not stay here on Wallach IX if the Sisterhood had determined to kill her.

They huddled for hours until the daylight around the hatch diminished, then the young man cautiously led the way up a ladder and pushed the underside of the hatch. It opened, revealing the lights of the landing field—and a waiting shuttle, its lights blinking in sequence from blue to green to red.

Brom looked at it, his eyes sparkling, his face wistful. "That is Reverend Mother Mohiam's shuttle—I saw it land just before I came to you. They're loading the cargo hold now." He swallowed, hesitating. "It'll depart soon. That is our chance."

Workers used machinery to lift small containers into an open hold. "You think I can get aboard? Ride it to the Heighliner, and be away from the Mother School . . ."

"We can." Brom stared intently across the field. Jessica watched the movement of machinery, the shadowy workers in the glare of the loading lights. They both saw their chance at the same time, reacted like components of a machine.

He leaped out onto the paved surface and sprinted forward. Jessica used her remaining energy reserves to follow, buoyed by the excitement, the chance. The air of Wallach IX was bracing as she ran right behind him, darting across the landing field. In moments, they had concealed themselves behind a container that had been unloaded with supplies for the Mother School. Other crates were ready to be hauled aboard.

Brom obviously knew more details of the landing field. "When we see a break, we'll cross the last gap and get on board. I can spot when the cargo handlers are off the ship."

She was just as alert and ready. She had trusted this bold young man this far, but their chances were still as thin as a frayed veil. When he nodded, they bolted for the shadows beneath the ship. They reached the rear of the cargo hold and loading ramp just in front of the shuttle's large engines. He slipped ahead and led her to a small access door. "This leads to an equipment room. We'll be safe there. Once the shuttle is locked inside the Heighliner, we'll have another set of problems."

Jessica did not think of the repercussions of Brom escaping with her. Just by breaking free, fleeing the Mother School herself, she would cause a tremendous uproar in the Bene Gesserit. She could never go back.

But she didn't want to go back to them. The Sisterhood had tried to kill her, and now she needed to get away. Had Xora already been dispatched on her assignment? To become the new Lady of Caladan?

If the two of them could stow away and ride the shuttle up to the Heighliner in orbit, they could figure out the next step from there.

They made their way into a cramped compartment that smelled of metal and oil, where they found a place to sit in a dark corner. Unspeakably weary, Jessica slumped back against the bulkhead and just let herself melt into a trance.

Light flared in the shuttle compartment, and a woman barked, "Stowaways! Exactly where you said they'd be, Mohiam."

Jessica blinked, trying to adjust her eyes. Brom lurched to his feet, ready to fight. A group of silhouettes stood outlined in the bright doorway, two dark-robed women, with others gathering behind them. With a sinking feeling, she recognized her old teacher, as well as the Mother Superior.

Mohiam strode forward with a harsh smile on her lips. "Didn't you think I could predict exactly where you would go, Jessica?"

The Imperial extravaganza was about to begin.

Shaddam looked at his Empress and extended his arm. "Despite all the efforts of my protocol ministers, my dear, you will outshine even our greatest show. And this is not a day I can afford for the public's attention to be diverted from the matter at hand!"

Her ornate gown was a vision of ruffles and ribbons, shining fabric, gauzy veils. Aricatha's dark hair had been bound back with soostones and Hagal emeralds intertwined with platinum chains. Her smile was the brightest treasure of all.

"You look quite impressive yourself, my dear husband." She reached over to touch the burnished buttons that ran down his chest, the gold braid on his collar, and the colorful spangle of ribbons and awards.

"We will make do together, my Empress." The two strolled off together through a wide corridor of the Imperial Palace. "My original idea for this would have garnered a lot of attention, but you added a twist that will resonate for years to come . . . despite the additional cost." He frowned, but could never remain annoyed at her. Aricatha always soothed him.

She guided him past lines of rigid honor guards and uniformed attendants and spoke close to his ear as they walked. "There are many ways to measure cost and benefit, husband. Wait until you see the profit you will gain in loyalty from your newest nobles, and for the price of only a few solari coins."

"It is millions of solaris, my dear. Far more than a few." They headed toward the vast open balcony that overlooked the murmuring crowds in front of the Promenade Wing. Still, he couldn't wait for the surprise.

Frustrated by the complaints of intractable nobles and merchants over his spice surtax, the Emperor had been planning this spectacle for a long time. The Landsraad, especially Lord Rajiv Londine, had demanded that the unnecessary tax be repealed immediately once the cost of the Otorio disaster had been recouped, but Shaddam's Mentat accountants kept finding new purported expenses, and therefore new demands on the Imperial treasury.

Today, he would demonstrate the success and prosperity of the Imperium by delivering a month of surtax revenues in a single load of solari coins, like an ancient treasure galleon from Old Earth. The glitter would astonish the people of Kaitain, and Shaddam would revel in it. With an additional surprise, thanks to the Empress. . . .

Moving gracefully together, he and Aricatha glided onto the Promenade Wing's balcony, which was the size of a small spaceport landing field. On cue, the crowds in the plaza let out a loud cheer to see the small, distant figures above.

The raging fountains gushed cannons of water high into the air, and he was pleased to see the marvelous hydroengineering. Today's event had nearly been delayed when his mechanics reported some malfunction in the ejector cannons or illumination projectors, but it had all been fixed, and now the show was as vibrant as he had hoped. Those fountains would project his benevolent image to the crowds all across Kaitain.

Standing on the open balcony, Shaddam smiled and waved to his people, while he muttered to Aricatha, "Hasimir should be here. I regret sending him away so abruptly."

"He made his choice, my dear, and you know he doesn't like big public events. He is a more private man."

Fenring always had important business on Arrakis, of course, but he had also disagreed with Shaddam about today's event, calling it a demonstration of Imperial greed and overreach rather than wealth and prosperity. The Count had been in a sour mood ever since losing a fortune in moonfish investments on Caladan.

Finally, Shaddam had snapped at him, "You are my Spice Minister on Arrakis. I am not completely convinced that you wiped out those insidious pirates who were stealing my spice wealth. Go find them. And by the way, you have no business investing in *fish!*"

Count Fenring had departed for Arrakis without waiting to witness this grand celebration. Still, Shaddam wished his friend could have been here to support him.

Now, with anticipation brimming, Shaddam stepped onto the speaking balcony, to the roar of applause and cheers. Just below, in the best seats, were representatives of the newly advanced noble families. The Emperor had rewarded his followers.

Out there, uniformed Sardaukar moved through the crowd in an intimidating show of force, maintaining security. With a subtle move of his fingers, Shaddam transmitted the signal to dispatch the carefully guarded treasury ship from its secure hangar to make its way across the sky toward the Imperial Palace. It was time for the show to begin.

Shaddam imagined the mounds of solari coins piling up here on the great balcony, the musical ringing sound as they poured out of the cargo hold in the open space before him, but Aricatha had convinced him that showing the generosity of House Corrino was more important than running his fingers through those coins himself. In a grand surprise, he would instead take all that revenue and redistribute it among these new nobles who had gathered to acknowledge him. Shaddam would relish the moment of genuine love and celebration.

He could simply tax it back out of them in the coming months.

The fountains rose higher, and holoprojectors activated. The glowing, idealized image of Padishah Emperor Shaddam IV appeared, spreading translucent arms projected on the mists, and he began his grand speech.

PATROLLING THE PROMENADE Plaza, making a careful circuit of the roaring fountains, Colonel Bashar Jopati Kolona maintained a level of alertness that only the Sardaukar could achieve. He looked up to see the small figures of Shaddam IV and his Empress standing at the broad balcony where the heavy treasury ship would land.

Pillars of spray rose even higher, nearly as tall as the palace towers, and then a shimmering image formed on the water, a live, holographic projection of Shaddam Corrino. He stood like a titan dressed in all of his Imperial finery, and the voice from the fountain image boomed as loud as the voice of a deity. His projected, kindly image was dominant but reassuring.

"All the Imperium has joined together to rebuild our treasury after the damages done by the Noble Commonwealth rebellion!" Shaddam sounded angry and the restless crowd grumbled, feeling his fury. "You have all done what was necessary to restore our Imperium, and I am immensely proud of you." His enormous, shimmering arms on the fountain mists gestured up to the sky, and all eyes turned.

On approach, the flashing Imperial treasury ship lumbered like a huge, fat bumblebee as it cruised above the capital city, carrying a load of commemorative coins that Shaddam had minted just for this occasion. Each of the shiny solaris bore his own image. Kolona didn't entirely know what the Emperor meant to accomplish by displaying such wealth, like some robber baron flaunting his treasure, but he was not a political adviser.

The Sardaukar officer smelled the cool mist of water droplets in the air. Not long ago, he'd been concerned to learn about possible malfunctions in the fountain holo-apparatus. He was suspicious by nature, but the pumping machinery checked out, and he could find nothing wrong with the water flow or the engineering, the solido projectors—no poison gas cannisters, no explosive devices.

The colonel bashar made his way through the crowd en route to the palace. His uniform was intimidating, and the people folded away from him.

Shaddam's speech continued, echoing around the plaza. "We are here to celebrate our thriving Imperium. Our success across countless worlds benefits all of my loyal subjects. Behold—"

Kolona had just reached the palace entrance and turned, when an extravagant outburst of water erupted from the fountains. As the fountain eruption cleared, Shaddam's projected image suddenly changed to an angry, evil countenance. "Citizens of the Imperium, heed my actions, not my words! Not my lies! I have stolen all this wealth from you while you toil and suffer." He bellowed an evil, cartoonish laugh.

The audience turned, puzzled, and Kolona felt a sudden chill of unease. He had reviewed the precise sequence of events on the schedule, and these were not the words Shaddam had planned to speak. Something was wrong.

He glanced up at the balcony. The small figures of the Emperor and Empress were still there, but the images on the fountain spray no longer mirrored what Shaddam was actually doing. In his fine robes, he gesticulated and shouted, clearly angry, while the gigantic projection spat out a damning diatribe of words that were not his own.

"Noble families rule their planets and work to feed and clothe their people, but I keep stealing your fortunes! I pile up my own wealth. That is what you see today."

Kolona touched his comm, sounding an alert as he bounded through the towering entry arches. "Watch the Emperor! Prepare to evacuate him!" A chatter of voices responded. He looked up at the sky behind him, where the large treasury ship cruised toward the Promenade Wing.

From outside, he still heard the booming words. "You are all fools to fatten my treasury, when you could instead be independent and free!"

Kolona bolted through the palace corridors and ran up a wide cascade of steps to reach the balcony level. The alarm had spread throughout the honor guard, and more Sardaukar raced toward the promenade balcony.

One of his underlings caught up and ran beside him. "Colonel Bashar, someone hijacked the amplifier! The holoprojector is coming from somewhere inside the fountain mechanism. We're sending engineers there to shut it down."

Kolona, though, remembered Otorio, where he had seen thousands of Jaxson Aru's holograms appear like ghosts throughout the museum complex. "Get the Emperor to safety—now!"

"We're guarding him, Colonel Bashar. There's no reason to fear."

"Of course there's a reason to fear." Kolona kept running, couldn't afford to be out of breath. "The rebellion won't be satisfied with just a speech. Jaxson Aru is behind this."

He burst out onto the expansive balcony where Shaddam Corrino was railing, but his voice pickup had been deactivated. No one heard his actual words, only the damning speech that someone else had recorded, mimicking his voice.

The crowd milled about, first confused, and now some were wise enough to feel fear, but there wasn't outright panic. Not yet. Kolona knew there was no time to sound a complete evacuation of the plaza. He had one priority.

"Sire! The emergency lift in the next gallery will drop you down to the armor-walled underground chamber."

Out in the plaza, the Emperor's image on the fountains transformed into a different person, a man instantly familiar to the colonel bashar. Jaxson Aru.

The Emperor issued brisk commands. "Shut down those fountains and stop that man's words. We must control the damage. I have to address the crowds and correct this!"

Jaxson Aru continued his tirade. "How much more will you let the Corrinos steal from you? The Imperium has ravished your wealth and prosperity."

Kolona looked around. "We will find him if he is here, Sire. But right now, we must take precautions. Come with me!"

Jaxson bellowed from the fountains, "I am Jaxson Aru, and I represent the Noble Commonwealth. As individual worlds, you could all thrive. You could achieve your own greatness, not give the lion's share—the *Corrino lion's* share—to this greedy Emperor."

The treasury ship cruised closer to the palace, and when Kolona saw it in-bound, fear and determination thundered through him. "Now, Sire!" He grabbed Shaddam and pulled hard enough to practically wrench the arm out of its socket. Two other Sardaukar swept up Empress Aricatha and raced her inside.

"Not now," Shaddam commanded. "I can't appear cowardly in front of that rebellious traitor. Shut him down and restore the amplifiers so I can speak!"

The colonel bashar propelled him along. "I respectfully refuse, Sire. You are coming with me." The honor guard charged ahead, clearing the corridors.

"I'll have you executed for this!"

"Only if you survive, Sire," Kolona said, and the steel in his voice made Shaddam falter.

His Sardaukar ignored the Emperor's protestations. In matters of his personal security, their priorities were clear. Even Shaddam himself could not command them otherwise.

Jaxson continued to roar out from the fountain projection. "The Noble Commonwealth will restore your prosperity! The wealth in that vessel is stolen from you! It does not belong to the Corrinos."

In the gallery ahead, the honor guard had moved a wall panel aside and opened the reinforced doors of an escape lift. As Jaxson finished his grim declaration from the towering fountain image, Kolona manhandled the Imperial couple into the large lift and went with them, while several Sardaukar piled in after them. Kolona activated the controls.

Suddenly the heavily loaded ship exploded above the plaza, turning a million metal solari coins into projectiles. Just before the escape lift doors slammed shut,

Kolona saw the roar of flame impact the balcony, slam into the walls, and spurt into the palace.

The armored chamber dropped as if propelled by rockets. The shock wave from the exploding treasury ship made even the armored lift ring out like a struck gong.

Outside, the wrecked hulk of the vessel careened through the air, gushing smoke. It crashed into the promenade balcony, and flaming portions of the hull rained down onto the crowd.

The escape lift reached its protected bunker. The Emperor and the few Sardaukar that had managed to escape all looked shell-shocked. Aricatha was surprisingly cool, though her eyes sparkled with anger. Colonel Bashar Kolona could only imagine the amount of destruction that had just occurred outside the palace.

Shaddam was darkly infuriated. "All those solaris. That was a month of spice surtax—and I meant to distribute it among the people! It was going to be my surprise, my gift to them." His lips drew back in outrage. "Now they'll never believe my generosity."

Kolona didn't imagine that would be the foremost concern to anyone else.

Secrets are best used by those wise enough to place a proper value on the information.

—Fremen admonition

When the man returned from the desert, he was desiccated and sunburned, his stillsuit damaged from the extreme ordeal. Esmar Tuek knew it was one of his people. And the man was a survivor.

Even though Beast Rabban and Baron Harkonnen had ceased their ruthless raids against the smugglers, Tuek's new camouflaged base was still protected by surveillance and scouting patrols. His people continued their work, which was sanctioned by Count Fenring, but none of them let down their guard.

Even though Staban had soiled his honor, he had taken on more and more responsibility for the harvesting patrols, swift factory runs, and the packaging of melange. Esmar still wrestled with what his son had done, but Staban was his blood, his only heir. His choices had been to kill the young man along with his own duplicitous wife, and ruin all possibility of a future . . . or to find some way to live with it. Staban was intensely aware that he remained on harsh probation, and he went about his days as if he were made of glass, easily breakable and trying to be transparent.

The survivor who dragged himself out of the desert was named Benak, a friend from Staban's youth. Benak and his companion, Corvir Dur, had been gone for days, ranging far in search of new spice sands while keeping their eyes open for the black-market spice harvesters. There was room for only one illegal operation on Arrakis.

Benak had staggered across the dunes, walking in the patternless Fremen fashion so as not to attract a sandworm, moving mostly at night. Still, he had left a trail of footprints that would be apparent to any airborne surveillance, until a windstorm erased them. Benak knew better, which meant he must be in his last hours of desperation.

As soon as the figure was spotted, Staban sent out a rescue team that swooped in to snatch the dying smuggler from the sands. They gave him water and tended him as the 'thopters raced back to the smuggler base, nursing him back to life. En route, Staban transmitted a report. "He's alive, Father, but Corvir Dur has been killed. They discovered something important, I think. Benak is delirious."

Esmar answered, "Let me know when he is able to speak, and deliver his report."

He retreated through moisture-sealed doors deep into the base, past the hangars that held their 'thopters and small spice harvesters, then sat at his desk in the secure office while he waited for the rescue party to return. He told his people to give Benak any water he needed, and even authorized moist bathing cloths so the suffering man could feel alive and whole again after his ordeal.

Perhaps Benak and Corvir Dur had found an answer about the spice thieves, information that Count Fenring badly wanted. A knot formed in his stomach.

To distract himself while he waited, he reviewed the most recent reports from Carthag and Arrakeen. According to the last information, the Count and Lady Fenring were back at the Imperial Court, and Esmar did not dare provide this valuable intelligence to anyone but Fenring himself. He would have to wait until the Count returned to Arrakis.

The cost of those spice thieves had already been unspeakably high, to his operations, to Rulla. . . .

The smuggler leader was not Fremen by blood, but he had adopted some of the harsher desert ways. Many tribes insisted that a child born of adultery was intrinsically evil, and they left such babies out on the sands to die. Rulla had betrayed her husband in the worst way, seducing his son. It was the most terrible crime he could imagine, and she had paid for it.

But the breathing room her execution had bought was running out. If Benak had discovered the real headquarters of the brigands who were stealing spice, Count Fenring could take care of them, and this nightmare would be over. . . .

When he could wait no longer, Esmar went to the quiet, cool temporary infirmary. Benak's tattered, nonfunctioning stillsuit had been stripped off, and a medic had wiped away the caked salt of perspiration . . . wasted water. The scout's skin had been burned into angry red patches, but he was awake.

Staban sat at his friend's side, feeding him crumbled corners of spice biscuits to give him much-needed energy. Esmar had seen people in far worse shape, and he knew this man would recover.

Seeing the smuggler leader, Benak struggled to prop himself up in bed. "Corvir Dur and I found their base, Esmar!" His voice was terribly hoarse, and the words croaked out. "They captured Corvir Dur." With a shudder, he closed his eyes to shut away the memories. "They drowned him in spice powder."

Esmar reeled, but he focused on the information. "What did you see? Where did you find these operations?"

"We saw a carryall and tracked it. There should have been no outpost there." Benak inhaled a deep breath. Staban remained at his friend's side like a bodyguard. The haggard man continued. "Nothing has been on the records for years. We thought it was shut down, destroyed."

"How will I know the place?" Esmar asked. "Can you show us on a chart?"

"The old Orgiz refinery complex. Someone restored the equipment and opened it up again. We watched full loads of spice brought in, then taken away in unmarked ships, probably to be sold somewhere off-planet."

"Orgiz?" Esmar's brow furrowed. "Right in the open? These smugglers must have powerful contacts."

"The desert is vast." Benak closed his eyes. He seemed entirely exhausted.

Esmar recalled the location of the place, far from any spaceport or any normal desert travel routes. He leaned closer to the man on the pallet. "Who did this? Did you see any banners, any identifying marks on the ships? Who is behind this operation?"

Benak shook his head. "There were no colors, no family crests. Corvir Dur let himself be taken so I could get away with this information. I . . . I watched them murder him. It was more than just a small base, Esmar! Much larger than our operations here, well funded, well organized."

"Corvir Dur's death will not be in vain. I will bring this vital information to the Imperial Spice Minister." Esmar looked at his son, who continued to tend the weak man.

Staban said, "You did well, Benak. I'm proud of you. Thank you." He met his father's gaze, defiant. Yes, this was another small step in which Staban had proved himself again.

"Rest and recover." Esmar squeezed the haggard man's shoulder. "We'll have you back working the spice operations in no time." He stalked out of the private chamber and headed for his sealed office, where he could sit and think.

Now he possessed the crucial information that Count Hasimir Fenring had been waiting for. He had to decide how best he could use this intelligence. By submitting this report, Esmar Tuek and his smugglers would make themselves invaluable and secure on Arrakis.

Emotions are an affliction to avoid in ourselves and exploit in others. Taking advantage of this weakness, this Achilles' heel, is an art form.

—MOTHER SUPERIOR RAQUELLA BERTO-ANIRUL

Captive again, Jessica faced an even darker future than before. What Bene Gesserit punishment would she face, now that her escape attempt had failed? She had no idea what had happened to Brom.

Sealed in the same isolation cell as before, Jessica prepared herself, mentally and physically, for whatever might come. Looking up at the high, narrow windows, she saw only weak gray light. During her brief periods of sleep, nightmares lingered in her thoughts and then faded, like sun burning through fog. But her powerful desire to survive was the sunlight dissipating the cold mist.

She controlled her mind and body. Removing her robe and dressing in a lightweight undergarment, she performed calisthenics, then jogged slowly around the perimeter of her large cell, faster and faster, speeding around the tight corners. Her bare feet kept traction on the floor, and she ran even faster, then from corner to corner. Burning off energy . . . building up energy.

She could not run away from the Bene Gesserit, but she could run away from her fear. *Fear is the mind-killer* . . . She could build her energy like a Holtzman engine increasing power. She practiced combat maneuvers, rolling on the stone floor and springing to her feet. With her feet, arms, and fists, she struck sharp blows at imaginary opponents. In her mind's eye she saw the enemies fall as Ruthine and Jiara had fallen. She used her rage to focus, to increase her strength, and she made sure she killed all of her imaginary opponents. No survivors.

Breathing hard, she stood in the middle of the cell and reached an epiphany. She had always been taught that rage was an emotion to suppress because it blocked the logical side of the mind and led inevitably to mistakes. But the endorphins she'd felt from her exercise, from letting her emotions rise, also lifted her mood, even simulated hope for her. Emotion didn't get in the way of her control; emotion was a tool. A weapon, if properly used.

She went to her small personal basin and splashed water on her face. Jessica felt ready now. She waited to learn what they would do to her.

I have to find some way out of this.

THE MOTHER SUPERIOR, Mohiam, and Reverend Mother Cordana extracted Jessica from her cell and led her into the cold forest. Seeing her teacher's stony expression almost unnerved her, but she resolved to face whatever they would do to her.

"Have you all come to kill me now, after Ruthine and Jiara failed? Is this to be my execution?" Jessica squared her shoulders.

Mohiam stopped, turned to give her a disappointed look. "Of course Harishka did not call for your death. Those others acted on their own, dangerous and rebellious, defying the orders of the Mother Superior. Both are being held so we can determine if this conspiracy against the Bene Gesserit is more widespread." Mohiam marched onward into the orange-and-gold forest.

Jessica's step faltered, and her limbs felt watery with relief. "What . . . what happened to Brom? He helped to save me."

"Brom is not your concern," Harishka said. "He will not be punished, if that is what you fear. He stopped a crime from being committed, and he saved the life of a valuable Sister." She narrowed her eyes, skewering Jessica with her glare. "If you can ever prove yourself to us again."

Jessica was filled with questions, but she kept them inside as the other women led her on a brisk and silent walk. Dry branches and brown-gold leaves rustled overhead, and the air had a chill dampness that always presaged winter. The Mother Superior moved with surprising energy for such an old woman, setting a fast pace as if she went on a wilderness hike every day.

Out here among the rocks and dense trees, Jessica could have left the trail and bolted into the forest. She might be able to elude all three of them, for a time, but they could call out extensive search parties. No, she needed to face whatever they had in mind.

With a deep sense of foreboding, she recognized that these trails led up to the sheer precipice of Laojin Cliff. Long ago, on the steep slope at the other side of the hill, Acolytes had been trained in dangerous special maneuvers, but many had died, and the exercises were no longer conducted. Her muscles tightened. Was Harishka taking her up there?

Then they surprised her by turning off onto a side trail through denser trees and rugged rock outcroppings, where the path switchbacked down the slope to a beautiful, secluded lake.

They reached the edge of the placid lake that reflected the gunmetal-gray skies. From here, they had a spectacular view of the stark rock wall of Laojin Cliff. Boulders along the silent shore offered places to sit, and Mother Superior Harishka chose a comfortable spot. Mohiam and the other two women took seats of their own, leaving one flat rock for Jessica.

Intent, though not submissive, she sat, stroking her skirt as a momentary distraction. Nearby, the lake stirred as a fish swam just beneath the surface. In the open air, the cool breeze whistled, and the cliff wall across the lake was like a stern glare.

The Mother Superior extended her hand and gestured toward the spectacular rock face. "Ten thousand years ago on the top of that cliff, Raquella Berto-Anirul, the founder of our order, threatened to throw herself to her death if the warring factions of the Sisterhood could not find a way to resolve their differences. She forced the issue and healed the terrible schism."

Jessica remembered the story from her history lessons. What was Harishka trying to say?

The old woman pointed off to the right side of the cliff. "Beyond that you can see the steep slopes where Sisterhood trainees went over the edge in a test of their courage and ability to survive. In ancient days, Sorceresses stationed them-selves on rock ledges to rescue them if necessary." She contemplated the rocky slope. "But some, notably Sister Valya, refused the safety net and leaped down the slopes on their own, to survive or die by their abilities." Harishka turned to Jessica. "Ultimately, Valya—a Harkonnen by birth—went on to lead the Bene Gesserit order, a lesson in survival of the fittest."

The Mother Superior rose from her rock and motioned her closer, then with odd gentleness, placed a hand on Jessica's shoulder. "Now why do you think we brought you here?"

Jessica regarded the steep slope, the test for Acolytes. There were countless possible answers. "To remind me that there are no safety nets in life, that all of us ultimately must survive on our own."

When Harishka's brow furrowed, Jessica knew she had not offered the right answer.

Mohiam said, "The Sisterhood itself is a safety net."

Jessica flushed and felt like a young student again.

"You have only answered half of my question," Harishka said.

Jessica concentrated harder, knowing that her life might depend on her an-swer.

Harishka prodded. "What else is there about this place that can teach us an important lesson? Reach into yourself. Apply what you've learned—or have you learned?"

Jessica gazed across the lake to the precipitous cliff face. No one could leap off that and survive, could they? She stepped toward larger rocks near the shore and climbed one of the lichen-encrusted outcroppings. From this vantage, she looked toward Laojin Cliff, where the precipice jutted out like a cantilever.

Ignoring the other women, her judges, she centered her thoughts, breathed slowly, and went inward, entering a prana-bindu meditation state. The answer was something important, she knew that. She considered her own life story, how she had gotten in so much trouble with her superiors, the decisions she had made, but did not regret. She heard voices, but none of their words were meant for her, and she blocked them out. Her vision clouded and then faded entirely, as did the world around her, until she was entirely focused inward, an island . . . a solitary planet drifting through space.

She lost track of time as her conscious and subconscious worked on the problem. The answer—*an* answer—was there, hovering in the background. When she emerged from her thoughts, fully aware again, she climbed off the boulder and returned to Mother Superior Harishka, confident that she knew. She just *knew.*

"As human beings we need to improve ourselves," Jessica said. "The Sisterhood elevates each of us through training, but there are always important lessons we must learn for ourselves. That boulder I just climbed represents the level I reached in my training at the Mother School, but beyond that is a much higher cliff face that I must climb on my own, until I reach the top. If I cannot ascend on my own, there may or may not be other Sisters to assist me. If I fall backward, there may or may not be other Sisters to rescue me."

She paused to consider her words before continuing. "In your eyes, I have fallen, Mother Superior. I know that. But I have *not* failed. I've just taken a different path to the top from the one you and the Bene Gesserit laid out for me."

Harishka's eyes flashed with surprise at Jessica's impertinence, then softened.

Jessica pointed to the summit of the sheer rock face. "Most people would see the top of the cliff as their goal, but our goal should be beyond that. The goal we set for ourselves should be to reach the stars."

Harishka exchanged glances with Mohiam, who wore an oddly satisfied expression, then she said, "An acceptable enough response. Reverend Mother Mohiam told me what an excellent student you were, what a sharp mind you have. You fell victim to your emotions, but I can see that you want to get up off your knees."

"I fell in love," Jessica said. "I did not fall to my knees."

Harishka let out a quiet, maternal chuckle. "As hard as it is for some to believe, I have deep emotions of my own, but I have been better at fighting them off, because I know our greater goal. I can see the top of the cliff . . . and the stars beyond."

Mohiam came closer to join them. "That is your weakness, dear Jessica—the reason you will never become a Reverend Mother. Eschewing the weakness of emotions is a sacrifice we made so the Sisterhood can stay focused on our goals."

Jessica still could not fathom how she could have any hope of breaking from their control, of returning to Caladan. Or was that door completely closed now? What would they make her do? What ultimatum or impossible task?

Harishka said, "You have made more than one mistake, Jessica, but I do not want to see you destroyed. I believe you can still do good work for the Bene Gesserit, provided you have learned your lesson."

"Provided you are *one of us.*" Mohiam joined her, and Jessica knew that these two had reached the decision together. "If you think you understand the Sisterhood and your role in it, then you will be given another chance."

Jessica was surprised at even the suggestion of a reprieve. "You still need me to prove myself to the order."

"Prove yourself to me," Harishka said.

"We are going to give you a narrow window and send you on a vital mission for the Sisterhood," Mohiam said. "If you succeed, then and only then, will the Sisterhood consider reassigning you."

Jessica felt a rush of hope and knew she would do whatever was necessary. "Back to Caladan?"

Cordana said, "Sister Xora has already been dispatched as the Duke's concubine."

Jessica tightened up. "Leto won't have her."

"Men are weak, and he's surely still angry with you. Maybe he doesn't want to ever see you again." Mohiam's smile seemed unnecessarily callous. "Xora may well fulfill her assignment."

Harishka ignored those comments. "If you prove yourself to us, Jessica, afterward there may very well be an opening for you on Caladan. There is other work you can do with Duke Leto . . . after we know we can trust you." She narrowed her gaze. "*Perhaps.*"

A spark of hope flared when she thought of seeing Paul and Leto again, but she braced herself for the Bene Gesserit punishment. "What do you need me to do?"

Looking back on the trail they had taken to the lake, Harishka said, "We will assign you to Viscount Giandro Tull on Elegy. His father was a great ally and strong financial supporter of the Sisterhood, but the new Viscount resists us at every turn. It is vital for the Bene Gesserit to have one of us at his side, in his head." She paused, and her next words came as blows. "You, Jessica, must become his concubine, his mistress, his love. Make him accept you. Do whatever you must and prove yourself to us. Show that you are a true Bene Gesserit."

Jessica looked out at the placid emptiness and stillness of the lake, and part of her died inside. They had done this to her on purpose! She was sure Mohiam had devised it. A second chance, a reprieve . . . but with a cost as great as the most terrible punishment.

She closed her eyes to shut out the tears and envisioned the beautiful seas of Caladan, and the rugged, ancient castle where she had spent so many happy years with her family. Could she possibly regain that?

I will find a way to go back, she thought. *I must!*

The depth of a wound matters less than how close it strikes to the heart.
—*The Assassin's Handbook*

Working through Harkonnen transportation ministers, Feyd-Rautha arranged travel for his twisted Swordmaster. No one could know who had hired Egan Saar until after he completed his mission. Then Feyd wanted the Atreides to know exactly who had hurt them so deeply.

Saar would depart in a government ship along with a handful of Harkonnen administrators and trade representatives. He would wear no Harkonnen uniform nor carry official papers, but everyone on the ship would know he was doing Harkonnen business, and no one would ask questions about his destination or his mission.

Before his departure, Feyd summoned the man to the flat rooftop, from which he liked to observe the throbbing heat and intensity of the industries, the insect-hive bustle of so many human beings helping to make House Harkonnen great.

Egan Saar came by himself, needing no escort and no bodyguards. He wore his loose, drab clothes and tattered cape, which covered his sword. The Swordmaster spurned the use of a shield belt.

As they stood together on the rooftop, Feyd considered how the man had rescued him in Forest Guard Station. For the past several nights, it had felt strange for him to sleep alone in his quarters, missing the loyal spinehounds at the foot of the bed. Blood and Bone had followed him wherever he went.

But his skin crawled at the thought of their predatory eyes, the blood on their muzzles, their fangs flashing as they turned on their master and tried to kill *him*. The sudden ice-water rush of his own mortality sent shock waves through him. The hunt master was dead, and no one but the twisted Swordmaster knew what had actually occurred out there in the wilderness. Feyd never intended for anyone else, particularly his brother or the Baron, to know.

He looked over at Saar, feeling petulant. "You haven't yet apologized to me for killing my spinehounds. They were rare and valuable animals."

The Swordmaster turned to him with a flat expression. "You want me to say I'm sorry for saving your life?" His eyebrows raised. He didn't add "my Lord."

"Well, that is an unorthodox apology." Feyd wasn't sure what he himself wanted to hear.

Saar continued, "I acknowledge that the CHOAM Ur-Director paid the Tleilaxu a great deal to have the hounds created for you, but I considered your life to be worth more." He paused. "My Lord."

Feyd smiled. "Good answer."

He thought about contacting the Tleilaxu to express his outrage at how Blood and Bone had turned against him, claim that their bonding was dangerously flawed, and demand that the Tleilaxu produce another pair of the vicious pets.

But as Feyd considered further, he decided against it.

He turned back to the matter at hand, feeling awkward. "In order to get to Caladan," Feyd explained, "you'll travel from here to Hagal, then Hagal to Kaitain, Kaitain to Ecaz, and finally the last leg to Caladan." The young man smirked. "Inconvenient, but there is no direct traffic from Giedi Prime to the Atreides homeworld, for obvious reasons." He chuckled, but the Swordmaster did not.

"Patience allows planning," Saar said. "I will not make a swift or clumsy strike, but a surgical one. That's the most efficient way to inflict the hurt that you request."

"Make whatever preparations you need," Feyd said. "You depart tomorrow."

The Swordmaster stood aloof. "I was ready from the moment I arrived here. I was ready when I killed your champion in the arena. And I am more than ready now."

"Good." Placing his hands behind his back, Feyd gazed at the tall thermal-exhaust towers on one of the large munition plants. Patrol ships and transport craft glided like hunting beetles across the smoky skies, and the people in the city below would look up like rodents fearing a bird of prey. The cruising aircraft gave Feyd a sense of security and confidence.

"Your strike has to be perfect, so that I can claim victory," he said. "My brother is so proud of his clumsy industrial sabotage on Caladan, killing off *fish!*" When Feyd frowned, his face acquired a pinched look. "That is not what our uncle had in mind when he issued his challenge, and there is sure to be blowback for what my brother did. The Landsraad might retaliate against House Harkonnen! Damaging a commercial operation has ripple effects throughout Imperial commerce. Other Houses trade in Caladan moonfish, and many nobles consume the stuff, though I can't stand the taste myself." Feyd grimaced. He had never actually eaten moonfish, but the thought of the Atreides left a bad aftertaste in his mouth.

"On a larger scale, of course, imagine if Duke Leto did something that disrupted the flow of spice from Arrakis! The nobles would turn on him like hungry scavengers." The nobles already grumbled because of Emperor Shaddam's harsh spice surtax, but they could do nothing about a mandate from House Corrino.

"That is not what you have in mind for me to do, m'Lord Feyd," said Saar. He also studied the skyline.

Feyd nodded. "We know very little about the inner workings of the Duke's homeworld. Go to Caladan, fit in among the people. Watch and observe. I don't want you to kill mere Atreides retainers or advisers—that would be a waste of your energy. Find a way to inflict pain . . . deep, soul-crushing pain."

"I've heard about Duke Leto," the Swordmaster mused. "He seems quite fond of his woman and his son. They are his vulnerabilities."

"I don't care how you do it. Kill his concubine or kill the boy, both if possible."

Saar nodded. "I am not in the practice of leaving jobs half-finished."

The most destructive weapon can be a trusted friend.
—The Assassin's Handbook

When reports of the new terrorist strike reached Caladan, Leto did not respond in the way Jaxson Aru must have intended.

As Thufir Hawat strode out to meet the Duke and his companions in the open castle courtyard, he presented newly arrived holoprojections of the flaming wreckage of the Promenade Wing, the bodies strewn about the plaza. "At least two thousand dead, my Lord. Several dozen prominent nobles, over a hundred members of Minor Houses." He had hurried from the Cala City Spaceport with the first reports from an urgent courier. Paul and Dr. Yueh had rushed out to join them under cloudy afternoon skies, with Duncan and Gurney close behind.

The Mentat shook his head as the images continued to play. "Not since the atomic obliteration of Salusa Secundus millennia ago has the Imperial capital suffered such a direct, devastating attack."

Leto was aghast. "This is almost as bad as Otorio. And Jaxson Aru thinks *this* will make me enthusiastic about his cause?"

Gurney Halleck grumbled, "God's below! Jaxson Aru is a wild dog and should be put down."

Leto lowered his head, clenched and unclenched his fists. "It's true that Shaddam was arrogant to boast about how much money he's taken with his spice surtax." He drew a long breath, let it out slowly, and looked over at Paul. "But he's still the Emperor, and the Imperium is far better than the chaos that would be result if it were destroyed. Imperial law is the safety net that binds human civilization together, and no fringe movement can be allowed to unravel the fabric of our society. Jaxson Aru must be stopped. I am utterly convinced of that."

Paul paled, looking at his father. "I'm glad you won't be joining him, sir."

Leto continued, "He'll call his act a bold strike against tyranny. He is blinded by his obsession and has no care for the collateral damage he does." As Hawat replayed the holo-recording, Leto noted that Jaxson used his former appearance in the towering image projected on the fountain mist, not his newly altered features. So, no one knew what he really looked like now.

Duncan prowled about with his sword drawn, though there were no obvious targets at hand. "I cannot believe that man came to the reef market to recruit you. Right here! We never should have left you alone, my Lord. That man could have killed you and gotten away with it. He's like a slime eel in mating season."

"Well, you and I were busy teaching Rabban a lesson," Gurney said. His grin stretched the inkvine scar on his cheek.

Hawat's brows drew together as he looked at his Duke. "I warned you to never go out without a full guard complement, Sire. From now on I insist—"

Leto raised his hand. "From now on, we will change tactics. As Duncan says, Jaxson Aru is as slippery as a slime eel. Emperor Shaddam and his Sardaukar have been hunting him ever since Otorio without a hint of success. No one knows his new disguise. Jaxson has extensive resources and wealth, even though his mother publicly disowned him. Noble Commonwealth supporters have their own treasuries, and the rebellion continues to grow. Shaddam is never going to find him."

The warrior Mentat pondered. "He makes his bold moves carefully, and the rest of the time, he remains invisible. I doubt he was even on Kaitain at the time of the recent attack, any more than he was on Otorio when he attacked there. He carries out his terrorist acts from a safe distance. Jaxson will not make a mistake and let himself be found."

Gurney hunched his shoulders. "'One does not look for shadows by bringing a light,'" he quoted from the Orange Catholic Bible. "How will such a man ever be found in the vast Imperium?"

"And how long before his next massacre?" Duncan asked.

"How can we help bring him to justice?" Paul asked. "Who can stop him?"

After a long pause, Leto surprised them all again. "I can do it."

Duncan and Gurney turned to him. Dr. Yueh raised his eyebrows and adjusted the long ponytail bound behind his neck.

Leto explained, "Jaxson thinks his new action will sway other followers to his cause. He believes that I have every incentive to throw in my lot with the Noble Commonwealth, that it will benefit the finances of Caladan and House Atreides. He made his argument to me, and he is just narcissistic enough to believe he can convince me to think the same way he does, as he has with other noblemen." He gave a cold smile. "Therefore, I will let him think that he convinced me."

He had kept the shigawire spool Jaxson gave him in the reef market, though he had not played it and had considered simply destroying it. He had also thought of delivering the spool to Kaitain in hopes that Imperial investigators, Shaddam's Mentats, or his Sardaukar detectives could uncover some damning information. But he knew Jaxson Aru was far too intelligent for that. In fact, Leto assumed that the moment he played the message, it would intrinsically destroy itself, and he was not ready yet. . . .

"He gave me a way to contact him." Leto saw the concern on his son's face, but he continued, "If I play along, I will have direct contact with the rebellion. I may learn of other imminent terrorist attacks before they happen, and do what I can to stop them. Once I have gathered the appropriate information, then I can expose Jaxson to the Emperor."

Duncan growled, "If you bring me with you, I could just strike him dead right from the start."

Gurney laughed. "Not unless I get to him first."

"Neither of you will accompany me, since it might breach any veil of trust. I need to bring down Jaxson Aru and root out the rest of the rebellion. That will stabilize the Imperium—for House Atreides and for our future." Leto lowered his voice. "Over ten millennia, there have been good Emperors and bad ones, but there have always been Emperors. I would not see it all erased. I'll respond to Jaxson Aru and pretend to be converted to his cause. That will let me get close to him."

Paul shook his head. "If my mother were here, she'd tell you this is dangerous and ill-advised."

Leto felt a storm growing within him, but he dampened it for his son's sake. "Your mother has surrendered her role as my adviser."

Troubled, Gurney paced in a tight circle in the open courtyard. "You saved the Emperor at Otorio, but it's clear that Shaddam doesn't entirely trust you. There's no other way to explain why Count Fenring came here to snoop around, not just as a benefactor. The Emperor thinks you may already have sympathies toward the rebellion."

"He knows I am an Atreides, and he knows that our loyalty is not subtle or conditional."

"Shaddam may not believe that," Dr. Yueh said quietly. "Treachery isn't always apparent, even to the one committing it. Paranoia makes an otherwise rational man suspicious."

"We'll ease the Emperor's fears by being completely transparent with him," Leto said. "Gurney, be my private courier. Take a message to Kaitain in secret and see to it that Shaddam knows I intend to infiltrate the Noble Commonwealth and bring them down from within. He must not let anyone else know, but make sure he is fully aware of my plans and that I am not disloyal. Never disloyal." The Duke looked at his warrior Mentat, at Duncan Idaho, at his Suk doctor. "The Emperor will surely embrace my scheme. You all know of my intent, and we will document it clearly as well. But with the exception of the Emperor, it must remain between us—only us."

Dubious, Paul turned to his father. "Are you sure you're able to do this, sir? I never imagined you as a spy."

"Not a spy—a righteous man. And I'll do what I need to." He placed a firm hand on his son's shoulder. "In all the Imperium, I am the best person for this job. I am willing to take a great risk because I know it can save countless lives."

He recalled the images of the mutilated and burned bodies across the Promenade Plaza.

Paul smiled at his father. "A brave and honorable thing to do."

"You're learning," Leto said.

AFTER THE DUKE dismissed them all, Dr. Yueh returned to his private quarters adjacent to the infirmary in Castle Caladan. He was always on call and ready for any medical emergencies that might occur. Although other physicians had offices in Cala City, Yueh was the only Suk doctor on Caladan, and he had served the Atreides for years.

He had been with House Richese for much of his early life and had helped Prince Rhombur Vernius with cyborg enhancements after a horrific explosion. But Yueh had remained here with House Atreides ever since.

Of late, he missed the Lady Jessica and their quiet conversations, but it was not his place to criticize her relationship difficulties with the Duke. Given the time she'd been gone, and the complete lack of communication, Yueh was not confident that she and Leto would come to a simple resolution, though he hoped for it. He was sure Leto did, too, though the Duke kept his emotions well covered. Jessica's silence since her departure was disturbing—but he knew it was how the Bene Gesserit operated.

The loss struck close to home for Yueh for another reason. He had not seen his own wife for many years. He and Wanna had been separated when she was assigned new Bene Gesserit duties. That was the way of the Sisterhood, regardless of what it did to a marriage. Yueh had understood that much long before Duke Leto Atreides. It was the price and the obligation of their order.

They had sent Wanna far away from him, and Yueh was forced to accept that. He knew she still loved him, wherever she was, and he still loved her with all his soul, even if a Suk doctor and a Bene Gesserit Sister measured such things by different parameters.

In his quarters now, he perused his laboratory specimens, cataloguing fungi and plant life he had gathered during the recent wilderness trip with Paul, Gurney, and Leto. Preoccupied, he didn't at first notice the message waiting for him.

An unmarked cylinder lay on the bureau where he kept his daily records, and Yueh realized it must have come on the same delivery ship that brought the news about Jaxson Aru's attack. He picked up the message container, turned it over in his hands. He was at first curious, then felt a growing sense of dread when he found a subtle mark of the Bene Gesserit Sisterhood.

As he unsealed it with his thumbprint, he wondered if it might contain a message from Wanna. Had she finally discovered a way to contact him?

He held his breath as he pulled out a sheet of instroy paper. It felt slick on the surface, meaning it was specially treated to erase the words in less than a minute. After all this time it seemed as if his mere thoughts of her had conjured this into reality . . . but he thought of Wanna often.

He read with deepening concern. The letter did indeed come from the Sisterhood, but not from Wanna. It was cold and brief, as the Bene Gesserit often were, a simple report that nonetheless put him on high alert.

> *Dr. Wellington Yueh, we must inform you that your wife has gone missing while on a private mission for the Sisterhood. At present, we have no further information. If Wanna makes contact with you, please inform the Mother School immediately.*

There was no signature, no identification. Yueh stroked the sides of his lips, reading the note several more times. The wording was innocuous, but the message itself was alarming. This wasn't some simple note to inform him of an insignificant matter. The fact that they would contact him at all indicated the depth of their concern.

But it had been years since he'd known even the smallest details of Wanna's duties. What could have happened to her?

He reread the few lines of text with increasing anxiety until the words faded and vanished.

He was too numb to cry now, but knew the tears would come.

Though bitter at how she had been trapped in a different way, Jessica remained determined. If this was her big chance, she would take it and do what the Bene Gesserit commanded of her. At least she would be away from Wallach IX. She would find some way to accomplish her task so that she didn't destroy *her* in the process.

My only chance to see Leto again, and Paul. And Caladan.

But how would that happen if her entire goal was to be accepted as the concubine for Viscount Tull?

In her traveling robe, she sat in a Heighliner passenger cabin, hardly noticing the blur of colors and shapes visible through her diamond-shaped porthole as the great vessel folded space. She was on her way to Elegy, the planet of House Tull— her new assignment, but she would not think of it as her new home.

The actual duration of the trip, while the ship's mysterious Navigator used Holtzman engines to alter space, was brief. Jessica felt the unsettled twisting, the lurch as the huge vessel traveled from one point to another without moving, and then they were in a different star system, above a different planet. But all the tedious boarding of shuttles, the loading and unloading, the waiting for administrative manifests and adjustments and course calculations, would take many hours.

While she waited in her private cabin, as befitted the status of a new concubine assigned to a noble house, Jessica controlled her anxiety and prepared herself. Knowledge and details would help her succeed, and at least she was out of the direct supervision and control of the Bene Gesserit—and that might offer new opportunities for her. But they knew that the hope they had dangled in front of her, the possibility of returning to her former life, would be enough to keep her under control. She reviewed a dossier provided by Sister Zoanna, former concubine of the old Viscount Alfred Tull, who had died not long ago.

After being ejected from Elegy, Zoanna wrote, "The old Viscount's son wanted nothing to do with me. I offered myself, used all of my training, but I could not succeed. He was very uncomfortable with my attempts at seduction. After all my years of dedicated service to House Tull, Giandro ejected me from his court and sent me away on the first outbound ship."

A virtual report floated in front of Jessica, and she stroked her finger in the air repeatedly, flipping the pages. Of course the new Viscount would object to the idea of his father's concubine offering herself to the son. A clumsy move. No wonder Zoanna had been sent away. Jessica's brow furrowed as she read.

> Not only did Giandro not want me, personally, I believe he has a deep distrust toward the Sisterhood. Alfred was extremely generous to us all his life, because of a perceived obligation, since a Sister saved him from misadventure when he was a boy. In gratitude, Alfred's father—Viscount Giandro's grandfather—gave large, continuous endowments to the Mother School, which enabled them to construct buildings and make improvements in the school complex. When Alfred reached adulthood and became Viscount, he continued the payments.
>
> But when his son recently took the role after Alfred's death, he cut off that funding completely. We must restore those endowments, but to do it, the Sisterhood must have eyes on Elegy. House Tull is involved in certain important affairs, and I caught only a glimpse of them. We must know what Giandro is doing.

Jessica flipped to a statement that Reverend Mother Mohiam had appended to the report. As the Emperor's Truthsayer, she herself had encountered the young Viscount at the Imperial Court, and she strongly disliked him, though she could not prove any treasonous activities. Mohiam wrote, "Not only did Giandro Tull show disrespect for our order, he is hiding something. We believe he expelled Zoanna to give himself more freedom to act. The Emperor's Sardaukar investigated Elegy, but despite thorough searches and interrogations, they found no evidence of involvement with the Noble Commonwealth. We need a new observer there—one of our own."

She also read a statement by a Sardaukar officer, Colonel Bashar Jopati Kolona, describing his investigation, which concluded that no further action should be taken against Giandro Tull.

Jessica absorbed more details from Zoanna's lengthy journal, but bypassed all the intimate details of the old man, now dead. She felt like a pawn. The Sisterhood was sending her on this mission for their own purposes—when did they ever do anything else?—but it also served as a test of her loyalty, proof of her willingness to serve the Bene Gesserit, without question, without hesitation. It felt like one of Thufir Hawat's Mentat instructional exercises, a complex scenario that resulted in impossible choices.

Would she find a way to walk that razor's edge? Could she find some clever solution?

Jessica had already built a wall around her heart, and now she shored it up further as she looked down at the planet below. Elegy was supposedly a lovely place, but she kept thinking of Caladan.

Nevertheless, she was resolved to succeed. Giandro Tull was in his late forties, a little younger than Leto. She was thirty-six—healthy, beautiful, and desirable, as well as intelligent and mature, able to draw on a wealth of experiences. Whether or not the new Viscount had connections to the rebel movement, he seemed to be an interesting person, an independent thinker. A part of her respected that the man resisted being influenced by both the Bene Gesserit and the Imperial throne. He seemed to have a clarity of purpose, and honor.

In some ways, he reminded her of Leto.

Maybe that was another reason they had chosen her for this mission.

The Heighliner was motionless, but Jessica heard a hum of activity around her as people left the cabins and shuttles and other craft departed. Here at Elegy, a new orbital station had been built to handle passengers and cargo, and smaller shuttles to go back and forth to the surface, almost exclusively for passengers.

She saw the new platform as she boarded one of the new small shuttles that would take her and perhaps fifty other passengers down to the surface. The station had windows all around and lines of lights; with the arrival of the Heighliner, it was full of people either disembarking from or boarding shuttles.

On the underside of the station she saw dump boxes of cargo being released to fall to the planet, while export cargo containers, called thrust boxes, were launched from the surface of Elegy. On the cargo box platform, bald Guildsmen coordinated everything, their unusual and sometimes highly distorted features visible through their sealed helmets. The operations looked very efficient to Jessica.

Half an hour later, as Jessica's shuttle dropped to the surface, she considered her own assertions of independence, wondering if they might align with Giandro Tull's. Having been raised and trained—irreparably molded—by the Bene Gesserit, a part of her had an innate desire to prove herself to her superiors, but her ultimate reason for this cooperation was personal, with the goal of earning her way back to Caladan.

Accomplishing her mission here would take time. Elegy was far from the Mother School, and she might at last be able to send a covert message to Paul or Leto. She clung to that hope, but did not know what lay ahead for her, and how much, if any, control she might have over her own destiny.

She would make her own destiny, however possible.

The shuttle crossed a hazy sky in the most beautiful sunset she had ever seen. The colorful light looked as if refracted through a prism. In her briefings on the planet, she knew that the landscape was lush with a local species of lichen that grew into fantastic shapes. One of Elegy's primary resources, the harvested lichens could be spun into exquisitely fine fabrics that were exported across the Imperium.

The shuttle landed at the main spaceport, and the passengers disembarked. She followed them, looking at her new surroundings. Would Viscount Tull welcome her, or rebuff her arrival? She smelled a faint perfume in the air, knew it was from the lichen. She saw some of it growing around the perimeter of the spaceport, and at this time of year, it had its characteristic little yellow berries—which were poisonous.

Considering how abruptly Zoanna had been evicted, Jessica was surprised to see an actual greeting party for her at the spaceport. Among them, she recognized Giandro Tull from the images in the dossiers, with shoulder-length dark hair and handsome features. He had come to get her himself.

She gathered her courage and stepped forward to meet him, wearing a cautious smile. His expression was stony, formal, and he gave her a stiff bow. "You have come to my beautiful planet, Sister Jessica of the Bene Gesserit, and I am honor-bound to receive you." His expression twitched into a frown. "I knew the witches would try again, so I may as well face this attempt openly, instead of waiting for something from the shadows."

Jessica had expected resistance from Viscount Giandro, and she responded with a reserved smile. "I'll try to be open with you, too, my Lord. I have spent little time at the Mother School in the past two decades. I've lived on Caladan, but in their wisdom, the Bene Gesserit thought you might find me acceptable." The words were difficult to speak. She bowed her head, turned her green eyes away with a hint of intentional shyness, as she had been taught.

"Caladan?" Giandro considered her for a long moment, then turned without asking further questions. "We prepared a place for you in the manor house. You'll be my guest, but not my concubine."

She met his gaze. "I respect your caution," she said, "and your boundaries."

"But the witches will certainly expect something on my part," he said with a weary sigh. "We'll go to my private hunting forest outside the manor house, where I've had a welcoming banquet laid out for us. It will let my staff become familiar with you . . . and we can talk more." The Viscount turned his back, and his retainers accompanied him, silently inviting Jessica to follow.

After the journey, she had hoped to settle in and adjust to the new time cycle, and to the subtle but perceptible difference in gravity. The passage from Wallach IX, her time on the Heighliner, the ride down in the shuttle, had all left her feeling rumpled, and space travel always unsettled her. She wanted to make a good first impression on this nobleman, *her assignment.* "My Lord, would you allow me to clean myself up a little? I'd like to be at my best for a formal reception."

He gave her his strange smile again. "You are a lovely woman. The Bene Gesserit have chosen well, and I cannot fault them for that." He kept moving. "Our dinner is already prepared. I'm sure the Bene Gesserit taught you to be resilient."

"As you wish, my Lord," she said. Another test? A simple enough one.

Tull wasn't as terse as she'd feared. Maybe Jessica could blur his unsettled memories of Sister Zoanna. She would have to navigate these waters carefully, but she longed to hear the whisper of Caladan seas.

As they headed away from the spaceport, the nobleman looked at her again, studying her carefully. He pressed his lips together in a smile, and she could not gauge his sincerity. "You aren't what I expected."

Retainers rushed ahead to prepare, and Jessica soon found herself in a well-manicured forest on the fringes of the manor house. A long, elaborate banquet table had been erected outside, in the midst of trees covered with clumps of aromatic lichen. Bright, multicolored berries were on full display. Beauty and poison together . . . perhaps a subtle message to her?

As darkness fell, the forested area was illuminated with unseen lighting hidden among the lichen clumps, as well as traditional candles on the wooden table. After Jessica took the seat of honor, the Viscount nodded to his servants, who came forward to present her with a spray of deep red roses, fanning out the large flowers in front of her place.

Despite the polite reception, Jessica noticed that since joining Viscount Tull's party, she had been watched carefully by men in uniforms. Whenever she looked at them, they looked away, but not before she caught a few rude expressions.

Giandro himself was a perfect gentleman, though. "Let me speak frankly, if I can. I did not want you here, nor did I invite you, but I am a man of noble blood, a well-respected member of the Landsraad, and I will be polite and gracious, until I am given a reason to do otherwise." He sipped from his glass of chilled white wine. "But that may change in the days to come. We will see if you warrant my traditional hospitality."

Careful to take no insult, knowing this man's prior experience with the Sisterhood, Jessica sipped her wine, tasted its crisp, subtle fruit flavors: peachberry, a mixture of spices, and oak from the aging barrel. She realized that he, too, felt caught in a web of obligations.

She half smiled. "I might as well enjoy this evening, then, and make certain that I earn nothing less than politeness from you. I hope I might be someone you'd like to know."

"Someone the witches would like me to know."

"Those two things don't have to be mutually exclusive." She studied him carefully. His long, lush hair had an almost feminine quality, but his profile was strong and masculine, with a bold brow and a firm mouth. At first glance, Giandro Tull was not of a sort that appealed to her physically, but she could see that he might easily disarm many women.

He noticed her studying him and met her gaze with his hazel eyes. "The Bene Gesserit sent you here, no doubt assuming you'd use their techniques to melt my heart. It's a form of manipulation. I am not a shy schoolboy giddy with the idea of romance."

That was exactly why they had sent her here, though she was trying to find her own place in the situation, an independent path. "I would not find a giddy schoolboy remotely interesting," she said. "You don't like the Sisterhood, do you?"

Scoffing, he lounged back in his heavy wooden chair under the trees. "That much is well known! My father gave a fortune to your Mother School, and I put an end to it. I never understood how the witches spent all that money."

She said, "The Mother School completed several major constructions, acknowledging the source of the funding with plaques prominently displayed on new halls, instructional, and residency buildings. They are very grateful."

He frowned and looked away. "They will have to find other sources of endowments from now on." He drank more of his wine as he collected his thoughts. "Unfortunately, I have somehow aroused the Emperor's unwarranted suspicions. I know his Truthsayer whispers in his ear, so perhaps if I let you stay here, that pressure will ease." His expression darkened. "But don't expect me to open the floodgates of funding again. My holdings have suffered a setback by Emperor Shaddam's destruction of our business partner House Verdun. I need to rebuild my own Great House."

Jessica saw an opportunity and felt her burden lighten. "Just having me here on Elegy will calm the Sisterhood, and I . . . I know Reverend Mother Mohiam personally. I can help."

He seemed surprised.

She nodded toward the uniformed men who stood under the trees, two of them hovering close, intense and intimidating. Was he just being cautious? He had good reason not to trust her from the outset. "Who are those men? Why are they so interested in me?"

"Security officers, assigned to make sure you are safe."

Jessica raised her eyebrows. Did that mean Viscount Tull had something he didn't want her to see? "Thank you for being concerned about my safety. Is this a dangerous world? Are there criminals lurking about, waiting to drag me off into the forest?"

"I would not want anything bad to happen to you," he said cautiously. "You are a Bene Gesserit, and as my important guest, you are under my protection."

She gave him a confident smile. "I am not helpless."

He looked at the uniformed men, who still hovered too close. He seemed to be speaking to them as much as to her. "Settle in, let your body adjust to this world, to my manor house. Feel free to go anywhere you wish—I have no secrets." He set his wineglass down on the wooden table, ran a fingertip along his lower lip, deep in thought. "Just don't be like your predecessor."

She needed to find a way past the bad blood between the Viscount and his father's Bene Gesserit concubine. "Since you never accepted Zoanna in the first place, I have no predecessor. I am the first concubine to report to you, Viscount Giandro Tull. I hope you will give me a fair chance."

He laughed. "You are quick. I like that. But you are not my concubine, and don't think you can seduce me." He smiled again. "At least not easily."

Jessica continued, "Let's consider this a friendly détente. I appreciate your gracious welcome, and I look forward to getting to know you, and this world, better."

Giandro Tull seemed relieved, even pleased. "We have an understanding, then, a truce of sorts." He extended his wineglass to her, and they shared an uneasy toast.

As she sipped her wine, Jessica's mind drifted to her dear Leto.

If we could overcome our fear and admit our shared goal, we would become invincible.

—JAXSON ARU, communiqué to the Noble Commonwealth

upile was an angry planet with smoky red skies and constant seismic activity. Even so, Ur-Director Malina Aru found the place comforting. The energy and chaos made for a powerful, exhilarating combination. Tupile was her home, one of the hidden planets that did not appear on Guild charts and served as sanctuary worlds for leaders of CHOAM or other exiles over the course of history.

She sat on her veranda, relaxed despite the constant churn of decisions working through her mind. She could think better here, and she had much to think about.

Har and Kar were content and sat on each side of her chair, ever alert and ready to protect her. They traveled with her whenever the arrangements made sense, but they preferred to be home. Sometimes, Malina wished her life could be as singular and simple as theirs. She scratched each spinehound's head. They panted, showing their long fangs, but they had never given her any reason to fear.

She was disappointed to learn through her spies that the two pups delivered to Giedi Prime had turned on young Feyd-Rautha Harkonnen, and been killed. She felt sorry for the animals, not for Feyd, and she would not arrange to procure any more pets for him.

Malina gazed into the ruddy sky and saw lines of smoke like dark finger paintings smeared through the atmosphere. Tupile's enormous moon hung there, covering an improbable portion of the sky, and she could make out the fissures and craters on its surface. It was waxing daily, which increased the tremors in the ground, but hydraulic stabilizers in her dwelling's foundation dampened the shocks so that she barely noticed them. Even so, the moon looked as it if might crash down on her head at any moment . . . like her plans to unravel the Corrino Imperium.

The careful, steady plans for the Noble Commonwealth were accelerating in a violent direction, spurred on by her son's provocations. Jaxson's recent attack at the Imperial Palace had been blunt and clumsy, like a dissonant brassy note in the movement of a symphony. The exploding treasury ship and the deaths of all those innocent bystanders should have resulted in widespread disgust and outrage, but rather it shone a bright light on how House Corrino had stolen so much wealth from other noble families. Even with so many tragic deaths, the loss of the ill-gotten taxation hoard undoubtedly meant little to Shaddam financially, other than the embarrassment. Few people felt the least bit sympathetic to the Emperor, even when he insisted unconvincingly that he had intended to distribute all that wealth to his subjects in a generous gesture.

Though still appalled by what her son had done, Malina realized that other members of the Noble Commonwealth did not feel the same reluctance, and she was beginning to listen to them. She saw that she could no longer control her steady, nonviolent course.

As if they were psychically connected to each other, Har and Kar pricked up their sharp ears and turned their heads in unison. The animals rose to their feet, and growls resonated in their chests. They looked into the large house, predatory eyes blazing.

Malina was immediately alarmed. Almost no one knew how to find her on Tupile, much less provide the required clearances. The number of people who could work the secretive Spacing Guild routes to reach this sanctuary planet could be counted on one hand.

She rose from her chair, felt her pulse racing. The loyal spinehounds remained close by, ready to attack an intruder . . . although any assassin who managed to make it this far would have resources enough to eliminate two guard animals.

The Ur-Director of CHOAM did not shrink from confrontation. Defiant, she walked with Har and Kar, letting the tense animals lead the way. "Show me." They prowled through the spacious halls of the domicile, leading her down a set of stairs to the open foyer.

A man waited for her there, facing her alone as she came down the staircase.

Malina Aru saw a ghost. Her husband, Brondon, had been dead for years, and she had not seen him in much longer than that. Once he'd gone into retirement exile on Otorio, whiling away his days with diversions on the family estate, Brondon was supposed to watch over their younger son, but he was seemingly oblivious as Jaxson grew more and more radicalized.

Malina had never felt much love or even affection for her husband, but now she looked at the face on the man in her home and felt a chill. She breathed his name, barely a whisper.

The stranger seemed to be waiting for something, and she realized that this wasn't Brondon, not exactly. The face was strikingly similar, but different. A brother perhaps? No, Brondon had no siblings. Was this an imposter? A clever disguise? And to what purpose?

"Who are you?" she demanded.

Har and Kar bounded the rest of the way down the stairs, and she thought

304 Brian Herbert and Kevin J. Anderson

they would rip the man apart. Instead, he leaned down to pat their heads, careful not to impale himself on their silver spines.

"I suppose that's a testament to the fine work of the Tleilaxu. I thought my own mother would recognize me."

Malina froze on the staircase and studied him more carefully. Yes, now she could see his original features, mostly subsumed by Brondon's. "Jaxson? What have you done to yourself?"

"A technique called facial cloning. It gives me a perfect disguise, and it keeps my father's image alive. Aren't you pleased?"

Malina processed all this in an instant. She came to the bottom of the stairs and stood in front of him, inspecting him closely. The spinehounds sat on their haunches, looking at Jaxson, who had once been a resident here in the household. She pursed her lips and nodded. "Excellent camouflage, but is it good enough to fool any identity scans?"

Jaxson smiled at her as if she'd given him great praise.

Malina said, "This is more subtle than your usual pattern."

"I do whatever is most effective, Mother. Right now, you and I need to have a lengthy discussion because we are reaching a crescendo. We have disagreed frequently on our tactics, but the most effective thing is for our activities to align. You cannot deny that I've shaken the underpinnings of the Imperium. If we work together—you and I and all of our allies—we can widen those cracks and shatter this ancient behemoth."

She walked slowly toward him. "I've thought about that a great deal myself. I ran thorough analyses, and I listened to impassioned speeches from Noble Commonwealth members." She saw the sudden reaction on his unfamiliar features. "You have more supporters than you know, Jaxson."

His mouth—Brondon's mouth—quirked in a smile. "What makes you think they haven't contacted me?" He let that weigh on her for a moment. She was unsettled, but didn't let it show. "If you'll admit that we seek the same goal, perhaps we can coordinate our activities and achieve success in a very short period of time."

After an awkward silence, Malina said, "I was forced to disown you, you know. It had to be done." She expected her tone to convey her apology. "Imperial Mentat accountants scrutinized all my dealings, and they could trace whether or not I had cut off your finances."

"Oh, I have my own finances, Mother, and you didn't manage to cut me off entirely. You know that full well."

She pressed her lips together and nodded.

He could not contain his excitement. "And I have high hopes that Duke Leto Atreides will join us soon! He has seen the corruption in the Imperium with his own eyes and has asked to join our cause. I just received an acknowledgment from him."

Malina blinked in surprise. "The Duke of Caladan? Leto the Just? I didn't expect that at all."

"It makes perfect sense. Think of the nauseating corruption and backstabbing he witnessed right there at the Imperial Court. Think of how House Corrino treated him, not just in the last year, but even when he first became Duke, how Shaddam worked to destroy him in the Trial of Forfeiture, but failed. Leto Atreides has no love for House Corrino. He will help us, and he will be a great ally."

Malina smiled at her son and welcomed him into her home. "Finally we may be able to work together."

I have never been adept at hiding or wearing a mask, but there comes a time when one must learn new skills.

—DUKE LETO ATREIDES, letters to his son

My words will stand for themselves," Leto said, leaning closer to Halleck and speaking with great earnestness. "But it's up to you, Gurney, to deliver this message. My cousin Shaddam must have no doubt that I remain loyal to him, even as I intend to work from inside this rebellion to bring down Jaxson Aru."

"I will tell him, my Lord," Gurney said. "I'll even sing him a song with your message in it, if that might help."

Leto chuckled, a much-needed moment of levity in the tense situation. "Only as a last resort." He held out a smooth ridulian crystal the size of a thumbnail. "I recorded my message here. Under normal diplomatic circumstances, I would write an official letter, seal it with my ducal signet ring, and entrust it in a secure wallet to be delivered. But we dare not take that chance. This is no political complaint, no filing of a bill of particulars. You must be absolutely unseen and unnoticed until you get to the Imperial Palace. Even then, no one but the Emperor can know what I'm doing—Noble Commonwealth rebels may have infiltrated the highest levels of the Landsraad or the court."

Standing in the private council chamber, with the door sealed against any possible eavesdroppers, Leto's group of closest advisers fidgeted, disturbed by the grim reality of what the Duke was saying. Looking on, Paul and Duncan exchanged uneasy glances.

Thufir Hawat motioned to Gurney and said, "Dr. Yueh will implant the crystal in your forearm and surgically seal it so that no one will find it—and it can never be lost."

"Not that I would misplace such a thing!" Gurney extended his left arm to Dr. Yueh. "Use this one, so I can still pluck baliset strings with the other."

Yueh wiped an antiseptic swab across the bare skin over Gurney's bunched muscles. "The procedure should not leave you with diminished dexterity, or even a scar once it heals."

As the doctor made a small incision, inserted the small crystal deep into the muscle, and sealed the wound, Gurney talked to distract himself. "With a face like this . . ." He tapped the scar on the side of his cheek. "I'm an ugly lump of a man, so I might still be recognized. The Spacing Guild has automatic identity scans, and if I intend to get into the Imperial Court, I can't carry false papers." He rolled his shoulders in a shrug. "But I'll keep a low profile. If I take my baliset along, should anyone ask, I can say I'm going to Kaitain to learn some folk ballads to play back here at the castle."

Finished, Yueh inspected his handiwork. "The woundskin will heal itself in a day or two." His dark lips curved down in a frown. "One of the Imperial surgeons will have to cut it out again so you can give it to Shaddam."

"Aye, that's a problem I'll solve when it comes time. Now, I must pack a travel bag and my favorite baliset before the Guild Heighliner arrives." He stood and rubbed his arm where he could feel the burn from the incision. "Don't worry, my Lord Duke. I *will* deliver your message."

WHEN HE ACTUALLY responded to Jaxson Aru's invitation in an ultra-covert way, Leto felt as if he were firing a weapon, perhaps at himself.

He remembered all the meetings with Thufir Hawat, the strategy sessions, the careful planning for how he would go meet the rebel leader. He had pondered his decision with the acuity of a Mentat, following lines of consequences and possibilities. He could not forget how that terrible man had slammed giant containers down on the Otorio museum and later sent the heavy treasury ship crashing into the Imperial Palace. Jaxson had been so convinced of his righteousness that he was blind to the hurt he caused. Just to make a point.

Leto had to make the rebel leader believe that he actually sympathized with the rebel movement.

Jaxson had answered Leto's message through private channels, a maze of messenger after messenger, with no possibility of being traced. Embedded in several layers of coding and security, unlocked only by Leto's thumbprint on this end, were instructions for how to meet Jaxson at a safe rendezvous. From there, Jaxson would take him into the heart of the Noble Commonwealth.

Leto activated the message, knowing it would only play once before erasing itself. Jaxson's holo-image greeted the Duke with confidence and warm pride. "Your transmittal came to me as welcome news, Leto Atreides! Your beloved Caladan will benefit when the Noble Commonwealth achieves its goals, just as our movement will gain strength from having you among us—you are a tremendous prize! I understand how difficult it must have been for you to reach this decision, but I knew you would, because I understand you, and I trust you to do the right thing." On the recording, Jaxson chuckled. "Maybe I comprehend your heart better than you do yourself."

The words stung Leto. Jessica had also told him she could understand him in ways that he himself wouldn't accept. It made him doubt who he was. He'd been considering the question a great deal lately, exploring parts of his personality that had remained buried, perhaps deservedly so.

Earlier, in going to Kaitain and playing the part of an ambitious nobleman, he'd been trying to become something that went against his grain, and he wasn't sure that he wanted to succeed. With this new secret plan, he would do something difficult but necessary in order to save the Imperium—which had done little to earn his loyalty.

But he wasn't doing this for Shaddam, and he knew Paul would understand. Before departing for the rendezvous point, whatever happened, he would leave a message for his son.

Gurney Halleck had departed the day before. The die had been cast, and Leto knew he could trust the man to complete his critically important mission. The web of the rebellion wound through many planets and noble families, and Jaxson Aru was clever, cautious, and alert for treachery. If one of his spies were to discover what Leto really had in mind. . . .

The Duke shook off the thought. Sitting alone in his spacious empty chambers at Castle Caladan, he gazed into the imager, paused, and thought. "After your mother's departure, Paul, I went to the Imperial capital and tried to strengthen House Atreides. I mistakenly believed that was important for when you become Duke, but I realized that the legacy I want to give you—and what I hope I've been giving you all your life—is the example and the tools you need to become a good leader."

Leto inhaled deeply. He poured himself a few swallows of Kirana brandy. The first sip burned his tongue, but he set the glass down and considered his thoughts.

"If something goes wrong, there are those who will accuse me of betraying the Padishah Emperor. Know that I take these actions of my own free will and strictly with the goal of tearing down the terrorist threat. I intend to trap Jaxson Aru into facing justice. The Emperor surely knows that I would never turn against him, but in these terrible times, I will make no such assumptions."

By leaving this recording, he knew his son would have something that was tangible to share, in addition to the implanted message Gurney carried. This recording to Paul would be his testament, and he hoped it would never be needed.

He spoke into the imager. "I—" He paused as his own pride and hesitation rose up. He just wanted to tell Paul that he loved him, but Duke Leto Atreides, the man so beloved by his people, had never expressed it in so many words to his own son . . . had never said it properly to Jessica either. Would that have made a difference?

Paul knew what his father thought of him, of that Leto had no doubt.

He activated the recording again. "I greatly respect you, Paul, and have the highest of hopes for you. I hope that in the end, Imperial historians will applaud what I have done, but if not, you will always know the truth."

Paul would keep this message safe and secure.

In his message, Jaxson Aru had instructed Leto how to book passage to an isolated and neutral meeting point, a new orbiting transfer station over the planet Elegy, where he and the rebel leader would meet. Jaxson included Noble Commonwealth techniques on how to cover his identity, and how to access funds from a shadow CHOAM account. The latter raised certain suspicions, but Leto was not surprised that Ur-Director Malina Aru might be aware of what her son was actually doing.

Leto finished the message to Paul with a heavy heart. Tears stung his gray eyes, and he convinced himself this was merely a safety measure, not a farewell recording. At another time, he would have left recordings for both Jessica and Paul, but he had still heard nothing from her . . . absolutely nothing.

Paul was his priority now, and Leto had to act for House Atreides.

He sealed away the recording and vowed that it would never have to be watched.

ARMS RAISED AT his sides, Leto allowed Dr. Yueh to examine him. "You've always been healthy, my Lord. Do you have any particular concerns?"

"Just being safe, Yueh. Where I'm going, I don't know what I might face."

Yueh checked his vital signs, noted the readings, and nodded. "Perfectly normal, Sire. Where exactly are you going? What is the name of the planet?" He hesitated. "You concern me with your words."

"There's good reason for concern, Yueh, but I am meeting Jaxson Aru at a rendezvous point. I have no idea of our final destination, intentionally so. I must be ready for anything." Leto became reticent once again. It wasn't a matter of trust. He had known the Suk doctor for years, and Yueh had never given him reason for doubt . . . but Jessica had once told Leto that his greatest weakness was that he trusted people to act with the same sense of honor that he himself did. She'd smiled when she said it, her green eyes bright, and now he wondered whether it was a compliment or a criticism.

Now with so much at stake, he couldn't take the risk.

Yueh stroked his mustaches. "With such turmoil in your life and in your family, you have been under significant stress, my Lord, but I see no obvious adverse effects to your health. You exercise regularly, eat adequately, although you could sleep a little more."

"I sleep well enough, because I know I'm doing the right thing," Leto said.

"As you have always done, Sire." The doctor bowed, his examination complete. "I am proud to serve House Atreides."

Though preoccupied, Leto realized that Yueh himself seemed troubled. His expression was sadder and more distracted than usual. "Are you all right, Yueh?"

Startled, the doctor looked up with a forced smile. "Are you conducting an examination now, Sire?"

"I simply like to know about my closest staff."

Making excuses, Yueh bustled about in his infirmary, putting away medical instruments, setting his kit beside biological specimens he had collected. "Yes, of course, my Lord. I am fine, no need to worry."

Leto responded with a friendly chuckle. "Thank you, Yueh. The Heighliner is already in orbit overhead, and I leave in a few hours on the shuttle."

After the Duke left the room, Yueh closed and locked the door of his infirmary office, then stood regarding the wall. With trembling hands, he took out the damning, terrifying message that had sent his thoughts reeling. It was unmistakably authentic—a secret transmission from Baron Harkonnen himself, the darkest enemy of House Atreides.

Early in his career Yueh had treated the Baron, back when his lean and muscular body had begun to change as he suffered the effects of the disease that made him so obscenely obese. Yueh had hoped never to speak to the vile man again. He had given his full loyalty to Duke Leto Atreides, backed up by his hard Imperial conditioning.

But now the Baron was demanding to see Yueh privately and in such a way that the Duke would never know about it. The threat in the words was plain. Yueh stared at the printed transmission.

Why would the Baron invoke Wanna's name?

Prove yourself each day, or perish.
—Ancient wisdom
(anonymous)

Languishing in her isolation cell, indignant at the irony, Ruthine sat motionless, while her mind was a whirlwind of thoughts and plans. Sadly, most of those ideas would not come to fruition now. She was angry at herself and at Jiara for the failure of their part.

But Ruthine took heart in knowing that one more wheel, one more gear of their plan turned on its inevitable course. Taula and Aislan were already on their way to Caladan. Xora would soon follow with her own piece of the plan, as a backup if nothing else. One way or another, the threat of Paul Atreides would soon be removed, and the boy would be dead.

Even if Jessica remained alive, the threat Lethea had foreseen would be gone. She took satisfaction in these things at least, and accepted the cost. Even though she sat motionless with her hands clasped in front of her, her face twitched in a smile. Her ringlets sagged around her head like greasy, limp worms.

Just then the door to her isolation cell unsealed, revealing Reverend Mother Cordana, shoulders at an odd angle with her twisted back, but she somehow loomed, full of questions and anger. Cordana always wanted to discuss matters more than she wanted to act. Discuss, discuss, discuss! Ruthine looked at her, knowing that even now Cordana's questions would overrule her actions. That had always been her weakness as much as her deformity. She had never been fit to be a high adviser to the Mother Superior.

"I know there is more." Cordana stood in the doorway with her arms crossed, as if she could pose some kind of a threat. "You and Jiara attacked Sister Jessica, but that's not all, is it? You intend to do more."

Ruthine spread her hands. "What more can I do? I am here in this cell."

Cordana grimaced. "I will not underestimate you, Ruthine, as you underestimated Jessica." She tracked her eyes up and down Ruthine's form, obviously enjoying the swollen bruises on her face, the black eye. "Even two of you were not enough to kill one woman locked in a cell."

Ruthine said up straighter, felt the aching muscles in her back. "You saw Lethea's warning scrawled in her own blood. Given her prescience, why do you give Jessica so many chances? I'll take care of her myself." She cackled softly. "To keep the blood off your pretty little hands. Bring her here to my cell."

"Jessica is gone from Wallach IX," Cordana said, lifting her chin.

This startled Ruthine. "Gone? Where?"

"Reassigned." Cordana smiled. "A new chance. She'll be the new concubine of Viscount Tull."

Ruthine reeled. "You should not let her go! After Lethea's warnings you can't let her loose. She may still find a way to bring down the Sisterhood."

"As you almost did? With your conspiracy against the Mother Superior?"

"Our leader failed to lead," Ruthine snapped. "Someone needed to take the necessary action."

"What else did you do?" Cordana pressed again. "I've investigated further. Sisters Taula and Aislan are gone, but the Mother School has no records of them being assigned or dispatched. I know they were your friends. I learned that they boarded a shuttle to a Heighliner—a Heighliner bound for Caladan."

Ruthine blinked at her. "I'm not in charge of the travel arrangements for other Sisters. I barely know Taula and Aislan."

"That is a lie," Cordana said. "They were your known associates."

She gave an annoying shrug. "See conspiracies in every shadow if you wish."

"Why would those two Sisters go to Caladan?"

Another shrug. She could see her reaction was bothering the other woman. "Perhaps to recruit more Acolytes, since the Mother Superior is so pleased with Jessica. Maybe she influenced a new generation of young girls on that backwater world. Whatever they're doing, I'm sure Taula and Aislan are performing the good work of the Bene Gesserit."

Clearly alarmed, Cordana looked like a startled goose. "What are their orders? I know they follow you as part of your conspiracy! Are they still working to overthrow Mother Superior Harishka?"

"As I said, I barely know them," Ruthine insisted.

"Liar," Cordana retorted. "Sister Jiara already confessed and explained what you intended to do."

Ruthine just laughed. "Now you're the one who lies. If you knew the answers to your questions, you would not bother to ask me."

Cordana hadn't moved, but her nostrils flared. Ruthine considered lunging toward her, attacking her, breaking the smaller woman's twisted back. A kick to the throat would kill her on the spot. It would be a futile gesture, but satisfying.

"I have heard enough," Cordana said. "Once I speak to Mother Superior Harishka, we will return—with a Truthsayer. We will extract the information from you, and your lies will not stand."

She spun about and left. Ruthine stared after her as the cell door sealed and locked. Her pulse raced, and her lips drew down in a frown. She knew full well that a Truthsayer could make her reveal everything.

Ruthine understood there was only one way she could keep her secrets.

DESPITE THE URGENCY in her adviser's voice, Mother Superior Harishka was reluctant to assign such motivations even to Reverend Mother Ruthine, who had already demonstrated her willingness to defy Harishka's explicit decisions. Ruthine's views had grown more extreme, and she had grossly overstepped, but it seemed inconceivable that she might actually try to overthrow the leader of the Bene Gesserit.

Cordana and Ruthine were bitter rivals, and their division had only grown greater as Lethea's rantings became more strident. Harishka was indeed furious with Ruthine and Jiara for what they had attempted, but they had been under extreme stress, distraught over Lethea's scrawled dying message. As with all of the old crone's prescient pronouncements, though, the meaning was far from clear. Harishka didn't see tangled, murderous plots or far-reaching schemes that extended all the way to distant Caladan. True, the departure of Sisters Taula and Aislan was unexplained, and the Mother Superior was trying to track down their travel itinerary and purpose.

For now, she hurried down the corridors to the isolation cells, accompanied by an agitated Cordana as well as Reverend Mother Hiddy—a skilled, patient, and utterly reliable Truthsayer. Hiddy was a handsome, unflappable woman with hair the color of dull steel.

"Make sure Ruthine can't twist her words," said Cordana, moving along with her uneven gait. "She's hiding much more—I could tell."

Moving along at a sedate pace, Reverend Mother Hiddy turned to her with a tight, skeptical expression. "So you are a Truthsayer now? You can read all the indicators. Then why do you need me?"

Cordana turned to the Mother Superior, who halted further comments with a gesture. "We will ask Ruthine our questions and get to the bottom of this."

They stopped at the doorway to the cell, and the Mother Superior straightened herself, composed her thoughts. Truthsayer Hiddy seemed to be in no hurry as Cordana worked the locking code and unsealed the door.

"Now you'll reveal the truth, Ruthine." Cordana entered the cell. "We'll learn exactly what you've planned against Jessica, her son, her Duke . . . and anyone else."

Ruthine sat there motionless, facing them but saying nothing. On her bland face, her eyes were open, and she stared forward. She didn't flinch or react, as still and silent as a statue. Harishka had a sinking feeling.

Cordana made another demand, but her words stuttered to a halt. Then she lurched in. "Ruthine!" She grabbed the other woman's shoulders and shook her.

Ruthine's head lolled to the side. Her eyes still didn't blink.

Harishka glided in and touched her temples, her neck, trying to find a pulse to detect breathing, but Ruthine's skin was cold, her muscles stiff.

As she looked into the glassy, dead eyes of Reverend Mother Ruthine, Harishka understood what must have happened—what any sufficiently skilled Reverend Mother was capable of doing.

"This is no accident," said the Mother Superior. "She controlled her body, her metabolism."

"Is it a bindu trance?" Cordana asked, shaking the motionless woman.

"More than that," said Harishka. "She stopped her heart and willed herself to die."

"No!" Cordana shouted. Her voice held anger, but also dismay.

The Truthsayer remained outside the cell at the door. "It appears she did not wish to answer our questions."

*Life is filled with experiences, and the quality of life depends on the breadth
and quality of those experiences.*

—DUNCAN IDAHO, reflections on Swordmaster training

His father was gone on an entirely different mission this time, and Paul
found himself again bearing responsibility for the world and its people,
as the heir of Caladan. Even so, he resumed his training. He did not have his
mother to continue teaching him Bene Gesserit techniques, but he was determined to fulfill his obligations and learn every skill he would need as the next
Duke.

Paul felt uncertain about his future, though. His father had said nothing more
about continuing to search for betrothal candidates, and he wondered if Jessica
had been guiding those considerations. Perhaps he did not need to think about
his future wife just yet.

When he'd spoken to Gurney, the troubadour warrior chuckled. "Right now,
don't worry overmuch about understanding marriage or alliances or family politics or love. I am far older than you, and I don't claim to be an expert. I just sing
songs about it." His grin twisted the inkvine scar on his face. "I let people make
their own interpretations, and thus they consider me a very wise man."

Duncan Idaho, however, did claim to be an expert on women, and had said
so with brash confidence on more than one occasion. That evening, Duncan
appeared at the door to Paul's quarters wearing loose clothes and carrying his
sword. He wasn't dressed as an Atreides House Guard nor in military uniform.
Instead, his shirt left his muscular arms bare, and when he grinned at Paul, his
rough, curly hair gave him a rakish look. "Time for me to continue your training.
As your Swordmaster and your friend, I feel obligated to do it in the right way.
You should enjoy your youth!"

"I prefer to continue my studies right here." Paul gestured to the ridulian crystal sheets, the shigawire spools, the crystal protectors on his personal desk. He
had been studying the structure of CHOAM, the web of Directorships and business alliances, considering the intricate rules. He wondered how House Atreides
might eventually acquire an important CHOAM Directorship.

Duncan scoffed at the documents. "I don't mean learning like that! I mean learning about life through experiences. Life and love! You're the heir to a Great House. No matter what happens now, you'll end up betrothed sooner or later. This is the proper time for a comprehensive approach—and some things are better done with your parents away." He flashed his smile again.

Paul groaned. "You've done this to me before, Duncan."

"And I will do it to you again, young Master. You are fourteen. Chasing love and flirting with pretty young women should be one of your most important goals."

"I'm the son of a Duke," Paul reminded him.

"Indeed you are, but the last I noticed, you were human, too."

Paul thought of his mother's training as well as Thufir Hawat's rigorous exercises, Duke Leto's steady instruction . . . and the strange and haunting dreams he continued to have. The mysterious, oh-so-familiar girl. . . .

"Human . . . ," he said. "I'll take that as a compliment."

Duncan crossed his arms over his tunic. "I've seen the sketches of that *particular* girl you keep imagining. I know what she looks like, and you thought you glimpsed her in Cala City. Just in case she is someone around here, instead of off in the sand somewhere, I kept my eyes open. I asked around." He raised his eyebrows. "There's someone I would like you to meet in an establishment you've never visited before." His voice grew more conspiratorial. "Your father would greatly disapprove if he knew I was taking you there, so this has to be our little secret."

Paul was suspicious. "Gurney took me to a tavern to enhance my experiences, but that did not turn out well."

"But it was still quite an experience, from what I understand! This one will be different. First we have to find you another shirt. The women already know you're the son of the Duke, but you don't need to intimidate them with stuffy finery."

THE ESTABLISHMENT WAS tucked away in a side street two blocks up from the lower docks, well lit and with many people going in and out, although the only identifying sign Paul could see was a placard with a purple Caladan rose.

Assembling the clues, Paul felt a knot form in his stomach. "Is this a brothel, Duncan?"

Flushing, the Swordmaster said, "Consider it a place where beautiful young women provide various personal services. You are a lordling and a most handsome young man, but you still have much to learn."

"And you think the girl I dream about is in there? In a brothel?" Paul pictured the elfin-faced girl, her dark red hair, and the desert canyons in the dusty sunlight. *Tell me about the waters of your homeworld, Usul.*

Duncan shrugged. "I tried my best to find her. You should at least meet her."

Paul braced himself, not sure he wanted to be here, but he pushed back his anxiety. Duncan clapped a hand on his shoulder, and the two entered. Paul remembered Thufir Hawat's admonition. "All of life is training."

The interior was lavishly appointed with artwork and plush furniture, but the details could barely be seen with the glowglobes tuned down low. A haze of dusty-sweet smoke hung in the air. Hypnotic semuta music was underscored by the low drone of conversation and accented by the tinkle of feminine laughter.

Duncan stepped up to a tall, older woman with dark skin and elaborate hair. A gleaming opal was affixed to her face high on her left cheek. "I made arrangements for a particular girl," Duncan said to her. "Shandrila. For the young Master here."

"Ah, so this is the young man." The woman smiled so broadly that her white teeth outshone the glint of the opal. "Shandrila is indeed reserved for him." When she looked at Paul, he suddenly felt light-headed. He couldn't think of anything to say. The woman gestured toward a long hallway. "The third door there, young man. Shandrila will make you comfortable."

"I'd like to talk," Paul said. "I want to find out if she's the girl I'm—"

The tall mistress twitched her hand and somehow silenced him as if she'd used Voice. "Shandrila knows what to do." She turned to Duncan. "Will you come back for him in an hour or two, or do you intend to stay?"

Duncan grinned. "Oh, I'd better stay, so I can be available . . . just in case."

Paul went to the indicated door and drew a deep breath. He was a small-statured young man, and at only fourteen, he didn't think he had the brashness to pull this off. But he reminded himself who he was. "All of life is training."

After knocking, he opened the door and saw a slender young woman in a chair next to a wide bed. She wore a beautiful Caladanian gown and a necklace of dull coral gems. Smiling, she rose to her feet. Paul was taken aback. His gaze took in her large eyes, her elfin features, her deep red hair. But there was no desert sun, no heat shimmers in the air, no canyon rocks.

Not like his dream, but still. . . .

"You must be Paul," said Shandrila. "I've been waiting for you."

"I've been waiting for you," Paul said automatically, but he quickly realized it wasn't her. Close . . . but not the same. Maybe this was the one he had seen walking in Cala City when he'd been with Thufir.

His hope turned to disappointment, as it had when he and Duncan went to the Caladan dunes down the coast. He should not have expected anything different. Still, Duncan had done an admirable job of finding a match to the dream girl he had sketched. Shandrila did resemble her.

Paul was the son of a Duke, but, as Duncan had reminded him, he was also human. Paul entered the room and closed the door.

WHEN DUNCAN FINALLY knocked on Shandrila's room two hours later, he was eager to hear what had happened. There was no response.

Growing concerned, because that was his job, Duncan knocked again, louder this time, and Paul's voice told him to come in. Swinging the door open wide, Duncan was taken aback to see the young woman sitting in her chair with Paul on the corner of the bed near her. He lounged back, his elbow on the blankets, propping his head up. "Are you ready to go, Duncan? I've had a fine time with Shandrila."

"I knew you would," Duncan said.

Paul rose, and the young woman looked at him with warmth suffusing her face. Her eyes shone, and her generous mouth curved in a secret smile. Duncan had seen that adoring look on the faces of many women.

Satisfied with himself, Paul brushed down his shirt, straightened his trousers. "Goodbye, Shandrila. Thank you for everything." He gave her a chaste kiss on the cheek.

"You always know where to find me, my Lord . . . Paul. I'd be happy to spend another evening with you, or many more."

He gave her a formal bow, like a Duke's son would offer a noble lady at court. Shandrila laughed.

Duncan led him out of the unnamed establishment into the shadowy streets late at night. Duncan's curiosity was ready to boil over, but Paul kept his words to himself. Duncan thought he looked smug.

Finally, after they had walked a block toward the brightly lit night markets, Duncan insisted. "And? Tell me what happened."

Paul gave him a half-hidden smile. "Would that be appropriate, Duncan?"

"I am your companion and bodyguard. I must know everything in order to keep you safe." He grinned again. "I'm also your friend. You wouldn't withhold anything from me?"

"Shandrila was not the woman from my dreams," he admitted, "although there is a certain resemblance."

Duncan was disappointed. "I hope that didn't stop you."

"It's not her fault she isn't the right girl, but she's fascinating in her own way. How we talked!" Paul increased his pace so that Duncan had to hurry to keep up with him. Once he started talking, the words poured out. "I learned all about her life and background, how her parents came to Caladan from Cuarte when they were young, but Shandrila was born and raised here. Her parents worked the docks and contracted on fishing boats, and they both died in a sea storm when she was only eleven. She was a very brave and ambitious young girl. I admire her resilience."

His voice fell. "We also talked about the ailar drug. She lost three friends to unexpected overdoses, and I think the spread of the drug was even worse than Thufir estimated, so many deaths never reported." He drew a breath. "But Shandrila is strong now and happy, with quite a sense of humor." Paul chuckled with a remembered joke that he did not repeat.

Duncan shook his head, unable to believe what he was hearing.

Paul continued, "It was good to get her perspective. My father always says that a leader must know his people. I'll probably talk with her again."

"*Talk?*" Duncan finally burst out. "You were with that beautiful and willing young woman, someone exactly your type because she looks like the person in your dreams—and all you did was talk?" He shook his head again. "Maybe you aren't human after all. I remember when I was fourteen . . ."

Paul stepped ahead, and he answered in a strange voice. "Why, Duncan, it is not my place to share everything, not even with you, my good friend."

The two were feeling so lighthearted and relaxed that neither expected the attack.

A pair of figures bounded out at them from the darkened streets, moving like panthers and dressed in garments woven out of shadows. The strike was coordinated, as if the attackers were mentally linked.

One engaged Duncan with a long blade in each hand, while the other dove directly for Paul. Duncan brought up his left arm to block, while with his right hand he snatched out his short sword. He managed to block the killing blow, but the razor edge cut into his forearm. If these assassins used poison blades . . . In that case, Duncan steeled himself to kill them both before any toxin could strike him down.

"Paul, your shield!" he shouted.

Duncan heard the activating hum as Paul slapped at his belt and countered the blows of the second opponent. As the first assassin lunged toward Duncan, he feinted back, caught the arm, and used their momentum to throw both of them to the ground.

Finally, Duncan registered that the loose whispering garments and veils covered female forms. Both attackers were women!

Paul had his own blade out now, and Duncan heard the click and ring of steel edges against the vibration of the shield belt. Duncan managed to activate his own shield as the woman sprang to her feet and shot toward him like a projectile. She struck too quickly, too recklessly, and her blade glided away from the personal shield.

Paul didn't speak a word or make a sound other than breathing as he fought his attacker. Duncan's neck tendons tightened, and his lips curled back with effort as he parried. He had to kill or defeat this woman so he could save Paul—but the young man was holding his own. Duncan knew how skilled the future Duke was in any kind of combat.

The first assassin came at the Swordmaster again, a spring-loaded fury of blades and precision. He brought up his own weapon to block, and the shield did part of the work. But now his attacker showed that she was also accustomed to the nuances of the Holtzman field, slowing her dagger to penetrate, intending to stab Duncan's side. He deflected her point and pushed upward with his blade, while reaching out with his bare hand. He clutched at fabric, tore a gray veil and exposed her face.

Duncan didn't recognize the woman at all—a small mouth, pointed chin, hard eyes, stray locks of dark hair around her face. She blinked in surprise at being exposed, and Duncan used the moment to crash into her, knocking her hard into the bricks of the narrow street's wall. He heard the *whuff* of her expelled air.

Paul fought in a blur, like his own attacker. Neither assassin was wearing a personal shield. The young man thrust hard with his long knife, hesitated out of habit, then drove the point into the target, piercing the woman's upper shoulder. As the blade cut into the meat and muscle, she let out a small hiss of pain, and Paul used the moment to retreat. He danced two steps backward to a safe, defensible distance, exactly as he had been taught.

Duncan's own attacker pushed off from the wall and sprang against him, driving him back. It all happened so fast. Paul's opponent clutched at her bloody shoulder, then bolted into an alley. The second woman—her face now entirely exposed—glowered at Duncan before she too darted off. They separated, a wise move.

"Paul, are you all right?" Duncan said, panting hard.

The young man joined him, his face flushed as he looked at the blood on his dagger. "I managed to stay uninjured." He looked at the bleeding cut on Duncan's arm. "Unlike you."

"A mere scratch. If there was any kind of paralytic on her blade I'd be feeling it by now."

Paul peered into the shadows where the attackers had vanished, but several seconds had passed, and they both knew it was too late for pursuit. By the time they called in the Atreides city guard to investigate, they would not find the would-be killers.

"Who were they?" Paul asked. "Why were they trying to assassinate us?"

Duncan, still wary, kept his blade out and made sure that he and Paul both maintained their personal shields. "As you've been taught every day of your life, young Master, there's always someone trying to kill the Atreides." Thoughts raced through Duncan's mind, and pieces fell into place. "They may have been Harkonnen operatives. Beast Rabban would surely want revenge after we attacked Lankiveil. I wouldn't put it past him to send murderers after you . . . and me, as a bonus."

Paul was restless, breathing hard, and he turned in slow circles, on the lookout for another attack. "Or Chaen Marek. He's already planted bombs in Cala City. He tried to kill me because of what my father did at the drug fields."

Duncan remembered facing off with the Tleilaxu drug lord in the barra forests in the north, the gnomish man's face, the dark glitter of his eyes. "I would not put such treachery past him . . . but he is a Tleilaxu. No matter how great his hatred for us, I can't imagine that Marek would have hired *women* as assassins."

"Then who else would be trying to kill me?" Paul asked.

Intensely aware, Duncan guided the young man out of the dark and narrow streets toward the brighter lights. He would not relax until they returned to the security of Castle Caladan. "Indeed, young Master, who else?"

The rush of the excitement seemed to be affecting Paul, though. He turned to Duncan and managed to smile. "Not exactly how I expected the evening to end, but considering we survived, I'll call it a satisfactory experience overall. All of life is training."

Being human means doing things we don't want to do, for our survival.
—LADY JESSICA, private journals

The Tull manor house was full of classical influences, finely appointed with frescoes, expensive furnishings, area rugs, and crystal chandeliers, along with a ballroom and grand staircase that connected to the upper level. While ruling Elegy for many decades, the old Viscount had often hosted lavish gatherings, dressing in finery and making memorable entrances onto the dance floor with his beautiful Bene Gesserit concubine on his arm.

Now that Zoanna was gone, the Sisterhood wanted Jessica to serve in that role for Giandro Tull. As concubine. Did they imagine that she herself had been nothing more than a decoration on Leto's arm? Even though the new Viscount had accepted her presence and allowed her to stay, as a provisional guest, she couldn't imagine gliding down the opulent staircase on his arm to a waiting crowd of planetary elite.

But she would do what she had to do in hope that she might be able to return to Paul, even Leto. She was still being watched, but she hoped to find some way to dispatch a private message to Caladan. How closely were the Bene Gesserit watching her now? Giandro's security observers, despite their numbers, could not possibly be as formidable as the surveillance she had faced at the Mother School.

Jessica had been given comfortable private quarters on the third level, not far from those of the Viscount. Over the past several days, he had grown more tolerant and even cordial, though still cautious. He wasn't sure he could accept her position, but willing to abide her presence if it calmed or deflected the suspicions of the Bene Gesserit and the Emperor. She even told him that being assigned here, to Elegy, was not her choice, and that seemed to make him look on her more favorably, rather than as an antagonist.

She had decided to be up front with Giandro, explaining to him her many years as Duke Leto's bound concubine, her fourteen-year-old son. Her relationship was a matter of public record, and the Viscount could easily obtain any details about her, so Jessica revealed it all. Despite her control, she could not erase her love for them in her voice when she spoke of them.

She was repulsed by the Sisterhood's command that she find a way to put the man under her thumb by employing the seductive arts of her order. The Mother Superior had been adamant that succeeding here was the only way Jessica could return to her old life and family. They were using a bludgeon on her.

She could have back what she wanted most, but her broken relationship with the Duke would need mending.

She rose early to take a walk outside, still familiarizing herself with the surroundings, the manor house, the nearby hills covered with lichen forests. The interesting architectural details of the manor house made her think of a palace. The three-story stone building was laid out around a magnificent garden courtyard decorated with lavish sprays of the distinctively beautiful Elegy lichens. A reflecting pool in the center sparkled as if tiny diamonds lay just beneath the mirrored surface. She made her way along a crushed-rock pathway, admiring bright flowers, decorative trees, and cleverly laid out rock walls with lichens growing on them.

She watched the gardeners at work, expertly snipping and grooming the lichens. When the workers gave her inquisitive but not unfriendly glances, she could tell that they assumed she was the Viscount's new woman, though he had not formally accepted her as concubine. Her routine here was just beginning.

As she paused on her stroll, she noticed uniformed security officers watching her, following her. Maybe they were more formidable than she'd been assuming. She steeled herself, recalled her own purpose.

At least she no longer had to wear the dark, frumpy Bene Gesserit robes from the Mother School. Just as in her role as the Lady of Caladan, she was part of this nobleman's household, and she wore elegant garments as if she were a noblewoman, shimmering fabric woven from the native lichens. They were warm and supple, giving off a prismatic light in the sun.

She strolled by heroic statues and a blue-leaf hedge she'd noticed from the balcony of her room. The hedge was laid out in the design of the Tull family crest, a sky-blue spiral. The statues, all men, had no name plaques, but she assumed they were Tull ancestors.

She took a seat at an outside table by the reflecting pool, where a setting had been laid out for her. One of the Viscount's liveried servants hurried up with a pot of coffee and a single cup, as well as a plate of dovina eggs for a light breakfast. She assumed that the Viscount would not be joining her this morning, but she would look for opportunities so they could talk. She sipped the strong coffee and stared at the water, watching it sparkle. The security men tried to remain discreet, but she still found them obtrusive. If she wished, she was sure she could use her own skills to elude them.

Footsteps crunched up behind her along the gravel path. She recognized Giandro's gait and turned only partway as he approached. The Viscount took a seat across the table from her and gave her a cautious smile, as if still trying to measure how much he was required to do with her. While servants set up for him to eat, he looked at her plate of small prepared eggs. "Not much of an appetite?" Giandro's long hair was secured by a blue clasp bearing his House emblem. "For myself, I like to begin each day with a hearty meal."

She nibbled at the flavorful blended eggs, which were delicious but rich. "This is as much as I need."

He chuckled. "It's about expectations. People say that men need the energy to inflict violence and mayhem on society, while women are calm and centered. I suppose building relationships doesn't take as much energy as embarking on a military campaign."

"Doesn't it?" She wasn't sure what to make of his conversation. "Maybe it's just a different kind of energy."

Giandro gave her an earnest look. "Then it could be we'll both need our energy today."

"Oh? Are we going off to war?"

He laughed again. "Or maybe laying the groundwork for a relationship? After all, we have expectations to meet."

As a liveried servant hovered close, Giandro asked for a large portion of thick sausages, a block of strong cheese, several slices of hearth bread, and a mug of coffee. When the servant hurried away, Tull smiled at her. "I'd rather not be seen eating dovina eggs—speaking of society's expectations."

Jessica took another bite, questioning. "Oh? What is wrong with them?"

"They're small and dainty, and considered foppish. Admittedly, though, they are bursting with flavor. Sometimes I sneak a taste of them when no one is looking." He licked his finger.

Jessica responded to his lighthearted conversation, not just out of her rote training, and she felt an awkward casualness forming between them. She had to encourage at least a friendly atmosphere. Giandro Tull was very different from her Leto, but she could see his worth.

"Your hospitality has been impeccable, my Lord. You have decided not to send me packing back to the Mother School, as you did with Zoanna?" She drank more coffee, met his gaze. "Thank you for giving me a chance."

His mouth twisted with distaste. "Zoanna served as my father's concubine for years, but she never filled any maternal role. He felt so beholden to the Bene Gesserit, was happy with whatever woman they sent him—she had him under her thumb. Then Zoanna tried to seduce me right after his death, as if nothing had happened!" He shook his head. "I thought you witches understood human nature better than that."

"We should." Jessica could only imagine how strange and unpleasant the situation must have been for Giandro. The Bene Gesserit were experts at covering or denying their emotions, but Zoanna had been *oblivious* to them. She must have analyzed the situation in strictly business terms, and felt she could simply remain in her position as concubine, except with a different Viscount. "I was imagining the conversation Zoanna must have had when she returned to Wallach IX." She smiled. "The Mother Superior would not have been happy with such clumsy work."

"Clumsy indeed! The very idea was quite unpleasant."

"So they sent me in her place," Jessica said. "I hope I'm not quite as . . . unpleasant." She ate more of her dovina eggs and, after a glance at the ubiquitous security watchers, slid the plate closer to Giandro, so he could sneak a bite while he waited for his own breakfast.

He offered an embarrassed smile. "If the witches are so intent on slipping someone into my bed, why not send a young, lascivious woman trained in all the techniques of seduction?" He seemed genuinely curious.

"You never asked me about my own training."

A flush came to his cheeks, and he acknowledged the point with a nod.

She continued, "Is that what you'd want? A giggly, young, well-endowed girl? I'd assume a Viscount could have that at any local brothel. The Sisterhood offers more than that. A concubine is a partner, not just a bedmate."

He regarded her carefully, analytically. "If I were to send you away, the Bene Gesserit would only try again with someone else, wouldn't they?" Giandro seemed shy, but he scooped one of the eggs she had offered onto a spoon for himself. "Yes, you are pleasant enough."

She let that hang in the air for a moment, while he ate the tiny egg. "Thank you for your kind sentiments. As you say, if you turn me away, they will likely try again . . . and then I'll be dispatched elsewhere. They'll consider that I failed in my assignment."

He looked suddenly concerned. "And they'll punish you? Rather than let you go back to Caladan?"

"The Bene Gesserit have many different categories of punishment." She set her fork down, leaned in, and gave him her entire attention. "Giandro, neither of us chose this situation, but maybe we can make this work to our mutual benefit. Let us get to know each other better."

A servant brought him his hearty breakfast and a large mug of steaming-hot coffee. He sipped from his mug, not bothered by how hot the coffee was. "Yes, it can be to our mutual benefit. Your Sisterhood has strong political influence around the Imperium, so perhaps I do need to repair my relationship with them—at least on the surface. I won't grovel to the witches, or be manipulated as my father so clearly was, but . . ." He paused to put cheese on a thick slice of bread, took a bite. "After Emperor Shaddam accused and then obliterated House Verdun, I confess that I've been tense—as are all Houses of the Landsraad. What will he do next? Shaddam already sent his Sardaukar here to inspect Elegy, to interrogate my people and me. I think his Truthsayer may have instigated it because I stopped the flow of Tull money to the Sisterhood."

Jessica boldly took a piece of aromatic white cheese from his plate. "And if you keep me here, then I can give you cover. Reverend Mother Mohiam—the Emperor's Truthsayer—was my old teacher. She knows me well."

He stiffened. "So, you're her spy?"

The cheese was strong, but Jessica liked the taste. "I am an observer, and I will observe whatever you let me observe. I can reassure Mohiam, and she will then reassure the Padishah Emperor."

Giandro looked past her, seeing but not acknowledging the not-so-subtle security men standing on the fringe of the garden. "My father's endowments to the Mother School cost my planet's treasury dearly. And Elegy will not be a slave to the Imperium either." He gave Jessica a sincere smile. "But your comments make sense, and it could be worthwhile to make a few concessions. Your presence here may be tolerable enough." He dove into his sausages with great gusto.

"High praise indeed." She ate another small dovina egg. "We can find our way through this." She had made considerable progress already, and she'd done it without being manipulative.

Would this rapprochement meet the objective that the Sisterhood had given her? How could she claim success with Viscount Giandro so that they released her? Surely she could smooth over the frayed relationship this nobleman had with the Bene Gesserit. But she doubted that would be enough. Harishka and Mohiam had also clearly instructed her to become this man's intimate adviser. Giandro had to publicly announce her as his new concubine, for all the Imperium—and Leto—to see. The thought was like hot lead in her stomach.

It was a test for Jessica. She had to prove that she was fully bound to the order, or they would never let her break free.

She kept replaying the nightmare of her last conversation with Leto, the look in his eyes, the cold wall he had built. Would he wait for her at all, or had he already turned his back on her? Jessica felt a deep ache as she realized that by now Xora might already be on Caladan. Xora would be assigned to do exactly the same thing as Jessica was doing here, trying to forge a bond as the new concubine for House Atreides.

Jessica looked up at the Viscount across from her. She had read the dossier from the Sisterhood, but it did not include the details. "Why did your father feel so indebted to the Bene Gesserit?"

Giandro turned his gaze toward the statues in the garden near the lichens. "Because of his own impetuous actions as a boy, and they saved him. He stowed away aboard a transport from Elegy and made his way to the Mother School because he wanted to see the 'witches' he had heard about. He hid in a storage container, was delivered down to the planet." Giandro's expression showed his amusement at the story. "My father was smart enough to figure out how to get to Wallach IX, but he did not plan the details very well. He was found nearly frozen to death trying to sleep in an unheated storage building. The Sisters nursed him back to health, and notified his family where he was. He almost didn't make it, but finally pulled through. For the rest of his life, my father saw to it that they were paid handsomely, to show his gratitude."

He frowned. "But I have other investments, important passions that require our funds. House Tull has given enough buildings to your Mother School."

Jessica understood. "One cannot mandate generosity—that defeats the purpose. You should do as you please with your family treasury."

He gazed at her long and hard, as if examining a puzzle box and trying to figure out which panel to slide open so he could get inside her head. Her frankness and honesty had thrown the brash nobleman off balance.

With a glance at the ubiquitous hovering security men, she recalled another part of her mission here—to watch and learn, to see exactly what Giandro's other "passions" might be.

As they talked, she remained pleasant and friendly, and she could tell he was warming to her company. She had been taught specific methods by the Bene Gesserit, but she had never needed to use them on Leto. When she'd been assigned to Caladan as a young woman, his relationship with Kailea Vernius had already been strained and dead. In an instant natural attraction, Leto had wanted Jessica . . . and she still wanted him.

And she ached for him now, but he was far, far away, in more ways than one.

Viscount Giandro's expression grew thoughtful. "If we are meant to be together, we will be together. We should believe in fate."

She smiled. "Sometimes fate needs a nudge in the right direction. The trick is to determine what that direction should be."

I am who I am. I am what I do—not what I appear to be, as a show for others.

—DUKE LETO ATREIDES, letters to his son

As Leto journeyed on the Heighliner, following Jaxson Aru's strict instructions, all contact was cut off from Caladan, his advisers, and his son.

The Duke wore common clothes, giving him the appearance of a nondescript businessman. Although Thufir Hawat could have created false identity certificates, Jaxson had provided counterfeit traveling papers, part of a complete camouflage so that Leto appeared to be no more than an executive merchant, a trader in various commodities from Caladan. He carried a manifest documenting shipments of pundi rice and trilium, unremarkable exports from his world. Claiming to be a trader in rare moonfish would have been too painful.

To mentally prepare himself for his new role, Leto spent time reviewing the intricate, challenging lessons Hawat had used when training him as a young Duke. The warrior Mentat had been thorough in his instruction, even if young Leto had considered it harsh at the time. Those lessons were burned deep into him, helping him to see an infinite constellation of influences, consequences, connections, and repercussions. He had learned how to be nimble in his reactions, how to observe, how to strike with the speed of thought, and how to wait, no matter how much he was tempted to lash out. Duke Paulus had also taught his son all he knew, raising Leto to be a leader, a commander, a statesman, a negotiator, and a formidable enemy.

As he planned for his meeting with the rebel leader, Leto promised himself he was ready.

After several tedious stops at other worlds, the Heighliner reached the obscure rendezvous point Jaxson had arranged. The planet Elegy had recently opened a new orbital transfer station, a modern travel hub where passengers and cargo could easily be shifted to appropriate routes without undue inconvenience. Traveling as a common passenger, Leto did not have his usual dedicated Atreides frigate, but after so much attention and scandal, he could appreciate being invisible, calm, and quiet.

But his thoughts were not quiet as he pondered what was to come.

Leto and more than a hundred other passengers disembarked onto the Elegy transfer station, a large, clean complex with many viewing windows that looked out upon the stars or down onto the planet. Gazing through a viewing window, he ignored the bustle of preoccupied passengers moving back and forth, looking at schedules, checking on when the next Heighliner would arrive to take them along different Spacing Guild routes.

The world below looked pleasant enough. Leto remembered Elegy was under the rule of Viscount Giandro Tull, whose father had recently passed away. The planet was known for exotic lichens and the distinctive fabrics made from them, some of which he had seen at the Imperial Court. But the bulk of House Tull income came from mining, processing, and distributing common metals from asteroid operations. Until recently, this had been done in a lucrative partnership with House Verdun. Leto knew this from the research he'd done on possible marriage candidates for Paul. Now that Emperor Shaddam had wiped out House Verdun, though, Tull might be facing difficult financial times. Maybe the income derived from this busy new orbital transfer platform would make up for it.

A man joined him at the plaz viewing window. "All the busy little creatures down there," he said. "Countless members of humanity with their own concerns, their own dreams, their own passions. But I see them as tiny fish caught in a tide pool. They have their own universe around them, and they are concerned with survival among the other creatures in the tide pool, never even imagining the great, wide ocean out there." Jaxson Aru drew in a deep breath and smiled. "It is our task to bring in the high water, Leto, so we can let the human race swim free."

Leto felt his pulse quicken. He looked over at the other man, frowned at the not-quite-familiar features. "Your disguise is quite good."

"We all wear disguises, my friend. Mine is just a bit more sophisticated." He laughed. "And in my wonderful projection on the fountains by the Imperial Palace, I intentionally used my old familiar features, so that no one would be looking for this face." He touched his cheek and stroked down with a fingertip as if it were a lover's caress.

Leto pulled together his thoughts, gathered his false persona, and hoped it would be good enough to convince the violent rebel leader. "You offered me a chance to participate in the Noble Commonwealth, yet I do so with continuing trepidation because I fear the violence you intend."

Jaxson just smiled. "But you are here because you also understand the end result. You know that a free and independent commonwealth will be far superior to a stagnant and corrupt Corrino Imperium." He lowered his voice amid the bustle of other travelers, possible spies, aboard the Elegy transfer station. "Let me tell you a story, Leto. On my family estate on Otorio, my father and I often spent time in the olive grove. The trees were large, magnificent, but ancient. There came a time when the trees were so old they stopped producing, and as much as we revered them, we had to cut them down, tear up the roots, and plant new, productive olive trees. That is the Corrino Imperium, my friend. We need to tear it down and till the soil so that something marvelous can grow in its stead."

Leto also kept his voice low. "And you do that by blowing up a treasury ship on Kaitain? Killing two thousand people who just happened to be in the crowd that day? You brought ships crashing down on a museum complex, to murder even more than that, Imperial citizens who simply answered their emperor's summons to a gaudy and meaningless display."

Jaxson's face darkened, and he turned away from the planet to look directly at Leto. "How is my incident at the Imperial Palace any different from what Shaddam's Sardaukar did to House Verdun? He wiped out an entire noble family, destroyed their holdings, burned down the capital city. The casualty numbers were far higher than my two demonstrations combined."

Leto wrestled with the comparison. "I never liked Duke Verdun, but I don't condone the actions taken against him. If we can stop that from happening again, then yes, I am willing to join you." The words made his throat go dry, but he knew his acceptance—though conditional—was what Jaxson needed to hear.

The rebel leader relaxed. "I know you can see deeper than the surface. There is subtlety and subtext to what I accomplished. All the strands connect in a larger tapestry. Now that you are joining us, my comrade, we have more threads to weave together, more goals to accomplish."

Leto remained cautious. "What do you have in mind? I agreed to speak with you and to meet other like-minded people."

"We are far beyond the point of discussion, Leto Atreides," Jaxson snapped. "Even my mother has come to realize that decades and decades of mere talk will not accomplish our goal. I have another hard but poignantly memorable demonstration planned." Together, they looked down at the cloud-scudded skies of the planet Elegy.

Jaxson's gaze seemed distant, filled with complicated plans.

"And you, Leto Atreides, are going to help me accomplish it."

A plan is nothing unless it succeeds.
—BARON VLADIMIR HARKONNEN

As the investigation continued, and the more Shaddam pressed and squeezed for answers, the more elusive the results became. Jaxson Aru would not have left any incriminating clues in the aftermath of the exploding treasury ship.

At the Imperial Palace, Shaddam's most demanding work was to control the fires of public outrage, calm the incensed Landsraad nobles who had the gall to turn against *him* instead of the violent rebellion. Looking aggrieved and with a downcast Empress Aricatha at his side, Shaddam had made a public statement announcing his original intent to distribute all that wealth as a reward to his loyal subjects. But the words rang hollow, and he couldn't make them believe. Lord Rajiv Londine had used the opportunity for another one of his maddening complaints against House Corrino.

He knew the best way to get the people back on his side would be to find the rebel leader and drag him into the damaged Imperial plaza, where he would create a far more memorable execution than any spectacle Jaxson Aru had conceived.

But even his crack Sardaukar investigators turned up nothing more than blind ends. Personnel records of the treasury frigate's crew, the transfer documents for all the solari coins in its hold, the dock manifests, the transport control listing—everything had been expunged. The crew members had been killed in the explosion, and some of them were surely coconspirators. Shaddam assumed they had hijacked the vessel from the transport hub, flown it on its suicide run—but the investigators couldn't even find their names.

Countless gleaming solaris were scattered across the blast zone, but everything else had melted into slag, blown up along with the treasury vessel. Because the coins did not have intrinsic value, but served only due to the backing of the Imperial Treasury, he knew it would not be economically feasible to extract any precious metals from the wreckage. Shaddam would simply mint new coins.

Intricate controls and electronic records from Kaitain's transport hub had gone offline just as Shaddam had started his speech from the promenade balcony. The harried personnel had worked so frantically to restore smooth operations across the entire Imperial capital that no one signaled the Palace until it was too late. Five ships of similar configuration to the treasury frigate had been docked or dispatched at around the same time, and those records, too, were wiped.

He increased his investigative team, demanding answers. More than that, he wanted Jaxson Aru.

THE DELAY IN Gurney's secret trip to the Imperial capital lasted for days while they waited for a replacement Heighliner. He found himself stranded at the spaceport on the planet Parmentier, frustrated, but unable to call attention to himself, or send word back to Caladan.

But this delay was not a critical problem. Back when Gurney was about to leave Caladan, Thufir Hawat had seen him off at the spaceport, attending personally to the security of his departure and to maintain secrecy about the nature of his mission. "We'd better have an understanding between us," Thufir had said. "I did not wish to criticize our Duke's plans when he has so much on his mind, but you and I should establish some timeframe. If I don't hear back from you within that time, I will send out inquiries."

"You worry too much, Mentat," Gurney had said. "I will not fail."

"But Thufir had insisted. Thirty days seems reasonable for you to get to Kaitain, deliver your message to the Emperor, and return to Caladan. By then, if I have not heard back from you, I would need to find out why."

"There is a certain risk in even sending out inquiries about my mission," Gurney said, thinking. "But I see your point. Yes, thirty days sounds right. And if I have not returned by then, you should take the risk to find out why."

"That is my exact line of reasoning."

Nodding, Gurney had said, "All right, we're in agreement." He'd grinned, wrinkling the scar on his chin. "But don't worry, I'll be back long before that deadline."

Now as he thought of this, a Spacing Guild apology was announced on an open comm in the old, busy waiting area. He strummed his baliset and tried not to grow furious as the hours passed. Many other passengers milled about in the large terminal building.

A wavering holo-image of a Guildsman in a silver suit spoke in an eerie voice to the thousands of passengers whose plans had been disrupted. "Thank you for your patience while we rearrange Heighliner schedules. Several of our largest vessels are undergoing refurbishment and technological upgrades. You will be rerouted appropriately to your final destination as soon as suitable Heighliner replacements are available."

Gurney's fingers produced a discordant jangle. He knew the Duke would already be gone for his rendezvous with Jaxson Aru, but Shaddam still needed to know his true motive.

"These schedule changes are only temporary," the Guildsman insisted. "Our apologies for this minor inconvenience." He went on to give specifics, explaining that some passengers—including Gurney, apparently—would be diverted to secondary routes.

"*Secondary* routes?" Gurney grumbled as the holo-image flickered off. "'All roads lead to the human heart,'" he quoted. "'And to the heart of the Imperium.'"

For millennia, the Spacing Guild had used ships with foldspace technology, guided by mysterious Navigators. They had always provided reliable transport, with remarkably few mishaps.

Well, Gurney would just have to finish his mission, get to Kaitain and make certain that he explained Leto's true purpose to the Emperor, and then all would be well. He calmed himself. *Travel is about solving problems.*

The sooner he reached Kaitain, the better. He just didn't know how long he would be stuck here.

HIS DAYS OF fruitless waiting at the transfer station on Parmentier were frustrating and uneventful. The planet had an intriguing history, including a famous slave revolt in ancient times, but at present, a weak House ruled the planet, and its industries were few. Parmentier was primarily an out-of-the-way place for people who didn't want to be seen or found.

The terminal building remained crowded. Other ships arrived and departed, but still not the vessel that would take him on his "secondary route" to the Imperial capital. He walked around aimlessly, chatting with the occasional person without revealing anything about himself, but he didn't exactly blend in. He watched formal, jumpsuited workers moving about, solicitous, their eyes hidden by reflective coverings. He recognized them as Wayku, a well-established group of stewards who had worked in Guild facilities and ships for centuries.

He also noted a few furtive types who moved in the shadows, avoiding contact with others. His eye caught a strange man on the other side of the large reception and waiting area, a small figure in a black cape, wearing a hat with a down-turned brim. Gurney smirked. If the man was trying to be inconspicuous, he had failed miserably. He also noted a number of dark-garbed, pallid people spread out around the lounge areas. Other passengers kept a suspicious eye on them, and he suspected they were pickpockets.

As he marked empty minutes and empty hours, sitting on a ledge beneath a window, Gurney kept a foot against his travel bag at all times, so he would feel instantly if anyone tried to take it, even if he was distracted by something else. He knew the game, and he would not fall victim to it. His baliset lay across his lap in its brown leather traveling case. He rubbed his forearm, where Yueh had implanted the message from the Duke. It was still a little sore, but the scar was difficult to see.

A flicker in his peripheral vision alerted Gurney to someone approaching from his right and another person coming from the opposite direction, a man and woman. He tensed, ready to react, but then relaxed when they met off to his side and began talking to each other, obviously acquaintances.

They were dressed colorfully, as if part of an entertainment troupe. The man wore a pale blue jacket, white trousers, and a rainbow-colored top hat, along with brown-and-white wingtip shoes. His companion was in a floor-length yellow dress covered with intricate lace designs. She wore a top hat as well, white with blinking, multicolored lights.

Now Gurney noticed more flamboyantly dressed visitors in the terminal lounge emerging from a room at the rear. Everyone in the unusual garb gathered around the furtive man he'd noticed before, and Gurney realized they were connected. Taking off the black cape and hat, the man handed them to a small companion, who put them on. It was some kind of performance, and he heard their voices accompanied by the lilting tones of a flute. The musician marched into the lounge from the back room to join the troupe.

Humming along to the familiar tune, Gurney made up the words of a fresh ballad. He began to sing along in a low voice.

The tall woman with the flashing top hat swept closer, startling him. "You have a rich and wonderful voice, sir."

Though he'd never been shy about singing in front of crowds at Castle Caladan, he felt oddly embarrassed now. "I didn't mean to disturb anyone."

Her companion joined them. "Keep it up! Would you be interested in accompanying us? At least for today's performance? Our troupe always has room for good singers."

The woman crowded closer. "What's in the case? An instrument of some kind?"

He chastised himself for drawing attention by singing. But now he had little choice except to speak to these people. "A baliset," he answered, then added with some pride, "I made it myself."

The man said, "I hear they're difficult to master."

Gurney smiled, rubbing the inkvine mark on his face while keeping the other hand on the instrument case. "I practiced enough."

"We are all on our way to Kaitain," the woman said with clear invitation in her voice, "to perform for the Emperor and his new Empress."

That caught Gurney's attention.

"And where are you going?" the man prompted.

"I'm just on vacation, traveling around a bit." They kept looking at the baliset case, and he knew they would like to hear him play. When Gurney offered no further details, the two backed off. The troupe began singing and playing more loudly, and the woman waved at him. "Feel free to come over and watch us practice. We'll be here for another seven hours."

"Or longer," the man said. "If they change the schedule again."

After a brief performance, the players retreated to the open back room in the terminal, and Gurney watched them, pondering. Seven more hours . . . He might enjoy playing his baliset with them, and if this troupe was en route to Kaitain, he might blend in better with them than as a man traveling alone. Camouflage. . . .

Through the open entrance to the back room, he heard them practicing, laughing. The notes of the flute skirled higher, joined by a stringed instrument of some type. Curious, and open to possibilities, he gathered his case and his traveling bag and went to the back room.

The troupe had moved chairs to create a makeshift stage area. Others smiled at him as he took a seat and watched while they ran through a range of practice skits, from sophisticated to bawdy.

An old, bald man with a large paunch played a stringed instrument of ancient design. He seemed too large for the chair he had chosen, but he made do. His nimble fingers smoothly ran through chord progressions and key changes, plucking the strings with metal picks on his fingers. He played an obscure style of music, while two women in heels and tight costumes clicked their toes rhythmically on the floor.

The man in the top hat stood off to one side, and when he noticed Gurney, he smiled in greeting. Gurney acknowledged him.

In that moment of distraction, someone reached from behind, grabbed the baliset case, and bounded toward an exit door. Gurney lurched to his feet and ran after him, bellowing. It was one of the furtive, pallid-skinned men, sprinting away.

"Stop him!" he shouted, leaving his other bag behind, not caring so much about his travel clothing. The baliset was more important. Had this all been a setup? Was the entire troupe working with the pale thieves?

He ran as fast as he could, rolling along with his powerful, muscular gait. The thief charged through the arched doorway and bounded off to the right, holding the baliset. Gurney closed in, his lips curled back in anger, ready to tear the man apart. The thief glanced back, then rounded a corner of the terminal building.

When Gurney turned after him, something struck him hard on the head, and he went reeling into a universe of pain.

"We got him, Piter!" a man shouted.

Piter? Gurney tried to focus on the name. It had ominous familiarity.

"He's one of Duke Leto's men. Our identification scans flagged him. I think he's one of those engaged in the recent raid on Lankiveil." The man had a thin, nasal voice. "Count Rabban will want to have him!"

Rabban?

"And take him apart piece by piece!"

Gurney struggled, tried to thrash at these men, but someone struck his head again and sent him into a pit of darkness.

When Ruthine caused her own death, she took all her secrets with her, like a drowning person weighed down by rocks. Jiara was also found dead in her holding cell. The Bene Gesserit felt that the scandal, and the problem, was over.

But Reverend Mother Cordana felt a knot form in the pit of her stomach, tightening and tightening into excruciating pain. The warm fire in the Mother Superior's council chamber did little to ease the ache in her body. Cordana paced back and forth while Harishka sat in her tall chair and downplayed the dire circumstances.

"You need to listen to me," Cordana insisted. "It is no coincidence that Taula and Aislan are gone, and I found clear connections between them and Ruthine, just like Jiara. Indications are that those two departed the Mother School for Caladan. The only conclusion is that they were sent to assassinate Jessica's son."

Harishka remained maddeningly calm and calculating. "I am skeptical when someone tells me there is only one way to look at something. It lacks imagination."

Cordana bit back a retort, calmed herself. "I would be happy to entertain alternative explanations, Mother Superior. In fact, I'd be relieved if you sent an immediate warning to Duke Leto Atreides—and it turned out to be a false alarm. But you must at least consider the possibility that this conspiracy against you is wider than just Ruthine and Jiara, that Jessica's son is in danger."

"But didn't Lethea predict that the boy *is* the danger? That Jessica *is* the danger?"

Cordana was taken aback by the comment. "And you decided otherwise, Mother Superior. You cannot allow a fringe group of extremist Sisters to countermand your own orders. Taula and Aislan were sent to kill Paul Atreides, I know it."

"There's no evidence of that," Harishka countered. "It is possible that they abandoned the order. Other Sisters are clearly dissatisfied with the Mother

School, and with me in particular. Those two were known to be disgruntled. More likely they ran away, left their robes on the Heighliner, and disappeared. It has happened before."

Cordana tried to control her breathing. "And Ruthine and Jiara just . . . coincidentally died in their cells, when we were about to make them face a Truthsayer?"

"Those two—as you said, they were clearly extremists." The Mother Superior raised an index finger to cut off Cordana's swift response. "Rest assured, I am making inquiries into the two missing Sisters, so we can be sure. It could well be that Caladan was not their real destination, but a red herring to throw us off, merely the easiest route on that particular outbound Heighliner."

Cordana didn't believe it for a moment, but she remained respectful in front of the Mother Superior.

Harishka continued, "It is fortunate that we have another operative en route to Caladan at this moment. Xora will present herself to Duke Leto as his new concubine, and I will dispatch word for her to remain alert, to keep watch in case the Duke's son is in unexpected danger. I am certain House Atreides has perfectly adequate security around the Atreides heir."

Cordana did not find the answer soothing at all. "Xora? But what if she is also connected? How do we know that Xora isn't acting with Ruthine and Jiara?"

Now Harishka's expression tightened. She rose from her chair and impatiently gestured Cordana out of the council chamber. "Then you are indeed seeing conspiracies in every corner."

CORDANA DIDN'T TRUST the dismissal, didn't believe there was nothing to worry about, and could not take the chance. That evening, she struggled with a decision, fearing that she might still be too late.

Yes, the Mother Superior had opened an investigation into Taula and Aislan. Once Xora arrived at Caladan, the Mother School would also dispatch a message asking her to be alert for any threat against Paul Atreides.

Too late. Too late!

Cordana had tried one more time to convince Harishka. For decades, the Mother Superior had led the Bene Gesserit order through a great deal of strife, and she refused to let emotions rule her decisions. Harishka would rationally discuss crises and responses, viewing the big picture through the perspective of the greater, overall Sisterhood.

But such calm rationality would not undo a disastrous misstep if Cordana's suspicions were right. She clenched her fist as she paced in her quarters, wrestling with her choices. She consumed spice to loosen her tight and aching muscles, and it also helped clarify her thoughts. The Mother Superior had selected her and Ruthine specifically because they were so diametrically opposed, because their sparring helped her to find a middle ground. But what was the purpose of a middle ground, when one side was right and the other was completely wrong?

She thought of Lethea's spiteful, possibly demented visions, her warnings, her prescience . . . or her delusions. Obviously, Ruthine, Jiara, and any other conspirators believed that the old woman's ravings were clear.

Cordana might not be objective either, but if Taula and Aislan killed a truly viable candidate to be the Kwisatz Haderach, better even than Xora's illicit son Brom, how long would it take for the Bene Gesserit to recover from that bloody mistake? Jessica could not just flit back to Caladan, into that tragedy, and get herself pregnant with another Atreides child.

The Mother Superior had forbidden Cordana from sending her own urgent alarm to Caladan, nor could she travel there herself. She had to obey the order.

But she could *selectively* obey.

There was one other person who might heed the warning and find a desperate way to act. If nothing else, at least Cordana would know she had tried, and her conscience—her instincts—would not let her do *nothing*.

She had already arranged for an urgent courier, looked up the arrival of a new Heighliner that would travel directly to the correct transfer station. Cordana had less than an hour to act, if she hoped to give a message to the courier.

Sitting at her small writing desk, she found a sheet of instroy paper and one of the unmarked message cylinders. With quick, sharp strokes of her stylus, she wrote a coded letter in a familiar but secure Bene Gesserit cipher.

She dispatched the sealed cylinder to Sister Jessica on Elegy.

AS DAYS PASSED on her new assignment, Jessica and Viscount Giandro fell into a regular routine. Each day, they met for meals, even occasional walks through the manicured grounds and hunting preserve. She was still just a guest, but the household staff and the citizens of Elegy seemed to recognize that the Viscount had a new lady in the manor house. The Bene Gesserit were waiting for him to announce her as his concubine, even if only a temporary one. They must have predatory eyes watching her progress.

Giandro made a habit of eating breakfast with her, and that morning on the garden terrace, he said, "Jessica, we both know your assignment here. There are expectations at every turn. If you are my concubine, in the eyes of the Bene Gesserit and the eyes of the public here on Elegy . . ." He drew a breath. "The Sisterhood chose well when they sent you here."

She agreed. "Under the circumstances, with this situation being forced on both of us, I could not have asked for a better situation."

He seemed embarrassed by his clumsy overture. "We are each dealt hands of cards at birth, and during life we pick up new situations and discard some. As we sit together on this beautiful morning, we have decisions to make about which cards to play and which to hold."

"I like your openness, Giandro, but I have to be frank as well. There is the matter of my previous . . . assignment. Elegy is beautiful, but my heart is still on Caladan."

"Caladan . . . " he said.

"I spent nearly twenty years there, with the Duke. He is the father of our son. I . . ." She forced herself to say it, realizing that he could use the words against her. "I loved him."

He looked away, then met her eyes again. "I can tell. Leto Atreides is known to be an exceptional man."

"And I will always love him deeply." Jessica paused, selecting her words carefully. "The end of the relationship was not my choice."

"Then he is a fool."

Jessica smiled. "It wasn't his choice either, but an entanglement of circumstances."

"And now you are here. On another assignment."

Without finishing her meal, she rose to her feet. "I'm sorry. I didn't mean to burden you with my troubles. None of it is your fault."

Giandro gave her a wan smile. "We're all entangled in circumstances, aren't we?"

As she paused at the balcony doors, she nearly ran into a flushed servant. He seemed to have been waiting for the proper moment to interrupt. He handed her a sealed, unmarked message cylinder. "This arrived for you, by special courier, my Lady."

The cylinder was bland, gray metal with no insignia, but she recognized its style—exactly the kind of message cylinder she would have used to smuggle a secret note to Caladan. Her senses were instantly alert. "Thank you. I'll read it in my chambers." Behind her, Giandro watched from the veranda.

As she left, clutching the cylinder, she tried not to rush, but her thoughts raced in circles. It must be some new command from the Mother Superior, or an announcement—or threat—from Reverend Mother Mohiam. She couldn't imagine who else from the Mother School would write her.

In her room, she used her thumbprint to open the cylinder and removed a piece of instroy paper. Translating the Bene Gesserit cipher in her mind, she read the message from Cordana with horror. She suddenly found herself not in life's metaphorical card game that Giandro had alluded to, but in a perilous war among malevolent forces, factions in the Sisterhood, fighting for her life. For Paul's life.

Returning to Caladan was no longer just a cherished dream, but a frantic need. Paul was under threat, and she had to do something. She could not spend weeks carefully winning over Viscount Giandro Tull.

Here on Elegy, Jessica was much freer than when she'd been at the Mother School. Maybe she could find a way to escape, somehow make her way to Caladan . . . but that was a mad and unlikely solution. With the Viscount's security forces watching her every movement so that she didn't stray where she was not allowed, she could never get off the planet.

And yet her son was in imminent danger.

She had one viable hope, one risky chance, and she had to take it. She would speak to Giandro directly and hope that he would allow her to go.

The Viscount was still sitting at the table with the remnants of his large breakfast spread out before him. He seemed to be pondering more than eating. He blinked in surprise and half rose from his chair. "Jessica? Are you all right? You look—"

"Giandro, I need to take you into my confidence. You're the only one I can talk to about this, the only one who . . . who can grant what I ask."

His face became determined. "You had better tell me."

Standing straight and proud, Jessica told him what the note said, adding key details about the Sisterhood's machinations and the damning words Lethea had spoken. She told him her son might be in terrible danger. "I have to go to Caladan. Right away."

He stepped away from the table, ready to leap into action. "I can arrange for transport, send an armed escort, if that is what you need."

Her heart lurched with surprise at his reaction, and she immediately started thinking through the obstacles. "We'll have to be very careful. The Bene Gesserit can't know that I have left here. I am not supposed to know about the threat—but I have to protect Paul!"

He gave her a hard, sincere smile. "Why would they need to know that you left? I will certainly not tell them. As far as they know, you'll be right here, staying inside my manor house."

"I don't know how you'll manage it," Jessica said. "But thank you. I need to save my son. I have to go to Caladan."

He didn't hesitate. "I'll arrange passage for you. Don't worry, I have ways of keeping your travel secret." He smiled. "I've used that trick myself a few times."

Jessica felt a trickle of relief, but she wouldn't let herself relax until she saw Paul and made sure he was safe.

"I can expedite your passage, arrange for the most direct flight from our transfer station. You will be away before you know it." Giandro's expression fell. "I hope you will come back."

She owed him a great deal. "I'll return as soon as I can, as soon as I know my son is safe. You're a man of many talents—some of them quite surprising. I can't possibly thank you enough." She thought again of the warning Reverend Mother Cordana had sent, the two Sisters supposedly with a mission to assassinate Paul. She hoped she had the opportunity to face them herself.

I would kill for my son.

I have never liked surprises. With the detailed projections I constantly run,
there should be few events I do not anticipate. And yet, it still happens.
     —THUFIR HAWAT, Mentat to House Atreides

With Duke Leto away on his journey into the heart of the Noble Commonwealth rebellion, and Halleck gone as well, Thufir Hawat prided himself on managing the security of Castle Caladan. He was on an even higher state of alert than usual because of the recent assassination attempt on Paul. His security troops had found no sign of the two female attackers.

Now there had been another attempted breach, and he was going to get to the bottom of it.

Standing at the main castle gates, he confronted the beautiful but haughty woman who had just arrived from Wallach IX. He said, "I was told nothing of this."

"Nevertheless, I am here, the official new concubine to the Duke of Caladan." The Bene Gesserit wore a black traveling robe and apparently expected to take her place in Castle Caladan without delay.

Hawat didn't budge, and his expression tightened. "I doubt that Duke Leto knows of this, or he would have informed me."

"In that case, I am informing you now."

The tall woman had bronze hair and striking blue, feline eyes. She reminded him of Jessica—which must certainly have been the Sisterhood's intent.

"I am Sister Xora, and I've been dispatched here on special assignment." She looked down at her bags. "Kindly have my luggage brought into the castle and taken to my new quarters."

Thufir pressed his red-stained lips into a stubborn line. "The Duke is currently off-planet. I am certain he did not request a new concubine from the Mother School . . . or from anywhere else, for that matter. Since the departure of Lady Jessica, he has been focused on other priorities."

Xora faced him, unsettled, and seemed to reassess her approach. "Duke Leto isn't here? How long will he be gone?"

Frowning, the Mentat stood in front of her, eye to eye. He had no inclination to allow her onto the grounds of Castle Caladan, nor to give her any further information. Her character was more insistent and aggressive than Jessica's had been. "The movements and the business of the Duke are not your concern."

"They should be," Xora said. "House Atreides is an important member of the Landsraad. Before the departure of Lady Jessica, the Duke relied on Bene Gesserit counsel for nearly twenty years. At this crucial time, I have come to fill the gap and assist him in all of his needs."

Hawat remained implacable, trying not to show his irritation. "Your assistance is not presently required. I regret that you have made a long journey here for nothing, but I will help arrange for your passage back to Wallach IX."

She stiffened, showing slight indications of going into a tense stance, and in response, his own muscles tensed. Despite his age, the warrior Mentat had no doubts about his combat skills, but he was aware of Bene Gesserit fighting methods and would not make the mistake of underestimating this woman.

Instead, he tried to defuse the situation. "The Sisterhood's offer of another concubine and adviser is very generous, but we should have received an advance communication from the Mother Superior about this. Then the Duke himself could have provided them with his answer."

With a shrug, Xora said, "I only know that I have been sent here with a specific purpose, and I know what my value can be to House Atreides." Though neither of them had moved much, they seemed to be doing battle with their eyes, and with slight adjustments in their muscles and stances. Now she relaxed, just a little. "It is best that I remain here until Duke Leto returns, and I can make my case to him in person. If he still rejects me, I would hear it from his own lips. Lady Jessica's quarters should be empty. They will be sufficient for me, while I am waiting."

The Mentat's face did not reveal his sudden anger at her comment. "The Lady Jessica's quarters are indeed empty, and they will remain so. Do the Bene Gesserit believe it's so simple to install another woman into House Atreides? Into the role of mother for young Master Paul?" He saw a slight change in her expression, a hint of surprise. His words became sharper. "You have greatly underestimated both Duke Leto and his heir."

Hawat ran rapid projections to understand what Xora was trying to accomplish. In the past, he had clashed with Jessica, disagreeing with her on certain matters of principle, but even when they were at odds, he respected her. More importantly, he knew that Leto respected her, even though the Duke had been thrown entirely off balance when she chose her loyalty to the Sisterhood over him. After she retreated to Wallach IX, the Mentat had spent much time considering whether Jessica might have been tricking and manipulating the Duke all along.

This new Sister, though, was losing his respect from the outset.

"I never expected to be made so unwelcome," Xora said.

He stood unflinching. "I will find accommodations for you, but they'll not be the Lady Jessica's quarters, nor will they be in Castle Caladan. We have stringent security protocols." He paused, softened a little. "Out of courtesy, I shall let you remain on planet Caladan until the matter can be resolved."

She bristled. "But you are not the Duke here, are you?"

"No. But I protect him. And you are not his concubine until he tells you so."

WHILE THUFIR HAWAT blocked Xora from barging into the castle, Paul was upstairs in his mother's rooms, unaware of the confrontation. Ostensibly, he had gone to Jessica's empty quarters looking for a filmbook they had watched together; he wanted to see it again, not because he had forgotten the material, but because he wanted to view it with a different perspective now that she was gone.

When Jessica initially showed Paul the filmbook, Leto had called it a Bene Gesserit propaganda piece. But she had patiently pointed out the value in it. She had convinced the Duke, and Paul in turn, that it accurately described long-ago events surrounding the death of the founder of the Mother School, Raquella Berto-Anirul.

Now, holding the filmbook in his hands, Paul recalled his mother's exact words, and he began to think deeply about the differences between history, legends, and propaganda. He heard her words clearly in his mind: "Long ago, as the old woman lay dying, factions fought for control of the Sisterhood, arguing over some matter of internal dogma. Since the end of that schism, for ten thousand years, the Bene Gesserit order has operated under a unified moral front. Ever since the overthrow of the thinking machines, their mission has been to improve the human race, seeking to enhance our qualities and potential."

Paul had asked her what the ancient schism was about, but she'd been reluctant to talk about the Sisterhood's internal teachings, even as she shared aspects of Bene Gesserit training and history with him. Paul missed her.

Now, as he pondered, two uniformed castle servants entered through the main door that Paul had left open. They were startled to find him there.

"Please excuse us, young Master!" the larger man said, taken aback. He carried a cleaning bucket, while the other servant held an armload of fresh linens. "There's a woman talking to Thufir Hawat, here from offworld. She announced that she's taking up residence here in your mother's quarters, but Hawat has not permitted her past the main castle gates."

The other servant said, "We came to make sure the rooms were ready for visitors, if need be."

Embarrassed, the two men scurried out before Paul could question them further. A woman from offworld? Asking to move into his mother's quarters? There had to be some mistake. . . .

He couldn't forget the two shadowy women who had tried to kill him and

Duncan the other night. Filled with dark foreboding, he stormed downstairs, looking for Thufir.

PAUL HEARD THE old Mentat's raised voice as well as an unfamiliar woman's. They were in a heated argument. Without hesitation, he stalked out to the gates, where Thufir and a striking Bene Gesserit Sister were standing face-to-face. They fell awkwardly silent when Paul approached.

The Mentat bowed slightly in the direction of the ducal heir. "Pardon my lack of decorum in this matter, young Master, but we're having a problem. I hoped to resolve it without disturbing you." He was cool and professional, but Paul sensed that Thufir was embarrassed.

"So I heard." He looked at the woman, who appraised him with intense blue eyes as if running him through an analytical scanner. She seemed surprised to see him. "The servants claimed that someone had asked to move into my mother's rooms, but that will not be possible." He stepped closer. "With my father gone, I make decisions on the Duke's behalf, and I am not inclined to open her quarters to a stranger, especially since we do not know when the Lady of Caladan will return."

The Sister, whom Thufir introduced as Xora, responded quickly. "Jessica will not return. The Bene Gesserit will choose another assignment for her." She cocked an eyebrow and seemed to stare right through him. "So, you are the son, the one who caused so much turmoil in the Sisterhood." She smiled at him with an approximation of warmth and compassion. "Do you know the origin of your name? Paul? It means 'rare, scarce, small.' It seems a fitting name for you."

The protective Mentat stepped closer to him. Paul tensed, remembering the women who had attacked him, but he did not show it. He frowned. "How have I caused turmoil in the Sisterhood?"

Xora laughed. "By being born!" She sighed, and her entire demeanor changed. "I have a son, too, a few years older than you. At least Jessica got to raise hers . . ."

Paul stood stern, like a Duke. "And my mother still has much to train me in—when she returns." He could tell she was attempting to work some of her Bene Gesserit wiles on him, but Jessica had taught him how to shrug them off.

"I hope we can be friends. I have much to teach you, too, now that your mother is gone."

Paul looked at Thufir, then at her with rising suspicion. "What do you mean? Why are you here?"

"Why, I am your father's new concubine, of course, assigned by Mother Superior Harishka herself. Caladan is my new home—which is why I intend to move into the appropriate castle quarters."

Paul could not believe his ears. "Did my father approve this?" His gaze burned through her, and he swung to face Thufir. "Did he request it?" Paul knew that the Duke had been hurt and angry with his mother, but he couldn't believe he would do this.

The Mentat straightened. "He did not inform me before he departed."

"Then I don't believe it," Paul said. "He didn't tell me either."

Xora shifted, paced around outside the gate and came back. She had a catlike way of moving, with coiled power in her muscles. She was trying to pull on their heartstrings. "I have no place else to go. You can't send me back to Wallach IX in shame!"

Paul looked at Thufir, remembering that this was his decision now, in Leto's absence. "What are we to do with this woman? She cannot stay here."

The Mentat's voice was hard. "I warn against letting her insinuate herself further into our lives, young Master. For the time being, we can find her accommodations in Cala City, if she insists on remaining until our Duke returns, although that could be some time."

Xora's demeanor changed. "My apologies if we had a bad beginning. I did not want it to happen this way." She did not look sorry at all. "You mean to put me in some sort of commercial lodging?"

"There are many pleasant establishments in Cala City," Paul said. "If you believe you will be staying on our planet, you should be glad of the opportunity. Staying in town will be an excellent introduction to the real Caladan."

AS SHE WAS summarily sent away, escorted from Castle Caladan by a young, low-ranking Atreides guard, Xora reassessed her plan. She had to think swiftly, be flexible. But she didn't have enough information to decide what to do about Paul Atreides.

Jessica's son was still alive!

Taula and Aislan must have arrived a week or more ago. By now they should have had ample time to attack and eliminate the young man, but if he was serving as the acting Duke and remaining within the security perimeter of the castle, how easily would the two Sisters have been able to plan a strike?

Many things had not gone as planned. Xora had expected some resistance to becoming the Duke's new concubine, but as Ruthine had said, if Leto's son were killed, his emotional walls would be down. He would need someone, and she could take advantage of such a vulnerability. Even though she had not been allowed to leave the Mother School for seventeen years, the Bene Gesserit had trained her in those skills. And she remembered.

Duke Leto was absent, so she needed to learn his destination, the purpose of his trip, and how soon he would be back. It would all affect her timing.

She expected that Taula and Aislan were still at large and nearby, possibly lying low in Cala City—where the Atreides guard was now taking her. Xora would find the other women and work with them to complete their deadly mission. Or Xora would do it herself, if only she could get into the castle and work her way close to the unsuspecting boy.

Much had changed. It unsettled her, yet she knew that changes and twists had a way of providing unexpected opportunities. She let the guard guide her down to the town, but Xora knew she would be back.

The moment just before a secret is exposed can be fraught with peril.
—Bene Gesserit training manual, "Analysis of Threats"

Count Hasimir Fenring did not gloat or boast, did not need to, but after proving his foresight time and time again, he wished Shaddam would listen to him more often.

Retreating into his duties as Spice Minister, Fenring had returned to Arrakis, where he would continue other intrigues in the name of the Emperor. He still felt stung that his friend so carelessly disregarded his advice against the bloated spectacle with the treasury ship. Rather than be part of it, the Count had withdrawn to the desert planet. And now this. . . .

Once again, as he had done for days, he went over images of the disastrous crash of the ship following yet another embarrassing speech from the terrorist Jaxson Aru. At least Grix Dardik was preoccupied with other projections at the moment, and Fenring did not need to deal with the Mentat's eccentricities on top of everything else. Such a brilliant mind, and such a difficult personality!

Lady Margot entered the Residency quarters she shared with her husband. She leaned close to kiss the side of his face. Her soft cheeks were flushed and dewy with a freshness so different from the leathery Arrakeen natives. He knew she must have just spent hours in the sealed greenhouse that served as her private sanctuary here. He could smell the mist and vegetation on her, in sharp contrast to the more prevalent dusty odors of unwashed bodies on this hellish planet.

She joined him in reviewing the horrific images again. "You warned him against holding the event, and yet he went on with it anyway." She chuckled as a thought occurred to her. "One wonders if you may have a hint of prescience, my love."

"It would take truly supernatural prescience to have predicted this." Fenring expanded the images, studied the wrecked Promenade Wing. "I've often joined him on that very balcony. For the first time, I'm glad I was here on Arrakis rather than on Kaitain."

Margot's expression flickered, and he saw her calming her emotions. "You and I would have been in attendance, right at the Emperor's side. And this time you would not have had Duke Leto Atreides to spot the threat in time to help."

"Yes, hmmmm. Leto was conveniently away this time . . ." He panned across the bodies strewn in the plaza, the smoke curling into the sky. "Shaddam will be vindictive. I wouldn't be surprised if he makes even more heavy-handed, reactionary decrees."

"I'm happy you are not there as a target for his ire. Best that we remain here on Arrakis." Margot stroked his cheek. "Keep our distance and do our work."

COUNT FENRING DID not expect good news, particularly from the smuggler chief Esmar Tuek. He was pleasantly surprised.

Tuek had bluffed his way past the Residency's outer ring of guards, then was given the proper pass phrases for the high-security area. The smuggler leader was a hard-bitten man with shaggy hair, darkly tanned skin, and a worn but well-maintained stillsuit. After being searched and stripped of his weapons, Tuek faced the Count in his administrative office, grinning through cracked lips. "I have information that will be worth a great deal to you, sir."

Fenring did not play the smuggler's game. "Ahhh, hmmm, I thought we had an understanding? Providing me with unfiltered information is your part of the bargain, and in exchange I turn a blind eye to your operations. If you wish to change the terms now, ahhhh . . ."

Filled with enthusiasm, the smuggler did not back down. "You'll understand the worth of what I'm about to tell you—so much so, in fact, that I will let you pay me whatever you think is warranted." When Tuek's grin widened, Fenring realized he had never previously noticed the man's teeth, which were brown and pitted. "We found them!"

"Who, or what, have you found?"

"The spice thieves we've been seeking! Extraction, processing, and shipping . . . it's a major facility in the deep desert, operating without Imperial oversight, and far more extensive than anything my smugglers have." His expression darkened. "It's the reason my Rulla had to die."

Fenring summoned the housekeeper, who hovered in the hallway outside his offices. "Bring us a pitcher of water! Cold water."

As the small desert woman scurried away down the corridor, Tuek produced a detailed chart printed on fine spice paper. He spread a topographic map of the mountains and desert basins on Fenring's desk. The Count leaned over to study the cartographic markings.

Tuek's gaze lingered on Fenring's face. "One of my men died to get this information, and another barely escaped with his life."

Fenring had just managed to orient himself with the charts when the shrunken Fremen housekeeper hurried in with a pitcher of water and two goblets. The old woman poured them each a goblet, but could not hide the hungry look in her deep blue eyes.

The smuggler leader took one goblet and drank gratefully, while Fenring continued to study the chart. "Tell me, ahhh, where might we find these thieves?"

The smuggler extended a finger, traced lines of steep mountains and rugged canyons. "The brigands have rebuilt the old Orgiz refinery complex."

"Orgiz, hmmm . . . That was destroyed decades ago."

"Indeed," said Tuek. "It has been resurrected."

From a hidden pocket in his stillsuit, Tuek produced a crystal, and glanced around Fenring's office until he located the Count's always-present player unit. Then he projected the images that Benak had taken—spice silos, barracks, a landing area large enough for carryalls, unmarked transit craft taking off with loads of spice.

Tuek added, "This is no mere scrounging operation, sir. Considering the carryall activity, we believe they have full-fledged harvesters and factory crawlers out on the sands. I find it highly offensive."

Leaning closer to the grainy images, Fenring noted hundreds of personnel working the site. "Where did they acquire all the equipment, and so many workers? How can they hide such major operations?" He dropped his voice to a deep rumble. "And who is behind all of it?"

"They are careful to hide their identity." Tuek drained his goblet and refilled it from the pitcher without asking. "They captured my man Corvir Dur and drowned him in a spice silo. Benak barely slipped away with this information, because he knew its importance."

"Sounds like your men were sloppy for one of them to be captured." Fenring pursed his lips. "I thought your people were good, Tuek."

"My people are exceptional. We found something that your Imperial scouts and Harkonnen search teams could not."

Fenring conceded the point. "Very well, hmmmm. We'll eradicate these thieves so that you and your crew will be the only sanctioned smugglers on Arrakis."

Plans rolled through the Count's mind. He considered calling an entire Sardaukar legion to grind these illicit operations to dust, but a chill went down his back. If he told the Emperor about the Orgiz refinery, Shaddam would know that his friend had lied to him, or at least exaggerated his success. He would be outraged to learn that Count Fenring had not, after all, taken care of the problem, as he'd reported. After Jaxson Aru's recent outrageous attack, he decided this was certainly not the time to reveal the extent of these operations on Arrakis.

"We already blamed Rulla for the black-market activities," Tuek said. "What will you say to the Emperor now?"

"Nothing." Fenring pinched the bridge of his nose. "I always meant for us to punish the culprits without Imperial intervention. We'll take care of it ourselves."

Upset, the smuggler said, "My people don't have the weapons or personnel to take down a complex like that. We have already done our part." Tuek defiantly drank more water. "We located them. Now you deal with them."

"Hmmm, ahhhh, I will do precisely that." He gave a formal nod of appreciation. "I'll contact Baron Harkonnen. He also has a great deal at stake here." Fenring sipped his water. "Together we will wipe out Orgiz, capture any workers, and put them through extreme interrogation." He smiled again. "We will find out who is behind this."

Jaxson Aru treated Leto Atreides like a business associate, using illicit rebel funds to buy them both an extravagant dinner in the best restaurant aboard the Elegy transfer station. The rebel leader seemed disappointed that the wine list didn't include any Caladan vintages, then chided Leto for his lack of distribution.

"We are still building our customer base for those products," Leto said.

"Perhaps your wines will make up for your loss in moonfish exports."

Leto seethed, but said nothing to the jab.

Jaxson ordered expensive Kirana brandy. He acted as if he didn't have the blood of many thousands on his hands, as well as plans to cause much greater harm.

Sitting uncomfortably next to him, Leto could have acted falsely enthusiastic, but Jaxson would never have believed him. So he searched for just the right tone as he sipped his brandy, rolling the burn around in his mouth. Leto continued to stare out the numerous plaz windows that gave the transfer station a bright and airy feel. "Are you intending to cause harm to Elegy?" he finally asked. "Did Viscount Tull offend you somehow?"

Jaxson wiped his lips with a fine-spun napkin made from lichen fibers. "This is just a transfer point, Leto. I have reserved a stateroom on a private frigate outbound on the next Heighliner, which will arrive within"—he glanced at the chronometer on the wall—"an hour, so be ready. We'll talk business once we are underway. For now, let us just enjoy the good company."

Leto didn't enjoy the company at all, but he managed to pretend, always reminding himself that each small step forward would lead to the end of this violent rebellion.

When the Guild ship arrived, Jaxson produced documents and receipts, and they joined other passengers boarding the frigate that would transfer them to the enormous hold of the Heighliner. The private compartment he and Jaxson shared had one small windowport, which at the moment showed only the inte-

rior of the hold. Countless vessels hung in place, each representing different noble houses, merchants, ambassadors, enemies, allies, or complete strangers. The
wealthy who owned private vessels mixed with the poor traveling to some new
hope . . . like countless fish in countless separated tide pools, Leto thought.

Once their passenger vessel was locked against the curved inner wall of the
Guild ship, Jaxson settled back and turned his weapon-like gaze toward his companion.

"Now, we can finally get down to business. For my next target, I've chosen to
be less overt, without such a grand and spectacular show." Jaxson smiled at him.
"I thought you'd appreciate that, my friend."

Leto wanted to shout each time the man said "my friend," but he kept a neutral expression in place. "Many are incensed by your bloody spectacles, Jaxson."

The rebel leader let out an impatient sigh. "Oh, there will be a great deal of
death and suffering, but I won't let myself be the scapegoat. I was willing to accept the responsibility before, but this time we'll let the Corrinos take the blame
and hatred from every side." He chuckled.

"That sounds like quite an accomplishment," Leto said, knowing he had to
gather and file away every possible detail. If he was this close and involved, maybe
he could stop the tragedy from happening. "What is the target?"

"Have you heard of Issimo III? A small, unimportant world ruled by an im-
poverished noble family, House Grandine. Earl Grandine has no clout in the
Landsraad, and few people know of or sympathize with his plight." Jaxson
grinned widely. "But they will."

Leto knew nothing about Issimo or House Grandine. The Imperium was
vast, with thousands of star systems and ten times that many planets. "What is
Earl Grandine's plight? Something you caused?"

"No," Jaxson retorted, then said in a quieter voice, "Not yet. Issimo III is
sparsely populated, probably fewer than five hundred thousand inhabitants even
though it was settled two centuries ago. Its sun is somewhat unstable, and in the
last five years it has transitioned into an active phase with intense solar flares."
He leaned closer as if revealing a juicy bit of gossip. "Those flares have caused
great damage to the environment. Radiation storms and yearslong drought devastated their agriculture, wiped out their crops, and now the people have little
to eat. Earl Grandine does not have the wealth to buy support or to bring in aid,
new equipment, different strains of crops. Because its population is so small and
Grandine's financial influence is so minimal, no one in the Landsraad hears his
pleas. But in his great 'benevolence,' Shaddam Corrino has dispatched an Imperial corps of engineers, a small group of a hundred or so bearing relief supplies.
They've been working for months planting new crops that can withstand the flux
from the solar flares. The people of Issimo III will have enough food to eat and
they will shower the Emperor with their gratitude."

"Whatever Shaddam's reasons," Leto said, "it was the right thing to do."

Jaxson's eyes flashed with intensity. He showed no notice of a slight shift as the Heighliner disengaged and began to move, but Leto knew that the thrum passing through the entire hull signaled that the Navigator was preparing to activate the Holtzman engines.

"Yes, I intend to take that away from him," Jaxson said. "It's quite perfect. In fact, I was inspired by you, Leto . . . or at least the tragedy on Caladan."

Leto was troubled. "How so? What tragedy?" He instantly thought of Jessica.

"The moonfish dying off—the deadly, invasive mite that Count Glossu Rabban introduced into your fishery industries."

Leto dreaded what this madman would say next.

"My people have obtained samples of the modified grains Shaddam's engineers are now planting on Issimo III, and we've adapted a deadly blight that specifically attacks those crops. You and I will release the blight. We'll pretend to be part of the Imperial corps, who are there as saviors to all those poor wretches. Their crops will wither and die after all, the people will starve, and they'll have no doubt that it was the Emperor who brought this blight. Word will get out, and everyone will blame House Corrino. Such a cruel act—an attempted genocide—is simply unconscionable, and the Noble Commonwealth will reap more and more support." Jaxson laughed out loud. "It is wonderful."

Leto knew he could not let this happen. "So House Grandine and their suffering people will be more innocent victims for you. They'll pay the price so you can get your message out."

"The Noble Commonwealth message, which will benefit all of us," said Jaxson.

"It doesn't benefit the people of Issimo III." Leto hardened his voice, but he knew if he pushed back too hard, Jaxson might become suspicious, might even abandon him here. Instead, Leto offered an alternative. "As you've said to me many times, we have numerous reasons to dislike the corrupt Imperium and resent the power of the Corrino Emperors, but you've not shown that the Noble Commonwealth is any better. If your acts are all reckless and destructive, how do you expect to win widespread loyalty? You must earn it by offering a better alternative, not through brute force." His thoughts raced ahead. "Prove in a tangible way that you are far better and care more for those people than Shaddam does."

Jaxson Aru looked defensive. For a long moment he stared out the windowport at all the other ships aboard the Heighliner. He wrestled with his anger and finally said, "How would you accomplish that?"

"We will offer a better alternative," Leto said. "I know the Noble Commonwealth has resources. You proved already that you have secret accounts possibly still connected to CHOAM."

Jaxson stiffened at that. "The Ur-Director of CHOAM publicly disowned me. You know that."

"Knowing and believing are two different things," Leto said. "I don't care where you get the money—I just know you have access to it. If Shaddam is making a token effort by sending a small corps of engineers to Issimo III, then you, Jaxson, can do far more. One of those extravagant gestures you're so fond of."

The man brightened somewhat. "I'm listening."

"For the cost of the destruction you're planning, not to mention the complexity of expecting others to understand the subtle blame you're trying to arrange, why not simply gather unmarked vessels and fill them with grain? Send massive amounts of agricultural equipment, greenhouse domes, food supplies so that all the people on Issimo III survive. Your rescue shipment will make Shaddam's efforts seem pathetic and embarrassing. You will demonstrate to everyone that the Noble Commonwealth serves the people of the Imperium, unlike the token effort that Shaddam Corrino made."

Jaxson Aru took a moment to digest the possibility. He turned away, and his shoulders were set, but not in anger.

Leto said, "Your grand gesture will win over hearts and minds, not just engender horror. The people will feel an appreciation for the Noble Commonwealth instead of just a hatred for the Corrinos. They will lose confidence in the Corrinos, though. Trust me, this is a better path to victory."

Though Jaxson remained doubtful, he gave a slow nod and leaned back in his seat. The stateroom and the entire passenger frigate vibrated as the engine power built up. "You are an unexpected man, Leto Atreides. And you may well become a great asset to us."

Around them, the ship, and reality itself, lurched as the immense Heighliner folded space.

Measure the journey not in distance, but in the toll it takes on the heart.

—Zensunni saying

At last she was on her way to Caladan, but Jessica had never been so terrified in her life.

Thanks to the intervention of Viscount Tull, along with substantial extra payments to the Spacing Guild, her trip was expedited. Giandro seemed to have mysterious connections, and he called in certain favors that he refused to explain to her. He would maintain the quiet fiction from his own manor house, and she would have time to complete her mission. The Sisterhood would never know she had left.

Still, Jessica was constrained by the routes and schedules of the Guild, and there was no direct Heighliner passage from Elegy to Caladan. The Viscount found a route with four segments and as many different Guild ships, making connections from one Heighliner to another with the shortest waiting time possible.

Dressed in a traveling coat, hat, and the common clothing of Elegy, Jessica waited with other passengers aboard the orbital station above the planet, watching the bustle of dump box and thrust box activity on a huge wall screen.

She found her faint reflection in the polished plaz startling. Her physical transformation had been accomplished in a matter of hours. The Viscount's personal stylist had cut her hair short and dyed it a dark brown, and the loose fit of the clothes disguised her physical form. A suitcase rested beside her, containing personal articles and travel necessities that Tull's servants had swiftly put together for her.

Though Jessica was preoccupied with her own fears for Paul, she realized how considerate and helpful Giandro had been, asking for nothing in return. His deep sense of honor and compassion reminded her of Leto. Such men were rare, and she counted herself fortunate to have known two of them in her life.

But Giandro Tull was not Leto Atreides, and she couldn't imagine ever feeling the same about him. Of course, the Bene Gesserit didn't want her to feel anything at all, merely to accept her assignment and prove herself. But she had put her body and her soul into her relationship with Leto, and they had been through experiences that bonded them forever.

Before it all cracked apart.

Jessica was supposed to reach Caladan in just under three days, a time that relied upon tight connections, transferring from one Heighliner to another. Now in the orbiting station, she kept watching a chronometer on the wall and looking outside for the gigantic ship to arrive above Elegy.

In the near distance, she noticed a ripple in space, and out of that ripple emerged a Heighliner, as if the cosmos were giving birth to the ship. The immense vessel crawled toward the orbital transfer station, and the call came for the passengers to board their shuttles and frigates to be moved over to the big ship.

As she prepared to take her place in line, a uniformed Guildsman strode up to her and gave a slight bow. He had a slightly misshapen head, as if some tremendous push and pull had distorted his skull. "Lady Jessica?" His voice was high-pitched, like a barely contained squeal. "Viscount Tull has arranged for an expedited escort at each stop in your journey, to make certain you do not miss a connection."

She was surprised Giandro had that much influence with the Guild, but she appreciated the gesture more than she could express. "Thank you. I have no time to waste."

The uniformed man looked at her strangely. "Neither does the Spacing Guild."

For the next three days, she met a series of devoted attendants. They took turns managing her movements from the orbital platform to the Heighliner, then the next transfer at the following star system. They also shielded her from too much attention. Jessica traveled as efficiently and as invisibly as possible.

She did not miss a connection.

CALADAN.

Through standard viewers, Jessica looked longingly at the green-blue planet that had appeared beneath the great Guild ship. Her eyes grew misty as she saw the precious gem of a world. All of her Bene Gesserit calming techniques could not keep her pulse from racing. She was so close to home.

The Sisterhood had given her many useful skills, and she could use her abilities now. She couldn't reveal that she had slipped away from Elegy, and she would not bring down another Bene Gesserit punishment on herself or Duke Leto.

But she *would* save Paul.

If she was not too late.

For an assassin, the choice of an assigned target is normally not personal.
But it can be.

—*The Assassin's Handbook*

The falsified documents identified Egan Saar as a merchant seeking to expand the trilium market, but his true business on Caladan had nothing to do with commerce. Fortunately, trilium was an uninteresting and inexpensive material used in construction, and the people of Cala City found nothing remarkable about it. The false identity allowed Saar to blend in, to watch and listen, and to cultivate his plans.

He would take as long as he needed.

Feyd-Rautha Harkonnen paid him well, yes, but Saar had never been interested in money. Before the famed Ginaz School had been destroyed fifteen years ago, interrupting his instruction, his core identity had been as a Swordmaster, and his subsequent unorthodox training only sharpened him. Having accepted this mission, he would do the job out of pride, no matter how many solaris were transferred into his account.

Saar paid for rooms at three different inns so that he could move about and not draw suspicion. His eyes and ears were as keen as his blade. Saar made no friends nor did he pick fights, though he occasionally bought a drink for someone who seemed talkative.

In his guise as a merchant, he made estimates of House Atreides finances, learned about the devastating invasive mites that had swept through the moonfish pools—Rabban's retaliatory scheme, he assumed. But Feyd's strike would be much more painful to the Duke. Saar would make sure of it.

He learned that the people of Caladan loved their Duke, calling him Leto the Just. Though the disguised Swordmaster pressed, he found few people willing to speak disparaging words about House Atreides. Although this complicated the process of gathering intelligence, it also made him realize that killing someone close to Duke Leto would be a devastating blow not only to him, but to the people overall. Feyd—and presumably Baron Harkonnen—would consider it a bonus.

In the tavern at one of the inns, the Song of the Sea, Saar bought ale for two new acquaintances, carpenters rebuilding town storefronts destroyed in a series of bombings. From their conversation, he learned that Leto Atreides had recently left Caladan for an unknown reason, and no one seemed to know where he had gone.

His new friends toasted him for the ale, toasted their Duke, then spoke with admiration about young Master Paul Atreides. One of the men even insisted to Saar that his construction boss might be interested in placing a large order for trillium; Saar took the name, though he had no intention of ever contacting the man.

Even if the people of Caladan were open and seemingly warmhearted, they respected their Duke's privacy. They talked among themselves in low voices, expressing concern for their leader, but since Saar was a stranger, they kept him out of their conversations. Nevertheless, he heard enough because he was attentive to nuances of words and phrases, and he noted at which point the conversation petered out.

He gathered that Leto and his bound concubine were having severe relationship difficulties. The woman no longer shared quarters with the Duke and was no longer in the castle, but the townspeople were closemouthed and determined not to gossip, especially when they saw him eavesdropping. Saar found that very interesting. Feyd had not given him any of those details.

His opportunities took a sudden turn days later, after he spent a few nights in a different inn, and then returned to the Song of the Sea. With his tattered cloak, he looked as if he'd had a hard day of business around Cala City. When he entered the tavern in late afternoon, before the fishing boats had returned for the day, he saw an out-of-place woman, beautiful and poised. She wore fine white garments adorned with green and black, the Atreides colors. She had bronze hair, and striking blue eyes. Observing closely, Saar noted that the woman had a Bene Gesserit way about her.

She argued with the innkeeper, but her dismay and displeasure were not directed at him, and the portly man with a full mustache understood that as well. He leaned closer, gave her an earnest look, as if sharing her pain. "It is the best I can do, my Lady. We run a clean, well-respected establishment, but I am sorry if the accommodations are not what you're accustomed to. This is what Thufir Hawat arranged."

"I am the Duke's concubine sent here by the Sisterhood," she retorted. "By rights, my quarters should be in Castle Caladan. Hawat is mad with power—I could see the ambition in his eyes. How can he oust me and send me off to stay in an inn? Vindictive Mentat!"

Listening intently, Egan Saar felt a tingle of excitement on his skin.

The innkeeper looked sympathetic, but Saar saw the flash of indignation that crossed his face. "Apologies, my Lady, but Duke Leto is gone, and he made it abundantly clear that in his absence, Thufir Hawat speaks for him and makes decisions in conjunction with young Master Paul. Perhaps if you spoke to the lad?"

The woman scoffed. "Young Paul would do me no favors." With a visible effort, she imposed control on herself. "Very well, I'll stay here until the Duke returns from his journey, and then we will resolve this."

The woman accepted the key from the innkeeper and stalked away. At the foot of the stairs leading up to the guest rooms, she paused, remembering to show courtesy, and turned back to the man. "I apologize, sir. I understand you have been put in an awkward position, and you are doing your best. I am the Lady of Caladan, and I will remember you once all this is resolved."

On high alert, Egan Saar decided it was the best time to return to his own room. In doing so he was able to watch the indignant concubine go to a door down the hall, the suite, of course.

Now he knew where she was.

He had been here for six days biding his time, trying to figure out how to slip into the castle and attack the Duke's son or an equally devastating target. Now this opportunity had fallen right into his lap.

I am the Lady of Caladan. . . .

In the countless battles he had fought as a Swordmaster, Egan Saar knew that luck was sometimes a significant factor. Twice, he had killed an opponent not because his own skill was superior, but because the victim had stumbled at the wrong moment, or been distracted by a buzzing fly.

Now luck had again worked in his favor.

The Duke's concubine was here in this inn. She was vulnerable, and the fact that she was quarreling with her Duke, that she had been ousted from the castle, only made the potential pain greater. Unless Leto truly hated her, which Saar doubted, the Duke's despair would be immeasurable after she was murdered. He would blame himself for whatever had happened to this woman, and his guilt would crush him.

Smiling, the twisted Swordmaster returned to his quarters to sharpen his blade and prepare himself. Feyd-Rautha would most definitely approve.

CALADAN HAD CHANGED little in centuries. Except for those who worked specific night duties or late business, most people got up early and bedded down not long after dark.

Saar waited until three hours past midnight when the Song of the Sea was quiet and full of shadows. The drinking and singing in the tavern below had stopped after the innkeeper chased the last customers out.

The concubine's room was quiet, and no one had disturbed her since a serving boy delivered a tray of food at dinnertime. The silence and darkness behind her door told the Swordmaster all he needed to know. No doubt the woman had fallen asleep, regretting her argument with Leto. She would be preoccupied with domestic matters such as how to salvage her relationship. Not even a stray thought about an assassin.

Saar crept along the inn's narrow hall. The other guest rooms were closed and latched. Caladan culture allowed for a simple privacy lock, but he had broken through far greater security. He easily moved the latch with just a quiet *snick* and eased open the door into the concubine's darkened room.

"I have nothing to steal, if you're a thief," said a woman's hard voice.

His eyes adjusted. She had left her shutters open, and moonlight streamed into her suite, the second floor up from the street. He stepped inside and closed the door behind him, holding his sword. "I am no thief." He flicked the latch again to secure the door.

He didn't have much time—nor would he need it. As a Swordmaster, Saar enjoyed a vigorous duel, not a simple slaughter, but if the woman screamed, the commotion would bring people running. He had to kill her and be gone.

He lunged toward the bed with his sword raised, but the concubine, in a black sleeping gown, moved like an angry cat, springing from the mattress and dodging his strike. She flung the sheets at Saar and twisted them around so they caught the point of his sword, dragging it down. He snatched back the weapon, and its razor edge slashed the fabric.

With a yell, the woman threw herself on him, clawing at his eyes. From somewhere she produced a dagger and swung it at him without hesitation, meaning to gut him. He squirmed out of the way, but her knife edge slashed down his arm.

"Guards!" she yelled, then lowered her voice to him. "I'll kill you myself before they get here."

He swung the sword in a hard, vicious blow, which she parried with her dagger, but the smaller weapon was no match for the sheer weight of his blade. His steel rang and he knocked her weapon away, onto the floor.

"Who are you?" she demanded.

"Your executioner."

She flung a water pitcher at him with perfect aim and struck his shoulder hard. He was amused. "The Duke trains his concubine to fight well."

"The Bene Gesserit trained me."

Now he heard loud voices in the corridor. Someone pounded on the door, and a heavy shoulder crashed against it. The latch would last only a few seconds more, if the concubine could evade him for that long.

Saar could see anger flaring in her, which he knew was a weakness. She threw herself at him screaming, a move that would have distracted any other opponent. She tried to land a heavy kick to his chest, but he caught her ankle, threw her to the bed. Before she could thrash, he raised his blade and brought it down with all his might, trying to decapitate her, but she spun out of the way.

She shot toward him from the side, and kicked his weapon hand so hard that he dropped the sword. Nothing like this had ever happened to him before.

She kicked the sword away, making it clatter against a wall, and placed herself between him and the weapon.

For a moment, they stood weaponless, glaring at one another in the moonlit room, their gazes flitting around desperately. Both of them saw her dagger on the floor at the same time, to one side and about the same distance from each of them. She lunged toward it, but he got to it first. In one smooth movement, he took up the knife, arced around, and slammed it into her chest. Even mortally wounded, she struck the side of his head with her fist, then fell on her back on the bed. Leaning over her, he pulled the dagger free, wiped the blood on her sleeping gown as she lay dying, and pocketed the weapon. Retrieving his sword, he looked back at her.

She lay on the bed, and blood spouted from her chest. Her face twitched and convulsed as she died.

He heard men throwing themselves against the door, attempting to break in. Wood splintered.

In a flash, Egan Saar sprang to the window, swung himself out, dropped to a secondary roof. He ran along it to jump onto a shed, before lowering himself to the street. He melted into the alley shadows even as the first horrified shouts rang out.

DAWN WAS JUST glimmering on the eastern horizon when Thufir Hawat got to the inn. Paul and Duncan came with him, looking grim. A minute later, they all stood staring at the woman's body and the blood-soaked sheets. Scarlet spray had fanned across the bed and the back wall. He remembered her indignant demands at the gate of Castle Caladan, her clear entitlement as the Duke's supposed new concubine.

But this. . . .

Out in the hallway, the innkeeper was violently ill, again and again. Horrified guests told their stories, trying to sound important, but Hawat quickly determined that no one had actually seen anything. The assassin or assassins had slipped away through the window, and no one had attempted pursuit until it was far too late.

"Why would someone kill Xora?" Paul asked, shaking his head. "Did the Bene Gesserit send her here and then dispatch an assassin after her?"

"That makes no sense," Duncan said.

"I concur," said Hawat, "it makes no logical sense."

Paul said, "Could it have something to do with the two women who attacked us in the streets? Those were skilled fighters, trained killers. But why would they target Xora? No one even knew her here."

Hawat drew his brows together as he went into deep concentration. "I wonder if this suggests some revolt inside the Bene Gesserit Sisterhood, factions turning against each other."

Paul paled. "My mother . . ."

Still studying the room, Hawat noted the discarded water pitcher, the slashed sheets, clear signs of a struggle. "She fought her attackers vigorously, but they were stronger and quicker."

Duncan pointed out, "If Xora was a Bene Gesserit, she would not have been an easy target. A common thief could not have made quick work of her."

"This was no mere burglar or cutpurse." Hawat shook his head, trying to derive some meaning from the shocked expression on the dead woman's face. "Duke Leto is gone, as is Gurney. Who would come here now?"

"They were trying to kill me the other night," Paul said, "But Xora was never accepted as my father's concubine—he didn't even know about her."

The Mentat looked up. "Someone intended to send a clear message." He shook his head. "But whatever it is, the message is not clear to me."

The timing of information can be as useful, or as dangerous, as the information itself.

— CHOAM memorandum

R abban!" the Baron roared. Buoyed up by his suspensor belt, he moved through the Harkonnen headquarters in Carthag. "Rabban!"

Members of the household staff wisely withdrew to hidden places or found suddenly urgent duties they needed to perform. His round face was flushed with anger and anxiety, and he had trouble breathing.

It had taken all of his control to hide his reaction to Fenring's news so that the Count would suspect nothing. He had managed to respond with shock and indignation, promising to offer all possible assistance, to gather his Harkonnen troops and pull together an assault team. He still felt ice in the pit of his enormous belly. The insidious Fenring would discover everything!

"Rabban!" the Baron yelled again, and his muscular nephew finally appeared, sweaty and panting from running.

"What is it, Uncle?"

"That damnable Fenring knows about our refinery complex, and he is hell-bent on razing it to the ground. He wants my help!"

Rabban looked dumbfounded and confused. "But you can't let him go there. He'll learn about our involvement."

The Baron often wanted to slap his nephew, and this was one of those times. "Somehow, you let the site be found, and now our secret will be exposed. Our only hope is for you to get there in time to scuttle the whole complex before Fenring makes me drag our army there."

"Scuttle it?" Rabban asked as if he didn't understand the meaning of the word.

"Blow it up. Level it. Crush it down to the last rivet and structural girder. Dispose of it, before the Count makes us do it for him."

"But, Uncle, that will cost—"

"It will cost much more if he discovers any clue that ties back to House Harkonnen. We have no choice, and we are out of time."

"Should I evacuate the crew? Maybe we can empty the spice silos, salvage—"

Though it sickened him, the Baron could not take such a chance. "If even one person slips away and Fenring interrogates him, then all is lost. We'll keep squeezing more spice out of this cursed planet, but we need to eliminate Orgiz. Leave no witnesses, no evidence. Go! You don't have time to waste."

"Scuttle it . . ." Rabban rolled the word around in his mouth. He seemed to like that part, at least.

THE NEWS WAS intriguing, even delightful, and Piter de Vries could not wait to share it with Baron Harkonnen and even Rabban. "I knew that man was up to something." His operatives had done excellent work in spotting him. He tapped his fingertips together as his thoughts raced in thousands of different directions, unreeling countless possibilities. "Gurney Halleck is not a man who takes vacations."

After the Atreides man had been captured and drugged into a state of long-term unconsciousness, Piter had calculated the best next move. Halleck had clashed with Beast Rabban numerous times, and the Harkonnens wanted him dead. But the twisted Mentat decided that Halleck was more valuable to the Baron *alive*, at least for the time being.

With Spacing Guild travel from Parmentier temporarily interrupted, Piter was able to whisk the captive away and hide him inside a sealed shipping container. He studied available routes to determine how quickly he could bring the captive to Giedi Prime, or to Arrakis, where the Baron currently was.

Frustrated with the lack of convenient options, he found an outbound Heighliner departing soon for Lankiveil, and decided that it was the most expedient alternative. Rabban's holdings on Lankiveil had recently been the target of an unexpected, illicit retaliatory strike by the Atreides, and Piter thought that the Beast would also like to exact revenge on this Gurney Halleck. He would let the Baron decide, and earn his favor.

Upon searching Halleck's baliset case, Piter found only a well-worn musical instrument, but no hidden diplomatic communiqué, no smuggled packet that would explain why Halleck had been traveling alone and heading to Kaitain. Still, the twisted Mentat did not underestimate the sheer value of the captive. He couldn't wait to tell the Baron!

When their ship finally reached Lankiveil and the Harkonnen group descended to Rabban's coastal holdings near the fur-whale fjords, Piter directed his companions to move Gurney Halleck to the office of a marine processing facility. The air was rank with the smell of fish, and Piter heard thrumming machinery, the clang of boat bells on the water, and the voices of workers in another part of the building. Only half of the facility was in operation, heavily damaged during the recent Atreides raid.

The twisted Mentat gulped a vial of sapho juice laced with a mixture of other drugs. The warmth and buzzing worked its way to the back of his mind as soon as the liquid went down his throat. So many ideas, so many possibilities!

Through a window, he watched a construction crew outside working to shore up a dock that had partially burned and collapsed in the Atreides sneak attack. Halleck would have to pay for this insult. Then again, he had many things to atone for. It would be a very pleasurable experience.

On his left, the captive lay on a medical stretcher on the floor, not moving. A constant infusion of drugs kept him sedated and weak, but still alive. Gurney Halleck was known to be a formidable fighter, and Piter took no chances.

He wished he could begin flaying him down to his core, to make his death as long and painful as possible, but he knew Rabban would be outraged if he murdered Halleck without permission, maybe even enough that he would kill Piter at last. No, he would wait. He wiped a drop of cranberry-red liquid from his lower lip. He would wait.

A Harkonnen captain in a black uniform said, "We should wake him up and interrogate him. At least we'll find out if he participated in the raid. Lankiveil will be more than a year rebuilding everything they destroyed."

Piter tapped his fingertips together again. "There'll be time enough for that."

Even sedated, Halleck managed to struggle against the drugs. He had been unconscious for days, which would likely have long-term physical effects. Piter's lips curled in a cruel smile. There were very few "long-term" things this man needed to worry about.

With a low groan, Halleck weakly thrashed. One of his arms reached up, as if clutching at something. Piter grabbed the wrist and pulled it down, shouting to two of the men nearby. "It seems we cannot trust the drugs. We need to bind him as well. Help me with this arm. We'll wrap him up like a cocoon."

As others lashed the Atreides man's wrist to the stretcher, Piter gripped the forearm, and his sensitive fingertips felt a lump there, and when he looked closely, a hairline scar, nearly invisible. He leaned closer, interested.

It was an odd place for an accidental gash. He pressed down with his fingers, worked them back and forth in a twisted imitation of a massage. Under the skin, he detected a hard, flat object about the size of his thumbnail. The Mentat's brows drew together. Shrapnel from some old injury? That made little sense.

No, with the line of the scar, it appeared that something had been *inserted* rather than removed. He looked up. "Bring me a knife. A sharp one."

The medical assistant rummaged in his kit and withdrew a laser scalpel. "Would you like me to operate, sir?"

"I'll do it myself." Piter switched on the blade, cut a smoking incision in Halleck's skin, and pried into the bloody wound with his fingertips. He dug until he found the hard object, something smooth and glassy. He extracted it, as if removing a nugget of precious metal from the dirt.

It was covered in blood, milky and translucent—a crystal. A ridulian crystal, on which messages were recorded.

"I think we may have learned why the famed Gurney Halleck is traveling undercover to Kaitain!" He wiped off the blood, exposed the smooth crystal, turned it around in the light. "Clean this, and bring me a player. Let us see what our captive has to say."

Within moments, Piter inserted the message crystal into the player, activated it, and watched breathless with delight. An image of the hated Duke Leto Atreides explained in detail how he would pretend to join the Noble Commonwealth in order to infiltrate Jaxson Aru's bloody movement.

Piter licked his lips. It was a delicious situation.

Jessica felt like two different people.

One of them, Jessica of House Atreides, the Lady of Caladan, had been to this spaceport many times with her Duke and their son. The buildings, the people, the landing zone and reception area—all were familiar to her. She was glad to be back there at last, breathing the salty air, looking up at the comfortable skies scudded with clouds. But this was not how she had wanted to come home.

She was a different person now, an invisible woman on a critical mission. She could not let word slip out that she had left Elegy, that she had openly defied the Sisterhood, but she had to stop Taula and Aislan. She needed to send a discreet word to Leto, alert Thufir Hawat, make sure that Gurney and Duncan kept Paul safe.

She longed to see them, speak with them . . . to hug her son and throw her arms around Leto.

Her every action, though, was fraught with danger. If Xora had arrived already, she might be part of the plan. Jessica didn't trust her. Right now, she had to learn as much as possible—and she had to hurry.

Disguised, Jessica took her bag and walked with other travelers across the arrivals area, and used public transport to Cala City. She hoped no one would recognize her with her short, dark hair and her formless clothing. The sunny day had a slight breeze, and she thought of times she and Leto had walked among the tide pools on the extensive beaches below the castle.

Giandro had provided enough funds to meet her needs, and she made her way to a part of the city she rarely visited. Jessica carried her own knife beneath her brown skirts. It would be easy for her to justify the weapon, as a woman alone on Caladan, although some might consider the blade too large for her. They could never guess just how adept she was at fighting, with her intensive training at the Mother School, the combat techniques she had taught Paul, as well as the Atreides methods she had subtly learned by watching Duncan Idaho and Gurney Halleck. She doubted she would need more of a weapon than herself, but she also knew that her anticipated Bene Gesserit opponents would be worse than any thug or petty street thief in Cala City.

She checked into an inn under a false name. Assessing her situation, planning her next move, Jessica ventured downstairs to a garden courtyard where she ordered a small lunch and a glass of paradan juice. As a young woman took her order, Jessica noticed that moonfish had been crossed off the menu, which she found odd. When she asked about this, the waitress explained that a terrible disaster had mostly wiped out the industry. The waitress seemed to think everyone on Caladan knew about the tragedy.

"So many awful things happening here," the young woman said, her face pensive. "The explosions in the old town caused by that Chaen Marek, all the moonfish dying off, and that horrific murder just last night! The Duke's new concubine stabbed to death right in another inn! And with Duke Leto gone off-planet now, heaven knows where." She shook her head, scandalized.

Jessica reeled, but used all her skills to cover her shock. The murder victim must have been Xora! She pressed the waitress for details, and fortunately, she was all too eager to spread fascinating gossip.

Jessica drank it all in. "And what about Paul? I mean, the Duke's son? Is he all right?"

"So far," the waitress said. "But is anyone safe these days?"

Jessica ate her meal, trying to rearrange the new information so that it made sense. If the murdered woman was Xora, claiming to be the Duke's concubine, why would she be staying in an inn across town? And who could have killed her? Xora was a well-trained fighter, just like Jessica, skilled in Bene Gesserit methods. No ordinary opponent would have been able to defeat her—but another Bene Gesserit would. Or two of them. Taula and Aislan?

But why would they have killed one of their own?

And why was Leto off-planet? Where had he gone? He'd never hidden his movements before. . . .

She left the inn, knowing she couldn't wait until dark. She needed to make her way surreptitiously to the castle and get word to Paul, alert the security forces. She believed that the old warrior Mentat was absolutely trustworthy. She could reveal the danger to Thufir Hawat, explaining what she knew. She knew that he, Duncan, and Gurney would give their lives to keep Paul safe.

But if she appeared at the main gates, or even tried to use one of the side entrances, she risked being recognized by the castle staff. Despite her disguise, she had been the Lady of Caladan for nearly two decades and was not anonymous.

But there was another way. After checking the time, she went to the harbor and hurried up the shoreline in the direction of the castle. In late afternoon, the tide was just coming in, so she moved along the rocky beach, familiar with the moods of the Caladan sea and the many secret ways around the headlands.

Shadows from the ocean cliffs extended over the water, and gloom settled upon the ocean. Rocky breakwaters extended away from the cliffs, and foaming waves from the returning tide turned the spit of rocks into a line of transitory stepping-stones. Jessica hurried along because the sea was rapidly erasing the puddle-strewn footpaths. Once beneath the sheer cliff, she could climb up one of the steep staircases to the ancient stone structure high above.

Ahead, she saw Duke Leto's private fishing shack tucked away in a rocky alcove with a small dock that he used when he went on boating expeditions. Leto considered the place a private, rustic sanctuary. The last time she had been there was to consider Thufir Hawat's initial list of betrothal candidates for Paul . . . a list that the Bene Gesserit had commanded her to alter. Although she'd had no choice, Jessica knew that altering the list was the first blow to shatter her stable life. . . .

A chill of foreboding reminded her that her family was in imminent danger. If need be, she could hole up inside the small, primitive shack, tucked away above the docks and the high-tide line. It might be a better base than the inn in town.

A narrow winding staircase ran up the cliff behind the shack, adjacent to the tracks of a rail-lift that could also be used to descend from above. She looked up the cliff at the high walls of the castle and identified which windows belonged to her son's rooms. *Please let him be safe.*

She picked her way over the moss-covered boulders exposed by the outgoing tide, and climbed a short set of rock steps to a deck adjacent to the shack. The little structure would be cold and dim, but she could activate the heaters and prepare it as a temporary shelter. Surprised, she noted that the door was slightly ajar, the latch broken. Had vandals been here? Looking around the corner, she saw a faint light coming from a small side window.

Her senses fully alert, she crept closer and looked in to see two lean and determined women dressed in unmarked gray garments that would have been ideal for hiding in shadows.

Taula and Aislan.

They saw her a moment later.

Jessica stepped back to face the two women as they burst out onto the deck platform. All three dropped into a fighting stance at the same time. Taula had blood-soaked bandages wrapped around a wounded shoulder.

Aislan hurled questions at her. "What are you doing here? How are you still alive?"

The comment brought a grim smile to Jessica's lips. "Maybe I am more difficult to kill than I appear. Jiara and Ruthine are no longer among the living. Their conspiracy is exposed—I stopped them." She did not explain about Cordana's letter; they didn't need to know. "I came here to stop you as well, and to protect Paul."

"Then you made a mistake," Taula said. "Lethea warned us all of the harm you and your son will cause. The Sisterhood can't take that risk." Despite being wounded, the woman moved forward, her eyes dark in the deepening dusk. The loud rush and boom of the incoming waves against the breakwater line was threatening. "But now you've come to us."

Aislan added, "We'll finish what Ruthine should have done, and then we'll slip into the castle tonight to kill your disgraceful boy, the child that should never have been born."

Jessica let out a taunting chuckle, though their training was solid enough that she could never provoke them into a sloppy mistake. "Paul has Thufir Hawat and Castle Caladan security to protect him. You'll never get near him." Jessica reached into her skirts and pulled out her own knife. With a surprising feeling of relief and confidence, she moved away from the isolated shack, down to the diminishing beach, her back to the rolling waves. She remained hyperalert, aware of the incoming tide, but the sea gave her protection; they could not attack her from that direction. "And I'll stop you first."

"You can try," Aislan said. The two women closed in, gripping long knives—assassination weapons rather than dueling blades. Taula's wound did not seem to impede her.

"We are two expert fighters against you," Aislan said. "How do you expect to kill us both?"

Jessica just smiled. "I fight for the life of my son."

Aislan dove toward her like a launched projectile, pressing her to the edge of the rocky beach. A wave curled in and splashed Jessica up to her calves, but she kept her footing.

The injured Taula jumped closer from the opposite side, raising her knife, but Jessica slashed sideways and cut her arm. More bright blood seeped through the gauze around Taula's wounded shoulder. The woman hissed and drew back, while her companion pressed Jessica farther into the wet sand as the salty waves retreated. As she felt the sucking current against her lower legs, she sprang onto a sturdy rock, the largest black boulder on the near end of the breakwater.

Aislan slashed the air with her knife, and Jessica moved like a cracking whip to avoid it. Her blade rang against Aislan's.

In cold, deadly silence, Taula drove Jessica back along the extending breakwater. She kept her balance on the spray-slick rocks, stepping on coils of seaweed, then leaping across a gap of water filled by the incoming tide. She landed on another uneven boulder, balanced and ready to defend herself. More waves crashed in as the tide encroached.

"The question is whether we dump your corpse on top of the cliff where the boy can see it," Aislan said. "That might provoke him into making a mistake."

"Or we could just dump you into the sea," Taula said.

"You have to kill me first." Jessica crouched in a fighting stance on the wet boulder.

Breakers curled in, foaming around them. Drawing them onward, Jessica jumped out onto the next stepping-stone just as Aislan bounded toward her. The woman landed on the adjacent rock as an unexpected wave splashed a plume of spray high. Aislan pawed at her own face to clear her vision and stumbled to her knees. The rough rock cut a gash through her skirts, slicing her leg.

Jessica instantly sprang back and darted in with the point of her blade as the other Sister tried to regain her balance. It was like the sting of a wasp, so sharp and fast, but deep, and Jessica braced her feet on the wet surface as she withdrew.

At first, Aislan didn't seem to realize she'd been stabbed. She clapped a palm to the back of her neck. Her eyes went wide when the blood started to gout, then she collapsed, slithering off the spray-slick rock.

Barely controlling her cold killing instinct, Taula bounded forward and drove Jessica back to what looked like a dead end, where the sturdy rocks were farther apart, separated by angry surf. Some boulders were already submerged, but Jessica still saw their tops. She found her footing, sprang backward, then jumped to the side, like a child's game of hopscotch.

Taula dove after her, slashing with her knife, trying to catch Jessica before she could find firm footing. But as she jumped to the next submerged boulder, Taula misjudged. Her foot hit a hollow in the rock, and she slipped, then dropped into the water.

Jessica launched herself back at her and raised her own knife. She felt no sympathy, no hesitation, only necessity. The Sisterhood had driven her to extremes, but Jessica, the Lady of Caladan, still had not reached her limit.

AS THE DARKNESS thickened and the tide swallowed the lower line of boulders, Jessica picked her way back to the narrowing beach. The roar of the incoming surf and the cries of gulls drowned out the noise of her heavy breathing. By now, much of the isolated beach was underwater, but Leto's fishing shack on higher ground would be safe and dry.

Behind her, she let the ravenous surf take the bodies of the two Sisters. They would be chewed and torn by the rough rocks, battered about until they were cast up on some other part of the shore.

The seawater turned red as it foamed around the bodies and pulled them out with the retreating waves. Tides ebbed and flowed, as was their nature.

She wished she'd had time to ask why Aislan and Taula had slaughtered Xora—it must have been them. But saving Paul had been her one priority. She had done her work. The two assassins no longer mattered, and Xora was dead.

Oddly, though, Jessica felt no sense of victory.

A good deed constitutes a victory in its own right.
—DUKE LETO ATREIDES, letters to his son

Guild Heighliners traveled on intermittent schedules to obscure destinations such as Issimo III, so the timing was tight and critical. The world should have been just a waypoint, a brief stop to unload one or two vessels on business for Earl Grandine or Imperial engineers providing token assistance to the ravaged planet.

Leto Atreides was astonished at how quickly the rebel leader managed to change his plans and organize an extravagant, unexpected response.

Jaxson Aru reacted with increasing glee as they sat in a small dropship waiting to depart for the surface of Issimo. Leto felt tense about traveling down to visit refugee camps and observe the Imperial corps of engineers. He wanted Jaxson to see the plight of the people on Issimo III, but he didn't want to be spotted.

"We'll have to be discreet," Leto urged. He shook his head, uneasy at the other man's self-satisfied grin. "I don't know how many relief supplies you arranged, but the people will appreciate it more than you can know. They'll remember the good work of the Noble Commonwealth." He tried to read Jaxson's expression. "That's how you want to be remembered."

"Oh, it's memorable, Leto. Memorable indeed." The man chuckled.

Leto smoothed his hand down the front of his uniform, which was marked with the red and gold of House Corrino. Somehow, Jaxson had managed to find them matching uniforms with the insignia of the Imperial engineers. The two men would blend in and watch how the unexpected supplies and equipment were received.

As the Heighliner opened its great bay doors above the bleak planet, Leto felt their small dropship disengage. Moments later, looking through the windowport, he watched another unmarked ship disengage, a cargo hauler moving in tandem with four dump boxes that also descended from low orbit. Leto leaned closer to the plaz, surprised and relieved. "I'm impressed, Jaxson."

The rebel leader kept smiling. "We're just getting started, my friend."

Even more unmarked cargo ships descended from the Heighliner. As the dropship descended into the atmosphere, it was followed by an entire armada of relief vessels.

Leto was amazed. "How did you arrange all this so quickly?"

Jaxson spread his hands. "The Noble Commonwealth is widespread, and we have logistics experts to deliver resources. Just look at what we can do."

Dump boxes passed them in the air on their way to the planet's surface, and the largest cargo vessels cut alongside them. Leto turned from the windowport. "Is House Grandine prepared to receive all this? It's an enormous amount of material—have they made preparations?"

"Of course not, Leto. They know nothing about it. You told me to make this a pleasant surprise."

Five other ships landed at the small main spaceport ahead of their dropship, and the rain of vessels continued. Once the landing zone reached capacity, some of the remaining dump boxes had to land in wasteland outside of the designated paved areas. The vessels opened up to allow numerous workers, construction porters, skilled laborers, crew chiefs, even some baffled agricultural specialists to emerge into the primary Issimo spaceport. All of the personnel wore similar red-and-gold Corrino uniforms, as if everyone had joined the corps of engineers. Leto knew that he and Jaxson could easily blend in among the bustle.

The other man emerged from the dropship, full of energy. "We'll just mingle and listen. This is what you wanted."

"It is," Leto said in a low voice. "Better than killing thousands of innocents."

Jaxson shrugged as if the issue might still be debatable.

Automatic hydraulic doors folded down on the sides of the unmanned dump boxes to reveal the cargo they contained. After the larger haulers locked down, their crews emerged and milled about, until crew chiefs barked orders, taking charge. None of the ships bore any markings.

"The paperwork will lead nowhere," Jaxson said with an ambivalent gesture. "Our funding is untraceable, but I hired all these crews, purchased enough supplies to feed the Issimo population for at least six months." He placed his hands behind his back as he looked at the crates and large machinery being rolled out of cargo holds. Bosses shouted orders, and well-trained laborers lined up to move suspensor pallets out into the spaceport common area. Supervisors reviewed manifests, double-checking the deliveries.

Finally, groundcars rolled in from the city proper, marked with the incongruous lightning-bolt symbol of House Grandine, along with Imperial vehicles bearing the actual leaders of the engineering corps. As they boiled out, the engineers and Imperial military officials looked flustered, barking questions, demanding answers.

A ranking officer approached a work crew leader. "What is this? We were expecting no deliveries. The Heighliner was supposed to send only a small shipment of garrison provisions."

The crew leader in the fake Corrino uniform spread his hands. "We were sent with all this because we know Issimo is in need."

Earl Grandine hurried up, a florid-faced man with a receding hairline and bags under his eyes. "A miracle! What have you brought us?"

"A miracle from the Noble Commonwealth," said the crew leader. His words landing like a physical blow, buffeting the genuine Imperial engineers into silence. The crew leader recited as if delivering a speech, "The Corrino Imperium cares only for its own profits, but the Noble Commonwealth wants all citizens to thrive. Independent planets can offer aid and cooperation when needed." The man gestured. "This is just an example."

While the head officer of the Imperial engineers appeared red-faced and appalled, Earl Grandine looked as if he might burst into tears.

Jaxson leaned close to Leto. "The man was paid a substantial bonus to memorize those words and deliver them. I believe he earned his money."

"So, he's not actually a member of the Noble Commonwealth?" Leto asked.

Jaxson blew air through his lips. "None of these people are, so they can't reveal anything under questioning—but they've all been paid very well. By the Noble Commonwealth."

"Here now, I object!" said the engineer.

Earl Grandine pushed his way forward to the rows of loaded drop boxes. "Greenhouse domes! Food supplies, filter film to protect against solar flares." He raised his hands in jubilation.

More of Issimo's citizens rushed toward the armada of landed ships. Surrounded by the burgeoning crowd, Jaxson Aru grew bold. He walked among them, chatting, and Leto followed. Pitching in, the two men used suspensor pallets and hauled out enormous crates of pundi rice, an irony that Jaxson thought Leto would appreciate.

"Purchased on the open market with no connections to you, my friend," he said, "but I considered it appropriate, since this was your idea."

Leto found the occasion bittersweet. The people of Issimo were receiving lifesaving supplies, but the Noble Commonwealth stood to gain even more. "I'm surprised you're not taking credit," Leto said, "since it's such a success."

Jaxson chuckled. "The Noble Commonwealth takes credit. That's the only thing important to me."

Instead of helping, several Imperial engineers used holo-imagers to capture the activity around them, no doubt for their report back to Kaitain. Leto pulled down his red-and-gold cap, while beside him Jaxson seemed aloof.

Leto was still amazed to realize that the population of Issimo had been saved. "In order to arrange all this, you must have access to countless distribution centers, not to mention cooperation among CHOAM and the Guild and countless Landsraad members."

"Don't jump to conclusions. You will know soon enough." He clapped a congenial hand on Leto's shoulder. "There were many times that I imagined the terrible blight among the crops here, all the starving, miserable people shaking their fists and cursing the name of Shaddam Corrino with their dying breaths." He let out a wistful sigh. "In many ways, that would be quite satisfying, but seeing this, Leto, I can appreciate your point of view. We will spread the word, announce to the entire Imperium that House Corrino failed these poor people, while the Noble Commonwealth saved them."

He walked at a brisk pace, leading Leto as they wound their way through the busy crowd. With a thrumming roar of engines, large agricultural equipment rolled out of the cargo ships.

"Where are we going?" Leto asked. "Should we speak with Earl Grandine? He needs to know what we've done."

"He can see what we've done," Jaxson said, heading toward their waiting dropship. "This is enough for now. You and I have to get back aboard the Heighliner before it departs."

Leto was surprised. "But we've just begun here."

"They know what to do. You and I have other commitments."

The comment put Leto immediately on his guard. "Where are we going?"

"To a planet called Nossus, where you will at last meet the core of the Noble Commonwealth."

The enemy of my enemy is still an enemy, no matter what they say. Harkonnens do not forget.

—BARON VLADIMIR HARKONNEN

On the fringe of the Harkonnen military field at the Carthag spaceport, the Baron prepared his attack squadron, though he was really just going through the motions. He had to stall Fenring. He could tell the Count was not impressed, but the man and his odd Mentat appeared to be fooled for the time being.

The ferret-like Imperial Observer flicked his dark eyes across the line of vessels as fueling crews moved among them. Grix Dardik stood at his side, making strange noises that were even more annoying than Fenring's mannerisms.

The Baron looked proud as he ostensibly supervised the work from the raised, shaded platform out in the heat-rippled air. Mechanics gave the suspensor and thrust engines a full rundown, others powered up the line of armored 'thopters, and pilots checked their own vessels. The troops were methodical, unhurried. One team made a point of repainting the Harkonnen griffin on the fuselage. Grix Dardik seemed to be counting complex numbers backward under his breath.

The Count's brow furrowed. "I, hmmm, expected you would have many more attack ships than this, Baron—considering the value of the spice operations and the frequent threats you face. Your military preparedness is sorely lacking. We need to go soon!"

The Baron actually had three times as many undocumented attack ships dispersed around Arrakis, but no records would show them, and Fenring didn't need to know.

Still, he did not have to feign his indignation. "My dear Count, I had many more ships ready to go—until recently. My men performed daily patrols to hunt down spice smugglers." He narrowed his black eyes in folds of fat. "But *you* ordered me to stand down against Tuek's smugglers and ignore their activities. *You* gave me explicit instructions they were sanctioned by the Emperor, and *you* yourself halted my crackdown." He sniffed in the dry air. "So I took the opportunity to perform much-needed maintenance on the entire fleet." He rocked back, slipping his thumbs into the suspensor belt. "The Arrakis environment is viciously hard on machinery and electronics. Even on a clear day, the dust, sand, and static wreak havoc. Oh, the number of carryalls, spice factories, harvesters, and spotters I have lost this year alone!"

The Baron shook his head, letting the burden visibly weigh him down. In truth, much of the equipment marked as lost, destroyed, or simply decommissioned had been repurposed for his secret spice operations around the Orgiz refinery.

"I know the numbers," Dardik said in a bright, happy voice. "Shall I recite them?"

"No," Fenring snapped, without truly paying attention. His face pinched, and his eyes flashed. "Your production inconveniences do not concern me, Baron. I require your full military strength right now so we can overwhelm that nexus of black-market spice production. It costs us all a great deal of money."

"Ah, yes, I will do what I can." The Baron gestured with pudgy fingers toward the fleet being prepped on the landing field. "Nearly a hundred ships—*Harkonnen* ships—should do the trick with an aerial bombardment on a simple pirate operation. It will be enough to dispense with some desert rabble."

"When, ahhhh, can we launch?" Fenring seemed both eager and nervous.

"As soon as the entire battle group completes its preflight checks." To give Rabban time, he had dragged his feet as much as possible in ways that would not seem obvious, and he still had a few more tricks up his sleeve.

Already five of the squadron ships had reported (false) malfunctions that would require a few hours to repair. The Baron had advised waiting for the entire group to be ready, but he also couldn't risk appearing incompetent.

"If a hundred attack ships are *more* than enough," Grix Dardik interjected, "and if we leave five ships behind, might that be *exactly* enough? Or is ninety-five still more than enough?"

As a deflection, the Baron turned his ire toward Fenring. "I am puzzled at the very need for this attack. What is this secret base you've found at the site of an old abandoned refinery?" He extended a finger toward the Count's pointed nose, ignoring the Mentat who rocked back and forth on the balls of his feet. "After all, *you*, Count Fenring, assured me that you had rooted out and executed the ringleader of these spice thieves. You showed me the images of Rulla Tuek being devoured by a sandworm, and you brought in urns of blood from other conspirators that you also killed. *You* told me the problem had been solved. You told *the Emperor* the problem had been solved! How, then, did this huge operation manage to slip beneath the notice of the Imperial Observer?"

"I, hmmm, seem to have underestimated the extent of their activities." Fenring was clearly embarrassed, which the Baron found most satisfying.

He pressed, "And why must *I* be the one to take care of it? If you insist on a rapid and overwhelming response, maybe we should contact Emperor Shaddam and ask him to send his Sardaukar here. They will certainly mop up all the leftovers you missed. I'd be happy to call for their assistance in such an important matter." Seeing that the Count was on the defensive for once, he couldn't let the opportunity slide past.

"That will not be necessary," Fenring said quickly. "As you yourself just said, a hundred Harkonnen ships should be more than adequate, ahhh, whenever they manage to be ready."

Surreptitiously, he glanced at his chronometer, knowing that a new delay would happen within moments.

On cue, a junior officer rushed up with a message printed on tan spice paper. "My Lord Baron, there is an urgent weather report! Storm overflight has sent us a warning of deteriorating conditions."

"A storm?" The Baron feigned concern. "There are always storms."

"A small Coriolis storm, my Lord, in the vicinity of our target. We will have to delay or divert the mission."

The Baron took the spice paper, frowned down at the ominous-looking weather chart. The images had been doctored well, but no one would know the difference, especially not Fenring.

The other man snatched the paper and scowled down at it. "If it is just a small storm, then perhaps we should risk it, hmmm? Why waste time?" His Mentat leaned close, too, but didn't speak.

"A small *Coriolis* storm," the Baron said. "A contradiction in terms. It would damage many of my ships, and I will not put my valuable men at risk just to soothe your impatience. According to the intelligence you shared, the Orgiz base has operated for some time, has it not? The site will be there tomorrow." He felt calm and satisfied. "Look on the bright side, the storm gives us time to complete our thorough maintenance and checking operations."

Fenring's expression darkened, but there was nothing he could say. Baron Harkonnen controlled all the decisions here.

If the Baron had seen his troops move with such ponderous deliberation at any other time, he would have punished them. But now the crews could take all the time they liked. The delay gave his nephew the time he needed to destroy the Orgiz base.

RABBAN TOOK THE controls of the lead attack craft, flying ahead of fifty cruisers loaded with incendiaries, high-yield explosives, and a battery of lasguns. They raced low over the desert, stirring up sand and dust from the surface. The lemon-yellow sky was clear, although false weather reports had been sent showing ominous storm activity in the area to deceive Count Fenring.

"Coming up on the canyon now, m'Lord Rabban," one of the scouts said over the comm.

He snapped a response, "Don't use names, fool! Follow orders." He increased acceleration, and the rest of his battle squadron followed.

The aircraft used only short-range line-of-sight transmissions, and on a private frequency, but Rabban didn't want anyone at Orgiz to hear them coming. He looked past the undulating sea of golden dunes to the stark mountains in front of him. He squinted as if he could make the approach come faster. "Weapons hot."

His comm hummed. "My Lord, are you certain we don't have time to evacuate the crews? They've worked hard for House Harkonnen. It would only take an hour or so for us to ferry them to a safe rendezvous point and then obliterate the factory facility."

"Are you questioning my orders?" Rabban growled. "That would mean questioning Baron Harkonnen's orders, and I have no intention of doing that."

"N-no, my Lord," the voice said.

Rabban scanned his comm panel to identify which ship had sent the impertinent request, but the pilot quickly switched off his unit.

He readied his weapons as the raw, black mountains hurtled toward him like a hand about to strike. The squadron rose up over the peaks, flew along the spine of the range, and then came down into the wide opening where the hidden refinery complex glinted among the canyon shadows.

As their approach was detected on surveillance screens, the Orgiz communications tower contacted them. "Unidentified ships, state your purpose. If you do not respond, we will open fire!"

Rabban was fully aware of the defensive batteries hidden among the rocks, but he had already bribed one of the men to sabotage them. The man had been happy to take the payment and do as he was told without asking questions.

"This is Count Glossu Rabban. We are inbound for a surprise inspection tour. Cease operations! All personnel are to present themselves in ranks as soon as we land."

That would delay them long enough, he knew. His attack squadron would need only a few minutes, and it would be over . . . long before his uncle and Count Fenring could arrive.

His squadron's incendiaries and larger explosives were prepared to drop down in a rain of destruction. Rabban looked below as they roared over the complex; he felt a new wave of angry disappointment to see the spice silos, two landed carryalls, the centrifuges and packaging lines. Rabban watched the unsuspecting workers line up below in military formation, rushing to get into ranks as ordered.

Swooping down, he dropped the first load, and the rest of the squadron was only a second behind. The workers stared upward, paralyzed for a moment, unable to believe what they were seeing. As soon as the bombs began dropping, they scattered, but not quickly enough.

The fiery shock wave was confined by the sheer walls of the canyon. The cliffs formed a funnel, and explosions thundered, bomb after bomb after bomb. The spice silos toppled, the barracks buildings collapsed.

Rabban finished his run, surely enough destruction already, but the Baron had commanded that he leave no speck of evidence behind. All of Orgiz had to be reduced to a puddle of slag.

He pulled up and circled around to come back over the mountains, this time activating his lasguns. He knew that none of the refinery's official buildings or personnel used shields, because the specter of the rampaging rogue sandworm in Orgiz remained stark and clear, but Rabban could not guarantee that some worker hadn't smuggled a personal shield belt out to the complex. He directed his lasguns toward the cliff walls instead, drawing a line of intense red fire that cut through the rock, slicing off tremendous slabs that tumbled down to the burning canyon floor.

Rabban felt such joy and power. Given enough time, he could have leveled the entire mountain range, piece by piece. But he didn't have time. His uncle had promised to stall Count Fenring for as long as possible, but the Spice Minister was wily, and Rabban needed to be swift. Behind him, other attack ships used their lasguns to pull down more massive chunks of rock.

Rabban circled around one more time and dropped the last of his explosives for good measure. Orgiz had been laid waste.

Although he resented the grim necessity of this action, Rabban was enjoying himself. He signaled the fighting squadron, and they arced away like ravens, heading out to a subsidiary Harkonnen base in the open desert. Rabban was sure his uncle would be proud of him.

AT LAST, AFTER a frustrating six-hour delay, the Baron's strike force lifted off from the Carthag spaceport. Fenring and his Mentat rode in the shielded observation ship behind the swift military aircraft, along with Baron Harkonnen. Although Fenring had acknowledged that the Baron would issue all orders, he activated the comm as soon as the ships flew toward the open desert.

Fenring announced, "We will seize control of the illegal operations and prevent any ships from escaping. You are authorized to use all necessary force to quell violent resistance, but make no mistake—we must have prisoners to interrogate."

"All necessary force," repeated Dardik. "So many things are necessary."

The Baron frowned at him and took control of the comm. "This is Baron Harkonnen. Please acknowledge the orders." He flashed a scolding glance at Fenring, who gave him a polite shrug, then nudged his Mentat. The squadron commanders responded. As far as they knew, the orders sounded perfectly reasonable. None of them suspected that the Baron actually desired something else.

As the heavy air squadron rumbled forward, he wiped persistent sweat from his forehead and worked the environment controls to cool the compartment. "I have much at stake in this, too, my dear Count. Those brigands steal money from House Harkonnen as well as from the Emperor. I won't tolerate being disrespected."

It was near sunset when they closed in on the mountains that hid the refinery complex. The Baron felt a wash of relief when he spotted plumes of oily smoke rising like a bloodstain of destruction in the sky.

Fenring frowned, but the Baron reached the comm first. "Scouts, report. What do you see up ahead?"

"Smoke and fire, my Lord Baron." The first scout ships roared ahead. "Images to come. It appears that Orgiz has already been destroyed."

Fenring pinched his nose, and his face darkened with rage. "Destroyed by what? That is not storm damage."

"Not storm damage," Grix Dardik agreed, unnecessarily.

"Let us wait and see," said the Baron. "We won't jump to conclusions."

As the swift squadron, followed by the observation ship, flew over the rubble, the Baron could see what a thorough job his nephew had done. He was satisfied with the total obliteration. This was even more impressive than the moonfish destruction Rabban had created on Caladan. . . .

"It appears someone did our work for us," the Baron said.

Fenring said, "Send forensic teams down there to comb through the rubble! Find any scrap that can help us determine who was behind the Orgiz operations."

"The obvious answer is a rival group of smugglers. They must be very powerful." The Baron managed to hide his sigh of relief. "But at least, we don't have to worry about Orgiz any longer."

Obligations are like shigawire—the harder you pull against them, the stronger they pull back.

—Bene Gesserit teaching

From all her years serving as the Lady of Caladan, Jessica knew every inch of the castle, every shadow . . . every loose brick in the massive outer walls, and every secret way in.

Thufir Hawat, the Atreides chief of security, had done an admirable job of locking down the castle and keeping Paul safe. She doubted that even Taula and Aislan could have succeeded in breaking in without being detected and stopped. Jessica was not merely a Bene Gesserit, though, but part of Castle Caladan as well.

She had to see Paul.

From what she had already learned in town, without calling attention to herself, Jessica knew that Leto was off-planet and Gurney Halleck had also gone away on some sort of mission. Still, Paul was protected by Duncan Idaho, Thufir Hawat, and the Atreides guards—as well as his own exceptional fighting ability. Jessica wasn't as worried for his safety, especially now that the bodies of the two Bene Gesserit assassins had been cast into the pounding surf beneath the cliffs.

She entered the castle through a covert door built by some previous Duke centuries ago and made her way through the back passageways and slip-corridors. She moved by feel, not daring to risk a handlight. The narrow tunnels were dusty and close, filled with cobwebs, insects, even a few mice who seemed astonished at the human intrusion.

As she furtively worked her way toward the castle wing where Paul's quarters were located, she wrestled with doubts. Since she had eliminated the grave threat to her son, her wisest course of action would be to slip back to the spaceport and simply return to Elegy, with no one the wiser. Her secret would be safe from the vindictive Bene Gesserit.

Yes, that might be the best course of action.

But she couldn't leave without seeing Paul, without attempting to resolve something.

Without stirring a whisper of air, she opened a hidden wall panel in his bedchamber and found the room dark. At first, she didn't think Paul was aware of her intrusion, but then she heard him moving as stealthily as she was. He slid from his bed and dropped into a hyperaware fighting stance.

Of course he had known about the secret wall panel. Thufir Hawat had trained him repeatedly that he must always have an escape plan, secret exits.

Only faint light came from the cloudy night skies outside, yet somehow Paul sensed her, knew her. "Mother?"

"I am here, Paul, but you cannot let anyone know."

"Thufir is on high alert," Paul said, sounding formal—like a Duke. "There's already been an assassination attempt on me and Duncan. Xora, a woman from the Bene Gesserit, has been murdered. She . . ." His voice caught. "She said she was here to take your place."

Jessica sighed. It would have been flippant for her to answer that no one could take her place, but the Bene Gesserit knew all too well what they were doing. "I came because I had to. You're safe from the assassins for now, two Bene Gesserits who were hiding in your father's fishing shack. I took care of them today."

"And Xora, the third Bene Gesserit? You killed her, too?"

"No. I had nothing to do with that."

"Who did it, then?"

"It must have been the pair that I killed, though I don't know their reason."

"You should be home again," Paul said. "You and I can work together. I'm acting Duke while my father is away."

"And where has he gone?"

"He—" Paul began, then froze. "I cannot say, because we are sworn to secrecy. And I don't know what happened to you. Why did you go away, and why are you back?"

"That's not something easily explained, Paul."

The young man hesitated, careful not to reveal anything. "But you should know that you can trust him, whatever you hear."

Jessica was surprised. "Of course I trust him."

"No matter what you hear," Paul said.

"I trust him," Jessica reaffirmed.

As her eyes adjusted to the faint light from the window, she could see his face: he was torn in many directions by his emotions, his joy that she was back, his concern, and his confusion. "I won't ask again where your father is, because you should not have to choose between your loyalty to him and your loyalty to me. Don't tell me. The Sisterhood can never force me to reveal something that I do not know."

Paul grimaced. "Why are they doing this to you, Mother? Why don't you refuse them?" He looked deeply hurt. "My father says you chose loyalty to the Bene Gesserit over him—over us."

"I didn't *choose* them, Paul," Jessica snapped, then regretted her tone. "I didn't choose anything . . . Nevertheless, I must obey. That is why you and your father and House Atreides are still in danger. The Sisterhood wields their power of obligation like a cudgel. They could destroy me if I don't do as they demand." She drew a quick breath. "And I would accept that fate if necessary. Worse, they might destroy you and your father—and I will not allow that, no matter what it costs me."

Paul stewed. "I hate the Bene Gesserit. I'd destroy them if I could!"

Jessica was about to chide him for his petulant comment, but with a chill she remembered what Lethea had said in her madness.

"They've forced me into a new assignment, one I did not request, and they dangled the promise that if I do as they say in this one thing, they will consider letting me return home . . ." She lowered her voice to the barest of whispers. "If Leto will still have me."

"We'll have you." Paul sounded so sure.

"I have to go," she said. "Always stay alert. Guard yourself. But the immediate threat was from an extremist faction of the Sisterhood, and I believe they have been eliminated. If I can make my way back to Elegy and the Bene Gesserit don't find out, then we will all be safe."

"Elegy? Why are you there?"

Jessica looked away, even in the shadows. "That is where they sent me. At least the Viscount is a good man. Don't worry about me. I love you, Paul."

"I love you, Mother," he said. "But I have so many more questions. I—"

"And they must remain questions. Please trust me. I'll be home when I can."

She melted back into the secret passageway, terrified that he would run after her, but she heard only silence and the pounding of her heart.

An important task of a commanding officer is to determine the enemy's plan in advance.

—Ancient tyrant, name lost to history

When Egan Saar returned to Giedi Prime and presented his report, Feyd-Rautha was sharpening his collection of blades.

The young man had weapons masters capable of performing the menial task, but he trusted no one but himself when it came to the security of his knives, kindjals, and swords. Here in this private, secure sanctuary, he liked the smell of the metal oil, the bright aroma of steel that made him remember the atavistic tang of gushing blood from an opponent's mortal wound. He found a singular focus as he moved the razor edge along the whetstone, saw the different sheen of a surgical edge. Previously, Egan Saar had remarked his admiration for Feyd's attention to detail.

Feyd had left standing orders that the twisted Swordmaster was to be brought to him as soon as he returned, and the young man had been expecting him for some time. Now Saar stood before him after being escorted by four armed guards. Seeing the satisfied expression on the man's face, though, made Feyd realize that he was not yet aware of his mistake.

If nothing else, Feyd would enjoy watching Saar's stunned reaction when the news hit home.

"My Lord Feyd-Rautha." Saar stepped forward and bowed—more respectfully than usual. He still wore his tattered cloak and loose clothes, with the sword at his side. "For a Swordmaster, the exhilaration of a job well done is its own reward, but I will accept my payment in solaris and be on my way."

Feyd set down the curved gutting knife he'd been sharpening and used a rag to wipe the metal oil off his hands. "You're being premature, Egan Saar. There was a condition before you were to be paid." His withering tone seemed as deadly as one of his dueling daggers.

"A condition, my Lord?"

"The condition that you actually *succeed*."

Saar straightened, indignant. "You gave me instructions to kill either the Duke's son or his concubine. The boy was cautious and well guarded, which was initially problematic, but the woman was vulnerable. I left her dead—no doubt of that." His brows furrowed.

Drawing himself up, Feyd stepped close to the larger man. "I don't doubt that you killed someone. You found an unfortunate woman, broke into her room at an inn, and stabbed her to death at night." He snorted. "Not the panache I expected from a Swordmaster, but effective enough." He threw his next words like a released spring. "But you killed the wrong victim."

Egan Saar opened his mouth, but no words came out.

Feyd continued, "The Lady Jessica, Duke Leto's bound concubine and the mother of their son, has been away from Caladan for some time. I sent my own spies there to keep their eyes and ears open, to send back any intelligence. I wanted them to watch you. I received their report two days ago."

Deep in his throat he made a sound of disgust as he rummaged among the paraphernalia on the tables in his sanctuary, moving aside the scattered blades he had been sharpening. He found a reader and an imprinted ridulian sheet containing the Atreides dossier. "I thought you would be more diligent and reliable." He called up the image of Jessica with her oval face, green eyes, bronze hair.

Saar stepped closer, still surrounded by a wall of silence as he studied the image. "There are some similarities, but this is not the woman I killed. She claimed to be the Duke's concubine."

Feyd scoffed. "I can claim to be the Emperor of the Known Universe, but that does not make it so! You were instructed to kill either the Duke's heir, Paul, or his mother, Lady Jessica. You did neither."

He called the escort guards from the corridor where they had been waiting. Saar tensed, and his hand strayed to the hilt of his blade. Feyd wondered if four trained guards would be sufficient against a twisted Swordmaster. Likely not. He glanced at the assortment of sharp weapons spread out in front of him.

Saar seemed to vibrate with building pressure inside him, but abruptly, his face smoothed. He drew in a long breath and took one step backward. "Then I shall return and finish the job properly. I apologize for the disturbance."

He spun about and then simply departed.

The guards didn't know whether they should stop him, waiting for Feyd's orders. As the young man considered this, an amused smile touched his lips. If the Swordmaster were a coward, he might simply vanish into the Imperium, which would then put Feyd in a position of having to expend the effort to hunt him down and punish him. But Feyd doubted that would happen. No, he was convinced that Saar would be even more intent on proving himself to his employer.

"I look forward to seeing how you impress me," he said under his breath.

THE OBESE BARON did some things that Piter de Vries found laughable, but he didn't dare show his amusement. Even an inappropriate chuckle would surely cost him his life.

After his long journey from Lankiveil to Harkonnen headquarters in Carthag, the twisted Mentat fidgeted at the doorway to the exercise room. The Baron's voice boomed, "Do not interrupt me until I finish my workout, Piter."

The twisted Mentat forced himself to contain his announcement as he stood next to several young male slaves who were prepared to assist the enormous man. Piter carried Gurney Halleck's baliset case as unnecessary physical proof for when he delivered his news.

Though supported by his suspensor belt, and protected by monitors that regulated his levels of strain, the Baron's exercise was surprisingly vigorous. The pale, puffy skin was greasy with perspiration, flushed with effort. After careful observation, Piter realized that the Baron was trying to burn off anger.

Some of the equipment used advanced technology to prime and tone specific muscles, while the design of other resistance machines had changed little in thousands of years. Even with exercise, though, the Baron's debilitating disease prevented his body from ever returning to the lean and muscular form he'd had as a much younger man.

The Baron chose a set of small hand weights, rested his bulk on a reinforced bench, powered down his suspensor belt, and began to lift the weights. "Remarkable, my Lord Baron," Piter said. *Such a ridiculously small amount of weight,* he thought. *He hefts more meat on a fork at mealtime, each time he takes a bite.*

With each raising and lowering of the weight, the Baron looked like he was wielding a bludgeon. Despite his enormity, he was a powerful man. Piter had seen him crush a victim's neck with one hand.

Piter was glad to see his master burning off energy, which made him less susceptible to violent outbursts. The Baron seemed satisfied as he finished his exercise, tossed the weights to the floor, activated the suspensors again, and rose from the solid bench.

Finally, the Mentat came forward to deliver his exciting report. "My Baron, I see you are refreshed and exhilarated, and I bring news that will improve your mood even further."

The Baron scowled at him, still preoccupied. "Aren't you supposed to be on Giedi Prime? Who is minding the business of House Harkonnen?"

Piter minced forward. "Ah, but this *is* the business of House Harkonnen, my Baron! Something that can bring about the downfall of your archenemy. We have an important captive—who was carrying a secret message that can destroy Duke Leto Atreides." The Mentat grinned with his sapho-stained lips.

"A captive? A message? What is this?" The Baron loomed closer to him. "And how do I destroy House Atreides?"

Piter removed the ridulian crystal he had dug out of Halleck's arm. The blood was gone, and he had played the recording several times. He held it forth as if it were a precious gem.

Before he could explain or activate the message holo, he noticed that Rabban had been listening in on part of the conversation. Rabban emerged from a steam room entirely naked, moisture glistening on his skin, which was more like an animal hide than human.

"We were just forced to destroy our Orgiz refinery, Mentat," Rabban said. "A tremendous loss to House Harkonnen. You'd better bring good news, or my uncle will kill you sooner rather than later."

Piter sniffed, feeling protected by his news. "This will surely prove my usefulness and my ingenuity to the Baron." He snickered. "And perhaps it will extend my life for quite some time." He was sure that Rabban hadn't told his uncle that he had used the Mentat's assistance in the highly successful plan to destroy the Caladan moonfish industry.

The Baron huffed. "Trying my patience will certainly not extend your life, Piter. What is it?"

The Mentat's report came out in a sparkling, enthusiastic rush. Rabban seemed to boil inside when he heard about Halleck. He looked ready to lurch off to wherever the captive was held, but Piter halted all conversation when he inserted the message crystal into a portable player. "This was found embedded in Halleck's arm—meant only for the eyes of Emperor Shaddam." His eyes widened with excitement as he activated the holo-image of Leto Atreides. "Obviously, the Emperor hasn't seen it, and never will."

On the recording, Leto explained his plan with intense, sincere words. Rather than watching it again, Piter observed the reactions of the Baron and his nephew. When the message ended, the fat man showed genuine pleasure, and a rumble of laughter resounded in his chest. "This has indeed granted you a few more months of life, Mentat."

"Where is Halleck now?" Rabban demanded. "Did you bring him here?" He looked down at the baliset case Piter carried. "Does that belong to him? Let me smash it." He grabbed the instrument from its case, clumsily dropped it to the floor. The sound of cracking wood and jangling strings was not at all musical.

"It would be much more painful if you were to smash it in front of his eyes," Piter suggested, retrieving the damaged baliset. "The captive is secured in your holding area on Lankiveil, my Lord Rabban. I know you two have a history. It was the safest place I could bring him, and swiftly. When we seized him at a junction station on Parmentier, we had to be quick." He lifted his eyebrows. "I thought you wouldn't mind. He is being kept sedated, until we decide what to do with him."

Rabban turned to the Baron. "I'll go there on the next transport, Uncle. Shall I bring him here for you?"

The Baron moved forward with oddly graceful steps and took the message and player from Piter. He didn't answer his nephew, but instead played Leto's words over again. His smile widened.

"This is most unexpected news, Piter, and it does make up for our recent setback. With the destruction of Orgiz, we'll have to charge CHOAM higher rates for their off-books flow of melange, just to recoup our losses. Ur-Director Aru will not be pleased." He tapped the crystal. "But this news offers a wide range of possibilities!"

Droplets of perspiration and steam rolled off of Rabban's skin, evaporating instantly in the dry Arrakis air. "I will go to Lankiveil and interrogate Halleck. I can squeeze more information out of him."

"Oh, I doubt that very much," the Baron said. "Halleck would die before revealing anything. That damnable code of Atreides honor." His thick lips curved upward. "But you can try. Yes, go to Lankiveil." He looked at Piter. "No one is aware that you've seized the Duke's man?"

The Mentat shook his head, already feeling the sapho wear off. "We were careful, my Lord. We whisked him away from Parmentier, smuggled him in a transport container. No one but our own people have seen him. I did not wish to cause an incident with the Atreides—that is for you to decide."

Rabban sneered. "He attacked Lankiveil, destroyed my holdings. We are entitled to our revenge!"

Backing away from his sweaty nephew, the Baron said, "Their attack was in response to your destruction of the moonfish industry. We aren't ready to invoke kanly just yet." Rabban looked disappointed. "But Leto Atreides will never accuse us publicly, will never say anything. Even if he believes we've taken his man, he can say nothing, or we will threaten to expose this message." He let out a rumbling laugh that grew steadily louder. "He's busy playing with the rebels, and no one—not even the Emperor—has an inkling that he isn't a genuine traitor. Oh, this is too good!"

Piter and Rabban looked at each other, sharing a rare connection, just as when they'd concocted the moonfish scheme together. "I didn't torture Halleck further, my Lords, because I thought Rabban might want to be present."

"Yes, I do!"

The Baron's expression became indulgent. "Rabban, I must stay here to organize a way to save our secret spice channel to CHOAM. You did do a good job destroying Orgiz, as I ordered. Despite our huge financial losses, you did protect House Harkonnen from being exposed . . . so, I will give you a reward. You also showed ingenuity and imagination with your scheme to wipe out the Atreides moonfish, even if you did leave clumsy fingerprints."

"You instructed me and my brother to hurt the Atreides." Rabban sounded defensive. "That is what I did." He shot a quick glare at Piter.

"Oh, there's no doubt you hurt Leto, and now you can go to Lankiveil and hurt Leto's man. Use your imagination. I don't need to know the details . . . unless I ask for them."

Rabban was both eager and relieved. "I have a brand-new torture facility, with state-of-the-art equipment to amplify pain, and prolong it. Halleck will be my first subject there."

"Fitting that it's an Atreides for your initial efforts," the Baron mused. "I can't wait to see what lovely Feyd does for his part in the challenge. Meanwhile, I have my own plan, another foothold in House Atreides." He chuckled to himself. "A weakness I never expected to find . . ."

Piter was fascinated. "What is it, my Lord Baron?"

"Not now, Piter. I have secrets even from my Mentat, but you can help me later. Rest assured, we are making an all-out attack on our enemy, through every back door they have left open. Everything except a full military assault, but that can come later. Now, help me to the showers." The Baron adjusted the suspensors and propelled himself toward a wide doorway. Rabban and the twisted Mentat followed, with three slaves behind them, moving to a large shower vault with water-retention pumps and moisture collectors. As the slaves rushed forward to disrobe him, Piter and Rabban waited just outside the vault. The air was lush with moisture, and Rabban practically salivated as he made his plans for Gurney Halleck.

When the Baron finished and the slaves toweled him off, Piter wondered if he would receive an additional reward for his foresight in capturing the Atreides man. He had been granted a few more months without the Baron threatening to discard him, which was a reprieve, but he hoped for more.

As soon as the big man was robed again and the slaves had made him immaculate, he glided out to face the other two men. He frowned at the instrument case that Piter still carried. "Take the baliset with you, and make Halleck sing for his life."

"But it's broken." Rabban pouted.

"You broke it," Piter muttered. "Damaged, not ruined."

The Baron chuckled. "What difference does it make, Piter? My nephew is tone-deaf anyway."

Rabban took the instrument roughly from the Mentat. "I shall make the great Gurney Halleck grovel and sing, grovel and sing. Maybe I'll cut off his baliset fingers first, and get him to sing in more than one way."

"Yes, yes, however you want to do it. It's your reward." He turned to Piter, glancing at the three slaves who had helped the Baron dress. "And, ah, a reward for you, too, Piter. I know how you enjoy a little wet work. These slaves are yours—practice on them as you will."

He and Rabban departed, leaving the Mentat to enjoy his reward. Piter slid out the stiletto he always carried. The slaves gaped at him as the Baron sealed the door of the exercise room behind them. Piter de Vries set about releasing his tension.

When one is caught in a nest of vipers, the best way to survive is to become one of them.

—*The Assassin's Handbook*

Duke Leto felt as out of place as when he went to Kaitain to play politics, but this was an entirely different kind of game, and certainly more dangerous.

As Jaxson Aru led him from transfer point to transfer point using multiple Guild Heighliners and false identity papers and travel certificates, Leto felt like a man wearing a blindfold. He had no idea where they were—which was likely the intent of the rebel leader.

Together, at what was supposedly their final destination, they emerged from the Heighliner in an unmarked privately owned shuttle. As they dropped toward the planet, Leto saw that, unlike the great flotilla of relief ships that had descended upon Issimo III, theirs was the only ship that departed in this system.

The world was small and nondescript, and he saw neither city lights nor signs of civilization on the nightside. The shuttle cruised over the dayside, descending above an open landscape of sweeping prairies dotted with lakes and occasional lines of rolling hills.

"This is Nossus," Jaxson explained with warmth in his voice. "It doesn't have the heart or nostalgia of Otorio, but I am trying to make it a new place of pride. We can accomplish great things from this place, Leto Atreides."

"You're very ambitious," Leto said.

Jaxson chuckled as the ship passed over intermittent farming settlements dispersed across open plains. He explained that the natives of this world had wandered to Nossus and settled here long ago, having no real connection to the Imperium or to human history. "But even if the planet's inhabitants are oblivious to politics, the Noble Commonwealth members who meet here are keenly aware of our actions."

The small craft finally came in to land among a cluster of other private ships on an expansive clear area near a large building under construction. Leto could see the structure was being erected in the style of a manor house, but rustic with thick logs stripped of bark. The building's framework implied rugged newness instead of stately ancient architecture. Part of the house was already completed, but additional wings were being added now.

Jaxson disembarked, happy and smiling. He spread his arms as he drew a deep breath of the dry, warm air. "You see, this is a new beginning. Look over there—I've already planted an extensive olive grove." He gestured toward geometric lines of small trees, each one marked and well watered. "My family considered the old olive grove on Otorio to be sacred. It grew on our estate for centuries. What we are starting now, Leto, will also grow large and strong, beautiful and important. Something to last even longer than the Corrino Imperium." He smiled. "Follow me."

Leto felt that the rebel leader was a contradiction. He did not reek of evil. His destructive plans were well considered and with a clear goal, and he was willing to plunge toward that goal, no matter the cost. No, Jaxson Aru was not evil—he was just *wrong*, in a very big way. He was misguided. And here, so close to him, Leto would have a chance to stop him, if he could maintain his own façade long enough.

As Leto looked at the other ships landed in the open areas around the isolated Noble Commonwealth headquarters, he was surprised to see a large frigate apart from the other vessels. Its engines were missing, the hull plates stripped away to leave only a skeletal framework, like a beached whale he had once seen on the shores of Caladan. He could still make out the lines, the design of the craft.

"That looks like an Imperial frigate," he said. Questions spun in his mind. "Are you building it for subterfuge? To slip into Kaitain with no one knowing?"

"We are not building it, Leto—we're taking it apart, stripping the vessel down so no one will find even a memory of it." Jaxson chuckled. "We took advantage of the uproar and whisked it away from the Imperial capital as swiftly as possible." His grin widened. He seemed to be waiting for Leto to assemble the pieces of the puzzle.

"An Imperial frigate . . . ," Leto said, then glanced up. "A treasury frigate. I saw the images when I reviewed the attack on the palace."

"You saw a decoy loaded with explosives instead of solari coins." The rebel leader chuckled. "Oh, I included enough coins to be scattered among the wreckage. No one suspected."

The two men stood before the hulk of the Imperial ship, and Leto imagined the hull intact, the markings of House Corrino, its compartments filled with cases of treasure.

"My bold statement was certainly effective, but I'm not a fool. The Noble Commonwealth requires funding for our operations. If I had the loyal followers to hijack a treasury ship and crash it into the palace . . . don't you think I could also arrange to have it swapped for a decoy?"

Leto caught his breath. "So you took the entire treasure."

"How do you think I paid for all those relief operations on Issimo III?" Jaxson turned toward the large house. He had a spring in his step. "The records were erased, and the real ship was slipped aboard a Heighliner, marked as CHOAM cargo. We were on our way while the fires still raged at the crash site!" He rubbed his hands together. "You see, my dear Duke, I can be clever as well."

Jaxson led the way to the completed section of the main building, ignoring dozens of local workers assembling a framework out of thick logs. Leto paused to look across the rolling pasturelands where wild grazing animals roamed. The wind whistled across the great open sky, and the long grasses whispered across the prairie where dark animals wandered.

He braced himself, strengthened his persona by reminding himself of why he was here, what he would accomplish and how he would save the Imperium. Thoughts weighed heavily as he considered Kaitain, the government that bound all the worlds of humanity. This, right now, stood to be the most important action Leto Atreides had ever taken in his life.

A man should leave something of himself behind, for the historical record of humanity.

He had to maintain his hold on who he was, but he also had to be someone else, raising not a shadow of a doubt among these conspirators. He would be aloof, confident, and impassioned. When asked, he would describe how the Emperor had harmed him, had *wronged* him, and he would talk about the needs of Caladan, which House Corrino refused to meet. If he failed, not only would he lose his chance to stop the insurrection, he would lose his life, undoubtedly in a most horrible way.

They stepped up to the door of the large wooden house, and Leto braced himself. Jaxson entered without knocking.

Inside the mansion, they found a sparsely furnished great room with bare wooden walls that smelled of fresh resins and oils, rugs on a hardwood floor, but the rustic nature did not imply a lack of wealth.

Jaxson called out, "I have arrived with Leto Atreides. Come out and meet our new partner, the Duke of Caladan." He motioned for Leto to walk down the hall with him.

Several people emerged into the hall from a large room, apparently a conference chamber. Even with their security concerns and the deadly nature of their sedition, the men and women seemed relaxed in casual dress, like nobles who had gone on a retreat. He recognized some of the faces because he had recently studied the most ambitious Landsraad members, those who were squabbling over the holdings left vacant after Otorio. He was amazed to see that some of those who had fought hardest and played Imperial politics were now in this inner circle bent on undermining that very Imperium.

"Very happy to meet you in person, Duke Leto," said a distinguished older man as he stepped forward. "I didn't get a chance on my recent visit to Caladan."

The man wore intense scarlet-and-orange garments, bright fabrics in a style that reminded Leto instantly of when he and Vikka Londine had dined together in the Imperial Palace. "I went to your beautiful world to secure a large moonfish shipment—one of the last shipments before the disaster, alas."

"Lord Rajiv Londine." He tried to control his reaction. Despite Fenring's suspicions, and Shaddam's outrage, Leto had wrongly dismissed the suggestions that this man had any involvement with the rebel movement. "I am surprised to see you here."

"We have many surprises. That's the way it's supposed to be," said a dark-skinned woman in a lilting, thin voice. Leto could not immediately identify her.

He felt a little dizzy as he wrestled with his questions for Londine. "But why would you so openly criticize the Emperor if you're part of the conspiracy? You only draw suspicions on yourself." Once again, he remembered the bitter ultimatum Fenring had given Leto before he could marry Vikka Londine.

"Oh, I've infuriated Shaddam, and he's made many accusations, but who would believe that a real rebel would complain so often in a public forum? A perfect camouflage, my dear Duke."

Leto did not entirely agree, but he saw the man's strategy.

Jaxson accepted a round of warm welcomes and congratulations, and he happily explained about the surprise armada of relief ships on Issimo III. "A complete success, and an innovative approach to the problem, thanks to Duke Leto."

Leto nodded as all eyes in the corridor turned to him. "It was a way to demonstrate the possible good work the Noble Commonwealth can do for the people."

Jaxson chuckled. "And once the natives there have full bellies again, they can think about the sheer incompetence of the Corrino engineers. Maybe they'll rise up and turn on the Imperial representatives after all."

Leto's brow furrowed, but some of the gathered conspirators muttered and smiled. "We can hope," said one man.

"We have all the resources we could possibly need," Jaxson said.

"So long as you promise not to cut off the other income streams," said Rajiv Londine. "Some of us rely on them." He gave an odd glance at Leto, who felt a chill, knowing he was missing some part of the conversation.

"The, ah, other income streams will remain," Jaxson agreed. "They form a foundation for an independent Noble Commonwealth, once we succeed." His eyes glittered as he looked from Londine to Leto. "I've heard that the Duke of Caladan might be courting your daughter, Rajiv. An Atreides-Londine alliance would be the beginnings of a powerful commercial empire."

"My daughter spoke highly of him." The old lord sniffed. "But Duke Leto did not continue his courtship. Apparently, he found my daughter unacceptable."

Leto saw his chance. "I found the *terms* unacceptable." He realized this was a good time to reveal what he knew, to provide another wedge that these rebels could use. "Count Fenring imposed a condition. He said that in order for the marriage to be sanctioned, I had to destroy you, Lord Londine. He wanted me to disgrace you, ruin you, and have you ousted from the Landsraad, if not killed outright. I refused to comply." He met the man's surprised expression, and suddenly a flicker of Jessica appeared in the back of his mind. He wondered where she was. Leto softened his voice. "I'm sorry if I hurt your daughter's feelings. She struck me as a fine woman."

Mutters of shock rippled around the people gathered outside the meeting room, but Jaxson was delighted. "You see! As if we needed more evidence of Shaddam's corruption."

Miffed, Londine gestured for them to enter the large conference room where the rebels were obviously holding some kind of meeting. Leto entered, not letting any of his trepidation show.

Two intimidating spinehounds rose to their feet, bristling, ready to guard the woman seated in one of the large chairs. She had short brown hair, a trim figure, and formal business attire, and she exuded a *presence* of manifest power without even moving. Leto had seen images of the CHOAM Ur-Director, Malina Aru.

He paused, trying to make the pieces fit together in his mind as Jaxson went forward to greet his mother. Leto said quietly, "So the family breach was just another fiction."

"Oh, it was real," Malina said, looking up at him without rising from her chair, "though perhaps exaggerated for public consumption. But my son and many other supporters of the Noble Commonwealth have convinced me to consider . . . alternative tactics to accomplish our goal in a more expedited manner."

Jaxson bent down to pat the spiny heads of the two guard animals. "And change the course of human history," he said to everyone gathered in the chamber.

"We're glad to have you among us, Leto Atreides," Malina Aru said. "We'll accomplish great things together."

Leto looked at all of them, remembering their faces. He offered them a firm smile that he hoped matched their own. "I am one of you now," he said.

He felt an emptiness in the pit of his stomach as he said the words. He had stepped beyond the line of safety, into a very dangerous unknown.

Is there a way to separate what we do from what we feel? Or, ultimately, is this only a fallacy?

—LADY JESSICA, private journals

Once she was back on Elegy, Jessica admitted to herself that the planet was indeed beautiful, especially the colorful, luxurious sunsets.

When she'd first come here, under orders from the Sisterhood, she had felt like a cornered animal, seeing only the walls that boxed her in. She had resolved to achieve the goal as quickly as possible, so she could be done. She had not wanted to be here—and Viscount Tull hadn't asked for her either.

But what Giandro had done for her, the consideration he had shown and the risks he had taken . . . all so she could save her son by another man, a man she still loved! Jessica realized that Leto would have done something similar under the circumstances, and that was one of the reasons why she loved him.

This Viscount wasn't a pawn to be manipulated or a tool to be used. Mother Superior Harishka had made it clear what was expected of her. The Bene Gesserit had given her the skills and training she needed, and if she used all of her abilities, even the irresistible bullwhip of Voice, she could break this Viscount Tull and wrap him around her finger.

A cold Bene Gesserit Sister would do exactly that, but Jessica would not. Giandro deserved more than that. . . .

After saving Paul, she had departed from Caladan as quietly, as discreetly as she had come, but she had left part of her heart there. The Bene Gesserit didn't know how she had protected her son, and they must never know she had left Elegy. The Sisters expected her to complete her mission with Giandro Tull and get him to accept her as his concubine.

On the second morning after her return from Caladan, Giandro went to the stables for a vigorous ride with five of his retainers. Jessica joined him there as he saddled up a powerful, well-bred black stallion, one of his family's famed horses. He was clad in a riding outfit with breeches, a tailored jacket, boots with spurs, and a helmet in Tull blue with a spiral design in front. He smiled at her and bade her good morning.

Jessica lowered her gaze. They had danced around the conversation ever since her return, but now she drew a deep breath. "Truly . . . I don't know how to express my gratitude, my Lord. What you did for me, for my son . . ."

He stood beside his magnificent horse, stroked the black mane with his fingers. He seemed shy, even awkward. "Truly, I had no choice."

Jessica faced him. "Of course you did. That's why it is such a tremendous thing."

He flushed. "I only did what I had to do as a nobleman, my Lady. After you explained the threat to the boy, how could I do otherwise? If I hadn't let you go . . . if your son had been killed after all, you would hate me every moment you remained here." He reached out to touch her hair. "And I could not bear that. I'm just amazed that you actually returned, of your own free will."

"I had no choice in that either. Duke Leto isn't the only part of House Atreides who has a core of honor."

He smiled at her, and swung up into the ornate saddle.

On impulse, she asked, "Can I join you?" Jessica recalled long, pleasant afternoons riding horses with Leto on the open Caladan beaches, far from the castle or town. She remembered seeing the Duke in profile, the bright smile on his face as they galloped side by side on the wet sand.

The Viscount's smile widened, then his expression suddenly changed. He glanced at his retainers. "I would love to ride with you, Jessica, but not today. My . . . friends and I have a special trip planned. It's rugged terrain, and I don't think you would enjoy it."

She was about to push back when she noticed something behind his eyes, an anxiety, even a hunted look. Remembering the shadowy watchers who always hovered nearby, she wondered again what he was hiding. One of the Mother Superior's other commands was for her to learn where the Viscount had directed the funding that House Tull previously sent to the Mother School.

Now she read the subtle differences in Giandro's expression, a flush that came to his cheeks, the flicker of his eyes. She knew he was not going on a simple ride for exercise and pleasure with a handful of retainers. Even with the secret they shared, he obviously didn't want her to know this other part of his life.

She nodded. "Some other time, then."

His expression became warm. "We will definitely ride together. Tull horses are the best in the Imperium, and you'll see that our fame is well deserved. For today, I'm sure you can find something else around the estate to occupy yourself."

She backed away as he nudged the stallion forward. "Of course, my Lord." She knew that wherever she went, the persistent watchers would keep her from straying outside any boundaries the Viscount had set.

Giandro headed out on his ride under sunny skies, and his uniformed companion soldiers followed him at a distance. He waved back at her. Glancing at his chronometer as if he had someplace else to be, he urged his stallion into a gallop. Jessica watched him ride into the thick forests and colorful lichen hedges of the sprawling estate.

Preoccupied, she did not return directly to the manor house on the main road, but instead took a trail through the exotic forest. As she walked along, she was aware that she was being followed, but she didn't acknowledge the usual watchful presence. Giandro had not prevented her from wandering the extent of the lavish grounds.

She considered how secretive he was. Though he was warming toward her, and he had certainly made her beholden to him by sending her to Caladan, he had built high walls around himself and his activities.

With the lucrative lichen industry here on Elegy as well as the materials-transfer business in the nearby asteroids, House Tull was indeed wealthy. Viscount Giandro was not miserly with his wealth, but he didn't seem willing to squander it on the Sisterhood. She didn't know his other investments, though.

The path wound up a hill, granting her periodic views of the manor house and the manicured boundaries of the estate. Giandro had already helped her save Paul. How much more could she ask of him? Perhaps if she could convince him to resume his stipend to the Mother School, that would certainly earn her favor. But he would resent the very suggestion . . . unless she could make him believe that it was a good investment.

She was ordered to become his concubine, using all the techniques available to a Bene Gesserit, and to prove she was a Sister first . . . and therefore reliable enough to be sent back to Caladan. *Her original mission.* And Caladan was where she longed to be.

But at what cost?

The trick was for Jessica to succeed in her assignment and satisfy the Mother Superior without becoming someone else's pawn.

She stood on the wooded path, looking across the colorful wash of spiky, tall lichens. Her minders had dropped back, no doubt in consternation, wondering where she was going. She had no plan, and the turmoil in her thoughts was not something that surreptitious watchers could observe.

Even here I have my private places.

From the high point of the trail, she looked across at the Tull manor house, which was not at all like Castle Caladan. If she accepted her new role here, as a dutiful Bene Gesserit, she could go through the motions and live a life of comparative ease and luxury.

And never think about Leto and Paul again. . . .

Impossible! She wouldn't accept that, not on those terms.

She noticed movement in the distance: Giandro continuing his ride, followed by his retainers. If she could learn his secrets, she would have another piece of the puzzle, another tool to use. But for whom?

As she headed through the forested hills, she walked in the general direction where she had last seen Giandro and his companions. The Tull estate had extensive grounds, but she had not explored into the wilderness. Now, though, her curiosity was piqued. In order to answer her questions, she had to lose her ubiquitous shadows.

Always before she had cooperated, biding her time. The men following her kept a discreet distance, but made their presence known. They were not inept, but neither were they subtle. Because she had been so cooperative, however, never pushing the boundaries, they'd grown somewhat lax.

Feigning nonchalance as she wandered along the leaf-strewn path deeper into the forest, she paused to look at a particularly jagged spray of lichen growths. The angle let her glance out the corner of her eye to note the watchers some distance behind.

Ahead, the path curved and descended out of sight into a thickly wooded hollow. She increased her pace, but not so much that the others would notice right away. She followed the curve where she was blocked from view, and instead of continuing along the path downhill into the dell, she slipped into the thick underbrush and darted up the slope, ducking behind trees. In the thick shadows of a bush, she crouched, watching in silence as the followers hurried along when they realized they couldn't see her anymore.

As soon as they were gone, Jessica worked her way in the opposite direction, rapidly climbing the steep side of the hill, working her way through thick lichens and obscuring deadfall. Trying to make no sounds, she ascended as swiftly as she could, working her way around the face of the hill. From behind and below, she heard voices. Hiding among the underbrush, she could see the followers hurrying back along the path, looking for her. She waited until they passed, then climbed even higher until she reached the top of the ridge, well obscured from the path below. Seizing her chance, she began to run.

Jessica meant no harm to him, simply wanted to discover what else Viscount Giandro Tull was about. She would take his measure—not for the Sisterhood, but for herself. From the top of the ridge she saw the extent of the Tull estate, the sprawling open lands, colorful lichen-forested hills, open meadows.

From her vantage, she spotted the group of riders. Giandro and his companions had reached an isolated meadow, where they sat on their mounts. She observed carefully, and realized they were waiting for something. From the way they searched the sky, she suspected a rendezvous of some kind. Why would he have a meeting deep in the wilderness that no one else could see?

Quietly keeping to the cover of the tall trees, Jessica made her way toward them. Giandro and his retainers faced the opposite direction, away from her sheltered hillside.

As she worked her way to the edge of the meadow, she heard a low thrum in the air, the staccato burring of wings. A camouflaged flyer came in from outside the boundaries, flying low. Giandro raised his hand, and his retainers dismounted as they rushed to prepare for the aircraft's arrival. They stationed themselves at what appeared to be natural rock formations, but Jessica realized were artificial structures.

She approached closer as the aircraft swooped in. No one was watching for her, and she crouched behind a thicket out of sight. She was close enough to hear Giandro speaking orders to his men.

The aircraft landed with a flourish as if the pilot were accustomed to military maneuvers or swift in-and-out missions. The retainers worked controls hidden in the rocks, and to her amazement, part of the meadow's grassy expanse shifted and blurred as a hologram faded to reveal a large landing area. A semicircular platform slid aside to reveal an underground bunker.

The cargo hatch opened on one side of the aircraft, and the pilot sprang out, a bearded man in rumpled old clothes. He waved at Giandro's men. "Unload quickly, and I'll be away!"

The Viscount made brisk gestures, and his retainers raced toward the landed flyer. In a swift, efficient operation, they removed unmarked crates and stacks of materials . . . explosives! Giandro strode forward to open one of the crates, inspecting weapons inside—lasguns, from what Jessica could see.

The unkempt pilot stepped up to the Viscount. Together, they watched the retainers finish removing the stockpile and lowering it into the underground bunker. "You've thrown yourself headfirst into the Noble Commonwealth cause, my Lord. You had a quick change of heart. It's a wonder the Sardaukar didn't find this stockpile when they did their search."

Giandro lifted his chin in pride as he looked to the sky. He swept his gaze around the hills of his estate, and Jessica shrank deeper into the thicket.

"The stockpile wasn't here then—nor was my intense dedication." He shook his head. "There's nothing like being accused and having your holdings threatened, nothing like watching one of your friends annihilated on the basis of no evidence whatsoever." He clenched his jaw, and the tendons visibly stood out on his neck. "It makes you realize what the cause is all about."

Jessica absorbed the information. Part of the rebellion! She had not suspected this at all, and she realized the magnitude of the dangerous information she now held.

If the Sisterhood knew what she had learned, they could control Viscount Tull, and force him to continue paying them. But the Sisterhood wouldn't know, Jessica vowed. She knew, and that was enough.

She didn't move, barely breathed, maintained her absolute silence and stillness, until the flyer was unloaded, the underground vault sealed up again, and the holographic camouflage restored. The surreptitious flyer took off and swooped away above the hills. Apparently pleased with the operation, Giandro and his retainers mounted up.

Jessica retreated into the forest. She would make her way back to the manor house, take a roundabout path far from anywhere that would raise suspicions. Whenever her shadowy watchers found her again, she would make up excuses, using embarrassed, lilting laughter to say that she had dodged them on a lark.

But she had much more to discuss with Viscount Giandro Tull. Accomplishing what she had to do would require a supreme effort, and all the skills and courage she could muster.

FOR DINNER THAT evening, Jessica dressed in a long white gown swirled with the blue spiral pattern of House Tull. She even wore earrings and a necklace of coral gems sealed in an airtight film, carried from Caladan as one of the few treasures she had been allowed to bring along. It was a gift from Leto in happier times. Viscount Giandro would not know their significance, but she needed this reminder tonight, to keep the love of her life in her mind. The effect was elegant, beautiful, breathtaking.

This kind man had let her save her son. He had helped her in her time of need. And now she knew his own dark secret. She needed a way to succeed without betraying him. A fine line to walk.

The Bene Gesserit order exerted their control over her, she knew. Jessica understood full well what she had to do here . . . the same assignment Xora had been given when dispatched to Caladan. But Xora was dead, Leto was gone. . . .

She longed to go home.

If ever she could return home.

If ever she convinced the Sisterhood that she'd done as they demanded.

For Jessica, the process was more than logic, it was balancing the logical and the emotional. Ultimately, she told herself, this was what a human being should be, balanced, not tilted to one extreme or another, not going through rote actions dictated by the Mother Superior and her advisers.

I am a person, I am an individual. I have the will and the power to do things in my own way. I can—and I will—figure out how to survive this situation.

The elegant meal with Giandro was a blur to her, but she made interesting conversation, like a courtesan might do. "As a Bene Gesserit I am an observer," she told him, "and I'm a student of human nature, human reactions. I also understand politics. Thanks to the Sisterhood, I'm aware of the tangled web of alliances and vendettas throughout the Landsraad."

Giandro chuckled. "You need not convince me that you're an impressive woman, Jessica, both beautiful and intelligent."

"No, but I may need to convince you of other things. The Sisterhood has laid down what I must accomplish before they'll set me free. I think we can help each other. I . . . I certainly owe you."

"I'd rather not keep score and count obligations," he said.

"Nor I," she replied, "but in order for us to accomplish what we need, I must be entirely in your confidence—as you are in mine."

He seemed embarrassed and also puzzled. "What do you mean?"

She altered her tone, even her body scent. She made the subtlest of key movements, holding nothing back. As expected, without even realizing it, he began to be receptive to what she had to say.

The Bene Gesserit had taught her a great deal.

But she also knew his secret.

Upon arriving on Elegy, she had been careful to establish an emotional barrier between them, like a personal shield, one that could be penetrated only by a fighter possessing great skill with the slow blade. If she approached Giandro with the proper speed and trajectory, could she allow him in close to her, and still remain safe?

"I have a proposal." Her pulse pounded, and she wrestled with her heart. "Shall we continue this in your private quarters, my Lord? We have much to discuss."

His answer was predictable, and she was only starting her work.

With her heart breaking, but knowing what she needed to do, Jessica followed him down the corridor to his chambers.

DEDICATION AND ACKNOWLEDGMENTS

This book is specially dedicated to Kim Herbert and Byron Merritt, who are officers of the family company, and who do so much behind the scenes to advance the work and legacy of their grandfather, Frank Herbert.

This book is also for our entertainment attorneys, Marcy Morris and Barry Tyerman, whose wisdom and sage advice have guided us through the intricacies of Hollywood. And for our tireless literary agents as well, John Silbersack, Robert Gottlieb, and Mary Alice Kier, who have been with us for so long, and have contributed so much.

And as always, we are eternally grateful to our wives, Jan Herbert and Rebecca Moesta, who have shared in our continuing and exciting journey through the wonders of the Dune universe.

—BH and KJA